"Come with me," Jen suggested softly, almost unwilling to believe how perfect the solution was. Bennett Vance was just what Apple Grove House needed. He was just what she needed. "Come back to 1999 with me."

Bennett looked at the first woman he'd ever loved enough to spend the rest of his life with. "Jennifer, what you are telling me about yourself and time is impossible. Surely you understand that."

"Bennett, think about it. There is something about this place that allows for weird things to happen in time. It has to do with cameras. But besides that, think—if you were with me in my time, we could save Apple Grove House from becoming another sideshow at an amusement park. Bennett, you have to come with me."

"Jennifer, even if the time thing is true, what makes you think Zach Schuster's camera can do it this time when he couldn't before?"

The light went out of Jennifer's brown eyes and the joy vanished from her face.

"Think this through," Bennett continued. "Even if you could stand up in front of Schuster's camera and it does flash you back to where you came from, what makes you think I could do it, too? What if the light only takes one of us?"

Jennifer shook her head. "No, don't even think that you can't come with me."

"But it is a possibility we would have to consider," Bennett whispered. "We could stand in front of that camera and be parted forever. . . ."

—from "An Autumn Bouquet" by Linda Madl

TIMELESS AUTUMN

Carol Finch
Kathryn Fox
Linda Madl

Zebra Books
Kensington Publishing Corp.

http://www.zebrabooks.com

ZEBRA BOOKS are published by

Kensington Publishing Corp.
850 Third Avenue
New York, NY 10022

First Printing: September, 1999
10 9 8 7 6 5 4 3 2 1

Printed in the United States of America

CONTENTS

THE COLORS OF AUTUMN

Carol Finch

Chapter One

"Julia, my dear, you have exceeded my greatest expectations! Wonderful job, just wonderful!"

Julia Harper glanced down from atop her stepladder and grinned at the stout, bald-headed mayor of Bugtussle, Texas. "Thanks, Pete. Painting this mural for your Octoberfest has been an enjoyable change of pace for me."

For the past two weeks, Julia had been staying in the laid-back community in hill country, working on the mural she'd been hired to paint on the broad storefront on Main Street, commemorating the town's one hundred twenty-five years of existence. Each year, Bugtussle celebrated by hosting a rodeo, a parade, a barbecue, and a street dance. This year, the city council had decided to depict life in the 1800s with a large mural.

"Sure you don't want to move your art studio down here from Fort Worth?" Pete McGrew asked. "Everyone in town has grown mighty fond of you, ya know. We'd love to have a famous artist to claim as our own. Why, the city council even suggested painting your name on our water tower, like the folks up in Yukon, Oklahoma, did for Garth Brooks.''

Julia reached up on tiptoe to put the finishing touches on the second-story railing of the nineteenth-century hotel depicted in her mural. Pete McGrew's offer was tempting. She could get used to living in this friendly community, where people treated her like extended family. It wasn't as if she would leave anything behind in Fort Worth, except a high-rise apartment and an art gallery. She had no family obligations, no close friends. Her dearest friend since childhood, Cynthia Phelps, had been transferred to Philadelphia. Julia hadn't seen her in a year.

No, there was nothing in Fort Worth that couldn't be packed up and hauled south. Julia could set up housekeeping in Bugtussle and still travel to the art festivals around the country.

"I'll consider your offer, Pete," she told him as she moved down two rungs on the ladder to paint green trim on the eaves of the old-time mercantile store.

"You do that, girl," Pete insisted. "You think about it good and hard, ya hear?"

Pete smiled in supreme satisfaction as he appraised the frontier shops, the horse-lined hitching posts, and wagons Julia had painted into the mural. "Wonder what it would've been like to live back in the days when Bugtussle first sprouted up. I'll bet our pioneer ancestors had a different approach to life back then."

"I expect so," Julia murmured as she painted.

Working on this mural had left Julia speculating for hours on end. While painting the portraits of the people on the street of this Old West town—using an old black-and-white photo from 1880 the mayor had retrieved from the archives—she had imagined herself on the frontier.

Each time she painted the signs hanging over the old-time mercantile store, the livery stable, the hotel, and the opera house, she wondered about Edwin Calloway, who founded the town and had his name plastered on most of the businesses.

Probably an arrogant old coot who got his kicks from seeing his name displayed up and down both sides of the street, Julia thought. Calloway had probably been a cocky demigod who made sure the townsfolk danced to the beat of his drum. His influential position had undoubtedly gone straight to his swelled head.

"How long do you think it will take you to finish up the mural?" Pete questioned as he glanced at his watch.

"Shouldn't take more than an hour," Julia told him as she climbed down the ladder. "All I have left to do is paint the young woman stepping down from the stagecoach."

Pete strode over to study the enlarged photograph propped on the windowsill. He shook his bald head and smiled. "Still can't believe you did this fantastic, colorful mural by looking at this grainy black-and-white photo. Sure wish I had your talent, girl. Must be nice to take a slab of plaster on this storefront and bring it to life with a painting. All I can do is draw stick figures for my grandkids. But you create something spectacular from nothing."

Pete grinned as he pivoted toward Julia. "If you decide to move to Bugtussle, would you consider giving art lessons? Lots of folks around here have been carrying on about how talented you are. Several of them would love to learn to paint. You've inspired a bunch of wannabe artists since you started this project."

"I swear, Pete, you are wonderful for my ego," Julia said, chuckling.

"Girl, you are damn . . . darn good," Pete corrected quickly. "This mural is so lifelike and full of depth that I swear I could walk right down the middle of that street into the Old West. I'll wager other communities in the state will be contacting you to paint murals of their frontier towns after they take a gander at your masterpiece. Mark my words, you'll have more offers than you can shake a stick at.''

Pete glanced at his watch again. "I gotta run. I have to make last-minute arrangements for tomorrow's festivities. Want everything to come off without a hitch, ya know.

"Save a dance for me tomorrow night, Julia. There are several eligible bachelors around here who want to twirl you around on the street, so I'm making my request before you're booked solid for the evening."

Julia was aware that bachelors had been eyeing her as if she were the flavor of the month. She drew a lot of attention while standing on a stepladder, her jean-clad fanny facing Main Street. At least a dozen men had stopped to pass the time of day while she labored over the mural. Julia hadn't accepted any of the invitations that came her way, because she didn't have much energy left after climbing up and down this stepladder a hundred times a day. Muscles she didn't know she had complained until she soaked her body in the motel bathtub for at least an hour.

When Pete lumbered off, Julia turned her attention to the faceless female who was stepping from the stagecoach. A wry smile pursed her lips as she mixed paint. She decided to give her mural a personal touch. In addition to signing her name on the artwork she was going to paint herself into this frontier town. *She* was going to become the woman stepping down from the stage into the Old West.

Impulsively, Julia gave the new arrival her own mop of curly blond hair, blue eyes, rounded chin, and oval face. When she put the final touches on her self-portrait the world began to tilt under her feet, then went completely out of kilter. A gray haze swirled around her and she experienced the peculiar feeling of being sucked into a vacuum. Darkness engulfed her, then all the flaming shades of autumn that she had used to paint the mural burst before her eyes. Unfamiliar sounds—rumbles, creaks and jingles—penetrated the dull roar in her ears.

Julia staggered clumsily when the scene from her mural came into sharp focus before her eyes. Her foot slipped off the metal step. She plunged from the *stagecoach*—not the *stepladder!*—and landed with a thud and a groan on the dirt street.

Dirt street? Julia braced her arms under her shoulders and jerked up her head to glance left, then right. *Lord have mercy!* What had happened to modern-day Bugtussle? There were no cars lining the street, but rather horses, carriages, and people dressed in nineteenth-century fashions.

Julia glanced at her own arms, noting she was no longer wearing a paint-splattered T-shirt. Her arms were encased in a colorful yellow gown, exactly like the one she had painted on the new stagecoach arrival in her mural!

"Good . . . God . . ." she bleated. "I must have painted myself into 1880!"

"You okay, ma'am?"

Panicky, Julia stared at the toes of the dusty cowboy boots in front of her. Her owlish gaze drifted up long, muscled legs encased in faded Levi's. Muscled arms and a broad chest were covered with a cream-colored chambray shirt.

Holy cow! What had she done to herself, and how was she going to get back to modern-day Bugtussle? She was supposed to be the guest of honor at the parade! Pete McGrew intended to present her with the key to the city.

She was scheduled to ride horseback in the opening ceremony at the rodeo!

While she was trying to deal with the realization that she had shot herself back into the Old West with her paintbrush, the man with the slow Texas drawl squatted down on his haunches to stare at her.

"Ma'am? Sure hope you didn't bruise or break anything when you fell. Can you move your arms and legs?"

Her legs, Julia realized, were buried beneath layers of petticoats and a long skirt. She'd never worn long skirts in her life. Formal attire had never been her thing. No wonder she had tripped when she stepped from the stagecoach. She wasn't accustomed to maneuvering around yards of restrictive fabric.

"Ma'am? Did the fall knock the wind out of you? You are Priscilla Flannigan, aren't you?"

Julia stared at the face attached to this incredibly masculine body. This was a man's man—a real man who didn't buff up with weights and work out three times a week at his local health club. From the looks of this brawny cowboy, he was accustomed to a hard day's work. His sun-bronzed face had so much character emanating from it that Julia felt the compulsive urge to grab her palette and paint his portrait.

Helplessly, she stared at him, memorizing every crinkle around his dark eyes, the high sweep of his cheek bones, the square cut of his jaw. His patrician nose had a crook in it, indicating it had been broken once. His lips were full and sensuous, and he wore a lopsided smile that Julia found endearing.

"Yep, must've knocked the breath clean out of her all right," someone drawled from behind her. "Let's stand her upright."

Julia stared stupidly as the cowboy and the stage driver

hoisted her to her feet. She nodded her thanks to the scruffy-looking stage driver, then refocused her artistic eye on the handsome cowboy, who tossed her another lopsided smile.

"Welcome to Bugtussle, ma'am. I've been expecting you. I'm Edwin Calloway. Folks here just call me Win." He turned to the driver as he took Julia's arm to steady her on her wobbly legs. "Would you grab Priscilla's luggage for me, Hester? I'll take the lady inside so she can get out of the sun and gather her wits."

Julia found herself swept up in powerful arms and whisked across the street, up the boardwalk and into the building, whose sign announced it was the Calloway Hotel. She still couldn't believe this was Calloway, the man who practically owned the whole darned town. He was nothing like she'd pictured him.

"I'll have Bea fetch you a sarsaparilla, unless you prefer the hard stuff," Win said as he carted Julia into the lobby and deposited her in a chair.

"No hard stuff," Julia chirped.

Win turned toward the registration desk. "Clarence, ask Bea to bring the lady a sarsaparilla. She took a spill when she stepped from the stage."

The young clerk bobbed his fuzzy red head, then scuttled off to find Bea Whoever-She-Was.

"Is there anything else I can get for you, Priscilla?"

"I'm not Priscilla Flannigan," Julia said as she shifted awkwardly in her chair.

Julia had no idea what had become of Priscilla. She had somehow managed to bump the woman off the stage like a standby passenger, then take her place. She felt bad about that—she really did.

Win frowned, bemused. "Priscilla was supposed to be on that coach. I was expecting her."

Julia thought fast, then displayed a bright smile. "Priscilla couldn't make it, so she sent me in her place. My name is Julia Harper."

"Well, Miss Julia, we are mighty glad you came." Win grinned broadly. "Everybody in Bugtussle is anxious to see your first performance at the grand opening of the new opera house."

Julia gaped at him. What had she gotten herself into? "Performance?"

He nodded as if she knew what the hell he was talking about.

She didn't have a clue!

"Ah, here comes Bea with your sarsaparilla."

Julia stared at the sturdy older woman, who lumbered from a doorway carrying a glass. Though her face boasted wrinkles that testified to hard living, she greeted Julia with a gap-toothed smile.

"Here ya go, hon. This'll put some starch back in your unmentionables."

Julia accepted the drink with a nod and a smile.

"Beatrice Garner, this is Julia Harper, our new songbird."

Songbird? Good grief! These people expected her to sing at the grand opening of the opera house? Julia didn't have extensive musical training. Oh certainly, her mother had enrolled her in all sorts of lessons while in grade school. Julia had done her stint with piano lessons, a year of voice lessons, four years of gymnastics, tap, and ballet, but the art lessons were the only ones that stuck.

Her only experience in music was singing alto in her church choir. In her book, that didn't count. And worse, she couldn't even think of a handful of songs that might have been popular in 1880. She was used to singing in front of a congregation, alongside eleven other people.

She had no specialized training in front of an audience, and she had the unnerving feeling there would be a drastic difference.

"Drink up, Miss Julia," Win urged. "I hope you'll feel up to a tour of the theater so you can get the feel of the place before doing your show. Then I'll take you to your room so you can rest up from your trip."

Julia chugged the sarsaparilla, then handed the empty glass to Bea. "Thank you. It hit the spot."

"Bea cooks in the restaurant," Win informed Julia. "Folks ride for miles to sample her meals. Her steaks melt in your mouth." He sighed audibly. "What she does with mincemeat pie is out of this world."

"Oh, go on, Win," Bea mumbled, clearly embarrassed by his praise. "Ain't nothing special 'bout my cooking."

Win winked at Julia. "She's also as modest as all get-out. The proof is in her pudding."

When Bea galumphed back to the kitchen, Win stole another discreet glance at Julia Harper. Damn, but she was easy on a man's eye. Blond curls that shined like nothing he'd ever seen cascaded over her shoulders. Wide blue eyes fanned with long lashes twinkled with so much inner spirit that it nearly took his breath away.

This songbird and actress had taken him by complete surprise. Most of the traveling musicians and actresses he hired had that hard, experienced look about them. Not this angel-faced beauty. Her skin looked as soft as silk and she had the kind of figure that could stop a stampede. Win was pretty certain that when word spread around town about the new arrival, the opera house would be filled to capacity. She was destined to acquire hundreds of male admirers before she opened that kissable mouth of hers to sing one note.

Damn, Win couldn't remember ever being so awestruck

by a woman's appearance. There was something rare and unique about Julia Harper. She had a look of intelligent awareness in her eyes, a worldly, sophisticated way about her. Yet she managed to retain a look of sweet innocence. A stunning contradiction, Win thought.

Before his betraying thoughts drifted off again, Win offered Julia his hand. "Do you feel up to the grand tour now?"

Julia took his hand, surprised by the combination of gentleness and strength in his callused grip. Edwin Calloway definitely was not what she'd expected. Although his name was plastered all over Bugtussle, he was an absolute hunk who exuded Southern hospitality. Julia wondered if he was married. Probably. He had to be considered a prize catch. Win obviously had money coming out of his ears and the kind of rugged good looks that attracted women from any era.

"Lead the way, Calloway," Julia requested. "I can't wait to see where I will be performing."

Win ushered her through the adjoining restaurant to a side door which opened into an elegant social club—elegant by 1880 standards, that was.

"I have decided to cater to everyone I can," Win said as he drew Julia into the cedar-paneled room. He gestured toward the bookshelves that lined the north wall. "This is the reading room. The card and billiard room is off to the right. Even though we are a small community, I want to offer folks the same kind of culture that draws crowds down in San Antone. The women in town want a place to come when they feel the need to get out of the house, so I stocked up on books for their reading pleasure."

"Impressive," Julia murmured as she appraised the carpeted room with its wide, spacious windows.

"You really think so?"

She nodded confidently. "Absolutely. Women around here will appreciate the fact that you have taken their needs into consideration. Seems to me that most towns . . . er . . . these days cater mostly to the entertainment of men."

"My sentiments exactly," Win agreed. "As long as you're in town, you're welcome to make use of the reading room anytime you please."

He clasped her arm to guide her past the chairs and sofas near the pot-bellied stove, then he led her through a lantern-lit hallway. "This is my pride and joy," he said as he opened the ornately carved oak door. "I expanded and remodeled the old theater to accommodate larger audiences."

Julia stopped short and gasped in surprise at the spacious room that yawned before her. The theater, which boasted spanking-new red velvet curtains, was equipped with a wooden stage, which had been polished until it gleamed. Elaborate balconies towered on each side and another balcony formed a semicircle at the back of the theater. There were enough chairs and benches to accommodate two hundred fifty people.

Good gracious! What made her think she could waltz onto this stage and perform in front of a crowd? She'd likely suffer a severe case of stage fright that would cause her vocal chords to collapse.

Win frowned at the horrified look on Julia's face. "You don't like it?" For some ridiculous reason he wanted to impress Julia. Why her opinion mattered to him, he didn't know, but it did.

"What's not to like?" Julia replied, flashing him a smile. "This place is spectacular. What actress wouldn't want to perform here." Too bad Julia wasn't one!

Win's shoulders sagged in relief. "Thanks. I've invested

a lot of time and effort into remodeling this place. I want to entertain the trail drivers who pass through here each spring and fall. It's better than having those lonesome cowboys shoot up the town for lack of constructive entertainment. Same goes for the men hired to lay railroad track," he added as he shepherded her down the steps. "Men looking for a good time need to be led in a positive direction. Otherwise you end up with gunfights and brawls. Bugtussle isn't going to be a hellhole, not if I can help it."

"That's a relief to know," Julia inserted. She had yet to acclimate herself to 1880. She wouldn't know what to do if she had to dodge bullets each time she walked out on the street.

Julia halted in front of the upraised stage. "You could use some stage scenery to add more color and give the audience a sense of place. I would like a variety of scenic backdrops. I'm calling my show Autumn Fantasia," she decided on the spur of the moment. "I would like to have scenes of faraway places to perk up my acts."

Win rubbed his chin thoughtfully. "Good idea. I've been too busy with construction of the opera house to consider the particulars. I'll see if I can find somebody to paint—"

"I can do it," Julia volunteered.

"You?" he eyed her incredulously. "You're an actress *and* an artist?"

"More artist than actress," she murmured quietly.

"Pardon?"

Julia flashed another grin. "You supply the paint and I'll supply the background scenery. Deal?"

"Deal," he said quickly. "You keep track of the hours spent on the work and I'll add it to your salary."

Julia jerked up her head. It dawned on her that she didn't have a penny to her name. She, who never had to worry about money, was totally without it. She couldn't even pay for her lunch. How embarrassing!

"Something wrong, Miss Julia?"

Julia was amazed at Win's attentiveness. The man's astute gaze missed nothing. "No, just thinking."

"You're sure?" he prodded, staring deeply into her eyes. "Seems to me that you were thinking troubled thoughts. Anything I can do to help?"

The man amazed her. Julia was accustomed to men who wrapped themselves up so completely in their own world that they didn't notice what happened around them—and some of them didn't really care. Win Calloway was in a class by himself.

"Are you married? You have to be married," she blurted out, then blushed furiously. "Sorry. That's none of my business."

"No, I'm not married," he replied with a lopsided grin. "Been giving it some thought though. You?"

"Haven't given it much thought at all," she admitted as she studied the sturdy four-by-four beams that spanned the ceiling. "Where I come from good men are hard to find and I refuse to settle for less."

"Where do you come from, Miss Julia?"

"About a hundred twenty years from here," she said half under her breath.

Win cocked a dark brow. "Pardon?"

Julia looked into those cocoa brown eyes, surrounded by such long, thick lashes that she'd swear they were fake if she didn't know better. She considered telling Win where she'd come from, but she suspected he would think she was loonier than he probably did already.

No, it was best to play along while she was stuck back in time. She would look upon this weird experience as a vacation—something like visiting a dude ranch. When the fascination wore off, she would simply paint herself back to modern-day Bugtussle. Until then, Julia would give her new profession her best shot and live the life she had imagined while painting the mural for Octoberfest.

This was a fascinating opportunity for her, she realized. She had arrived in a place where everyone's previous expectations and conceptions of her were nonexistent. She didn't have to live up to her own modern-day expectations either. She could be anyone she wanted to be. The thought was exhilarating.

"I come from Fort Worth," she told Win belatedly.

"Rowdy town," he grunted. "The kind I don't want Bugtussle to become. After serving in the war, I've seen more than my share of blazing bullets and battles. I'm ready for peace and quiet."

"I'm sorry," Julia said sincerely. "It must have been awful to live through that kind of hell."

His easygoing smile vanished in a heartbeat. Julia sensed that he had become a captive of nightmarish memories. Some things, she knew, would never change with time. War was one of them. No matter how sophisticated or unsophisticated the weapon technology, war had to be absolute, unequivocal hell.

"It wasn't anything I'd wish on any other idealistic sixteen-year-old kid who decided he should do his part to save his way of life. When you're in the trenches, your ideals fall to pieces. You never forget what you went through. Never want to forget so you won't let it happen again."

While Win led her through the theater to show her the remodeled barroom, Julia asked herself if Calloway's nonchalant manner concealed deeply embedded anguish. She suspected post-traumatic stress was a modern term that also applied to the nineteenth century. Tormented emotions were bound to exist, even without a clinical label attached to them.

The thought reminded Julia to watch what she said and how she said it. She had already drawn peculiar glances from Win with her comments. She had to make certain that she didn't expose herself by blurting out phrases and terms that hadn't been invented yet.

Well, Julia, here you are, zapped back in time for a couple of weeks. It's time for you to give some serious thought to how you're going to pull off your stage performances. Better come up with something clever and innovative to distract audiences from your lack of musical talent. How are you going to give these folks their money's worth so they won't boo you out of town?

Good question. Julia decided she'd better come up with a good answer pretty damn quick.

Chapter Two

Julia surveyed the twelve-by-twelve hotel room with its featherbed, lowboy, commode, small table and chair, and brass tub. A lantern sat on the nightstand. The closet wasn't large enough to turn around in. Compared to the spacious walk-in closet in her apartment and the elaborate bathroom with its whirlpool . . .

Julia swallowed uneasily. When she considered all she had left behind on the teetering edge of the millennium, she nearly panicked. She had no cosmetics, no moisturizing soaps, no television to keep up with world events, no microwave oven, no computer E-mail to stay in touch with Cynthia Phelps in Philadelphia.

Dear heaven! Cynthia hadn't even been born yet!

Overwhelmed, Julia plunked down on her bed. She was totally isolated from all she had known and she was going to have to make drastic adjustments to her lifestyle.

Maybe it was a good thing she hadn't left a lover behind.

The truth was that Julia had given up all hope of finding the man of her dreams—a man who was more interested in her than the vast inheritance and insurance settlement she received when her parents were killed in a car wreck eight years earlier. She'd had money out the gazoo and more would-be boyfriends than she could shake fistfuls of dollars at. She had even fancied herself in love once, only to overhear a conversation from Mr. Right—who turned out to be all wrong. Robert Dorsett had boasted to his friend that Julia was going to become his meal ticket.

Julia had been so hurt and outraged by the discovery that Robert was only interested in her money that she had sworn off men and refused to date for three years. Looking back—or forward, as the case happened to be—Julia realized that she had turned to her fiancé in desperation after her parents' tragic deaths. She had needed a friend, a strong shoulder to lean on for compassion and moral support. Instead, she had settled for an arrogant premed student who wanted to get his hands in her pockets. She should have known that he didn't really love her, because he rarely considered her wants and needs, and a physical relationship never developed. As it turned out, Robert was tomcatting around on the side to compensate for his lack of physical interest in Julia.

Older and wiser, because of the morally crushing experience, Julia had dated casually now and then. But since she couldn't separate herself from her money, she didn't trust the male of the species to love and want her just for herself. In short, she had developed very low expectations for the male gender.

Julia chuckled at the irony of her situation. She had certainly been separated from her money now, hadn't she? She was going to find out in one whale of a hurry if she had the kind of appeal and personality that attracted men.

Win Calloway didn't behave as if he had fallen head over heels after spending the past hour with her. She, on the other hand, had developed an immediate fascination for him. His looks alone made him appealing to the feminine eye, but his laid-back manner and his sincere concern intrigued Julia. She noticed that Win had taken time to speak to everyone who approached him, and he always seemed willing and eager to help if there was a problem to solve.

From all indications, Win Calloway was well respected and well liked in Bugtussle—not the arrogant, domineering demigod Julia had imagined. No one around here resented the fact that his name was plastered all over town or that he appeared to be a pillar of frontier society. Heavens, what was there not to like about that brawny hunk of old-fashioned, good-hearted cowboy?

Well, if Julia thought this was going to be some grand romantic adventure in time, she might as well nip that foolish fantasy in the bud, here and now. She hadn't bumped some wealthy aristocrat off that stagecoach and dumped the poor woman who knew where! Julia had to impersonate an actress and singer. She had to create a spectacular stage show to ensure Win Calloway got his money's worth. Thus far, he had been kind and generous by allowing her to stay in his hotel for nothing. Julia couldn't bare the thought of letting him down . . . .

A firm knock at the door jostled Julia from her thoughts. "Come in."

"Can't. You'll have to open the door for me," Beatrice Garner called from the hall. "Got my hands full here, gal."

Julia scuttled over to open the door. The mouth-watering aroma of food floated up from the covered tray Beatrice clamped in her hands. Julia took the tray, passed it under her nose, and sighed appreciatively. "Ah, Bea, how did you know my stomach has been growling something fierce?"

"Didn't." Bea ambled into the room to survey the spacious suite. "It was Win's idea. He figured you might be hungry after chowing down on stage rations. This meal is on the house, of course. Win asked me to bring it up before the noon rush got underway in the restaurant."

"He has been exceptionally kind," Julia murmured as she set the tray on the nightstand.

"Heart as big as Texas," Bea readily confided. She plopped down on the edge of the bed to give herself a much needed rest. "Ain't hardly a soul in town who ain't beholden to Win—one way or another.

"Take me for instance," Bea continued as she braced her arms behind her and sprawled leisurely. "My husband got sick and died while we were headed west in our Conestoga wagon. At that time, there was nothing here but Calloway Ranch and the stage station Win agreed to run. He hired me on to cook at the station and I've been here ever since.

"Then there's Clarence Potter, the young man at the registration desk."

Julia nodded recognition. "He seems like a nice young man."

"Is now. Wasn't when Win took him under his wing. Clarence's ma was worthless. She just up and left with a gambling man one night while Clarence was asleep in the shack. Win trained Clarence to man the registration desk and saw to it that he stayed out of trouble."

"Who manages Calloway's Mercantile Shop?" Julia asked curiously.

Bea grinned, exposing the gap between her teeth. "You catch on quick, gal. Everybody who manages Win's businesses has his own hard-luck story to tell. John Witham runs the store. He came up from San Antone a few years back. Not a penny to his name. Nothing but the clothes on his back. The drought caused him to lose all he had. He was ready to end it all. Then Win convinced him that he would be the perfect manager for the dry goods shop, seeing how Win was so busy constructing new businesses to accommodate the influx of people that he didn't have time to run the ones he had.''

Given what Win Calloway had confided to Julia about serving in the war, and hearing Bea's testimonials, Julia wondered if the town founder had compensated for the lives he'd seen lost in battle by providing hope and new life for the poor souls who wandered into Bugtussle.

"Win Calloway is the closest thing to a saint in these parts," Bea said as she dusted specks of flour off her calico skirt. "Win finds a place for everyone who needs a helping hand. He's extended credit to so many folks around here that he sort of fell into organizing the bank. Then he put Otis Fletcher in charge of managing it."

Julia was duly impressed—and a little ashamed that she hadn't become the kind of humanitarian Calloway was. She hadn't put her money to good use. She'd just stashed it away for a rainy day and lived comfortably, taking care of no one but herself. She had closeted herself in her art studio and protected her wounded heart and her feminine pride from the hurt her ex-fiancé had caused. Calloway, however, had given his time and money to help those who were down and out.

Bea regarded Julia for a pensive moment. "The only thing Win has done wrong is let that twit who's set her cap for him think she's got a snowball's chance in Hades of putting a wedding ring on his finger."

"And what twit might that be?" Julia asked.

Bea pulled a sour face. "The Fletcher twit. Her daddy

is another hard-luck story, but Otis's newfound success in
Bugtussle has bored into his wooden head like a plague
of termites. Otis used to be some hot-shot newspaper man
before the war destroyed his business and his home in
Louisiana. He seems to have forgotten who gave him this
new lease on life. He struts around town like a peacock,
and he and his wife, Matilda, have spoiled their daughter
so badly that she's as ripe as a three-day-old dead fish.''

Julia chuckled at the comparison.

Bea's gray brows puckered over her deep-set green eyes.
"Think it's funny, do you? Well, it ain't. That Fletcher twit
has run off three prospective brides who were worthy of
Win Calloway's affection. You asked me, it's time Trudy
Fletcher got what's coming for her lying and manipulating.
In fact—''

Julia raised a brow when Bea paused to regard her ponderously. "In fact *what*?''

"You want to see these tasty meals showing up at your
door three times a day?'' Bea baited.

Julia glanced at the covered dishes that had her stomach
growling in anticipation. "Certainly. Who doesn't want
three tasty squares a day?''

Bea grinned triumphantly, braced her hands on her
knees, and leaned forward. "I ain't asking you to do nothing underhanded or illegal here, you understand. You
seem a fine sort of woman to me.''

"Just what is it you want me to do to earn these delicious
meals?''

Another smile spread across Bea's lips and her green
eyes sparkled. "I want you to play up to Win Calloway.
Show an interest in him. I saw the way he was looking you
over when he thought no one noticed.''

Julia blinked, startled. "He did?''

Bea nodded her frizzy gray head. " 'Course he did. The

man ain't blind, ya know. You're a very attractive woman. Win never gave any of the other traveling musicians the grand tour. Never took anybody's arm to escort them around either. Usually he keeps a respectable distance in public, but he didn't seem to mind standing close to you every chance he got.''

"Just exactly what do you expect me to do to earn my meals?" Julia wanted to know that very second.

"Don't get your feathers ruffled, gal," Bea snickered. "I just want you to be nice to Win. That shouldn't be difficult. Just make that Fletcher Twit jealous enough to expose herself for what she is. She's all sugar and smiles around Win; then she turns into a witch when she's around the rest of us. She's snippy and shrewish and altogether unpleasant, unless Win is in hearing and seeing distance.''

Julia didn't want to get involved, hadn't planned to be in the Old West long enough to expose the Fletcher Twit for what she was. But Julia supposed that, being beholden to Win Calloway—like everyone around here—she should do what she could to save him from a bad marriage. Win had given her his best suite at the hotel and had agreed to let her design the scenery. In short, he had gone out of his way to be kind to her.

"Will you do it, gal?" Bea prodded. "It's not like a woman has to *pretend* to be interested in Win Calloway. What woman wouldn't be? If I was thirty years younger I'd give that snotty Trudy Fletcher a run for her money—''

Bea's voice dried up when footsteps resounded in the hallway. Julia glanced up to see Win's sinewy profile in the shadows of the partially open door.

"Did you get settled in? Need anything?" Win questioned as he poked his head around the corner.

Julia gave him her best smile. "Everything is fine. The

room is nice, and you have been exceptionally generous. Thank you."

Win noticed the tray on the nightstand. "Glad to see Bea has delivered lunch. You won't be disappointed."

"I'm sure I won't be, but since Bea and I are getting acquainted, I haven't taken time to sample the food."

"If you're free this evening, I'll accompany you to the restaurant so you can enjoy another meal, as well as Bea's slice-of-heaven desserts."

Bea slanted Julia a discreet glance, but Julia didn't let on that she had been bribed. "It's kind of you to offer. I'd love to join you this evening."

Win stared curiously at Julia. "You sure have a strange accent for somebody from Fort Worth," he commented.

Julia smiled breezily. "Stage training," she said by way of explanation. "Have to enunciate clearly in the theater, you know."

"Oh." Win shifted from one booted foot to the other. "Well, I guess I'll see you this evening."

While Bea was mentally rubbing her hands together in glee, Julia strode toward the door before Win could exit. "There are a few things I'll need for my act. I wonder if I could impose on you to help me round them up this afternoon."

"Sure, I'll be happy to do what I can," he offered magnanimously. "Come downstairs after your meal and we'll see what we can do about getting you set up."

When his footsteps receded, Bea grinned. "You need anything at all, gal, you let me know. Hear? I can't bear the thought of that Fletcher twit sinking her claws into a good and decent man like Win. He deserves better than that. Teach that twit a lesson she won't forget and I'll be your devoted friend for life."

After Bea lumbered off, Julia ate the sensational meal,

then unpacked the luggage that had been carried upstairs for her. To her dismay, she discovered that Priscilla Flannigan's wardrobe and stage costumes were outrageous! Black mesh leggings, satin garters, diving necklines, and skimpy skirts? Julia was going to look like a second-rate Las Vegas show girl if she wore these god-awful getups.

Priscilla Flannigan had no sense of style or fashion. Julia would have to make a few alterations and hope she didn't come off looking like a sleazy harlot during her performances.

"Make the best of this," Julia told herself as she hung the garments in the closet, then tucked the undergarments in the chest of drawers. "With a little imagination you can alter these costumes and produce an entertaining stage show."

Although Julia had agreed to be especially nice to Win—in an attempt to infuriate the Fletcher Twit—the deception made her uncomfortable. Well, she amended, she wasn't really going to be devious. She did find Win Calloway extremely attractive, and it would be refreshing to respond instinctively to a man for a change, rather than standing on guard, expecting the worst to happen.

There was only one hitch here, Julia realized. The roles had been reversed. Now Win Calloway was the one with all the money. Would he be as cautious as she was? How did one go about building trust when money was involved?

"Stop analyzing the situation to death," Julia scolded herself as she wiped the dirt stains from her yellow gown. "You're stuck in a new place in time. You can be whoever you want to be for as long as you like. This is a once-in-a-lifetime adventure, so relax and enjoy it. After all, Bea Garner didn't ask you to throw yourself in Win Calloway's bed. You can do this, Julia."

After having the heart-to-heart talk with herself, Julia

strode determinedly toward the door. She was going to have some fun with her new career as a performer and make a place for herself in old-time Bugtussle. She was going to relax and enjoy the company of the man who had drawn her immediate interest. She might miss the modern conveniences she had taken for granted, but things weren't bad here. This really might be fun. She should stop fretting and just go for it!

"You want to *what!*" Win gaped at Julia as if she had sprouted antlers. He shifted his attention from her to the beams that spanned the new theater, then frowned on her sunny smile. "You can't be serious!"

"You want a theater act that provides thrills and attracts crowds, don't you?"

"Well, yeah, but—"

"Then all we have to do is rig up a harness that fits under my costumes, attach fence wire to a rope-and-pulley system secured to those three sturdy overhead beams, and *poof!* we'll have a spectacular performance that rakes in money for you."

The grand idea of flying through the air while singing in her mediocre voice had come to Julia on her way down the hotel steps. She had decided to employ the kind of special effects and razzle-dazzle that Garth Brooks used in his concerts. True, technology to provide flashy light shows hadn't come along yet, but she could improvise.

Win stared dubiously at the beams. "I don't know of any women who have attempted such daring acrobatics during their performances."

"Exactly my point. Give the audience something they aren't expecting," Julia said. "My act will be unique. You want crowd-drawing entertainment in here, don't you?"

"Yeah, but not at your expense," he was quick to add. "I don't want you to break your neck. Bad for business."

Julia snickered at his comment and his lopsided grin. "I appreciate your concern, but I'm in tiptop physical condition. I've had gymnastics and aerobic classes to keep in shape."

Win's brows beetled over his dark eyes. "What kind of classes?"

Julia muttered under her breath. She kept forgetting that while her body was trapped in 1880 her brain was still operating on 1999 intelligence levels. "Exercise classes," she corrected herself. "I keep myself in good condition. Everyone should remain physically active."

Win couldn't help himself. His gaze slid over Julia's shapely figure and he smiled rakishly. "Lady, there is absolutely nothing wrong with your shape and I doubt there ever was. A man would have to be blind in both eyes not to notice you."

The compliment, coming from Win Calloway, was exceptionally flattering. For the first time in years Julia accepted a compliment without cynically searching for ulterior motives. Win didn't know she had been wealthy. To him, she was a performer for hire who flitted around the country making a modest living in one frontier town after another.

"Thank you," she replied. "Not that I am responsible for my God-given attributes, but the point is that I enjoy being active."

"How old are you?" he asked out of the blue.

"Thirty. How old are you?"

"Thirty-five." Win shook his head in amazement. "I would have guessed you to be no more than twenty-five. Women your age haven't held up so well out here on the frontier. You must be living right," he added with a lopsided grin.

Living in some other time when life didn't pelt people with so many hardships, Julia silently corrected.

"Now then, about my harness-and-pulley system," she prompted. "When can we start gathering what we need?"

He stared into her smiling face and lively blue eyes, noting her determined stance and enthusiasm. Then he gave in without much of a fight. He was still skeptical about the safety of her proposed acrobatics, but she was convinced her idea would work.

There was something intriguing about Julia Harper. She appealed to Win on a level that went deeper than physical attraction. True, she was damn easy on the eye, but there was so much more. Her lively manner, her unusual turn of phrase, her undaunted spirit—they were all infectious. Escorting Julia around town while she gathered necessary equipment was a good excuse to spend more time with her.

Oh certainly, Win knew that a woman like Julia would come and go like the seasons under the sun, that she wouldn't be interested in settling down in a laid-back place like Bugtussle. She would want to appear in all the theaters and music halls that had sprung up around the country. But Julia was here now, for a couple of weeks, at least. Win, who had been so preoccupied with helping friends and neighbors get their start, had allocated very little time for personal diversions.

Except for Trudy Fletcher, he amended. She was constantly after him, making a nuisance of herself. She didn't appreciate it when Win took an interest in a woman, but she had to learn that Win didn't like to be chased. Maybe escorting Julia around town would help get through to Trudy that she needed to find another romantic interest and leave him the hell alone.

Win cut Julia a sideways glance as they ambled toward

the mercantile shop. He wondered if she was being nice to him because he had money. She didn't act as if it mattered to her. She appeared genuinely interested in making the grand opening of the opera house a smashing success.

Smashing. Win winced. He sure hoped this lively female didn't smash herself up when her pulley system malfunctioned. Win had pulled too many mangled soldiers from the front lines. He didn't wish anguishing pain on a living soul. Since those hellish years of battle it seemed he had been rescuing someone or another from calamity. He didn't consider himself a saint, but he had seen so much death and injury that it had become reflexive to ease suffering.

"Hello, Win," John Witham greeted cheerfully. "What can I do for you today?"

Julia instantly remembered what Bea had said about the shop manager, who had fallen into a state of depression because he had arrived in Bugtussle penniless. Since Win had made a place for John Witham at the store, he had become Win's loyal and devoted friend. Admiration and respect were written all over John's lean face.

For a moment Julia became lost in memories of her "future" life, her self-imposed isolation. She had been so busy protecting old hurt that she hadn't developed new friendships, hadn't given of herself the way Win Calloway had.

Damn, why couldn't he have been born a century later? Why couldn't he have been one of the eligible bachelors in modern Bugtussle who stopped to chitchat while she was working on the mural?

If nothing else, her association with Win Calloway was bringing out the best in her, teaching her to give more of herself to relationships and friendships. She should do something constructive with the modern-day fortune that awaited her. She had made Cynthia Phelps her beneficiary, but there was plenty of money to donate to worthwhile programs and charities, as well as set Cynthia up for life.

"Come here and see what you think, Jule," Win requested, rousing her from her pensive thoughts.

Julie strode forward to appraise the neatly stacked supplies in the tidy store. John Witham certainly had made Calloway proud, she realized. The manager had placed everything in alphabetical order, testifying to his organizational skills. The store was free from dust and litter, and everything was in its place.

Julia glanced down at the leather mule harness Win held up for her inspection. "Perfect," she said. "Now what about ropes and pulleys?"

"Right this way, Miss Julia." John smiled cordially as he ushered her down the aisle. "Most anything you need we keep in stock. If we don't have it we can order it. That's Calloway policy, you know."

"Obviously so." Julia scanned the shop again, noting there was indeed a little bit of everything in stock. "I'll also need a pair of gloves and an extra heavy-duty rope."

Win did a double take. "What can you possibly need another rope for?"

She grinned impishly at him. "You'll see. I know what I'm doing."

"She's a daredevil," Win confided to John, who lugged the heavy coil of rope from the shelf. "Don't miss her act day after tomorrow. It might be her first . . . and last."

John dumped the coiled rope on the counter, then dusted the hemp from his jacket. "This must be some newfangled kind of stage act that I've never heard of. I thought performers just juggled or sang or danced."

"I want to be more innovative," Julia insisted. *Innovative for this day and age,* she qualified. "We are going to need extra lighting, too. You can take these extra expenses out of my salary."

"Won't hear of it," Win insisted. "I'll pay for what you need. Get whatever you think it will take to keep you *safe.*"

The comment provoked her to smile. It was refreshing to meet a man who was concerned about *her*, who cared what happened to *her, not* about her money. It made Julia even more determined to repay Win's kindness by making his newly expanded theater the talk of Texas.

By the time Julia finished buzzing around the shop like a whirlwind, gathering paint for stage backdrops and supplies for her flying contraption, Win had to hail several men off the street to cart the goods to the theater. But he didn't fuss or grouse about the extra expenses, Julia noted. She had made a second offer to pay for the additional supplies, but Calloway flashed her a stern glance on the way out the door and told her that since he had hired her he could fire her if she didn't agree to his terms.

Smiling, Julia strode down the street, wondering if men like Win Calloway really did come along once in a century.

Sure looked that way.

Chapter Three

Bubbling with excitement and fantastic ideas, Julia accompanied Win to the theater. When she saw a younger female approaching—decked out in a grape-colored ensemble, complete with a matching parasol and a ridiculous hat that boasted a purple feather that could have served as a radio antenna—Julia knew this had to be the Fletcher Twit. The shapely brunette, who looked to be in her early twenties, batted her eyes so rapidly at Win that her lashes were just short of launching into orbit.

"Oh, Win darling, I'm so glad I happened on to you."

Julia silently smirked at Trudy Fletcher's syrupy, breathless voice. *Happened on to Win?* Ha! Not damned likely. Julia would have bet her right arm that Trudy, dressed fit to kill, had been lying in wait.

"Papa insisted that I invite you over for supper this evening," Trudy cooed. "He wants to talk to you about some bank business."

Julia was quick to note that Win was polite to the gushing twit, but his face didn't light up like a laser beam when Trudy homed in on him. Obviously, he took Trudy's blatant interest in him in stride, for he wasn't sending out signals that indicated a fierce attraction to her. Julia would have been disappointed in him if he had. Bea was right. This twit wasn't good enough for Win.

Julia had promised herself that she was not going to interfere in any relationship that looked to have possibilities, even if Bea was pushing her in Win's direction.

"Trudy Fletcher, this is Julia Harper," he introduced. "Julia will be performing at the grand opening of the opera house day after tomorrow."

Trudy, Julia noted, looked down her nose, as if Julia didn't measure up to her lofty standards. "A dance hall girl?" Trudy sniffed distastefully. "Oh dear ..." She backed up a few paces, indicating she was much too good to rub shoulders with the likes of Julia.

"Actress and singer," Win was quick to clarify. "You'll see how talented she is when she gives her performance. You might want to buy your ticket early, because the place is going to be packed."

For that comment, Julia could have hugged the stuffing out of Win. He didn't know how good or bad Julia's talents were, but he had come to her defense. Win Calloway, good and decent man that he was, didn't put up with Trudy's crap. Julia liked that. She'd never had a man stand up for her before. It felt good. Damned good.

Trudy hurled Julia a vicious glare, then turned her one-hundred-fifty watt smile on Win. "I'm sure Miss Hooper—"

"Harper," he corrected.

"Yes, whatever. I'm sure she will give an adequate performance to satisfy the simpleton cowboys and track layers who swarm around town. Now about the supper invitation, I—"

"Sorry, Trudy, but I already have plans," Win interrupted. "I'll stop by the bank to speak with Otis after I get things squared away at the theater."

"But—"

"It was nice to meet you," Julia cut in as she started forward.

Julia didn't care if the twit finished another sentence in that nauseatingly sweet, wispy voice of hers. It only took one short encounter to realize what a fake Trudy Fletcher was. The twit was spoiled, self-absorbed, and manipulative when it came to getting her way. Win Calloway needed someone who was as generous and kindhearted as he was, someone who put the needs of others above her own, someone who cared about Win and wanted to see him happy.

Trudy Fletcher, who obviously suffered from the Beautiful Bitch Syndrome, was not that woman.

"Sorry about Trudy," Win murmured as he held open the theater door for Julia. "Her manners leave a lot to be desired. Most of us around Bugtussle don't pay her much mind."

"I think she perceives me as a threat," Julia commented. "Correct me if I'm wrong, but Trudy seems to be casting about for a marriage proposal, and she doesn't want competition hovering around the man she's set her sights on."

Win squirmed awkwardly. "I've been getting the same feeling."

Julia had never been confident of her ability to attract men, but she felt the need to attempt flirtation with Win. She liked him, really liked him. She moved a step closer, near enough to catch a whiff of his alluring scent, to feel the power and strength that was only a touch away.

"What feeling do you have about me, Win Calloway? Not the same vibrations Trudy sets off, I hope," she said as she stared directly into his midnight black eyes.

Desire hit Win like a stack of bricks. He couldn't honestly say he hadn't seen it coming, because he had suffered an immediate and startling reaction to Julia the moment he scraped her off the street and scooped her into his arms. She appealed to everything masculine in him. She was bubbly, vivacious, quick to laugh and smile, enthusiastic . . . and she had the most kissable mouth ever etched on a feminine face.

It was too soon to test his reaction to her. He might offend her if he came on too strong too fast. Hell, they had only known each other for a few hours, though he felt as if he had waited a lifetime to meet someone like her—someone different, someone forthright and independent, not helpless and clingy. Too many people around Bugtussle looked up to him, relied on him. He didn't want a woman who offered more of the same. He wanted someone who could stand strong beside him and offer him the kind of support and enthusiasm he usually heaped on everyone else.

Even while Win told himself it was too soon to make amorous advances he wanted to kiss the breath out of Julia. He could feel his head moving toward hers, compensating for the differences in their height. He longed to taste those petal-soft lips and sip the sweet nectar within.

An instant jolt of awareness sizzled through Julia when she realized that Win meant to kiss her, that she *wanted* him to kiss her. For a woman who had been extremely cautious around men, Julia was tempted to throw her arms around his neck, hug him close, and discover if this really was the man of her dreams, even if he had been born a century too early for her.

She waited with bated breath, wanting him to be the one who made the first move, because that was important to her. She needed to know that he was feeling these same tingling sensations.

"Hey, Win! You'll have to show us where to hang these pulleys and ropes."

Win snapped up his head and Julia silently cursed the well-meaning men who waited on the stage.

Win stepped away, his easygoing smile back in place. "You'll have to ask Jule. She dreamed up the idea for this contraption."

Julia squared her shoulders and moved swiftly down the aisle, wondering if the magical moment she anticipated simply wasn't meant to be. Probably not. If she let herself get too attached to Win Calloway it would be difficult to paint herself back into the future. She didn't need to be carrying any emotional baggage when she traveled through time again.

This is just an adventure, she reminded herself sensibly. *You have been playing it safe and cautious the past few years. It's time for a change. Enjoy every moment. Don't take yourself too seriously here. How can you possibly, for Pete's sake? You are about to become a theater performer and you don't know squat about it.*

"Now then," Julia said, taking command of the situation. "We will need a ladder to reach the overhead beams. Win, do you have one handy?"

"It's out back of the hotel," he replied.

"I'll fetch it," a stout, redhaired young man volunteered immediately.

When Carrot Head scurried off, Julia smiled, wondering how Win had helped this particular citizen get a new lease on life. There was another hard-luck story here, she suspected.

"What I have in mind," Julia told the volunteers, "is to stretch the rope and pulleys across the ceiling so that I can fly above the audience."

The men stared at her with their jaws scraping their chests.

"One rope needs to be anchored in the wings of the stage so someone can direct the speed of my flight."

"I will be in charge of manning that rope," Win insisted.

Julia wasn't surprised by the firm command. Win held himself personally responsible for everyone in town. She had become part of his extended family, and he was watching out for her safety.

"Then I will be in competent hands," she said without hesitation. She directed the men's attention to the rear balcony. "I want the long coil of rope secured to the beam so I can swing from the back balcony to the stage for the finale."

"Swing?" all five men parroted incredulously.

"Sure, just like Tarzan."

"Who?" Again in chorus.

"Friend of mine," she said with a dismissive shrug.

Win shook his head and frowned. "I swear, woman, you are way ahead of your time with these ideas for your stage show."

"Really? You think so?" He had no idea!

"Way ahead," he readily confirmed.

"While you're securing up the ropes, I'll work on the stage backdrops," Julia informed the men. "I'll be back after I change clothes. We'll get everything set up so I can make a trial flight this afternoon."

"Whoa, woman," Win spouted at her departing back. *"I* will be testing the equipment."

Julia wheeled around. "No," she told him firmly, "you will not." *She* had to test the rigging, because it might be her one and only rehearsal for the act she had yet to dream up. "Since I will be the one doing the flying, I will be the one doing the testing."

She saw another side of the easygoing man when his dark-eyed gaze riveted on her. His mouth flattened into an uncompromising line and he took on an intimidating stance. Tough yet gentle, she thought. Add those redeeming qualities to generous and reliable and what you had here was one helluva man.

Julia countered his black scowl with a brilliant smile. "Trust me on this one, Calloway. I know what I'm doing." She hoped.

"So you keep saying," he grumbled uneasily. "But it makes me twitchy to think of you taking a bad spill."

"Look, if I flop, literally, you can hire another performer for your grand opening—someone who doesn't mind keeping her feet planted firmly on the stage. I'm not holding you responsible. You are *not* responsible for *everyone* on this planet, Calloway. Just chill out."

When Julia whipped around and trotted through the side door, Win let out his breath in a rush. "Ever met a woman as independent, headstrong, and quick with strange turns of phrases as this one?" he asked the group of men.

The general consensus was no, not even close.

Win kept having mixed feelings about this fireball female he'd hired. He admired her daring spirit, but he felt a fierce need to protect her so she wouldn't get hurt. Most women he knew yielded to a man's command when he pressed an issue. Not Julia "I Can Fly" Harper. Hell, you'd think she had wings tucked under her yellow dress. You'd swear she had taken care of herself all thirty years of her life and had never allowed herself to depend on a man. Damn, she beat anything Win had ever seen.

"So, Win, where do you want to start?" Ben Grover questioned when he returned with the oversize ladder.

Win stared pensively at the rafters. If Julia was bound and determined to fly, then he sure as hell was going to supervise the construction of her flight contraption. The ropes and pulleys would be securely anchored so that he could control the speed and direction of her flight. That woman was not going to splatter her gorgeous body on the floor of his theater, because he intended to double-check every rope and pulley and ensure they could hold at least twice her weight!

Wearing the tight-fitting, ridiculous-looking knickers she found in her luggage, Julia returned to the theater. She was not about to tramp around in a dress while she painted stage scenery. First thing tomorrow, she promised herself, she was going to consult the local seamstress about designing clothes that suited her active lifestyle. Flouncy dresses with enough yards of fabric to mummify a horse definitely had to go!

While the men climbed up and down the ladder, connecting and securing the ropes and pulleys, Julia spread a tarp, then mixed her paint. She decided on a jungle scene, since safari settings were all the rage in modern-day Dallas and Fort Worth.

With the kind of enthusiasm and excitement she hadn't experienced in years, Julia set to work on a background of palm trees, ferns, and tangled vines that opened to a spectacular waterfall. She didn't have time for extensive detail on this first mural, since she was working on a short clock, but the scene came together nicely. She had decided to make several sets of portable stage screens, which could be changed easily during the course of a week. She wanted something new and different to lure Win's audience back to his theater. Even if her singing and dancing were mediocre, the scenery would be eye-catching.

The mural she had painted for the Frontier Day Octoberfest had been good practice, she realized as she worked. She had made amazing progress on the jungle scene when Win called her over to test the rigging.

Julia smiled in satisfaction as she appraised the leather harness that was hooked to two wires connected to the overhead ropes and pulleys. She stepped into the harness that supported her hips and shoulders, then waited impatiently for Win to man the dangling rope that hung in the wings.

"I'm ready!" Julia called to him as she slid her gloves on her hands.

Win grabbed the rope and braced his legs. "All right, daredevil, let's hope this holds you up."

Julia improvised by making two stag leaps, which she had learned years ago in gymnastic class; then she lunged forward, her arms outstretched, and swooped off the stage. Although Win squawked in frustration, because Julia hadn't cued him for her leap, he managed to yank down on the rope so that Julia sailed above the rows of chairs and benches. When he yanked downward again, she soared higher and higher.

"Let me down lower!" Julia called to him. "Then pull me back toward the stage!"

Win strained against the rope, his gaze glued to the riggings—in case they broke loose.

"Okay, now let's try it again," Julia called out. "Swing me from the stage all the way to the back balcony."

Again, she breezed over the chairs, arcing toward the rear balcony. Gracefully, she reached out to steady herself on the railing, pirouetted, then stood up to grab the dangling rope that Win had hung above the back balcony.

When she unhooked the harness wires the men gasped for breath. Julia stood precariously on the railing—with nothing but her sense of balance to steady her. She grabbed the second rope, drew up her legs, swished through the air and swooped toward the stage. She slid her hands down the rope while in midair so that she could alight on the stage.

Problem was, Julia misjudged how far to slide her gloved hands down the rope. She came too close to the edge of the stage, bumped her hip, spun like a top, then windmilled across the floor.

Win charged across the stage when he realized Julia was about to make a crash landing. She plowed into him before he could set his feet. They cartwheeled across the polished floor and landed in a tangle of arms and legs—with Win on top.

Julia instantly forgot about her miscalculation. The feel of Win's muscled body pressed intimately to hers sent shock waves radiating through her. When he looked down, his raven hair flopping over his forehead, his eyes wide with surprise, Julia forgot to breathe. His knee was squarely between her thighs, his chest meshed to her breasts.

He felt good. He felt right. He felt as if he belonged there, body to body, heart to heart, she thought to herself.

"You okay?" he murmured, his gaze focused on her parted lips.

"Perfect," she whispered up to him.

"Jule . . ." he said and groaned low in his throat.

"Hey, is everybody up there all right?" Ben Grover called out.

Win tore his gaze away from her tempting mouth, amazed at how easily he forgot they weren't alone. Odd, when he was this close to Julia, the world shrank to a size no larger than she occupied. Although the man in him begged him to stay where he was a little longer, Win forced himself to shift sideways. He propped Julia up beside him, then combed the tangle of blond curls from her flushed face.

"We're fine," Win assured his friends. "Nothing broken. Bruised a little maybe."

Julia bounded to her feet, flashed a smile to disguise the shaky sensations that had nothing whatsoever to do with her acrobatic crash landing. Damn, the effect Win Calloway had on her was startling. She had wondered how it would feel to be intimately close to him, to have his muscled weight pressed to hers. Now she knew.

There was something instinctively explosive about her attraction to this man. Julia had the unmistakable feeling that if Win Calloway ever kissed her—et cetera, et cetera— it would be all over but the shouting.

Julia suspected there would be a lot to shout about, too.

Determined to get her stage landing right, Julia walked through the theater and bounded up the balcony steps to grab the swinging rope. She tied a knot at the precise place that would allow her to touch down on the stage without another mishap.

"I'm coming down again," she hollered at Win. "Get out of the way so I don't plow over you."

"No, damn it," he exploded. "You're not going to kill yourself! I won't allow it! You were lucky the first time. Now get the hell off that balcony railing!"

The group of men gaped at Win. He scowled. He had never once raised his voice to anyone in Bugtussle. He had learned to control his temper and his emotions years ago—during that hellish war, to be precise. But Julia's shocking effect on him and her reckless daring were getting to him. Win kept telling himself it was only concern that roiled inside him, but he didn't make it a point to lie to himself. Hell! He had to turn away from the other men to conceal the bulge in his breeches. Damnation, he hadn't been this randy since adolescence struck half a lifetime ago!

Muttering, Win stared up at the balcony, where Julia was perched like a parrot, refusing to obey his order to abandon her stunt. She stood there with that glorious mane of curly gold hair cascading over her shoulders, her eyes alight with excitement, her curvaceous body outlined in those tight-fitting pink pants and that skimpy blue camisole. She was defying him outright.

Funny, he thought as he met her stare for stare, he had never minded a woman displaying her assets before. Now, he felt damned possessive, compelled to march up there and cover Julia so the other men, who had been gawking at her while she painted the background scenery, couldn't speculate on how she'd look in the altogether.

"And double damn it, Jule," he erupted again. "Don't you dare say trust me on this one! I've heard that one time too many already! Now get the hell down!"

Her playful laughter wafted through the theater and floated toward Win. He knew what this infuriating imp was going to say before the words were out of her mouth.

"Hey, trust me on this one, Win. This is going to work. No problem!"

Win stood there at center stage, his feet askance, determined to catch her if she misjudged the length of the rope again. While he watched her plunge through the air, her legs sweeping back and forth, a delighted smile on her lips, he realized this woman who had come into his life like a misdirected cyclone had added the kind of excitement and challenge he had been missing.

Julia hit the stage with a perfectly executed cartwheel, then bounded up in front of Win to fling her arms around his neck. Her bubbling laughter echoed around them.

"Told you so," she said elfishly.

Again, desire hit him like a runaway locomotive. "Damn it, woman, you're making me crazy. . . ."

"Win Calloway, what is going on in here?"

Julia stepped away when she heard the clanging voice rolling from the doorway. Before she turned around, she knew who had arrived on the scene. Trudy Fletcher's sugar-coated voice had turned sour. She glared patriot missiles at Julia as she flounced down the aisle.

"Really, Win," Trudy chided from the orchestra pit. "I am appalled that a man of your status would carry on with this floozy in front of an audience of your friends! She is making an embarrassing spectacle of you!"

"Now hold on, Trudy," Win said as he surged forward. "You have no call for insults. Julia is rehearsing for her performance."

"Is that what you call it?" She smirked disdainfully. "That isn't all this two-bit harlot is working on. It is plain to see that she is after your money and she is using that indecent getup to lure you in! I will not stand aside and let this shameless hussy spoil what is between us!"

"There is nothing between us," Win told her flat-out.

Julia watched Trudy's face turn the exact shade of her fashionable ensemble. The younger woman looked furious enough to commit murder.

Before Trudy further exposed her nasty temperament, she managed to regroup, then tipped up her chin. "Papa sent me over here to ask you if you could have a conference with him now. He has some spare time."

"Go ahead," Julia insisted, refusing to dignify Trudy's murderous glower with more than a fleeting glance. "The rigging has passed the test. I want to work on the backdrop this evening and then practice my songs with the pianist. I can manage on my own."

Win glanced back at her and she smiled reassuringly.

"No more trial flights, I promise," she assured him.

"I'll hold you to that. We don't have a doctor in town yet, so I'd just as soon you didn't break or twist anything that Bea Garner and I can't fix."

When Win strode off the stage, Julia kindly thanked the other men for helping with the construction project. The men dispersed and Julia returned to her landscape painting. She had made an enemy of the Fletcher Twit, she knew. Julia made a mental note to check the ropes for evidence of tampering before each performance. She wouldn't put a staged accident past sweet little Trudy. The woman was determined to nab Win for her husband, by hook, crook—or severed ropes.

Julia wasn't the least bit surprised that Win didn't return in time to escort her to supper. No doubt, Trudy had schemed and manipulated him into coming to her home for dinner. Not that Julia could spare the time right now anyway. After working on the stage scenery, she had to rehearse with the pianist who played in the barroom.

Despite arthritic fingers, Daniel Spencer was a master pianist. Julia wondered where this old man had wandered in from to become one of Calloway's lost-then-found flock.

"You know "The Flying Trapeze," I hope," Julia said to Daniel. She wasn't sure when that song had come into existence. She sincerely hoped it was before 1880.

"Sure do, hon." Daniel limbered up his stiff fingers,

then plunked down on the piano bench in the orchestra pit. "I play by ear, as well as read music, so if you can sing something I can pick it out and play along. My friend Edgar plays the banjo. He said if you wanted him to play for you he'd be glad to do it. He owes Win a favor or two."

"Now why am I not surprised," Julia mused aloud.

When Daniel showed her several pieces of sheet music he had on hand, Julia asked him to play so she could sing along. He sent her a few curious glances when she stumbled over the unfamiliar words, but he didn't comment. Apparently, he was surprised that she didn't know the popular songs.

Julia promised herself she would know the words on all the sheet music in time for her first performance, even if she had to stay up all night memorizing them!

After two hours, Julia had gained command of the songs she planned to perform. She asked Daniel to pick up the beat of two tunes to make them more lively. He accommodated without missing a single note. The man was damn good. Julia figured Daniel's talent at the piano, plus Edgar on the banjo, would carry her mediocre voice through her theater acts.

I can do this, no sweat, Julia told herself repeatedly. The audience would be distracted by what she was *doing,* not focused on how well she sang while she buzzed over their heads like an oversize bee.

"Thanks for the help, Daniel," Julia said as she returned his sheet music. "I've taken up too much of your time. Sorry about that. I suspect you're due at the bar already."

Daniel shrugged his thin-bladed shoulders. "Not to worry, Miss Julia. Most of the men in the bar come to drink themselves deaf and blind. Rarely do they remember whether I was at the piano or not. But this"—he winked at her—"is going to be very interesting. I heard gossip that you aren't planning to spend a whole lot of time standing at front and center stage."

Julia grinned at the kindly old man. "You heard right. I plan to be all over the place, so don't be surprised where I cue you from."

He eyed her pensively, grinned, then nodded. "I'm thinking a woman like you is full of interesting surprises. Where were you about forty years ago, girl?"

When Daniel strode away, Julia sensed that she had made another friend in Bugtussle. Daniel's talented knack of filling in notes that weren't on the sheet music added a perky beat to liven up the simple songs. Julia suspected he had played other places besides bars in frontier towns. The man was teeming with talent, and Julia was certain he would make her sound much better than she was when she sang.

Exhausted, Julia trudged upstairs. To her delight, Bea was waiting with a tray of steak, homemade biscuits, and apple pie that put Julia's taste buds on full alert.

"You've had a big day, gal," Bea said as she plunked down on the end of the bed. "And productive, too, from what I hear. Thought you'd be hungry since that Fletcher twit finagled Win into going to her house for supper. Told you she was scheming to get her hooks in the man.

"He's like my own son," Bea added. "Don't want some half-baked female like Trudy making his life miserable."

"Bea, about this plot," Julia began as she dived eagerly into the steak. "I don't do devious very well. Don't get me wrong here—I want what's best for Calloway, too. He's a very special kind of man, but—"

"But nothing," Bea argued. "There ain't nothing dis-honest about you showing interest in a man you obviously like and respect. Just don't hold back your feelings on account of that Fletcher twit. You've seen how she operates. That twit has no consideration for anybody but herself. She's rude and insulting to anyone who threatens what she wants. You need examples? I'll give you a few."

"Fire away," Julia offered as she attacked her delicious dinner.

Bea plucked up a biscuit, chewed, and swallowed. "There was the time when Win hired a schoolmarm who turned out to be sweet on him. Trudy became insanely jealous, so she lured in one of the cowboys who works at Win's ranch and convinced him the schoolmarm was sweet on him. Then Trudy sent a message to Win and he came right on cue to find them sprawled on the sofa together. Trudy had drugged their drinks.

"The schoolmarm was thoroughly humiliated when she woke up to find her dress unfastened and the cowboy's shirt gaping open. The poor woman was forced to leave town because Otis Fletcher insisted she was unfit to teach the children. He loaded her up on the first stage out of town, and Win didn't know she had left until she was long gone."

"You didn't tell Calloway what happened?" Julia asked between bites.

" 'Course I told him when I found out the whole thing was staged, but it was too late. The teacher wasn't around and Win just went back to helping the next poor soul who showed up in town. Ask me, he liked the schoolmarm well enough, but there wasn't any magic. Gotta have magic, same as there was with me and Rupert."

Julia watched a faraway look settle on Bea's wrinkled features. Clearly, the old woman had loved her husband dearly.

"Gotta be magic," Bea murmured, smiling. "Gotta be lightning striking if it's the lasting kind of love. When it happens, you just know it. Wham, it's there and it don't go away, not in all the years to come. It nearly killed me when Rupert died. I had no family of my own, but Win's kindness and encouragement gave me new purpose.

"Now maybe a traveling gal like you never stayed in one place long enough to find the magic, but I'm here to tell you it exists. Too often women just settle for what's handy and available, because they want a home and security, because that's what's expected of them. Demanded of them sometimes."

The fact that Julia felt the makings of "magic" when she was up close and personal with Win made her uneasy and eager at once. She was out of her time and place temporarily. She couldn't expect anyone here to understand that, but she had no idea where her future would lead. She had to paint herself back into the twentieth century sooner or later. She had left unfinished business. Her car was parked across the street from the mural she'd painted. She had a high-rise apartment and her art gallery and a dear friend in Philly . . . .

"Well, I gotta go, gal. Kitchen needs to be spiffed up before we close down for the night." Bea rose from the bed, then patted Julia on the shoulder. "Bugtussle ain't a bad place to settle down if you get the hankering. One or two troublesome folks like Trudy around, but otherwise a good-hearted lot. If I were you, when Win looks at you the way he does when he thinks nobody sees, I'd be testing the waters. 'Course, if you only stay long enough to stir up that Fletcher twit so she makes a grand fool of herself I'll be mighty beholden."

Bea ambled toward the door. "Breakfast is at six, gal."

"I'll be in the restaurant," Julia insisted. "No need for

you to cart a meal up here. Heaven knows you've got enough to do already."

Bea halted, then spun around. "You're a good woman, Julia Harper—nothing like the usual traveling performers Win hired in the past. Daniel Spencer said the same thing to me a while ago."

"He was an accomplished musician, wasn't he?" Julia guessed.

Bea nodded her fuzzy gray head. "Back in Boston," she confided. "His own brother tossed him out in favor of a starlet who caught his eye. He used Daniel's talent to give her a strong start. Damn shame when you're own family stabs you in the back like that. Broke Daniel's heart and soul, it did. Took to drinking, but Win found out he played piano and put him to work. Wouldn't pay him with anything but poker chips that first year. Daniel could only redeem the chips for food, lodging, and clothing from the mercantile shop. Win dried the man out and treats him like family. Daniel never forgot the favor."

When Bea exited, Julia shook her head in amazement. Win Calloway was definitely a rare gem. Good men were so hard to find—at least men who met Julia's high expectations.

For a whimsical moment Julia let herself imagine what it would be like to give in to this attraction, to explore it, to be unafraid of putting her heart on the line.

Fat chance of anything developing in the short time she had here, Julia thought to herself. Calloway appeared to be a man accustomed to restraining himself. He proceeded with casual patience. His dealings with his oppressed flock of lost souls indicated that he set a slow, steady pace. Unfortunately Julia didn't have a couple of years to hang around in 1880. Before long, she would be listed as a missing person, then presumed dead. She had to go back to the future and wrap up loose ends.

Mulling over that thought, Julia grabbed the slinky negligee from her luggage and collapsed in bed. She needed her rest if she was going to paint more scenery and choreograph dance steps to distract the audience from her average singing voice!

Chapter Four

Win Calloway paced in the wings, nervous as a caged tiger. He hadn't seen Julia except in passing all day. She had been working intently on finishing one set of stage scenery; then she had begun another. Watching her work assured Win that Julia was an intense person. She attacked a project and didn't let up until she reached her goals—same way Win had a habit of doing.

They hadn't spent a private moment together for two days. He'd been busy with last minute arrangements of rounding up ticket takers for both evening performances, checking inventory in the bar, and fending off Trudy Fletcher who popped up like a jack-in-the-box to flaunt herself at him.

Certainly, Win knew Trudy was up to her manipulative games. She'd become more aggressive since Julia arrived. Trudy had dragged Win to a nonexistent conference at the bank with her father, who had been in a meeting with one of the local farmers who needed a loan; and Win had no choice but to visit Otis after bank hours.

Win had put his foot down firmly when Otis declared he had decided to foreclose, since the down-and-out farmer couldn't make another installment because of crop failure. Otis was letting the power of his position go to his head. He was behaving as if *he* owned the blasted bank and had the power to turn out struggling farmers and ranchers at will.

It was not going to happen. Win wouldn't let it. After a long discussion with Otis, Win had declared that Otis was not going to foreclose on anyone without his express written consent; otherwise the pompous banker could look for a new job.

To top off the frustrating evening, Trudy had appeared on the front porch, dressed in a clinging gown that showcased her feminine assets. She had thrown herself at Win and nearly kissed his lips off before he could untangle her octopus arms and skedaddle. Win was pretty sure Trudy had plotted to set him up—she had a history of that—in hopes that her father would see them and demand a wedding to compensate for the blemish on his precious daughter's reputation.

Win had come to the conclusion that helping the Fletchers had been the one mistake he had made in Bugtussle. The other citizens had turned their lives around to make new starts. In the Fletchers' case, man, wife, and daughter had allowed financial success to go straight to their swelled heads.

Although Win had apologized to Julia for breaking their dinner date he still felt bad about it, but he'd had to get things squared away with Otis before that struggling farmer with mounting loans was forced off the farm he'd built with his own two hands.

Win checked his watch for the fourth time and stewed about where Julia was. The grand opening performance was due to start in less than thirty minutes. Where the hell was that woman?

"Win! You gotta see this!" Daniel Spencer called from the door that opened onto the street.

Frowning in concern, Win sprinted down the aisle. To his amazement, he saw Julia dressed in a colorful, formfitting costume that was covered with blue sequins, driving a carriage that was surrounded with signs that announced the evening performances. The cattle drovers who had camped west of town had left their herds with a skeleton crew and come trotting after her. Railroad track layers, off duty for the evening, were also at her heels. There were virtually hundreds of men from outlying areas forming a line behind Julia.

"First time I ever saw a traveling performer drum up this much business," Daniel said, shaking his gray head and grinning in amusement. "There is no way all these folks are going to fit into two performances, not when the whole town plans to attend, too. None of the citizens around here want to let you down, not after all you've done for us. Everybody will be here tonight with bells on."

Win wasn't paying much attention to what the pianist said. His gaze, and his thoughts, were focused on the alluring costume that attested to Julia's well-conditioned body. Heaven knew Win had speculated on how she would look naked—more times than he cared to count. For all his casual nonchalance, the woman aroused him, even when she wasn't trying, even when she was simply bubbling with laughter or swinging through the air during her devil-may-care plunge over the stage. Damn it, he could just look into those sparkling blue eyes and forget everything except his want of her.

What the hell was wrong with him? He'd never been so instantly attracted to a woman before. He was always in control—polite, reserved, patient. But this vivacious woman tested his willpower every time he got within ten feet of her.

No telling what he might have done when he found himself sprawled on top of Julia after her crash landing on the stage if they hadn't had an audience! That wasn't like him. He had a reputation for treating women with consideration and respect, but Julia inspired sensations that he had to battle willfully to control. What was there about that woman that sent logic and honorable intentions flying off in the wind?

He'd only known Julia for a couple of days and already he was a walking mass of unruly urges! This had to stop!

"Better open both doors, boss," Daniel suggested. "This place is going to be filled to capacity pretty quick." He flexed his fingers. "I better go warm up in the bar. Got a feeling I need to be at my best tonight."

The hired help came running to set up the ticket booths and light the extra lanterns Julia had placed in the theater. Conversation and laughter filled Main Street as Julia approached like the Pied Piper.

Win's knees wobbled when Julia bounded agilely from the carriage, waved her arms in enthusiastic gestures, then flashed him a blinding smile. He just stood there looking stupid, wearing an idiot's grin . . . until Trudy appeared beside him and clung to his arm like Spanish moss.

"My God, Win, that woman is making an absolute spectacle of herself again, isn't she? I suspect you are embarrassed to no end by her costume and her shameless theatrics."

Although Trudy was trying to plant negative thoughts in Win's head, he was wise to her scheme. Furthermore, he wasn't embarrassed. He was flattered that Julia had gone to great lengths to ensure the success of the newly expanded opera house. No one had gone to such extremes for him before.

Oh certainly, he had been properly thanked for his generosity and had acquired scores of lifelong friends who were willing to lend a hand when he needed it, but this was different. This was a stranger who had opened her heart to him, to this town. She had worked extra hours to provide spectacular stage scenery to brighten up his theater.

The woman was a talented artist, in addition to her other admirable traits. Win never imagined having such impressive scenery in the opera house, but Julia whipped them up and behaved as if it took no special effort. He knew better, because he had seen her busting her fanny for hours on end.

Win moved aside when the eager crowd surged toward the double doors. He turned to see another boisterous crowd enter from the side exit that adjoined the bar. In fifteen minutes, the theater was packed, and Daniel appeared with Edgar, the banjo player, in the orchestra pit. Daniel struck up with soothing music—Bach and Beethoven, if Win was guessing correctly—to keep the crowd from starting a ruckus.

Making his way behind stage, Win waited for Julia to arrive. She bounded toward him like a jackrabbit, all smiles and customary enthusiasm.

"Okay, Win, here's the deal," she said as she halted in front of him. "I think the crowd is large enough to warrant a third performance this evening. I want the gate for bringing in extra business."

Win felt disappointment crawl through him. Maybe he had given Julia more credit than she deserved. "Fine, you can have all the profit from the third performance," he said flatly.

"What you collect from the third show will go into a fund for families in need," Julia insisted. "The only salary cut from the profit goes to Daniel and Edgar, not to me. Deal?"

"Deal," Win readily agreed, his faith in Julia restored—tripled was nearer the mark. "We'll call it the Harper Relief Fund."

"Thanks, Win. I don't want you to be the only one around here having all the fun of extending a helping hand to those in need."

He eyed her for a long moment. "The ravages of war taught me to spare my fellow man from suffering. What motivates *you*, Jule?" he questioned curiously.

Julia flung her arms around his neck impulsively, then reached up on tiptoe to press a hasty kiss to his lips. "You do, Win Calloway. You restored my faith in men and gave me a rewarding purpose. You treated a virtual stranger like a welcomed friend. I owe you."

She bounded off like the hurricane she was. "My first act will be a dance performed on stage to Daniel and Edgar's lively music. The second act is a song and dance. The third is a sing-along song to keep the audience involved. After that, I'll come to you so you can hook up the wires for the harness. I'll be off and flying in the fourth act. Any questions?"

Yeah, what the hell am I going to do for enjoyment when you board the stagecoach and take your acts on the road again? "No, I'll follow your cues," he said instead.

Julia put her nervous energy to good use by limbering up for her first act. She had choreographed a combination of gymnastic stunts and aerobic routines she had learned at her health club. She hoped the razzle-dazzle and acrobats would grab the audience's attention and help her work through her nervousness.

By the time she had to sing and dance, she hoped her voice would be steady. Daniel's ad-libs on the keyboard would entertain the crowd, too, and the sing-along would have the rafters vibrating. She hoped her grand finale would put praise on the lips of the theatergoers as they exited. With any luck, the crowd would be compelled to return the following night. Of course, that would mean Julia would have to constantly add new songs and dance routines to keep her acts fresh, but she looked forward to the challenge.

Julia was determined to give the audience all she had to add enjoyment to their long workdays. Before her leap into the Old West, she had never felt so uninhibited, so free to express herself. This unprecedented experience had given her a new perspective. She wanted to share her pleasure with everyone she came into contact with. She wanted to live every day to its fullest.

When Julia heard Win's voice carrying through the opera house, announcing her as a celebrated star of stage and theater, Julia inhaled a deep, steadying breath. As the curtains opened, Julia gave Daniel his cue, and she put her heart and soul into pleasing the crowd with her lively dance and acrobatic routine.

His mouth gaping, Win watched Julia bound around the stage in rhythm with Daniel's and Edgar's fast-tempoed tune. She cartwheeled, she somersaulted, she shimmied and flung out those shapely, mile-long legs in a performance that exceeded every expectation and outshined any show he had ever seen or heard of!

It was amazing, absolutely amazing! Apparently, Win

wasn't the only one who thought so, because the crowd was hooting, cheering, and bursting out with wolfish whistles and applause. The woman was spectacular and every man in the opera house was all eyes and broad smiles.

When Julia completed her first unusual dance routine, the crowd roared for more. The applause shook the rafters. As soon as Julia burst out in song and danced back and forth across the stage—using every square inch of it—the audience settled in to watch and listen.

Win couldn't say how good Julia's voice was, because he was so busy watching her graceful body movements and hand gestures. He was lost in an erotic fantasy—and he knew exactly why Julia had entitled her performance Autumn Fantasia. He couldn't imagine how any future acts he booked for the opera house could compare to hers—and she hadn't even gotten to her grand finale yet . . . !

The thought jolted him back to his senses. He whipped around to double-check the pulley system, though he'd already checked it four times that afternoon.

When Julia raced toward him, amid catcalls and uproarious applause, her face flushed with exertion and excitement, fierce need hit Win squarely below the belt buckle. He just stood there, absorbing the essence of this lively female, this crowd pleaser who was giving her audience more than their money's worth.

"Hook me up," Julia said.

Win shook himself from his daze and groped for the wires that were to be attached to the rings of the harness on her shoulder blades. "Be careful when you swing from the back balcony," he cautioned. "Don't miss the stage."

"No problem."

"That's what you said before we both went winding. Not that I didn't enjoy it—"

"Me, too, Win," she said before she bounded off to incite another uproar.

Did that mean Julia didn't mind him being sprawled on top of her? Was she hinting she welcomed his advances? The speculation sent hungry anticipation flooding over him, and Win had to give himself a mental slap before he got so distracted that he forgot to look for his cue.

With a wave of her arms, Julia signaled Win to lift her off the stage as she burst into the first verse of "The Flying Trapeze." The audience cheered as Julia soared toward the balcony, then twirled herself around in midair as she swung back to the stage. Then she propelled herself sideways—which was not the way she had rehearsed!—to glide gracefully toward the audience seated in the side balconies. Win waited until Julia lost momentum before he tugged on the rope and launched her toward the rear balcony again.

The audience twisted around in their seats and gasped as Julia teetered on the railing and reached back to unhook her harness. While she belted out the chorus, she swooped through the air, hanging on to her rope. Win held his breath, but he worried for naught. Julia alighted as gracefully as a butterfly to take her bow.

If Win thought the roar of applause was deafening before, it was thunderous now! There was so much whooping and hollering from cowboys and track layers that the sound drowned out the music. Every face in the crowd beamed like a beacon—with one exception. Trudy Fletcher sat in the front row, glowering at Julia.

Win suddenly recalled every stunt Trudy had pulled to discourage other women Win had taken a temporary interest in the past few years. He didn't like the hatred etched in Trudy's puckered face, and he wondered to what extremes she would go to destroy Julia's moment of theatrical glory. Win would have to keep a close watch on Trudy. If she did anything to ruin Julia's happiness, he would be all over that chit like lice on cattle.

The uneasy moment was forgotten when Julia rushed toward him while he closed the curtains. She wasn't looking for his praise; she just flung her arms around him and hugged him excitedly.

"Was that fun or what?" she bubbled, her eyes sparkling. "I didn't realize I was such a people person until tonight."

Her odd comments flew over his head—the same way she whizzed over the audience singing at the top of her lungs. All Win could think to do was wrap her tightly in his arms and deliver the kiss that had been interrupted the first day he met her.

Julia's legs turned to the consistency of cooked noodles in a heartbeat. The easygoing, reserved Win Calloway delivered a lip-sizzling wallop when he got down to the serious business of kissing! She wasn't accustomed to this level of emotional intensity. Nothing had prepared her for the sensations Win stirred in her. Maybe the thrill of her successful performance added fuel to the sensual fire he ignited. She didn't know, didn't have time to figure it out. All she knew was that she felt as if she had been lightning struck . . . .

Oh my God! It's just like Bea Garner described. The magic! According to Bea, it was either there or it wasn't. Julia had been there lots of times with other men when it *wasn't*.

It was most definitely *here . . . now . . . .*

Wild, rippling sensations cascaded through Julia like an electrical current while Win plundered her mouth with a desperate impatience to match her own. He hauled her against his muscled contours, and Julia realized instantly that he was fully aroused. He had pressed his hips against her in a frantic gesture that indicated he couldn't get close enough to satisfy the need boiling between them. She knew exactly how he felt. The barrier of clothing and theatrical harness provided a frustrating obstacle. It didn't matter that this wasn't the time or the place. What mattered was this explosive, ungovernable need that had come to life and burned like wildfire.

Julia gave as fervently as she got in that breathless moment. She didn't know if this was pure physical desire and nothing more, on Win's part—but spontaneous wanting was mutual and it was feeding on itself.

Moments later—maybe a century or so; Win couldn't tell for sure—the roar of the crowd demanded an encore. Win staggered back and steadied himself by grabbing the curtain. Nothing had ever hit him this hard or fast—except maybe an unexpected punch in the barroom brawls he occasionally broke up. He should apologize for dragging Julia against him and sucking the breath out of her, but he couldn't form the words. That kiss was there between them, erasing everything that had come before. It was just there, tingling through him until his toes curled up in his boots and the throb in his lower extremities made him want to drop to his knees and howl.

"Jule?" That was all he could get out—one word, swear to God. One croaked syllable that was his pet name for her.

"Win?" She peered up at him with dazed, rounded blue eyes. Her mouth was swollen from his ravishing kiss and she was swaying on her feet.

The crowd began chanting: "Julia, Julia, we want Julia." Nothing was going to shut them up except her reappearance on stage.

"Damn," she wheezed, then managed an impish grin. "When you kiss a woman, you don't hold anything back, do you, Calloway? My jazzy song and dance routine doesn't hold a candle to *your* performance."

Julia made a hasty return through the opening in the curtains, then cued Daniel and Edgar to play the song they had rehearsed that afternoon. Julia ad-libbed with a few lively kicks and hand gestures, then bounded down the steps that led from the stage to the audience seats. Encouraging the crowd to their feet, she motioned them into the aisles and out the doors.

Men followed her eagerly, which was a darn good thing, because her repertoire of nineteenth-century tunes was still limited and her head was still spinning from the aftereffects of Win's scorching kiss.

Julia definitely needed time to catch her breath and compose herself before her next scheduled performance!

Win Calloway was full of unexpected surprises, she mused as she trotted around the opera house to enter through the kitchen. She wasn't used to the kind of sensual excitement Win Calloway provided when he stepped from behind that wall of polite reserve to become a sensual wild man!

During the week that followed, news of Julia's high-energy performances at the opera house spread far and wide. The autumn season for cattle drives kept cowboys pouring into town, and track layers made the return trip from their camps to be entertained. Folks from other nearby communities drove to Bugtussle to catch Julia's show and filled the barroom and restaurant to capacity.

Julia was performing three times a night for packed houses, and she spent her days busting her butt to create new and colorful stage scenery. She learned three new songs that Daniel Spencer had composed, and she studied the sheet music he brought to her so she could provide varied performances for the large crowds expected for the Saturday night show.

In her spare time—what little she had—Julia picked up scrap lumber behind the theater and bought a roll of fabric from the mercantile shop so she could construct a painting canvas. She had to work on her modern-day painting of Bugtussle so she could make her return trip to the future.

The inescapable truth was that she was getting entirely too attached to Win Calloway. Her growing affection for him was making her nervous. She had to return to her own life before she fell so deeply in love that she would be miserable in the future.

Although Win had withdrawn into his reserved shell, offering no repeat performances of that blazing kiss, he was always nearby, checking the riggings for her flight contraption, asking if there was anything she needed. Julia was vividly aware of him and she longed for more than the easy friendship and camaraderie between them, even though she considered those sensuous thoughts risky business.

What was she supposed to do in this peculiar situation she found herself in? Sit Win down and say: *Here's the deal, Calloway. I came here from the end of the twentieth century, but I'm afraid I'm dangerously close to falling in love with you. So . . . do you want to take a quantum leap through time with me and see if we can make a go of it?*

Somehow complete honesty just didn't seem to cut it. Julia decided to play it cool, to enjoy this unusual vacation of hers and then return to 1999 and make a meaningful contribution to society—as she was doing here and now. Or *back then*, as this case happened to be.

Fact was, this was the first time Julia felt as if she belonged somewhere in almost a decade. She was no longer isolated, no longer afraid of being hurt. This launch into the past had brought out the best in her, left her living up to full potential, meeting new challenges. She hadn't been this happy and carefree since childhood.

Damn, she felt as if she were being pulled in two directions at once. She didn't want to turn her back on the friendships she had developed in the Old West. She wanted to explore her relationship with Win, because he attracted her the way no man ever had. But this wasn't her time and place. Every day she struggled with the fact that she knew what the future held, yet she also knew she couldn't change history. How could she possibly live beyond her time?

Julia had a real conundrum here. What her heart, her mind and her feminine body told her to do was in constant conflict. She knew she should leave, but she wanted to stay just a little while longer.

"My goodness, Jule, what are you painting?"

A warm tingle skittered through her when she heard Win's rich baritone voice rolling down the theater aisle. She pivoted away from the new stage set she was working on to see Win striding toward her.

"Too far out, do you think?" she asked. "I'm calling it science-fiction fantasy. *My* vision on the future, so to speak."

Win halted at the edge of the orchestra pit to appraise the unfamiliar vehicles with dark tires and surrounding glass. He studied the tall buildings that lined a road, which looked as if it were paved with mortar. Then he recalled Julia's odd turn of phrase. *Too far out?* She sure had a peculiar way of saying things.

Win climbed the steps to stand beside her on the stage. "This new stage setting for your act isn't going to entail more rigging for flight, is it?" he asked warily.

Julia flashed him an impish grin. "How'd you ever guess?"

"Because I think I've gotten to know you pretty well this past week. You like to stretch the limits. Not that I don't shake my head in amazement like the rest of your mesmerized audiences, because I do. And don't get me wrong, I appreciate all your extra efforts in my behalf, but no one else I've hired to entertain has gone to such extremes to make my theater such a success." He stared at her ponderously. "Why are you doing all this? Why do you keep turning down the extra pay I offer you?"

"Because I'm enjoying what I'm doing and I like you." That much Julia could tell him without revealing too much of her feelings. "I've developed a fond attachment to everybody in town. Everyone has made me feel welcome and wanted, and I enjoy helping other people. It makes me feel good. For the first time in a very long time I feel as if I'm giving something back. The roar of applause makes me want to create new ways to please and entertain."

"I can't imagine how this town could be so much different from the other places you've performed. I suspect your impressive talents draw enthusiastic crowds everywhere," Win insisted.

He watched Julia—ogled her shapely backside was more accurate—as she turned to work on the scenic backdrops. Truth was Win couldn't keep his eyes off her—and it got progressively worse with each passing day. He had tried to keep his distance, knowing she wouldn't be in town much longer, but damn it, this woman stirred him up.

"Um . . . Jule? I know I hired you for only two weeks, but I was wondering if maybe . . . Well, I don't know what your schedule is, of course, but . . . er . . . would you be interested in staying another two weeks?"

Julia set aside her paintbrush and smiled up at him.

Desire hit him hard and fast, just as it always did when he was with her. It had become such a reflexive reaction that Win couldn't control it. He dreamed up excuses to stop by to see her while she worked.

True, Julia wore the most unconventional garb he'd ever seen—odd-looking garments she had designed and had the local seamstress whip up for her. But on the inside, where it really counted, Julia was one hell of a woman. Her fun-loving personality and tireless energy impressed him.

"I think I could squeeze in another couple of weeks in Bugtussle," she replied.

"Good." Win figured he was wearing another of those idiotic grins that crept to his lips every time he gazed into her sparkling blue eyes. He didn't really care. She made him feel good all over. "And something else you should know, Jule. I like you, too."

"You do?"

"Yeah. I came by to see if you could spare time to ride out to my ranch with me. I asked Bea to pack us a picnic lunch. You've been working nonstop for a week and you deserve some time off—"

"Win! Yoo-hoo, darling!"

Julia glanced toward the door to see Trudy Fletcher make her dramatic entrance in a matching ensemble of pink. The twit reminded Julia of a giant bottle of Pepto-Bismol. Which was a good thing, because Trudy could be very nauseating.

"I think we should go to lunch so we can talk privately," Trudy declared, refusing to acknowledge Julia's presence while feasting her greedy eyes on Win.

"Sorry, Trudy. I have other plans."

"But—"

Win replaced the lid on the paint can and took Julia's

arm. Julia could feel the heat of Trudy's glare burning through her clothes as Win led her across the stage to the adjoining door. Despite the hatred Julia knew was brewing in Trudy, Julia was delighted with the prospect of touring Win's ranch and spending an uninterrupted afternoon with him.

Trudy's venomous jealousy was quickly forgotten as Julia rode beside Win in the buggy, headed for the rolling hills that were alive with all the glorious colors of autumn.

Chapter Five

Julia sighed appreciatively as she surveyed the two-story stone ranch house, with its covered porch and whitewashed outbuildings, huge barn, and corrals, which were tucked against the north side of the hill to block off cold winter winds. The urge to paint this peaceful, scenic retreat was overwhelming. Julia sketched a mental picture of the ranch and promised to commit the beauty of the area to canvas as a parting gift for Win, first chance she got.

"Oh, Win, this place is lovely!" Julia said as he reined the carriage toward the front lawn.

"Thanks. I've had a lot of help keeping the place fixed up. I can't take credit for its appearance."

Julia smiled to herself as he lifted her from the buggy. No doubt, several folks in need of jobs had been hired to keep the ranch immaculate. This was yet another example of Win Calloway's technique of helping neighbors when times were hard.

"The ranch has grown to excessive proportions," he told Julia as he led the way up the stone path. "I had a small cattle herd, a few sheep to keep the lawn clipped down, and several acres of rich bottomland beside the river, which produces winter forage for the livestock."

He opened the front door and Julia halted in her tracks to absorb the ambiance of the cozy, wood-paneled parlor and its grand fireplace. Lord, the room, though very masculine in decor, drew her gaze and held it fast. The homemade furniture was polished to a shine—just like the stage floor.

Julia eyed him curiously. "You did this, didn't you?"

He nodded as he escorted her to the spacious dining room and then to the sprawling downstairs bedroom with its adjoining sitting room. "When I first moved here, there was nothing but open spaces and plenty of timber. I couldn't afford to send off for furniture, so I made my own."

"You definitely have a gift," Julia complimented. The oak table and chairs were finely crafted. The headboard of the bed, the carved highboy, and the dressers were wooden masterpieces.

"I haven't had time to furnish the three upstairs bedrooms," he told her as they returned to the foyer. "The community of Bugtussle just sort of fell into my lap, because there was a need for a mercantile store on the cattle trail to the railheads in Kansas. The stagecoaches needed a station where fresh horses were stabled and passengers could take a meal and stretch their legs."

"So you supplied what people needed, and the town sprang up beside your property?" she asked.

"Actually, the town sits on my property," he clarified. "The original stage station is now the seamstress's shop where you had your unique clothes made. The mercantile shop is the same, except that I had to expand it to accommodate the needs of the growing town.''

When they exited the house, Julia scanned the wooded hills, which were alive with spectacular shades of gold, orange, red, and brown. She remembered the park Mayor Pete McGrew had shown her the day he had insisted on taking her on a tour of modern-day Bugtussle. The mayor had mentioned a waterfall tucked back in the hills, but time hadn't allowed for Julia to hike off, because she had been pressed to complete the mural before the Frontier Day festivities.

Julia was glad to know this panoramic countryside would become a park, that the wildlife and natural beauty would be preserved and appreciated. Win would want that, she suspected.

"I've had to hire a bunkhouse full of cowboys to keep up with the growing herds," Win explained as he lifted Julia onto the carriage seat. "Cattle drovers coming up the trails have a policy of shooting calves that are born en route. The young calves can't keep the pace of moving herds. I take in the newborns and bottle-feed them, until they are old enough to graze with my herds. As a result, drovers bring their newborns to me to prevent destroying the helpless calves."

Julia wasn't surprised by Win's policy of taking in helpless critters. Win Calloway was a man who refused to let anyone or anything suffer unnecessarily. Impulsively, she leaned over to press a kiss to his sun-bronzed cheek.

"You're a good man, Win Calloway. The best. The world needs more people like you."

"Like I told you," he said as he sent the buggy rolling west, "when you suffer through the hell of war, you realize no one really wins and everybody loses. You hear the anguished cries of the injured and dying and you have the intense need to ease their pain, because you know damn well it could have been *you* crying out for assistance and compassion."

A rueful, tormented expression passed through his eyes as he stared into the distance. "The day I found my older brother beside the road and realized the troop of soldiers ahead of me had walked past him without stopping to make his last minutes comfortable, I . . ."

When his voice trailed off, Julia squeezed her eyes shut. Her heart went out to Win. She couldn't begin to imagine the horror young Win Calloway had experienced that tragic day. She suspected that everyone Win had helped since that traumatic day had become his attempt to compensate for the one life he had arrived too late to save.

"My brother was a lot like you," Win murmured, lost in bittersweet memories. "So full of life, laughter, and tireless energy. I worshipped him, admired him. He was all I had left in the world and he was gone before I could say good-bye."

"So you made the people in your corner of the world your family," she surmised, then wished she had turned her hurt outward rather than inward when she'd lost her parents. Win had made the world a better place, while Julia had isolated and insulated herself against the pain.

"Yeah, I guess I did create my own family after that," he admitted. "Loneliness was a difficult thing those first few years after I moved here. I had my ranch and carpentry to keep me busy, but it wasn't enough. Material things weren't enough. I had seen homes and businesses blown away in the blink of an eye during the war, but nothing seemed as vital as the lives those battles affected. I needed more than this ranch. I needed to make a difference."

Win shook himself loose from the bad memories and gestured to the north. He had brought Julia here to enjoy her company, not to dwell on things he couldn't change. "There is a waterfall a quarter of a mile from here. I thought you might like to see it. According to the legends, this was once a Comanche haunt—a place were spirits whispered in the trees and murmured in the rapids and waterfall."

Julia bounded from the carriage without waiting for Win's assistance. "I've heard about that."

"You have?" he questioned as he grabbed the picnic basket. "From Bea? She's the only one from town who has seen it, other than the ranch hands, of course."

Julia smiled and reminded herself to watch what she said. "Then it must have been Bea who mentioned it. Come on, Calloway. I'll race you!"

Julia sprinted off, hoping her careless comment would be quickly forgotten. Despite the fact that Win carried the wicker basket, he overtook her with his long, graceful strides. Losing the race was immediately forgotten when Julia spied the small waterfall that tumbled from a ledge of rocks to form a pool that flowed over the rapids to a meandering stream.

"I definitely have to paint this landscape," she said, panting for breath. "Absolutely, no doubt about it. It has to be done in the shades of autumn."

Win set aside the basket to admire the serenity and majesty of the falls. "I'd pay handsomely for a landscape painting to hang over my mantel. Name your price, Jule."

She turned her blinding smile on him. "For you, I'll do it for nothing."

He looked at her, so vibrant and alive, standing against

the backdrop of colorful leaves and glinting falls, and felt
need strike like a thunderbolt. He wanted Julia the way
he'd never wanted another woman. It wasn't just a reaction
to the physical urges he'd been holding in check and
refused to appease with any of the calico queens who constantly propositioned him. This kind of need went deeper,
pulsated stronger. It was fierce and consuming and it made
him shake with unexplainable sensations.

Win had tried to keep a respectable distance the past
week, telling himself there was no future for this wild
attraction. Julia would be here and gone and she wasn't
the kind of woman who wanted complications in her life of
traveling cross-country. He'd told himself all those sensible
things, repeated a mouthful of consoling platitudes about
how his life was rewarding and he shouldn't ask for more
than he had. But all those mental pep talks fizzled out
when he stood this close to Julia—all alone here in the
wilderness.

"Jule, I have to be honest with you," he said huskily—
his need for her was having as potent an impact on his
voice as his male anatomy. "I brought you out here because
I wanted to be alone with you without unexpected interrup-
tions. Truth is that I've been starving to death since that
first backstage kiss. If you don't want a repeat performance,
then you better tell me to go chew on a fried chicken leg,
because I've got a powerful hankering to kiss you again."

Julia went utterly still when she saw the flickering desire
in his coal black eyes. She had tried to tamp her own
need down so often that she'd grown tired of fighting the
feelings. If they started something here, something that
led to intimacy, she was taking a terrible chance with her
future. The way she felt about this ruggedly handsome
hunk of man could invite complications that might follow
her back to the future. And yet, the prospect of taking

part of Win Calloway with her to the new millennium held a tempting appeal. If their tryst produced a child, she would have someone to love, someone who would love her back. She would have a family of her own again.

"Jule?"

She found herself walking toward him instinctively, wanting to consummate these electrifying sensations that roiled through her, wanting what she'd never had before. She had the inescapable feeling that this was the right time and place, the right man—who hadn't come along while she was living in the "future".

"Let's save the chicken for later," she whispered as she traced the sensuous curve of his lips, the strong line of his jaw.

Her quiet invitation had Win groaning. He wrapped his arms around Julia and sought her lips with fiendish urgency. The world went out of focus when her mouth parted beneath his. He plundered her mouth the way he ached to posses her body. He longed to become a part of her radiant fire and spirit. She unleashed emotions in him that he thought had died during the war. All his generosity toward his fellow man didn't give him anywhere near the satisfaction he discovered when he took Julia in his arms and felt her melt against him. She created an intense need in him—and only she could appease it.

His hands moved of their own volition, mapping the luscious curves and swells that he had previously caressed with his gaze. She was firm yet oh so shapely, and his hands trembled as he cupped her breasts and brushed his thumb over the pebbled peaks concealed beneath the cotton fabric.

When she moaned softly and arched toward his hands, a wave of possessive jealousy roiled through Win. He knew this alluring performer must have known other men, had been touched intimately before—and probably would again when she left town to satisfy her craving to roam. But suddenly he needed to leave his brand on her, to plant his memory in her mind as a reminder of a time in Nowhere, Texas, when she had been loved well. Not just because of her luscious body and bewitching face, but because of the way she made him feel.

Julia's mind reeled when Win tunneled his hands beneath the cotton blouse to caress her nipples. He was giving her such wondrous pleasure that the flame of desire burned her inside and out. She wanted to return these scorching sensations, to assure him that she was willing to give as well as take the shimmering pleasure he aroused in her.

Her shaking hands fumbled over the buttons of his chambray shirt. Julia wanted to press her hands to the solid wall of his chest, feel his masculine power beneath her fingertips. She wanted to know this one special man the way she knew no other man—as a lover, a friend, and a business associate.

"Lord, woman . . ." Win groaned when her palms splayed over his hair-roughened chest. "I told myself I'd settle for just a few kisses, but—"

"I'm tired of *settling*," Julia interrupted as she stared straight into his eyes. "I want you, even if today is all I can have."

"Sweetheart," he said hoarsely, as he scooped her up and carried her toward a grove of trees. "Considering the way you make me feel, I doubt one day is going to be enough."

Julia caught her breath when he laid her down ever so gently in the grass, then reverently pulled away her blouse. He stared at her as if she were a masterpiece; then he bent his ruffled raven head to skim his lips over her nipples.

Fire raged through her at first touch. Need burned out of control when he suckled her, plucked at her with his fingertips.

The murmuring waterfall drowned out her surrendering moan and she trembled helplessly beneath adventurous caresses that trailed along the band of her drawstring breeches.

Julia felt as if she were a drowning swimmer going down for the last time when his hand drifted sensuously across her abdomen, then skimmed over the fabric between her legs. She desperately wanted his hands on her skin without the slightest scrap of fabric between them. She wanted to discover where these aching sensations led and what it took—if anything—to satisfy them.

At the moment, Julia swore nothing could ease this wild, burning ache that followed the wake of his unhurried touch. She'd never felt so hungry for a man, so hopelessly out of control.

Win had called her a daredevil, and maybe he was right. This new lease she had on life, this uninhibited persona, seemed to have overtaken the cautious, hesitant woman she had been. She trusted and respected Win too much to let herself believe he would hurt her intentionally.

Now that Julia was living each day to its fullest, savoring every moment, she knew she wanted to share the deepest intimacies with this man. When she was with him, feeling his gentle caresses and kisses, she swore she could spread her wings and fly, just as she did during her stage performances. Only this time, it was this man's passion that put wind beneath her wings. It was this one man whose touch created that special magic that had been missing in her life.

Brazenly, Julia reached up to pull off his shirt. Her questing fingertips glided over his belly to the noticeable bulge in his breeches. When he pressed against her hand and groaned, Julia experienced a newfound sense of feminine power. It thrilled her to realize she could make him respond as ardently to her as she did to him. It was gratifying to know they had the same devastating effect on each other. She'd never sensed that with her ex-fiancé. Their limited interludes never involved this much heart and soul. They were merely rehearsals for this moment, which entailed so much more.

Julia's bold caresses played hell with Win's resolve to proceed slowly and patiently. He hadn't wanted fast and furious with Julia, not if today was all they had. Yet suddenly, he couldn't peel off those peculiar-looking breeches of hers quickly enough to satisfy himself. He wanted to bury himself inside her soft heat, to let this unparalleled firestorm of desire run its course. Then maybe the second time he could make love to her without being in such an all-fired—literally—rush!

While Julia lay there naked and open to him, looking up at him as if he had hung the moon and every last star in the universe, Win wrestled with his boots and breeches. But his fingers had become thumbs and he felt like a clumsy fool trying to undress in record time.

When he came to his knees, Julia's admiring gaze swept over him. He was amazed by the blush that crept to her cheeks. There was a sweet innocence about this worldly, independent woman that never failed to surprise him, making her even more alluring to him. Even if she had been with other men she had a way of making him feel as if this moment was special.

Special. That was what he wanted, even if he was fighting like hell to keep his animalistic urges under tight rein. Julia's wild blush and all-consuming gaze prompted him to slow down, to prolong each moment of pleasure before passion took absolute control of his mind and body.

With that determined thought in mind, Win eased down to lightly caress the silky flesh of her inner thighs. "You're beautiful. Absolute perfection. You know that, don't you?" he murmured as he brushed his lips over her belly and let his hands wander where they would.

"Am I?"

Her breath hitched as he grazed the nub of passion, then dipped his fingertip inside her. Knowing she burned for him, that the sight of him, the feel of his caresses aroused her, intensified his own desire. Again, he dipped his hand in liquid fire and felt her passion burn all the way to his soul.

"I want to savor every sweet inch of you, woman," he rasped, then smiled when she caressed his fingertips in the most intimate way imaginable.

"Oh . . . God . . ." she wheezed. Her eyes fluttered shut; her body melted around his stroking caress. "Oh . . . God!"

Win eased between her legs, holding himself above her as he brought her to another pinnacle of shimmering pleasure. He bent to take her lips at the same moment that he pressed intimately against her. Knowing she was ready, willing, and waiting, he drove into her tenderest flesh . . . and realized instantly that he'd ventured where no man had ever been before. There was no mistaking the hidden barrier he had broken. He saw the tense lines that suddenly bracketed Julia's mouth as she stared questioningly at him and he knew he was not mistaken. He had definitely been her first!

Stunned, he jerked back and stared bewilderedly at her. "Damn, I'm sorry. I didn't know. I thought—"

"That I did this sort of thing all the time?" Julia smiled

at the concern and bafflement in his rugged features, then shifted, trying to adjust to the feel of his masculine invasion.

"That sounds bad," Win said through his clenched teeth, trying to still the innate urge to drive to completion. "Considering your age and your profession . . . Hell, that didn't come out right either."

Julia grinned in the face of his obvious discomfort. *"This* is going to come out right eventually, isn't it? You aren't going to storm off thinking I'm trying to trap you into a commitment you don't want, are you? It's not like that, Win, not at all," she told him earnestly. "The truth is I never wanted to experience this kind of intimacy until I met you. No pretenses, no traps, just you and me blending into the glorious colors of autumn . . . in this perfect place, in the perfect time with the perfect man . . . ."

Maybe she was an accomplished actress, but her words were spoken with such sincerity that Win believed she meant what she said. There was such a look of hope and wonder in those blue eyes—which matched the color of the sparkling waterfall—that it touched his heart.

Julia was nothing like Trudy, who plotted and schemed for a marriage proposal she was never going to get from him. Trudy was insensitive and superficial, while Julia was honest and straightforward. She had depths of character Trudy would never realize existed.

Win couldn't find the appropriate words to respond to Julia. He preferred to show her what the gift of her innocence meant to him. He reached between their bodies to caress that sensitive nub and saw her eyes widen and glow with rekindled passion. He moved slowly, deliberately toward her, felt her relax and accept him. He ordered himself to proceed with the patient tenderness Julia deserved. But when she arched up to meet his gliding thrusts and gave herself wholeheartedly to him, his good intentions cartwheeled over the waterfall and plunged into the rippling pool below. In an instant Win was riding the rapids, lost to the sweetest, wildest pleasure he had ever known.

Need erupted like a geyser. Wave after wave of mind-spinning sensations whirled through him. He held on to Julia as desperately as she clung to him. With each penetrating thrust he felt himself losing his grasp on tenderness. And too soon—too damn soon!—his male body betrayed his need to make this wondrous moment go on forever.

Win cursed under his breath when he shuddered helplessly in her arms. He was sure he had failed to meet Julia's expectations . . . until he felt her nails dig into the muscles of his back and heard her cry out his name. He felt her body caressing him as he tumbled over the edge of oblivion—pulsating inside her, matching her pounding heartbeat, her desperate attempt to breathe.

A long time later, when reality returned, Julia lay there staring up at the darkening sky, marveling at the indescribable sensations she had experienced in Win's arms. She still felt as if she were soaring, as if she were swinging from the rafters in the opera house.

Magical, she caught herself thinking. It was just as Bea had said. It had taken a quantum leap through a time warp for Julia to find the magic. What a shame she had been born a century too late.

Thunder rolled and rained splattered from the overhanging clouds. Odd, when Julia was with Win, she didn't even notice the rainstorm was rolling across the hills until it descended on her. The storm had sneaked up on her . . . the same way love had . . . .

Julia tensed when she realized she had given far more than her innocence to Win Calloway. Even though she knew the hazards of falling in love with a man from the past, her heart hadn't been paying the slightest attention to common sense.

"Sorry. I'm probably crushing you," Win murmured, mistaking the sudden stiffening of her body for discomfort.

When he tried to move away, Julia clutched him close. "No, I like you just where you are," she assured him. She lay back on the ground and opened her lips to taste the replenishing rain, not caring if she ended up all wet. She wasn't ready to face the "awkward moment" after their spontaneous lovemaking.

"Julia, it's . . . um . . . raining," Win pointed out.

"I know. Do I look like I care?" she asked, grinning up at him.

Win stared into her beguiling face and smiled. "No, you look like you don't have a care in the world."

"You?"

He shook his wet head. "No, but I don't want you to catch cold and sneeze your way through the air during your grand finale. I think we're looking at an indoor picnic." He grinned roguishly. "And I'm not sure you spent enough time carefully examining the craftsmanship of my bedroom furnishings. Maybe you should take a closer look."

Julia giggled at his invitation. "Can we bring the waterfall back to the house with us? It would look breathtaking on your bedroom wall while we're . . . er . . . studying your craftsmanship."

Any awkwardness Julia expected to experience washed away when the sky opened and rain came down in torrents. Laughing like children, they grabbed their discarded clothes, gathered the picnic basket, and dashed madly for the buggy.

Julia's smile evaporated when they veered toward the house to find the Fletcher Twit camped out on the stoop.

Trudy's dark hair had wilted around her face and her elegant pink satin ensemble was drenched and splattered with mud. Trudy's gaze leaped from Win to Julia, arriving at suggestive implications; then she glowered furiously at Julia. For a moment, Julia swore she could see steam rising from Trudy's lacy collar and billowing from her reddened ears.

"You scheming Jezebel!" Trudy railed at Julia. "Don't think the citizens of Bugtussle aren't going to hear how you lured Win out here to angle for a proposal so you can get your greedy hands on his money! You aren't the first woman to try it, you know! But you won't get away with it, I promise you!"

"That's enough, Trudy," Win snapped as he bounded from the carriage to help Julia to the ground.

"Enough?" Trudy fumed, her chin going airborne. "Don't be a blind fool, Win Calloway. You think this third-rate actress has any real interest in you? You think she hasn't slept her way from one theater to another from one coast to another? She's a tramp, just like the rest of her kind—"

Win grabbed Trudy's rigid arm and gave her the good shaking her pampering father had neglected. "You apologize this instant."

"I will never apologize for stating the truth," she howled in outrage.

"I want you off my property. And don't come back," he snarled at her. "I've tolerated your nonsense for too many years, but it ends here and now. Julia Harper is more woman than you can ever hope to be."

"She has bewitched you!" Trudy railed, glaring hatefully at Julia.

In a burst of tears, Trudy plunged off the porch and scrambled into her carriage. She tore off down the muddy path, oblivious to the downpour.

Julia had a very bad feeling about this confrontation. Trudy assumed correctly that Julia and Win had become lovers. The jealous female couldn't tolerate the thought of losing the man she had designs on. The self-centered creature appeared to be the type who harbored resentment and made a habit of getting even with anyone who stood in the way of what she wanted.

Trudy Fletcher wanted Win Calloway and the power of his position in town quite desperately. She wanted to become the reigning queen of Bugtussle and she wanted Win as her doting king. Win's harsh words had destroyed her illusions. That made Trudy exceptionally desperate and dangerous.

"I think I should return to town," Julia murmured as she stared after Trudy.

"You're right. Better stop the spread of vicious gossip before it takes root. I hope you don't mind eating our picnic on the go."

"It won't be the first time," Julia said as she dashed toward the carriage.

"I'm really sorry, Jule," Win apologized as he drove toward town. "Trudy can be very difficult and I've been too lenient. No one has ever taken her as seriously as she takes herself, but this time she has gone too far. Her behavior is inexcusable."

Julia couldn't agree more, but she wasn't sure how to cure Trudy of her severe case of selfish spite. Julia had the unshakable feeling that she and Win were on a collision course with trouble. Yet it was Win that Julia was worried about. Loving him as she did, she felt fiercely protective and she refused to see him hurt.

Julia preferred that Trudy direct her vengeance at her. Win was the pillar of this community. He had given the town life and made it breathe. If Trudy destroyed his rapport with the citizens of Bugtussle, Julia would never forgive herself!

Chapter Six

"Well, damn it all," Win grumbled when he saw the "science-fiction" backdrop Julia had been working on. Globs of paint had been splattered on the portable screens. There was no way to salvage them.

"Trudy certainly doesn't show any signs of creative artistic ability, does she?" Julia said as she stared at the screens.

Win whirled around, startled that Julia wasn't as outraged as he was by Trudy's destructive retaliation. "Hell's bells, Jule. She ruined hours of your hard work and that's all you have to say about it?"

Julia smiled, touched by the outrage Win felt in her behalf. "It won't take me long to whip another copy of this stage set, because I have this one as a model. Instead of getting all bent out of shape, I think we need to figure out how to deal with Trudy."

"*Deal* with her?" Win said and snorted. "I was planning to strangle her!"

"Why?"

"Why?" he blustered. "Because she is striking back at you and I don't like it!"

"And you are in the habit of protecting all the members of your flock," Julia speculated.

"Well, yeah, I suppose so. I seem to have been elected, by unanimous decision, as law enforcer and judge. People expect me to handle all the problems that arise. I have to do something about Trudy. I have to teach her a lesson she won't soon forget."

Julia was a little disappointed by his reply. She supposed she wanted Win to give an indication that what was between them was vitally important to him. But why should she expect him to make an earth-shattering confession of love when she hadn't found the nerve to tell him how she felt?

Julia was pretty sure that, although the world changed drastically with times, affairs of the heart were much the same from one era to the next. Admitting private feelings between a man and woman was intimidating, because no one wanted to become vulnerable, hurt, or played for a fool.

Julia was feeling her way through this affair with Win, wondering how he felt about her, wondering how to proceed without coming on too strong—or not strong enough.

"Let's appraise the situation with Trudy rationally," she suggested.

"Rationally?" Win scoffed. "I want to do Trudy bodily harm for this prank!"

"This from the man who is usually easygoing and nonchalant?" she teased.

"Well, I have my moments of madness occasionally," he assured her. "Seeing what Trudy did to your stage scenery makes me furious!"

Maybe Win didn't love her the way she loved him, but he did feel something, Julia assured herself. Even if nothing came of her affection for Win, she could return to the future knowing he cared enough to be protective.

"What is it that Trudy wants more than anything?" Julia asked.

Win frowned thoughtfully. He admired Julia's ability to get to the root of problems. She was intelligent and insightful and he needed to set aside his irritation and focus on a solution to this problem.

"Trudy craves attention," he said after a moment.

"Scads of it," Julia agreed. "But not just from everyone in town. Mostly from you."

Win shifted uncomfortably. "I know. I guess I just kept thinking she would grow out of her infatuation and take interest in someone closer to her own age. I've been polite but standoffish most of the time. She just never took the hint and focused her affection on somebody else."

"Why would she want to do that?" Julia quizzed him. "She sees you as extremely attractive. I can't blame her for that, because I find you impossible to resist myself."

Win smiled for the first time in an hour. "Yeah?" He waggled his eyebrows at her.

"Yeah." Julia pressed a quick kiss to his lips. "But in Trudy's case, your wealth and prestige in Bugtussle are vitally important to the image she perceives for herself. You claimed that no one takes Trudy as seriously as she takes herself. She wants to feel important, to be taken seriously, to have her opinions matter to everyone. She isn't satisfied unless she is standing in the limelight, unless she is dressed fit to kill, unless she is soaking up constant attention."

Win shook his head and sighed. "Damn, Jule, how and where did you learn to analyze people so accurately?"

Instead of telling him she'd passed Psychology 101 with flying colors in college, she merely shrugged. "The thing Trudy probably fears and resents most is being overlooked and ignored. She sees me as an intolerable threat, because my stage performances have drawn considerable attention and I'm stealing her thunder. That infuriates her. She is accustomed to being doted on and getting what she wants. The fact that I have an interest in you and you have been spending your spare time with me makes her even more determined to manipulate the situation."

"Maybe it's time I marched up and told her I'm never going to marry her," Win mused aloud. "That is pretty straightforward. Maybe if she hears the words from the horse's mouth she'll believe it."

Julia smiled ruefully. "Resenting me the way she does, Trudy will only convince herself that I've cast my wicked spell on you and that she has to save you from my evil lure. Her ego won't allow her to admit that she doesn't have what it takes to win the man she set her sights on."

"So where the hell does that leave us?" Win questioned.

"I haven't figured that out yet," Julia admitted. "Maybe—"

"Well, there you two are," Beatrice Garner interrupted as she galumphed through the side door, grinning from ear to ear. "Had to see for myself how this sordid, shameful affair was coming along." She halted in front of Win, still smiling in amusement. "Funny, you don't look like you're trapped under the wicked spell Trudy claims you are." She glanced wryly at Julia. "And where's your cape and pitchfork, gal? The way I hear it, you're the devil incarnate and I should run for cover."

Win swore under his breath. Having Julia's name slandered made him angry. Trudy was ruining what had been a perfect afternoon. His protective instincts for Julia were in full scale riot. Ordinarily, Win tackled the problems that arose without letting his emotions and feelings get in the way of sensible logic. But when it came to his feelings for Julia he couldn't remain emotionally detached. She mattered too much, and he thought he mattered to her, too. She definitely wasn't the kind of woman who cavorted with a man on a reckless whim. Their afternoon of lovemaking lent testimony to that.

"I suppose Trudy has been buzzing around town, flapping her jaws," Julia commented.

"Fastest tongue in the West," Bea declared. "Problem is that folks around here are so fond of both of you that no one has paid Trudy much mind. In fact, the whole town agrees you two should tie the matrimonial knot so we can keep our star performer here forever and get our town founder settled down once and for all."

Julia shifted uneasily, then darted Win a discreet glance. He was staring at her, pondering Bea's suggestion. As much as the prospect of sharing a future with this special man appealed to Julia, she had unfinished business in the final countdown to the twenty-first century. She had to return to put her business in order and tell everyone that . . . That what? That she had decided to live in the past— literally? What if after she launched into 1999, the cosmic alignments changed, and she couldn't return to 1880? What if these next few weeks were all she had with Win? And heavens, what if she couldn't make the return to the future and everything was left undone? How would she feel about that?

"You know, Jule, Bea might be on to something here." Julia blinked. "Are you proposing?"

"If I did, would you accept?"

"About damn time," Bea cut in gleefully. "I had a feeling about you two—I surely did." She whirled around and
headed for the doors that opened onto the street, then
paused to say, "I'll spread the word about your engagement."

"Wait!" Julia's shoulders slumped when the door
banged shut behind Bea.

"Well, Jule?" Win prompted. "Better speak now or hold
your peace, because Bea will have the news spread from
one end of town to the other pretty damn quick. This
doesn't have to be official, if that isn't what you want. It can
be a temporary engagement, until Trudy simmers down. If
you decide to go on the road, your problems with Trudy
will be behind you, you know."

Suddenly Win sounded a little *too* rational for Julia's
tastes. Maybe she had turned into a hopeless romantic
during her leap through time. Perhaps her deep feelings
for Win were making her ultrasensitive to what he said,
but she wanted a commitment of love, not a solution to
the problems with Trudy. Julia didn't want this betrothal
to turn out as badly as her first one. The hurt she suffered
had dictated her actions over the past eight years. She
didn't want to spend the rest of her life trying to get over
Win Calloway. Damnation, it would probably take dying
to get that done!

"Jule?" Win framed her face in his hands, demanding
her undivided attention. "I will never tie you down, if that's
not what you want. I can understand if you haven't satisfied
your craving for travel and adventure. I felt that way until
the war changed my perspectives and folks started settling
in around me to become the family I'd lost."

Julia peered into those chocolate brown eyes surrounded by impossibly thick lashes. This man had her

heart and she knew she could love him for all times, but only in *his* time. He wouldn't be happy in her high-tech world, because in bustling modern society, on the eve of the millennium, things that were critically important to him—like friends and family and his secluded ranch— often became lost in the scramble for financial and professional success. People had become enslaved to their elegant homes, apartments, and convoys of luxury vehicles. Their material possessions, and the loan companies, *owned* them.

Julia had gotten caught up in her own world of art, so she knew how easy it was to lose focus on the simple basics of life. She was ashamed to admit it, but it was true. She had become upwardly mobile, putting too much stock in her professional success and making a name for herself.

She couldn't imagine how this old-fashioned, good-hearted cowboy would deal with the future world that was totally foreign to him. Julia was certain it would be easier to go *back* in time than to go forward. There were too many blanks to fill in without the natural progression of changing events.

Despite the conflicting emotions thrumming through her, Julia felt herself reaching out to happiness, to the chance of a lifetime—if only in this lifetime. Even if this engagement turned out to be temporary, she would take the pleasure she could grasp and run with it until time ran out.

"All right, Mr. Edwin Calloway, you've got yourself a fiancée," Julia agreed as she looped her arms around his broad shoulders. "For as long as you want me . . . In order to resolve this problem with Trudy, I hereby consider myself engaged."

Win bent to brush his lips over Julia's lush mouth and drew her against him. The now familiar throb of need pounded through him. He no longer fought to control it—he accepted it. "I consider myself likewise engaged, Miss Julia Harper . . . for as long as you want me."

When his lips descended hungrily upon hers again, Julia felt the floor shift beneath her feet. It was hard to think straight when he kissed her senseless, but Julia had just enough mind left to note that Win had said, "For as long as you want me." He hadn't attached any stipulations, as she had. Did that mean . . . ?

Oh hell, thought Julia. Sometimes she did entirely too much thinking for her own good. Right now, she was simply going to feel and enjoy and pray that the solution to the problem with Trudy didn't invite another set of problems.

Win stood at center stage for the first evening performance. He stared at the eager faces of the audience that filled the opera house to capacity. Although Julia was concerned that a public announcement of their betrothal would set off Trudy and incite another retaliation, Win was convinced his statement would persuade Trudy to turn her attention elsewhere.

"Ladies and gentlemen," Win boomed. "I am pleased to inform you of my upcoming marriage to Miss Julia Harper."

The crowd cheered enthusiastically. It was as Bea Garner predicted. Folks hadn't paid much mind to Trudy's cruel gossip. That in itself should assure Trudy—who was seated in the second row—that she had no influence over the good citizens of Bugtussle.

Win was quick to note the mutinous scowl that puckered Trudy's face. Although she glared pitchforks at him, he ignored her.

"When's the big day, Calloway?" someone called from the rear balcony.

Oh damn! Win hadn't anticipated being pinned down so quickly.

Behind the curtain, Julia heard the pregnant pause. Hurriedly, she burst onto the stage to rescue Win. He took her hand in a display of affection—for appearance's sake, at least. Julia smiled, silently assuring him that whatever fictitious date he dreamed up would be fine with her.

"We've decided on this Saturday night, right here in the theater, so there will be room to seat everyone who wishes to attend the ceremony," he declared.

This Saturday? Julia managed to hide her surprise behind a beaming smile. *This Saturday!* That was only four days away! Had Win lost his mind? A temporary betrothal was one thing, but a wedding was something else entirely. They would be committed to each other for all times. As she recalled, divorces weren't easily acquired, or common occurrences, in the 1880s. When she returned to the future to tie up loose ends she might not make it back. She couldn't leave Win wed to a woman who disappeared into thin air. She had earned his trust and respect, and it would kill her if he believed she had betrayed him by leaving town without a word of good-bye.

This Saturday! If she went through with this wedding, she might never be able to return to the future before she was listed as a missing person or presumed dead.

The crowd cheered enthusiastically—all except for Trudy, whose face had turned the color of raw liver. Although Win was sure this tactic would squelch Trudy's interest in him, Julia wasn't so sure. She predicted Trudy was sitting there plotting her next move—and it would be a desperately drastic one.

"Seven o'clock Saturday," Win added as an afterthought. "Julia's wedding gift to you will be a spectacular stage performance, and my gift will be free admission."

To Julia's loving amusement, she watched Win double at the waist and drop into a spectacular bow that would have done the crowned heads of Europe proud. The crowd cheered loudly when he pressed a kiss to her wrist, then swept his arm in an expansive gesture, cueing her to begin her lively dance routine.

Julia threw herself into the jazzy number she and Daniel had cooked up for tonight's performance. She told herself not to think about what she and Win were getting themselves into. She danced her heart out, much to the delight of the crowd—save one.

The audience *ooh*-ed and *ah*-ed over the new stage scenery when Win opened the curtain for Julia's second act. Trudy hadn't managed to destroy the new panels Julia had tucked backstage—probably hadn't had time before Julia and Win returned to town. The new scenery depicted a tropical island with sparkling blue water, white sandy beaches, and a volcanic eruption in the background.

Julia had tailored her costume to match the brilliant colors of the backdrop. Apparently the crowd approved, because they clapped along with the lively beat while Julia used her combination of gymnastic skills and aerobic routines to leap one way, then the other.

When she concluded the number, she had the crowd sing along with a familiar tune; then she performed three *glissade tour jétés* to reach the wings so Win could hook her up to her flight contraption.

"I double-checked the ropes and wires," he murmured as he fastened the hooks. "But I can't be absolutely certain Trudy didn't tamper with the equipment. Don't get carried away when you go airborne. I don't want my fiancée swan diving into the audience."

"I plan to make three sweeps above the crowd tonight," she informed him quickly. "I've rehearsed with Daniel and he'll play the chorus three times. When I flap my arms, you can send me soaring to the rear balcony."

"Got it," he said before she darted to center stage.

While Julia fluttered above the audience, swinging to and fro, singing her ditty, Win braced his legs, worked the rope, and smiled to himself. Since the minute Bea decided to play matchmaker, the thought of marrying Julia had appealed to him. It was high time he took a wife and gave thought to having his own family. Although he believed Julia cared for him, he sensed she was withholding something from him. He hadn't pressed her to bare her conscience. He'd hoped she would confide whatever was troubling her. So far, she hadn't said a word.

Was she hiding something from her past? How bad could it be? It wasn't as if she were capable of committing murder. Was she afraid staying in one place would bore her eventually? Win didn't have a clue, but he knew something was troubling her. He was determined to make things work between them for as long as Julia would have him. As for Trudy, she'd better not cross him, because he'd had his fill of her manipulative interference. Even if Trudy's father managed the bank, and her spitefulness caused a rift, Win wasn't going to lose the happiness he'd found with Julia.

Things would work out, he told himself optimistically. He would ensure they did.

Clasping the rope tightly, Win pulled down when Julia gave her cue. The audience hooted in delight when she soared over their heads and balanced on the balcony to unfasten her harness.

Oh damn! Panic raced through Win when he remembered that he hadn't inspected the rope hanging over the rear balcony. Julia could plunge to her death and it would be all his fault!

Before he could halt her performance, she swooped down. Win froze and prayed like hell that the rope would hold. To his sheer relief, it did hold. Julia—who was forever altering her routines in midperformance—made another flying sweep toward the back of the theater. On her return flight, her gloved hands slid down the rope to hold on to the knot and she alighted gracefully on the stage.

Win sagged against the curtain. One more performance had gone off without a hitch, but he was going to stand guard between shows to make sure Trudy didn't tamper with the equipment. Win almost wished she would, so he could have it out here and now. He still maintained that strangling the vicious little snip would be the quickest, easiest solution.

Julia pulled the modern painting of Bugtussle from beneath her bed and studied it pensively. She had begun the painting after Win made their wedding announcement. She kept wondering if she should paint herself into the future and tie up loose ends, then hope she could return before the scheduled wedding. It wouldn't give her much time, but she could call Cynthia Phelps and ask her to handle what Julia couldn't fit in.

But what if she got stuck in the future and missed the wedding? What if she painted herself forward in time and got the sequences all screwed up?

Pensively, she stared at her left hand, then toyed with the elegant ring Win delivered to her that afternoon. His generosity touched her deeply. The man never failed to amaze her, and she wondered if it would be the same if they had a lifetime together.

Yet as stunning as the engagement ring was, Julia wanted something Win hadn't offered her. Love. He hadn't come right out and said how he felt. She wanted the kind of love Bea and Rupert shared. The kind her parents had experienced. She didn't want this upcoming marriage to be a solution to anything, but rather an honest, heartfelt, mutual commitment. Could Win give her that? Should she live on the hope that he would come to love her as intensely as she loved him?

The firm rap at the door jostled Julia from her thoughts. "Yes?"

"It's me," Win called softly.

Julia tucked the painting under her bed. "Come in."

He did, but he stopped to lock the door behind him. When he pivoted around he had that look in his eyes, and he moved quietly, deliberately toward her.

"I know you probably think I'm—"

Julia kissed him, assuring him that she was glad he'd come. That pleased him immensely, because he hadn't been able to get her off his mind. He'd given her the ring and she'd seemed pleased with his choice, but he couldn't overcome this uneasy feeling that something was going to sneak up on his blind side and spoil his happiness. That sense of unease had him juggling his various duties so he could spend some private time with Julia.

Since the first time they had made love, Win couldn't stand sleeping alone in his bed. It seemed natural that she should be there with him. She belonged beside him. Crazy as it sounded, he could almost thank Trudy for forcing his hand. But he kept remembering what Julia had said that first day, about not giving any thought to marriage. He hadn't planned to rush her until Trudy had gone on the rampage.

Oh certainly, Win knew Julia was too bright, too talented,

and too good for him. It was humbling for a man who usually exuded self-confidence, but that was the way he felt, as if he was trying to grasp the vaporous trail from a passing comet.

Win had come here, wanting Julia in the worst way. He needed to hold her in his arms and assure her that he wasn't using her to resolve his problems with Trudy Fletcher. He still hadn't worked up the nerve to tell Julia, straight-out, how he felt.

Soon, he promised himself.

When Julia backed from his arms and smiled in the playful way that never failed to make his heart flip-flop, he eyed her curiously. "Now what?"

She unbuttoned his shirt, then drew it from his shoulders and tossed it recklessly toward the chair. She missed her target by a mile. He hissed between his teeth when her hand glided over his aroused flesh that strained against the fly of his Levi's. When she unfastened his jeans with maddening patience, Win groaned aloud.

"Woman, I better warn you that it won't take much to set me off. I haven't been able to keep my mind on business all day because of you."

"Really?" She sounded enormously pleased by the admission.

"Really. I—"

His voice dried up and blew away when she knelt in front of him to trail her hand over his sensitive flesh. Every nerve and muscle in his body clenched when she released him from confinement and glided her forefinger from base to tip. When she held him gently in her hand, then whispered moist kisses against him, Win swore his legs would fold up and dump him on the floor.

The sensual impact of her touch was staggering. Never in his life had he allowed a woman the kind of intimate privileges he granted Julia. His sexual encounters had been brief and uncomplicated—a simple appeasement of physical needs. But there was something extremely personal and complicated about his feelings for Julia. She aroused him to the most startling degrees—like a thermometer reaching its boiling point.

Heat spiraled inside him when her lips and tongue grazed his most sensitive flesh. "Jule?" he wheezed.

Her free hand drifted over his washboarded belly to encircle his male nipples. "I want to show you what delicious pleasure I experienced our first time together. I swore I was about to die when you touched me."

"I'm already dying," he rasped. His voice shattered when she took him into her mouth and nipped lightly with her teeth. "Damn . . ."

"That bad?"

Win didn't know whether to laugh or scream in sweet torment. "That good," he groaned. "You're setting me on fire."

Julia smiled against his velvety strength. That was what she wanted: to send him up in flames the way he'd left her to burn that first time. Inexperienced though she was, she wanted to learn how to please him, to know him as intimately as he knew her. She wanted to show him that this spur-of-the-moment marriage Bea had cooked up for them held real possibilities, as far as she was concerned. She wanted him to realize that giving him sensual pleasure aroused her. Each gliding touch and intimate kiss was a silent whisper of *I love you*. She wanted him to want her desperately so he would know exactly how she felt.

Never mind that Julia hadn't figured out what to do

about traveling back to the future. Here and now was all that mattered. Win was all important. He had given her life new meaning, opened her eyes to the simplest, most rewarding pleasures in life.

"Stop!" Win groaned in sweet torment. "I swear you're killing me. Come here now!"

The desperation in his voice and the raging need in his dark eyes thrilled her beyond measure. The way his strong callused hands shook as he peeled off her blouse and breeches delighted her. To her surprise, he grabbed her to him and sent them tumbling across the bed . . . .

The slats gave way instantly and Julia giggled when Win jerked up his head and looked around as if he had been bushwhacked.

"Definitely going to have to come up with a better support system for these hotel beds," he said, a lopsided smile twitching his lips. "Should have foreseen this problem when I decided to marry a lively acrobat."

All the while, his hands were sweeping over her, sensitizing her, exciting her as she had excited him. "Just proves that you leave me spinning out of control," he whispered.

Julia gasped when he moved down her body, leaving a row of sizzling kisses on her breasts, her ribs, her belly. His hands glided between her thighs, his fingertips parting her, filling her, leaving her moaning with need.

"I want you," he murmured against her quivering flesh. "I want to taste all of you . . . ."

When his mouth glided lower and he flicked out his tongue, Julia couldn't draw breath, couldn't remember why she needed to. His wildly intimate kisses left her aching to possess him completely. At that precise moment she knew that, no matter where fate led her through time, she would never allow another man to touch her the way Win

had. It would always be *his* memory that lingered, *his* masculine scent that filled her senses to overflowing, *his* caresses
and kisses that enflamed her body and soul.

When he came to her, she tasted her own desire. His
tongue plunged between her lips as he buried himself
deep inside her. Julia clung to him, knowing her nails were
leaving marks on his back, unable to loosen her fierce
grasp. Sensation after wild sensation converged as they
moved in timeless rhythm, satisfying the demanding needs
of their passion-racked bodies.

Waves of ecstasy crested over her. Julia swore all the
glorious colors of the rainbow were arcing behind her
eyelids as she matched Win's urgent thrusts. He shuddered
above her, his face buried in the tangle of her hair, his arms
wrapped tightly around her. Julia felt herself cartwheeling
through space without leaving the magical circle of his
arms.

Paradise, she thought dreamily.

God, she didn't want to go forward in time, didn't want
to take a chance of never coming back. She had discovered
the magic she would be missing if she became lost in the
twenty-first century.

That frantic thought prompted Julia to hold on to Win
as if she never meant to let him go. She rested her head
against the muscled wall of his chest and told herself that,
although she thought she could live only for the moment,
her heart knew it would never be enough.

"Jule?" Win lifted his head when she kept her death
grip on him. "What's wrong?"

She smiled, her eyes misty with unshed tears. "Nothing.
Everything is perfect."

"You're sure?" he persisted.

"I'm positive."

With all her heart, she wished she could confide everything to him, but Julia knew this secret wasn't meant to be shared. She loved him and that was all he would ever need to know. Very soon, she hoped she could work up the nerve to tell him exactly how much.

Chapter Seven

Julia was more nervous than she had been when she made her stage debut to perform for the packed theater. She had been working frantically to replace the damaged stage scenery for her Saturday night performance, then to rehearse the new acts. She had picked up some pieces of stained glass from the mercantile shop to pass in front of the lanterns in the theater, hoping to give the rudimentary appearance of psychedelic lights during her "science-fiction" performance.

She had spared a few minutes to rush down the street for the final fitting on her wedding dress, but she hadn't taken time to complete the modern painting of Bugtussle. She had put the background of the shops in place and sketched her body, but she hadn't put a face on the woman who stood in front of the hardware store directly across the street from the mural she painted for Frontier Days.

Julia kept telling herself she should have tried to make

the leap through time, but she kept procrastinating. First, she'd decided to make the return trip the *day before* the wedding. Then she'd decided to put it off until the *day after* the wedding. Now she was wondering if she dared risk the uncertain trip at all.

You've turned into an absolute fool, Julia chastised herself. She'd told herself that she needed Win's confession of love before the wedding ceremony. Now she was ready to settle for his friendship and his lust. What a hopeless cause she was! She had reduced herself to settling for whatever affection Win could give her, just for the chance to share part of her life with him.

When Julia heard the rap at the door, she turned the modern painting against the wall and set aside her palette.

"Come in. I hope that's supper, Bea. I'm starving . . . ."

Julia's voice evaporated when she wheeled around to see Trudy Fletcher poised at the door. A shiny pistol was clamped in her hand—and pointed directly at Julia's chest.

Damn. Julia had been so preoccupied with last-minute preparations that she had forgotten about the Fletcher Twit. Obviously the Fletcher Twit hadn't forgotten about her. Trudy must have spent these past few days plotting her next move. From all indications, Trudy had come up with a plan to ensure Julia didn't arrive at the wedding on time—if at all.

"You think you're going to get what you want, whore?" Trudy hissed spitefully. "No chance. You aren't the only woman who tried to stand between me and Win Calloway. But you will be the last, I assure you."

Julia stared at the spitting end of the Colt .45. Trudy's eyes were wild with demented fury and vengeance. She was long past rational thought. The attention Julia had been receiving from her packed-house performances had been working on Trudy's inflated ego like poison. Everything Trudy valued was being threatened and she considered Julia the source of her woes.

"Gather up your luggage, whore," Trudy spat. "You are leaving town."

Julia decided not to argue with the loaded pistol, since Trudy's index finger lay against the trigger. Furthermore, Julia didn't want anyone else to blunder onto the scene and get hurt. Bea was due to arrive with a supper tray and help Julia dress in her wedding gown. If Bea fell in harm's way, Julia would never forgive herself. If Win rushed in to rescue her—and he would; he was the type—Julia couldn't bear the thought of seeing him hurt. He meant too much to her, to this town.

"Hurry up," Trudy snapped impatiently.

Julia quickly gathered her belongings and crammed them into the three carpetbags stashed in the bottom of the wardrobe closet. Trudy monitored every move with the pistol barrel—just in case Julia tried to pull a fast one. When Julia reached for the paints and the canvas she had been working on, then tucked them into the oversize bag, Trudy produced a short piece of rope.

"Wrap this around your wrists," she demanded.

Julia did as she was told—though it wasn't easy. She figured Trudy planned to put the finishing touches on the makeshift handcuffs when time permitted.

Julia had to give Trudy "The Madwoman" Fletcher credit, because she had arranged this abduction carefully. Trudy nudged Julia down the back staircase with the pistol, then gestured toward the wagon that had been parked in the alley. Julia was instructed to lie facedown in the bed.

"A pity you won't be around to watch *my* upcoming performance of pretended innocence," Trudy taunted as she tossed a tarp over Julia. "I will outdo you by a country mile, whore."

Julia felt the tug of more rope being bound around her. Trudy, it seemed, had pretty much thought of everything to ensure Julia didn't make an unexpected escape. But at least no innocent bystanders had gotten in the way. For that Julia was grateful.

The wagon rolled down the alley, and Julia heard Trudy snickering fiendishly. "By the time I present my version of what happened today, everyone in town will know that I was right about you and they were wrong."

"What do you plan to do? Stage a tryst between me and some low-life slime bag you paid to ruin my reputation? Sort of like you did when you learned that the schoolteacher was sweet on Win Calloway?" Julia questioned from inside her tarp cocoon.

"Hardly," Trudy snorted as she veered down the tree-lined path that weaved around the hills. "I'm far too clever to repeat myself. This plan is even better. It's perfect, in fact. No one will be around to contradict my story—certainly not you, whore!"

Julia squirmed uneasily. This did not look good. Trudy had progressed beyond petty schemes. It sounded as if she planned to dispose of Julia—permanently. Damn it. She hadn't given this lunatic enough credit. That could prove to be a costly mistake. Julia could lose her life to this crazed maniac!

Beatrice Garner rapped on Julia's door, then waited an impatient moment. "Hey, gal, I brought your supper. We ain't got much time before the nuptials. What are you doing in there?"

Still no answer.

Concerned, Bea set aside the tray and opened the door.

Her eyes popped when she realized Julia's belongings were gone. "Oh, no!" she howled in dismay.

Bea made a beeline down the hall and scurried down the steps to see young Clarence Potter manning the registration desk. "You seen Win lately?"

Clarence shook his fuzzy red head. "Nope. Don't think he's come back from the ranch yet. He was going home to get gussied up for the wedding and put some finishing touches on the bridal suite. He should be back in a few minutes. Is something wrong?"

"Yeah, something is definitely wrong," Bea muttered. "Julia and all her belongings are gone."

"What!" Clarence tweeted. "She is going to leave Win at the altar? That doesn't sound like something Miss Julia would do!"

"That's what I was thinking," Bea grumbled, her mind racing. "Go see if you can find that Fletcher twit. I'd bet a steak dinner she has something to do with this. And pass the word around town that Julia is missing," she added hastily. "We'll need the whole town to serve as a posse if we're going to find Julia before something awful happens."

"You think Trudy—"

"Go on. Git, boy," Bea ordered, flapping her arms in expansive gestures. "We ain't got much time!"

Bea barreled toward the door. Clarence was one step behind her. Bea borrowed the first buggy she came upon. It belonged to Otis Fletcher. Bea figured that was fitting since Trudy was probably involved in Julia's disappearance. Bea had tried to warn folks that Trudy was trouble, but everybody tolerated the twit's foolishness and didn't take her very seriously, hoping she'd mature eventually. Her pa should have taken a paddle to her backside years ago. Instead he spared the rod and spoiled that girl rotten!

Bea popped the reins over the horse's rump. The elegant

buggy whizzed westward. She hoped she would intercept Win on his return trip to town. Otherwise, more time would pass before Win could take command of this alarming situation. He was good at decision making, a born leader. If ever there was a time Win needed to think fast it was now, because his future bride might be whisked from his life—for good!

Win stood in the doorway, appraising the changes he'd made in the spacious bedroom suite. He had accomplished the effect he wanted—one he was sure Julia would appreciate. Everything was in its place for that memorable moment when he brought his bride home for their autumn honeymoon retreat. They would hike through the hills and have that picnic by the waterfall that had been postponed. They'd ride off at sunrise to familiarize Julia with the ranch and inspect the far-flung cattle herds. Then they would spend splendorous nights in this bed . . . .

Smiling in anticipation, Win turned away, then checked his timepiece. He had a couple more surprises to arrange before the wedding and theater performance.

Win grabbed his Stetson from the hat tree in the hall, checked his appearance in the mirror, then strode outside. He still had an hour of daylight left in which to tend his last-minute errands. Then he would grab a bite to eat before the wedding.

Everything was going to be perfect, he told himself as he drove toward town.

Win frowned curiously when he saw a buggy barreling toward him at breakneck speed. He squinted, trying to determine if the driver had lost control of a runaway horse. When he recognized Bea, alarm clamored through him. Something was wrong! Damn it!

Snapping the whip, Win sent his carriage racing forward. He stamped on the brake when Bea waved frantically and skidded to a halt beside him.

"Julia's gone!" Bea panted. "Her belongings went with her."

For a stunned moment, Win sat there gaping. Julia had abandoned him? He knew she had reservations about their marriage, but he thought it was something from her past that troubled her. He had never once considered the possibility that she'd get cold feet and bail out at the last minute. Surely she wouldn't do that. Not Julia. She was reliable and dependable. If she said she would do something, then she damn well did it.

"And before you even think that gal would run out on you, stop!" Bea muttered as she reversed direction. "I'll wager that Fletcher twit is at the bottom of this. I had Clarence race off to alert everyone. Ten-to-one odds says that twit is nowhere to be found either. All the townsfolk are gathering up for a search, ready to follow your orders when we get back."

"Damn it all to hell," Win muttered as he raced toward town with Bea a horse-length behind him.

He had gone too easy on Trudy. He should have confronted her, rather than let Julia talk him out of it. If something happened to Julia it would be his fault. He hadn't protected her against the possibility of disaster. He wouldn't make that mistake ever again . . . .

If Julia lived that long . . .

The tormented thought incited a turmoil of emotion. Win told himself to calm down and think clearly. Julia's life could very well depend on his ability to ensure the rescue brigade functioned effectively. He needed a plan of action and he sure as hell better come up with one fast!

The moment he reached town, he saw the crowd standing in the middle of Main Street. The crowd parted to let him pass, and all eyes were on him as he stood up in the buggy.

"Who has seen Julia in the past two hours?" he questioned.

Daniel Spencer's hand shot up. "I did. We rehearsed the new numbers. Then she went to her room to eat and dress for the wedding."

Win whipped around. "Bea, when did you discover Julia missing?"

"Thirty minutes ago."

"Has anyone seen Julia on the street since then?"

The townspeople glanced around, but no one responded.

"Then we have to assume that Julia was taken into the alley to make an inconspicuous exit. Who was the last person to see Trudy Fletcher?"

"Now see here, Win!" Otis Fletcher hooted. "I don't like the implication!"

"This is no time to defend Trudy," Win snapped brusquely. "Everyone in town knows she has tried to interfere in my life the past few years. Trudy destroyed Julia's stage scenery in a fit of jealousy. I'm wondering if she didn't have a hand in Julia's disappearance. Until proven otherwise, Trudy is our prime suspect."

"I saw Trudy after lunch," John Witham, the mercantile store manager, piped up. "She came to borrow my wagon. Didn't say why, didn't even ask. Just said she needed it."

"I saw Trudy dart around the alley about an hour ago," Agnes Jones, the seamstress from the boutique, added. "I was on my way back to the shop to put the final touches on Julia's wedding gown."

Win's stony gaze swung back to Otis and Matilda Fletcher, whose faces had turned pasty white.

"Granted, Trudy has developed quite the obsession for you," Otis bleated uncomfortably. "But surely she wouldn't do something like this!"

"Oh yeah?" Maynard Thompson blurted out. "What about the time she drugged my drink and set me up in that embarrassing scene with the schoolteacher who was sweet on Win? You ran the poor woman out of town on a rail, but it was all Trudy's doing. I tried to tell you so, but you refused to listen."

Otis shifted awkwardly. "Well—"

"And don't forget about the time the young widow who worked in Agnes's boutique took an interest in Win," Bufford Hawthorne, the livery stable manager, put in. "Trudy started the rumor that the widow wasn't a widow at all, that she had left her husband and two children to find herself a man rolling in money."

Otis and Matilda turned another shade of pale.

"None of that matters now," Win said urgently. "What matters is that we have to track down Trudy before she harms Julia. Does anyone remember seeing a wagon driven by someone who fits Trudy's description?"

"Oh, blast it!" Bufford Hawthorne grumbled. "I saw a wagon veering from the alley and headed toward that dirt road that winds up into the hills. I was coming back from treating old man Taylor's foundered mare."

"Headed south?" Win asked anxiously.

Bufford nodded. "Yeah, the road that weaves toward those caverns just east of Taylor's property."

"Every able-bodied man should grab a horse or buggy and head south," Win insisted. "We'll fan out to see if we can track them. Bufford, you're in charge of the first patrol. Maynard, you set up your squadron, and I'll take some of the men and drive straight to the caverns. If anyone

encounters Trudy, send up two rapid-fire shots to alert the
rest of us.''

People scattered like quail to leap into buggies and vault
onto horseback. Win quickly named his rescue brigade,
then turned his buggy around in the street. He was suffering horrible visions of Trudy shoving Julia down one of
those bottomless pits reported to be in the caverns. He
had given some thought to exploring those winding tun-
nels and setting up tours, if he deemed the place safe
enough. But he had been too busy with renovations for
the opera house to begin that time-consuming project.

The very last thing Win wanted was to explore those
gloomy shafts in search of Julia's mangled body . . . .

The uneasy thought served to remind Win that he
needed lanterns and torches for the search. He jerked
back on the reins, then bounded toward the mercantile
store.

He exited a few minutes later to see Bea ensconced
on the seat, stretching out her arms to take the needed
equipment. "I'm going with you, so don't tell me to wait
here in town," she said sternly. "I'm especially fond of
that gal. If she needs medical care, then I will be there to
give it. You and I are the closest thing to a doctor this
town's got. Which reminds me that you need to round up
a certified physician for our growing community."

Win didn't argue with Bea. He was too busy speculating
on all the horrors Julia might be facing. He drove off as
if the hounds of hell were nipping his heels.

During the frantic ride toward the caverns, Win kept
thinking how empty his life would be without Julia. She'd
brought him joy and pleasure and excitement. She had
given him something to look forward to besides serving
the community that looked to him for support and encouragement. Now, in the course of one fateful evening, all

his hopes and dreams were teetering on the brink of calamity. He would not allow Trudy's spiteful jealousy to ruin his chance at happiness! No one was going to make excuses for Trudy's unpardonable behavior this time, not even her parents.

Trudy Fletcher was going to pay full retribution for abducting Julia before she and Win could speak their vows!

Julia waited tensely when she felt the wagon creak to a halt. She heard the sound of Trudy dragging the carpet-bags from the wagon bed and wondered what phase two of Trudy's dastardly scheme entailed.

"Sit up, whore," Trudy spat. "If you don't, I'll blast holes in you with this pistol. The devil and the buzzards can fight over what's left of you."

Julia did as she was told. When she squirmed into an upright position, Trudy untied the ropes and yanked off the smelly tarp. Julia glanced at the looming hill and then stared at the shadowy entrance to a cave. *Uh-oh,* she thought, swallowing apprehensively. From the look of things, Trudy had picked out Julia's sepulcher.

"You've plotted everything out, haven't you?" Julia said with more bravado than she felt. "I'm impressed. It's a shame you don't use your intelligence to spread goodness instead of catering to your selfishness."

"Just shut up!" Trudy hissed. "If I want to hear from you, I'll let you know. Now get out of the wagon and start walking. If you make one careless move, I'll plug you with a bullet. Don't think I won't. We're close enough to the cave for me to drag you inside now."

Julia didn't doubt that Trudy would do as she threatened. It was best to wait until she ducked into the cave before she attempted escape. Perhaps in the darkness Julia could catch Trudy off guard.

Musty odors greeted Julia as she stepped into the bowels of the earth. A candle flared to life behind her. Damn. Trudy had indeed thought of everything.

"Take your bags," Trudy ordered sharply. "I don't want any trace of you found anywhere. In fact, I prefer you didn't exist at all. You've been nothing but a nuisance since you got here, whore."

Julia reached down with bound hands to hoist up the carpetbags; then she stumbled when Trudy kicked her in the backside.

"Keep moving," Trudy snarled. "Veer right. There is a convenient pool for you to drown in just beyond the winding tunnel. It sits under a spire of hanging stone."

"Stalactite," Julia said. "It's called a stalactite."

"Shut up! I don't care what it's called, Miss Know-It-All," Trudy growled. "If you don't prefer drowning, then there's a nice deep pit at the far end of the cavern room that you can fall into. Take your pick. I don't care one way or the other, just as long as you're gone and Win realizes I'm the one he wants and needs."

"He doesn't love you, Trudy. Never has, never will," Julia said as she tramped through the winding tunnel.

"Yes, he does!" Her wild voice echoed through the cavern. "Folks in town will sit up and notice me when I share his power and prestige. They'll be sorry they didn't take me seriously!"

In a fit of fury, Trudy plowed into Julia, knocking her off balance, sending her plunging into the black pool.

It was deeper than Julia realized. She had to tread icy water while Trudy stood on the stone bank, holding her flickering candle in one hand and the pistol in the other.

Trudy reached down to grab the carpetbags Julia had dropped, then flung them in the water. Julia's hand shot up to snatch the bag that contained her canvas and paints. Given half a chance, she would paint herself out of the catastrophe facing her. . . .

The hopeful thought vanished when Trudy cocked the trigger on the Colt and smiled nastily. "Farewell, whore. Fascinating, isn't it, how quickly a person can vanish without a trace? I want you to die knowing that Win Calloway will be in my bed very soon—"

"Julia!"

Win's booming voice rumbled through the cave like thunder. Trudy whipped around and cursed foully. While the maniac was distracted, Julia surged toward the far end of the pool. She wrested her hands from the rope that bound her wrists and pulled herself onto solid ground.

"He won't have you!" Trudy sputtered. "He'll be mine or he will have no woman at all!"

Dropping the candle, Trudy hiked up her skirts and charged through the mazelike tunnel. Julia considered giving chase, but Trudy had a head start and Julia feared the maniac would hear footsteps and blast away. Bullets would ricochet off the stone walls, and there was no telling who would wind up dead. Win might catch a bullet before he saw it coming. Julia couldn't bear the thought of having Win gunned down by that crazed lunatic!

Hurriedly, Julia grabbed the canvas she had painted of modern Bugtussle. She dipped her brush in the pool and mixed paint. The only light she had to work by was the discarded candle that gave off a dim flicker.

"Win! Be careful!" she yelled at the top of her lungs.

"Julia!" he called back from the distance.

Hands shaking, Julia hurriedly filled in the features of

the faceless woman on the canvas and prayed that the quirk of fate and cosmic alignment that sent her catapulting through time and space were still in effect.

She heard pelting footsteps echoing in the tunnel while she completed the facial features of the woman's face. And suddenly there came an eerie silence.

Two rapid-fire shots exploded in the distance. Julia feared the worst. Although she had completed the painting of the woman standing on the street of modern-day Bugtussle, her attempt to save Win had obviously failed. Oh, God! Trudy had fired at Win before he knew what hit him!

A sob burst from her lips as she bounded up and ran through the darkened corridor. If Trudy had killed Win—

"Oomph!" Julia squawked when she plowed into the solid wall of a male chest.

"Jule? Thank God!"

Julia was enormously relieved to hear that deep voice and feel those sinewy arms close around her. She flung her arms around Win's neck and practically squeezed him in two.

"Are you all right, sweetheart? I heard you scream, but I couldn't understand what you were saying. Where's Trudy? I was afraid she—"

"I'm fine." Julia stepped back on shaky legs, her mind reeling in an attempt to come up with a believable explanation for what had happened in that moment when Trudy went charging off to fill Win with lead. "I need to gather my luggage." *And my wits!*

Julia scooped up her bag, then nudged the canvas with her foot, sending the painting into the black pool.

Win looked around, baffled. "Where did you say Trudy was?"

Julia hadn't said—yet. The truth was that Julia had *painted* Trudy into the future before she shot down Win, but Julia couldn't tell him that. He would think she was as batty as Trudy.

At this very moment, Trudy was probably standing across the street from the mural, dressed in her flashy blue ensemble, wondering where the hell she was and how she'd gotten there.

It would only be a matter of time before the police picked Trudy up for carrying a loaded weapon and carted her to the hospital's psychiatric ward for observation.

The perfect place for that raving lunatic as far as Julia was concerned.

Slowly, Julia turned to meet Win's questioning gaze. "Trudy stashed me here to die . . . then she . . . er . . . took off on the horse she had waiting outside the cave. She went berserk, carrying on about how she was going to put an end to me, then move off to another town where no one knew her."

Well, that's pretty close to the truth, Julia congratulated herself. No one in modern-day Bugtussle would have a clue who that homicidal maniac was or why she was dressed in a Frontier Day costume long after the celebration ended.

"Well, wherever she ends up is a damned good place for her," Win muttered angrily.

"I was thinking the same thing," Julia murmured.

"If you'd come to harm, I promised myself that Trudy would spend the rest of her days locked in the penitentiary." He grabbed the one remaining carpetbag from Julia's hand and led her from the tunnel. "We don't have much time before the wedding. Nothing and no one is going to stop the ceremony."

"You don't have to go through with this now," Julia reminded him. "Trudy is no longer a threat."

"Don't argue with me right now. I can't think rationally after being scared witless. We can discuss the particulars later, honey. The whole town is expecting a wedding and a wedding is what they'll get!"

Julia found herself propelled outside to see a crowd of anxious citizens awaiting her. Cheers went up in the twilight, assuring Julia that everyone was relieved that she hadn't been harmed. It was in that defining moment that Julia knew she had finally found the place where she belonged. It was here, and the citizens of Bugtussle were her extended family. This was where she would stay, even if Win Calloway hadn't learned to love her as intensely as she loved him. He was willing to make a go of this marriage, and Julia vowed to love him enough for the both of them.

After the wedding ceremony and the spectacular "science-fiction" theater performance, Julia and Win were cheered enthusiastically as they left for the ranch. Win didn't have much to say during the short jaunt. He just kept smiling, leaving Julia to wonder what secret he was harboring.

"Right this way, Mrs. Calloway," he said as he opened the door, then bowed gallantly.

He took her hand and led her down the hall to the bedroom suite. Julia screeched to a halt when she saw a dozen bouquets of flowers placed on every piece of finely crafted furniture. Sweet scents filled the room. Candles flickered on the matching nightstands by the bed.

Her mouth fell open when she turned her attention to the portable stage screens that depicted an African jungle setting, the nineteenth-century skyline of New York, and

the tropical island paradise she had used in her performances. The scenery gave the room the appearance of
being the center of every spectacular view in the world.

"I would like to take you to all these places, Jule," Win
murmured as he came to stand behind her. Then he glided
his arms around her waist. "But to me, you represent all
these marvelous places, all the wonders of the world. You
are my touch with a paradise island, the excitement of a
tropical jungle, the sophistication of New York."

Julia turned in his arms and stared into those fathomless
eyes. Then she watched a lopsided smile spread across his
lips. She tried to speak, but fierce emotion clogged her
throat.

"I know something has been worrying you, something
that's made you reluctant to marry me. Something from
your past perhaps?" he asked softly. "You are afraid to
confide in me, but you need to know that it isn't your past
that concerns me. It's *you*. I want you here and now. I want
a future with you."

He cupped her chin in his hand, then bent to press a
feathery kiss to her quivering lips. "I want forever with
you, but if you grow restless to see the wonders of the
world, I'll go with you . . . anywhere. We can tour to your
heart's content, so long as we come home now and then."

He spoke so tenderly, so sincerely, that tears clouded
Julia's eyes and dribbled down her cheeks. "It isn't my
past that has been bothering me or a restless need to
remain on the move," she choked out. "The problem was
that I wasn't sure you loved me. I wanted our marriage to
be created from love, not as a solution to a problem."

"You don't think I love you?" Win threw back his head
and laughed at the absurdity. "*I* fell in love with you the
moment *you* fell from the stagecoach and landed at my

feet. I knew when you looked up at me that I was staring into the *future*."

He didn't know the half of it!

"You mean that?" she asked hopefully. "You're not just saying that because I nearly got myself killed tonight, are you?"

Win scooped her up in his arms and carried her to bed. "Julia Calloway, smart as you are, I thought you already figured out that you stole my heart when you went soaring across the theater, wearing that devil-may-care smile and leaving me quaking in fear that you'd break that gorgeous neck of yours. You worked tirelessly to make the grand opening of the opera house an astounding success. Then you insisted on taking the profits from the third performances to raise money for needy citizens in Bugtussle.

"Not love you?" he chuckled as he tumbled with her onto the satin bedspread he had purchased in honor of their wedding night. "How could I do anything but love you, Jule?"

Julia cuddled up beside him—she in her elaborate wedding gown and he in his elegant three-piece suit. "I'm relieved to know that, because I didn't want to be the only one in this marriage who was hopelessly, helplessly, crazy in love."

He went very still as he held her gaze. "Do you truly mean that, Jule?"

She unbuttoned his vest, his shirt, and his breeches. "All I want in this world, Win Calloway, is *you*, anytime, anyplace, forever and ever."

He grinned rakishly as he stripped her down to her silky skin and treated every inch to worshipping kisses and caresses. "Trust me on this one, sweetheart. That is exactly what you're going to get—*me*, anytime, anyplace, forever and ever . . . ."

Then he showed her how much he cared by giving his heart, his soul, and all that he was to her. They made wild, sweet love in the center of a magical universe created by their mutual love. He came to her, whispering promises for all times, promises radiating with all the timeless colors of autumn . . . .

AUTUMN LOVER

Kathryn Fox

Chapter One

"The pumpkin is like a woman heavy with child. Round, full of promise." Ian caressed the pumpkin's smooth surface with a gnarled and knotted hand. Bushy white brows and a shock of snow-white hair blended to shadow his grin.

Leigh Hunter smiled despite her sour mood. "That's very poetic, Ian, but I'm still not buying a pumpkin for Halloween. It's a silly holiday and downright dangerous."

"Silly? What is silly? Who decides, eh?" His accent was indistinguishable, a mixture of something Old World—Scottish maybe—with a dash of New York. "This is not silly?" He pointed to the forest of skyscrapers that shaded the Manhattan street and the river of people rushing past them.

If anything could look out of place on a Manhattan street, his ragged produce cart did, its wooden sides worn from use and shaded with tattered burlap. Alongside new, gleaming stainless steel vendors' carts, his looked as if it had dropped onto the New York street from another time and place.

"Now celery—*this* is silly." He waggled a stalk of celery at Leigh, its tiny green leaves flapping like a chicken's wings. "What good is celery? What would life be without silly? Look at people who pass." He waved at the crowd that hurried by. "Look at their faces. So serious." He mocked the intensity that characterized the upwardly mobile.

"Just tomatoes today," Leigh said, smothering a smile.

With a resigned sigh, he replaced the celery and removed the pumpkin from the shelf, carefully placing it in a cushioned crate at his feet.

"You do not need tomatoes," he grumbled as he snapped open a paper bag. "You need imagination, carelessness, impetuousness."

"I have imagination. I'm a television producer. Creativity is my best asset." As she said the words, she wondered why she defended something of which she was so certain. No one else had ascended to the top of the network chain of command as quickly as she. No one else had raised the Neilsen Ratings twenty points over all the network shows. Yet even as she mentally ticked off her assets, the wisp of truth in his words haunted her.

With a wink, he handed her the paper bag. "I'll save the pumpkin just for you." He held up a long, bony finger. "You will change your mind."

Leigh took the bag from his hand, noticing the age spots that dotted his skin. He was one of few constants in her changing world. Every day, rain or shine, he opened his stand and greeted every customer with a smile. Consistency and a kind soul—those traits were often rare commodities in her world.

She felt a twinge of regret as she turned away from his

cart and walked toward her tall gray granite office building. The bustle of Manhattan closed in around her, completely absorbing her. But the towering obelisk that was home to Triton Broadcasting, Inc., no longer impressed her, she realized as she looked up at the glass structure, which stretched toward the sky until the morning sun's glare obscured it from view.

The revolving door swallowed her and she emerged into a wall of people. Molly, her office administrator, met her in the lobby, day planner in hand.

"You have nine o'clock coffee with Mr. Umstead." She shoved a dog-eared script into Leigh's hand. "Here's the latest rewrite for *Sally,* and it's not any better than it was before." Molly peered pointedly over her thick glasses. "I think we should bury this corpse before it starts to stink."

Leigh smiled as she took the script. Molly was efficient and smart, and she minced no words. Thumbing through the document, Leigh noted that comments in the margins had been edited and those edits edited again. She sighed and tucked the package under her arm. "I'll deal with this after coffee. Anything else?"

Molly rolled her eyes and shoved her glasses up on her nose. "Mr. Perfect called and wants to take you to dinner. At least he's willing to feed you. I don't know why you put up with him, Leigh. He's like one of those sweet white chocolate candy bars that aren't good for anything except to induce a sugar coma."

Leigh moved toward the elevator without comment. Molly was right. Bryan was about as deep as a birdbath, and they used each other by mutual agreement. No strings, no expectations.

She stepped into the elevator and the door slid shut. As the sensation pooled in the bottom of her stomach, she wondered just when her life had become completely devoid of emotion.

Leigh crept from the bed, padding across the plush carpet and into the bathroom. The Hollywood lights flickered on, and she leaned forward to peer into the mirror and pluck at a stray dark curl that flopped onto her forehead. Bracing both hands on the countertop, she studied her reflection.

When she first came to New York, her eyes had sparkled with life. Now, after eight years of stress and fast living, she looked and felt older than her twenty-eight years. She flipped off the light and tiptoed through the bedroom to the kitchen, glancing once at Bryan's sleeping form beneath her comforter.

In the kitchen, she selected a bagel from a bag in the freezer and popped it into the toaster.

"Hey, Leigh. You want to do this again tonight?" Bryan sauntered into the kitchen, naked. He stood with his arms crossed over his chest, as if appearing in her kitchen naked was the most natural thing in the world.

Leigh let her gaze rake over him. Molly was right. He was too perfect. Blessed with natural blond hair and brilliant blue eyes, he set female hearts atwitter every afternoon in the most popular soap opera on the air.

And she felt . . . nothing. They met almost every night for wonderful sex, but that was all it was—sex in its most elemental form. No endearments, no vows, no future. A simple coupling of two beings for the purpose of pleasure.

Except the pleasure had gone out of it.

"I don't think so, Bryan. I have a late meeting with the

executive producer and then drinks with a new sponsor. Maybe tomorrow."

He shrugged, turned, and sauntered away with a twitch of his backside. "Your loss," he threw back over his shoulder.

The toaster popped and Leigh snatched her bagel out, took a bite, and walked to the broad window that looked out over Central Park. The trees below were ablaze with fall color. As she studied the palette before her, she picked out, as she did each year, the red maples, flamboyantly waving to her from amidst the common oranges and yellows.

She took another bite and thought of the red maple that had stood in the corner of her yard as a child. It had offered shade in the summer, a place to feed the birds in the winter, twirling seeds to play with in spring, and a brilliant show in the fall.

Memories of long-ago Halloweens flashed through her mind and she closed her eyes, seeing cheesecloth ghosts swinging from the limbs as trick or treaters trudged up the walkway.

"I'll see you on the set later. Okay?" Bryan paused at the door, now dressed, flashing her his perfect smile.

For a brief instant, Leigh entertained the thought that there might be something behind his words, some honest hope of seeing her, but then she slammed that door in her mind shut, remembering that his contract was due for renegotiation next month.

"Yeah. See you there."

He took the doorknob in his hand, then paused. "Are you okay, Leigh? You seem a little down."

She shook her head. "No, I'm fine."

" 'Bye." He disappeared—a little too quickly, she thought.

"I will not alter this storyline." Leigh slammed her palms down on the glossy mahogany table. Uncomfortable looks passed between the man and woman on either side of her.

"Look. We've altered this plot three times since the first of the year. First, Tom and Beth get married. Then, his first wife rises from the dead in a display that Lazarus would envy because Joan Becker throws one of her famous temper tantrums in the exec's office and demands to be written back into the show." Leigh began to pace the room, drowning in the anger seething within her. Her patience was at an end.

"A few months pass and Joan's off on another one of her pouts and Tom and Beth are back together. A month later, Joan's romance with an Egyptian archaeologist doesn't work out and she's demanding to be written back into the show for the second time. Enough is enough. There's a limit to even these kind of shenanigans on daytime television."

Mr. Corleoni, coproducer of *All That Glitters,* cleared his throat and toyed with his pen. "Leigh, we all recognize your talent on behalf of this show and acknowledge that you have single-handedly raised the point spread between us and *Thunder Bay* to a wide margin. But I am sure that by now you realize we are dealing with artists here. Joan Becker is one of the reasons that this show is still on television. The audience loves to hate her."

"She's become impossible to work with. I cannot change the scheduling, change the actors and the production schedule to accommodate her irresponsible lifestyle."

Mr. Corleoni raised his eyebrows and glanced down at

his expensive, marble-patterned pen. Some small part of Leigh recognized that she might have crossed an imaginary line, but she'd lost three of her best crew members due to Joan's temper and she wasn't about to lose another.

"Perhaps I should speak to Joan," he said in a voice that carried a hint of a warning.

Leigh reined in her temper and bit back the words she so wanted to say. "Thank you."

"Now," he said, shifting in his seat. "On to the new show. What are your opinions of the new script for *Sally?*"

"The edits are unacceptable." Leigh opened the script to where spiderwebs of corrections filled every available margin.

Corleoni stared at her. "Michael Dulton made these edits himself. Surely the head writer can satisfy you, Leigh?"

She bristled at the condescending tone of his voice. "No, he hasn't."

"Neither has Bryan apparently." The comment was murmured from the other end of the table. Leigh scanned the faces before her, but each expression was guiltless.

Corleoni glanced around the table, then back at his pen. He stood. "I think we'll all do better work tomorrow when we're fresh. Meeting adjourned."

Chairs glided across the rich plush carpet and Leigh's coworkers filed out of the room in silence.

"Would you please stay for a moment, Leigh?" Corleoni asked as he gathered up his papers.

Leigh sat down and waited for the tongue-lashing she was sure to get. *Sally* was Mr. Corleoni's pet project—one he was adamant about getting in next fall's lineup. The heavy double doors swung shut, closing them in the enveloping quiet of the room.

He carefully tamped the papers down until they were even; then he laid them in his briefcase.

"You know you've been like a daughter to me, Leigh. I'm speaking now as a friend who cares for you. If something is wrong, you know that you can come to me, off the record."

"I know that, Mike. There's nothing wrong. Honestly, the script is just plain bad."

Mike ruffled the edge of his papers. "You've lost your edge, Leigh. When you first came to work here, you had one of the best instincts in the business. You were a natural for this job. Now, I see you back away from risks. You're afraid to take chances. That's a deadly combination in this business."

A pain started between her eyes and radiated out into her temples and across the top of her head. "I'm just as sharp as I ever was. I'm just tired of Joan's shit. She's run up tens of thousands of dollars in production costs. We've lost the art director and one of the makeup artists. No, I haven't lost my instinct, Mike. My instinct tells me that this is bad business."

Mike's stare was cold and calculating, and Leigh knew that he'd now dropped any personal overtones this conversation had had.

"Joan Becker is one of the best things that ever happened to Triton Broadcasting. She gets whatever she wants. Is that clear, Leigh? A whole handful of production crew members aren't worth one of her shoes. See to it that she's written back into the storyline even if you have to fire all the writers and start all over again."

Leigh stared into his eyes and knew that she'd lost not only an argument, but an ally. "Perfectly clear, Mr. Corleoni."

* * *

A cold autumn wind whipped at her skirt as Leigh stepped through the revolving door and into the five o'clock rush. The flow of human bodies swirled her into their midst and carried her along like a leaf in a swift river.

Storefronts were decked out in Halloween decor—everything from plastic skeletons to rubber masks of the latest big-screen ghoul. A group of teens ran by in the opposite direction, plastic masks of Clinton and Monica attached to their faces with slim rubber bands. Leigh calculated mentally and found that Halloween was two days away.

The throng split into two streams as they approached the subway terminal. Leigh glanced at Ian's produce stand. A lit jack-o'-lantern grinned at her from the counter. She veered away from the crowd and moved toward the stand.

He smiled slowly. "You changed your mind about the pumpkin, didn't you?"

She stared into his weathered face. "Yeah, sure. What the hell. I'll carve it and sit it in the window. At ten floors up, maybe a passing pigeon will appreciate it." She shifted her briefcase and rummaged in her purse.

He reached behind the counter and carefully removed the pumpkin from its nest of shredded newspaper.

"How much?"

He shook his head. "No money. I give this to you."

Leigh held out a ten dollar bill. "No, please. Take it."

He shook his head. "No. This is special pumpkin. I bring it just for you. You take and enjoy. It will make you very happy."

Knowing there was no use in arguing, she crammed the bill into her coat pocket and lifted the pumpkin into her arms. "This should be an interesting subway ride. I'll see you in the morning. Do you think you'll have any artichoke hearts?"

He smiled slowly, reminding Leigh of a sly, sleepy cat. Then he reached across the counter and took her hand. Despite his hand's bony structure, his fingers were supple and warm and gentle. "Tomorrow you will not be interested in artichoke hearts. Tomorrow you will be interested only in human hearts."

Chalking up his odd comments to old age, she smiled and nodded and waddled toward the subway entrance, but just before she plunged into the human river again, she turned around. Ian's produce stand was gone, leaving only a whirlwind of autumn leaves.

Leigh juggled her keys in one hand and balanced the pumpkin on her knee. Peering over the edge of the pumpkin, she managed to get her door unlocked and stumble inside. She tossed her briefcase to the chair and set the pumpkin on her kitchen counter.

By pumpkin standards, Ian was right. This one was perfectly round, just the right uniform shade of orange, and free from flat places where it had lain in the field. As a child, she'd accompanied her father to the country to select just the right pumpkin for carving and then worked magic with a knife and a large spoon under her father's careful instructions.

The smooth orange skin begged to be touched. She ran her hand over the ridges and a tingle raced up her arm. She yanked her hand back, puzzled. After all, she reminded herself, she'd had two drinks before heading home. Maybe she should consider herself lucky she was feeling things and not seeing them.

She flopped onto a leather-upholstered chair, raincoat

and all, and rubbed her fingers. She had thought about carving the pumpkin into a jack-o'-lantern, despite her declarations of the silliness of it all, but now, she thought she would leave it whole, perhaps add some autumn leaves, and keep it until Thanksgiving.

She struggled out of the overly soft chair and shucked off her raincoat, dropping it over a chair back. Her shoes went next, one under the coffee table and one under the television set. Stocking feet sliding against the carpet, she stepped into the bathroom, turned on the water, and poured a small amount of bubble bath into the tub.

"What the hell?" she muttered, turning the expensive bottle over and pouring half into the filling tub.

She fixed herself another drink—a stiff one—stripped out of her clothes down to her satin underwear, and reveled for a moment in how good it felt to be unfettered. Simple pleasures no longer had a place in her fast world. Pleasures were bought or coerced, she thought jadedly.

Then another unbidden memory rose. She and her sister, about five or six, running in and out of the sprinkler in the backyard, wearing only cotton panties while Mom and Dad laughed and watched.

Clutching the glass, she sat down on the edge of her bed, long-suppressed sadness emerging unexpectedly. The elation of remembering those days was cut short by the remembered pain of losing both parents in an automobile accident when she was fourteen and her sister Karen was twelve.

Shoving herself off the bed, Leigh tried to stem the tide of emotions returning to her heart. She walked down the hall to the bath, slipped off her underwear, and slid into the warm, fragrant water. As the bubbles tickled up her neck, a sudden jarring memory of her sister's death only a few years ago barged into her mind. Karen had died in a breech childbirth—a tragedy that had cost Leigh both her sister and her newborn nephew. Her brother-in-law could never reconcile himself to the loss, so he moved back to California and the loving support of his own family.

Leigh set her glass on the edge of the tub and scooped up a handful of bubbles, blew them away, and watched the trembling rainbows pop and shower her with soapy bits. She and Karen had taken bubble baths, splashing and shrieking until Mom came in and dragged them out.

"Stop it, Leigh," she warned herself out loud.

Leaning her head back against the bath pillow, she directed her thoughts to return to the events of the day, from the conversation with Bryan this morning to this afternoon's fiasco with Mike.

Of all her liaisons with men—and there'd been no shortage of seekers—she'd never entertained the thought of marriage, but now, tonight, her treasured independence just seemed like plain loneliness. Bryan, and all the other perfect male bodies seeking career advancement by romancing the executive producer, had only been toys, bodies to amuse herself with for a few hours, then cast aside. They wanted entanglements no more than she did. Leigh stood and wrapped a towel around herself. She trailed a path of wet footsteps to the kitchen, where the pumpkin sat on the counter. Somehow drawn back to it, Leigh touched it with one finger. A trilling sensation ran up her arm and fanned out across her shoulders and back.

She smiled and touched it again. The sensation wasn't painful or unpleasant, so she ran a hand across its smooth surface. The shock was more intense this time, but still not unpleasant.

Leigh tucked the towel more firmly around her and grasped the pumpkin with both hands. She felt as though every nerve ending in her body had suddenly awakened and begun to transmit messages to her brain. She was aware of everything: of the roughness of the towel against her skin, of the smoothness of the pumpkin, of the beating of her own heart.

The room began to spin. She struggled to remove her hands and found she could not. Fireworks went off in her brain, raining brilliant sparks of light behind her eyelids. Then the world was no more.

Chapter Two

"Oh, my. The poor dear's fainted."

Leigh heard high-pitched voices through the fog in her mind. She struggled to sit up, but strong hands pushed her back down.

"You rest, child. I fear you fainted."

The stilted speech and the illusive scent of lilac swirled around her. "Are you guys EMTs?" She shook her head to clear her vision and stared up into three identical faces that hovered over her. Triplet EMTs? the rational side of her brain asked. And women at that.

"Why no, dear. We're Smiths," said one of the faces.

"Where am I?" She put a hand to her head and found that her hair was now dry.

"The poor dear is delirious," another of the faces whispered with urgency. "She must be ill. You better go get Doc Watson."

A set of feet hurried away, reducing the hovering faces

to two. "I'm okay. If I could just sit up." New York must be desperate for emergency medical staff, she mused, because these were the oldest paramedics she'd ever seen. "Never let it be said the Big Apple isn't an equal opportunity employer," she muttered beneath her breath, shaking her head to rid it of the annoying buzzing.

"She's ill," another voice whispered. "Maybe with some dreadful disease. What kind of girls has Miss Eva brought these poor men?"

Leigh blinked and stared up into the canopy of a red maple wearing its best fall foliage, a brilliant blue sky beyond.

"How did I get outside?" She sat up. "Oh, God, the building didn't burn, did it?" she asked, remembering the vibrating electrical sensations touching the pumpkin had produced.

The sight that greeted her defied anything she'd ever seen. She seemed to be in the center of a town square, lying in the grass beneath a tree. Beyond the edge of the spotty grass, horses waited at hitching posts and men with guns and holsters stood on a wooden sidewalk, their arms crossed over their chests, staring at the spectacle she must surely present.

Standing to her side were two old women, white haired and identical down to their peach cotton print dresses that swept the sandy ground and straw hats with bouncing flowers atop.

"Has anyone sent for Miss Eva?" one of the ladies whispered.

"Oh, yes. I sent Tom after her immediately," the other answered.

Leigh clasped her head with both hands. She reached for the towel she'd been wearing to pull it tighter about her. In its place was a very tight cotton dress.

Her fingers traced over the line of buttons leading down the front of the dress and up to her neck. If she could just get these damned buttons undone, she might be able to breathe.

"Dear child, we're here to help you."

Someone shoved something under Leigh's nose, and the scent pierced straight to the center of her brain, making her eyes pour tears. She batted away their hands and twisted her head from side to side.

"Leigh? Are you all right?" A fourth lady hurried toward her across the grass, her long black skirt hitched up in her haste. She dropped to her knees beside her. "I should have known you weren't feeling well on the stage."

"What stage? Hey, are you guys from the Fox Network? Is this some kind of *X Files* joke? Look. We really don't do that well against you guys Sunday nights."

The woman picked up her hand and patted it with pudgy, soft fingers. Leigh followed the chubby arms to a kind face and a gentle smile. "You're probably overwrought. I've seen it many times with the girls I bring here."

Leigh stared at the woman, her thoughts swimming as she tried to piece together something that made sense. "Who are you and what kind of girls?"

The woman's face spread into a lovely smile. "Why, surely you remember, dear. We've spent three days together on the stage in anticipation of this blessed event."

Leigh withdrew her hand slowly. "Look, lady. I don't know what you're talking about. I don't know you and I don't know anything about any blessed event. All I want is to know where I am."

"Pardon me, ladies," a masculine voice cut into her next thought. Someone stepped between her and the sun, casting a long shadow across the grass. He knelt down on one knee, touched Leigh's forehead with his fingertips, then began to unbutton the neck of her dress.

"Matthew Sutton! This isn't proper," the trio sang in chorus.

Cool fingers undid the top three buttons and pulled the material away from Leigh's neck. Cool air swept over her skin, and she took a deep breath. Surely, he must be an angel.

"Matthew. This isn't seemly. You can't do this." Miss Eva leaned closer. "You're not married yet," she whispered.

Leigh stopped breathing. Married? She blinked and squinted up at this angel. He was tall and slim. His hands pushed back her hair and pulled at the material at her neck. But the sun blocked her view of his face.

"Miss Eva, there's nothing improper about giving a soul a breath of air," the rich voice drawled. "With all the paraphernalia you girls wear underneath your clothes, it's a wonder half the town isn't stretched out in the maple grove gasping for breath."

"Matthew! You mustn't speak of such things. Whatever has gotten into you?" Miss Eva huffed off a step or two, hastily checking the neckline of her own white blouse.

Then he leaned closer to Leigh and winked. His skin was weathered and tanned. Fine brown hair tumbled over deep brown eyes and carelessly teased the tops of his ears. "I'm Matthew Sutton. I'm sorry we have to finally meet under these conditions."

"Finally meet?" Leigh stared up at him. Did everybody here know something she didn't? "Look, I don't know what's going on here, but I don't like it."

One corner of his mouth twitched slightly and he glanced up at Miss Eva. She solemnly shook her head.

"Leigh dear, this is Mr. Sutton, with whom you've been

corresponding for some time." She turned to the Smith sisters. "Is Doc Watson on the way?"

The old lady shook her head. "He's out at the Sims place delivering a baby."

Matthew stared down at Leigh, his eyes full of laughter and mischief. Then he carefully pulled the cotton material back loosely across her neck. "Perhaps she would like to come home with me until she feels better."

Leigh glanced at the women, reading the horror on their faces. If this was a dream, it didn't matter what she did, she reasoned. If this was some altered state of consciousness, some diversion in the flow of time, some . . . mystery that science-fiction writers salivated over, then what the hell? Quickly, she calculated her options. She could stay here with these women in their too starched clothes and too tight viewpoints . . . or go with him. Whoever or whatever he was.

You need imagination, carelessness, impetuousness. Ian's words came back to her.

She looked back at Matthew and smiled. "Yes, I would like that very much."

The women's gasps changed the oxygen content of the air around them.

Matthew returned her smile, stood, and scooped Leigh into his arms.

"Oh, dear. Oh, dear," Miss Eva muttered, fanning her now flushed face.

"Miss Eva." He shifted Leigh more securely in his arms, snuggling her closer to his chest. "Miss Leigh and I will be going along now. I don't reckon this is any reflection on you. She's my responsibility from this point on."

"But . . . but the wedding isn't for two days. And you don't have a chaperon."

Wedding? Leigh stiffened, but Matthew held her firmly.

"I don't think we'll be needing a chaperon, Miss Eva.
I'll have her back at the boardinghouse before dark. A
nice carriage ride'll do wonders for her and we can get
acquainted."

Miss Eva opened her mouth to protest, but snapped it
closed, and Leigh got the impression that not many people
interfered with this Matthew Sutton.

He moved away down a dirt street, carrying Leigh as
easily as if she were a child. From her new vantage point,
she saw more of the town—a picture straight out of a
Saturday morning cowboy movie. Heads turned as he carried her across the street toward a wagon hitched to two
bay horses.

She risked a glance upward. Dark stubble shadowed an
angular face with a firm jaw. The rough blue denim shirt
scratched pleasantly against her cheek. Every logical brain
cell she had should have been screaming at this moment.
She should have vaulted straight out of his arms and
headed back toward people and safety, but curiosity over-
rode caution. Perhaps she hadn't lost her instincts after
all.

Effortlessly, he placed her up on the wagon seat, then
swung around the team, trailing a hand across their necks
and faces and murmuring something to each one. The
wagon lurched to the side as Matthew climbed up and sat
down, then flicked the reins, and they rolled forward. As
they passed the square, Miss Eva and the three sisters
watched, their mouths agape. A tiny thrill darted through
Leigh, a tantalizing sensation of being naughty.

Leigh clutched the hard wooden seat as the wagon
moved along at a rollicking gait. On the edge of town,
a sign above the sidewalk proclaimed the *Aurora Sentinel*
newspaper was housed there. Leigh turned her head at the

huge banner in the newspaper office window announcing a Halloween dance.

Halloween, 1899.

Another wave of weakness swept over her. *If this is a dream,* she told herself, *it's more interesting than most of my dreams.*

The landscape quickly changed from neat wooden buildings to flat fields and forests ablaze with autumn colors. Piles of yellow hay lay in the fields and ripe, orange pumpkins lay amid their dying vines, their color in stark contrast to the lingering green of summer's grass. Leigh shivered, remembering her own mysterious pumpkin.

The pumpkin. Realization hit her with a start. She had been touching the pumpkin when the world disappeared. Pieces of jumbled suspicions began to fall into place. Ian and his produce stand had vanished once she accepted the pumpkin he wanted her to have. And when she touched it . . .

"That's ridiculous, Leigh," she mumbled beneath her breath, mentally discarding such a ludicrous notion. She was just dreaming. A very vivid dream, but a dream nonetheless.

"I beg your pardon?" Matthew sat hunched forward, the reins threaded through his long fingers. He slanted her a quizzical glance from the corner of his eye, then turned his attention back to the road ahead.

"Nothing," she said with a shake of her head.

"You seem very different from your letters."

"Letters?"

He glanced at her again, but didn't meet her eyes. "The letters you wrote me."

"Oh, those."

"You don't seem shy at all."

"I said I was shy?"

"No, but you seemed that way from your letters."

"Well, I'm not."

"I can see that."

They rode on in silence, the horses' hooves making little clopping noises against the hard-packed ground. Leigh scanned the horizon, still clinging to the hope that she would see a camera crew driving across a field.

"This reads like a really bad screenplay," she muttered to herself. *Didn't we reject something like this last week?*

Although Matthew glanced at her quizzically from time to time, they rode on wordlessly, then entered a sparse stand of birch. A two-story white house sat amid the trees, freshly turned flower beds puddling at its base. A porch surrounded the house and elegant gingerbread work coiled into the corners.

"This is my home." He drew the team to a stop and set the brake. "Do you like it?" Pride was evident in his voice, but there was a plaintive expectancy in his eyes.

"It's lovely," she said, and a warm, slow smile spread across his face.

"I painted it last week."

Leigh was about to leap off the seat when she saw him hurrying around to her side. He lifted her free of the wagon and set her on the ground. His hands lingered on her waist for a second, then quickly dropped to his side.

"Come inside." He beckoned toward the house and sidestepped up the walkway, looking back over his shoulder with childish enthusiasm.

The house was indeed freshly painted, every rung of the porch railing carefully trimmed. He opened a screen door, and she walked beneath his arm and into the cool interior of the house. The scent that met her was jarringly familiar.

Home.

Sharp, bittersweet memories surged back, vivid and

unexpected, rare recollections of her own childhood, the only idyllic time she could remember.

Rugs were strewn across the floor, and delicate white curtains danced in the morning breeze that poured in through open windows. An afghan was draped across the back of a settee, and a large painted vase of sunflowers sat on the bottom step of the staircase.

Leigh touched the bumpy black center of one of the flowers. Was this his doing?

"You said you liked sunflowers so I planted a whole row of them out back."

He blushed an enticing, embarrassed pink to the edges of his hair. She looked back at the sunflower, touching its velvety petals. How real this all seemed. The idea that this was a dream was rapidly fading and a deeper explanation was taking its place. Had she somehow taken someone else's place in the world? Apparently, a very loved and anticipated someone?

Lucky girl.

"Matthew . . ." She turned to confess, no matter that she would sound like even more of an idiot than she felt, but he whipped out a bouquet of autumn wildflowers from behind his back.

"These are for our room." His eyes darkened briefly; then he smiled. "I thought you might like to take them up."

She took the blooms from him, and their hands brushed together beneath the mixture of leaves.

"Ah . . . we were supposed to be married by the time you came here so . . . I tried to make the bedroom nice for you." He released the flowers and stepped backward.

Panic rippled through Leigh as the pieces fell together in an epiphany. She had somehow dropped into this time as if through a trapdoor, dropped dead into someone else's life. But where was this someone else?

She glanced around frantically, still hoping to find out if this was a joke or a dream or hallucination.

"Leigh?" Matthew's gentle voice brought her gaze to focus on his face. "Are you all right?" His hand caught her arm and drew her toward him. "Perhaps you should sit down," he suggested.

"No. I'm fine," she lied and forced a smile. "Really."

His answering smile was gentle and sincere, and Leigh turned her attention to evaluating him. He was a man unused to elegant words and cunning statements—a man who spoke straight from his heart, lived by simple ideas and simple promises. These things she sensed in him as he stood before her, his heart in his eyes.

For someone else.

"Do you want me to take these?" He tugged gently at the flowers gripped in her hand.

"No. I'd like to take them up." She started up the stairs, eager to be alone for a moment, to try to gather her scattered thoughts. She paused once to look back. He didn't follow, but stood at the bottom of the stairs. With one hand thrown over the banister, he stared up at her.

She stepped up onto a landing that squeaked softly. Her unruly imagination immediately conjured more soft night sounds. Going downstairs for a glass of milk. Padding through the dark to check on a baby.

"You've really lost it," she said through clenched teeth. "You're going *Little House on the Prairie* here."

Two rooms opened off the landing. She looked back down, but Matthew was no longer watching her. She stepped into the room to the right. A huge four-poster bed sat in the center of the room, a quilt sweeping the floor on either side. Scattered braided rugs protected bare feet from the rough hewn floorboards. Gauzy white curtains admitted the sweet scent of sun-dried, dying leaves.

Someone had meticulously cleaned the room. The faint scent of lemon still lingered in the air. A small dressing table with a mirror sat to one side, a large, cut-glass vase on its delicate top. Leigh arranged the flowers in the vase, pausing to move one or two blossoms, feeling as though she were intruding on something very intimate and private.

She walked to the window and looked down on the yard below. Matthew was leading the horses around the house, soft words drifting up to her, their meaning lost, but their intent evident from his soothing tone. How on earth would she make him understand that she was not his Leigh, that she was an interloper in time, a soul out of place? How could she make him understand when she didn't understand or believe this herself?

She glanced around the room again. This was obviously meant as a bridal chamber—a tenderly orchestrated welcome for the woman who would occupy Matthew's house and his heart. She had to find some way to tell him before things went too far. The thought sent a strange chill racing up her back and along the hairs that curled at the nape of her neck.

The landing creaked softly and Leigh started, then felt a flush heat her cheeks.

"The room is lovely, Matthew." She didn't want to turn and see the unasked question in his eyes, see his eagerness to please this phantom woman whose life she was living.

"The bed is new and the dressing table was my mother's. I . . . thought you might like it."

Leigh turned, hoping that seeing his face might somehow evoke the words she would need to explain this. But his face cleared all explanations from her mind. Want and loneliness were almost tangible in his stare, and a slight flash of panic passed through her. What kind of man would send for a mail-order bride? Was there something wrong with him?

He moved to the window and pointed down below. "I've already turned up the beds for you, and next spring we'll plant flowers all around the house."

Leigh moved to his side, fighting down a willingness to lose herself to this fantasy. How easy it would be to block out all else except this seemingly idyllic moment, to buy into the notion of forever.

"I plan to put roses over there by that bench." He pointed to a small raised bed area, a birdbath in the center. "The birds come there in the evenings."

Again, an explanation sprang to her lips—evidence of a rehearsed life of saying exactly what she meant when she meant it. Quick, curt explanations designed for efficiency, not politeness. But the childlike trust in his face stopped her as he turned again to gaze at her.

"You look just as I imagined you," he said softly. "You said your hair was curly and that you didn't like it." He raised a hand, hesitated, then took a strand of her hair and let it slide through his fingers. "But I do. It's so soft."

The magnetism she had felt before as a slight tug became a reckoning force. Intuition surged into her thoughts, chasing away grim reality and logical reason. His arms would be warm and strong, his chest firm and comforting, some inner voice taunted. And when he pulled her against him it would be with no ulterior motives, no bargains or deals. His love would be a precious gift, given only once.

"Would you like to see the barn?"

When he spoke, she realized she'd been staring at his mouth, wondering what his lips would feel like against hers. "Ah . . . yes. I'd like that very much."

He led the way out of the house and across the yard to

a large red barn. *Cavernous* was the word that came into Leigh's mind as he swung open the huge double doors, and the pungent scent of cows, manure, and hay spilled out.

"Ugh," Leigh said, covering her mouth and nose with her hand.

"What's wrong?" His startled expression said she'd just made a fatal error.

"That smell."

Matthew smiled. "That's just the cows and the horses. Didn't your father's barn smell like this?"

Leigh's thoughts raced as she hastened to recover ground. "Of course. It's just that . . . I guess all at once . . ."

"I guess a weeklong ride on a stage and I wouldn't want to smell any more livestock either."

"Yes, that's right." She checked his face to see if he'd seen through her, but his attention was directed to the stalls to their left.

"Patty's bred and she'll drop a colt anytime now." He stroked the bay's head that jutted over the stall door. "You're my girl, aren't you, Patty?" He scratched behind her ears and the mare answered with an affectionate butt of her head against his chest. "She and I cleared the front field, didn't we, girl?"

He moved down the row of stalls and laid a familiar hand on the head of a black-and-white cow.

"Julie—she'll drop a calf about the same time." Large liquid brown eyes blinked once and a huge tongue snaked out and licked her wide pink nose. Matthew turned, his face animated with enthusiasm. "Her stud was the best bull in the area. Old Black Jack over at Tom Simpson's place. He throws a calf every time and most of the time they're heifers."

Leigh tried to look as though she understood every word

Matthew said. But her eyes kept wandering to his face, to his eyes, and to his lips, and all the while, she scolded herself for such nonsense.

He continued down the length of the barn, patting the cows and horses and explaining the recent romantic encounters of each one. They went out of the barn to investigate the chickens and, lastly, the one lone mule, Lucy.

When Matthew finished explaining Lucy's parentage, the sun was drowning in an ocean of color, banners of orange and pink painting away the last of the daylight. Leigh felt her eyelids begin to droop and her knees threaten to buckle as fatigue settled in.

"I should get you back to town before Miss Eva sends the sheriff out here looking for you." Matthew put his arm around Leigh's shoulders and pulled her against him.

Leigh roused herself at the mention of Miss Eva. "Back to town?"

"When I saw you lying there in the grass—well, it frightened me." He took her hand and rolled her fingers in his hand. "I saw then that you'd just fainted. But you looked as if you needed rescuing, and I just couldn't wait for you to see the place." He grinned and looked down at his feet. "The only way I got away with bringing you out here was to promise her I'd have you back by dark."

"Uh-huh," Leigh said, fighting off the overwhelming tiredness now claiming her every muscle.

"There's a dance tomorrow night. A Halloween dance. Would you like to go?" He moved in front of her, blocking her path.

Leigh stared up the length of him, finally reaching his face. "I'd love to," she heard herself mumble.

"Wait here," he said when they reached the front porch. "I'll get the team."

Leigh sagged against a porch column, trying to remember when she had ever been so tired. Harness buckles rattled and the team plodded around the side of the house. Matthew helped her onto the seat and, with a flick of the reins, drove them off into the fading sunset.

Chapter Three

The moon was a faint promise in the eastern sky while the last of the sun drowned in a sea of magenta and red. Leigh wrapped her arms around herself for warmth as the increasing chill crept beneath her thin cotton dress.

"I should have thought to bring you a wrap," Matthew said, stretching an arm across her shoulders and drawing her close to him.

Leigh slid against him, grateful for the warmth of his body and too tired to protest. A pleasant soapy scent rose from his shirt as she laid her cheek against the fabric. She jerked awake as they entered town, knowing only then that she'd slept leaning against his shoulder.

He pulled the team to a stop in front of the boarding-house and set the brake. He wasn't off the wagon seat before Miss Eva appeared, a lantern held aloft.

"Thank goodness," she breathed, clasping closed an old thick wrapper. "I was beginning to worry, Leigh dear."

A cloth around her head held in check bits of rags wound into her hair like curlers. They bobbed in the dark like moths.

Matthew helped Leigh down and her knees threatened to buckle as his hands left her waist. "Now, Miss Eva. You don't trust me?"

"Of course I do, Matthew. It's just that her safety was entrusted to me and after today . . ."

He took Leigh's hand in his. "I have brought her back to you as pure as when she left." He bowed low and kissed Leigh's fingertips, winking at her as his lips left her skin.

"Come inside, dear. You've had a long day." Miss Eva nudged her toward the open door.

"Wait." Leigh stopped, a hand on either side of the doorframe. Now was the time. *Tell him now. You can't let this go on any longer.* "I'd like to speak to Matthew a moment please."

Eva frowned. "Leigh, you've had ample time and we *are* standing out here for all the town to see."

"Please? Only a moment?"

Eva pursed her generous lips and crinkled her brow. "Only a moment." She hustled away with a swish and shut the door all but a tiny crack.

Leigh turned slowly to face Matthew. The dim light softened his features as he watched her with an expectant expression.

"There's so much you don't know about me," she began, desperately searching her soul for words to explain the unexplainable.

"I know that you are kind and that you love the sun and the morning air, as do I." He stepped closer, and his expression sobered. "Love is a simple thing, Leigh." He hovered above her a moment, leaning down, his lips only a breath away. The magnetism that followed him like a second soul enveloped her in its spell. Leigh closed her eyes, anticipating his kiss. A cool wisp of air passed between them, and when she opened her eyes, he had stepped away. "The rest we will find out in two days."

Before she could find an excuse for him to stay, he was gone.

Funny how a few hours could change so much. Matthew padded barefoot across the moonlight-patterned floor and stood by the bedroom window. A cool breeze ruffled his hair and pushed open his unbuttoned shirt. Night was well on its way to dawn and sleep still had not come. He closed his eyes, imagining Leigh again standing in the window, tendrils of her hair swirling around her face on the tiniest of breezes. She'd only been here for a few minutes and already the house was imprinted with her presence.

He ran a hand across the smooth wood of the windowsill. He'd planed and nailed each board of the house himself, cleared every acre of the new land—all in preparation for a bride who had never become his wife. Sweet Mary had died, along with her parents, in a fire that had blazed obscenely against the dark night sky. Since then, he'd thrown himself into his land, clearing, building, toward what goal he hadn't known.

The nights had stretched long and empty, but his work had kept him isolated and alone. Then, Miss Eva had swept into town, bringing with her young women from the East who sought homes and husbands. She'd already made several successful matches with local bachelors, having the uncanny ability to see beneath one's skin and read what was in her heart. So he'd approached her and she'd introduced him, via letter, to Leigh.

From their first correspondence, Leigh's letters had

been neatly scripted, her words carefully chosen. She'd seemed kind and intelligent and loyal, and he'd fallen in love—a love as gentle and predictable as each of her letters.

But as their correspondence continued, it seemed that she lacked the passion and curiosity for living that fueled his soul. Every element of nature struck wonder into him. Every blade of grass was a marvel, every birth a miracle. He'd written these things to her—his most intimate thoughts and musings.

Her responses were beautifully worded and carefully agreeable, but she offered no thoughts or observations of her own. If only, he'd wished, she'd disagree with him or offer an intimate glimpse into her soul. Even as he carefully wrote the words asking for her hand, he wished she possessed the same passion as he.

But now, seeing her in person, he sensed in her a quivering energy not evident in her letters, a passion waiting to be discovered. While her letters painted her as shy, she appeared self-confident; while she described herself a simple person, she seemed complex, promising a fascinating journey to discover all that she was.

He slid the window closed against the cold wind, then turned. The bed mocked him with its neatness, giving wing to thoughts that had sprung to life since he'd touched her hand. He ran his hand across the quilt, a gift from his mother just before her death. His eyes drifted closed and he drew a shaky breath, imagining tangled sheets and bare shoulders beneath it. A niggling worry intruded into his thoughts. There was something disturbing about her, some unnamed thing that his mind could neither ignore nor explain . . .

He placed a hand on the cold glass. Another day, just two more sunrises, he would be alone, and then he'd be alone no more.

* * *

A cold wind swept in the window, reminding Leigh that behind the sweet lethargy of autumn would come the bitter promise of winter. Her chest hurt as she breathed in the bitter wind. Closing her eyes, she searched her mind, trying to remember the last time she'd noticed a cooling breeze. Ensconced in her environmentally controlled apartment, riding in the stifling subway, wheeling and dealing in her stale office—the only time she noticed the weather was walking to or from the subway station a block away. And only then if it was raining.

Another breeze, this time more moderate, caressed her cheek, promising a few more days of autumn. She opened her eyes and stared out across the sleeping town. Moonlight gilded the simple dwellings and no lights shone to rival its beauty. Dawn was only a few hours away.

Wondering where she was and how she'd gotten here had given her a headache, but no answers. She rubbed her throbbing temples, arching her shoulders against the confining cotton fabric of the nightdress she'd found in a bag in the room Miss Eva had identified as hers. Did she no longer own thin, silky nightgowns and delicate underthings? Did she even own her soul? She fingered the smooth cotton. Would the sensation of touch be so real in a dream?

She moved to the dressing table, peered into the mirror, then reeled with surprise. Who was this person staring back at her? She leaned closer. She didn't look the same. Her hair was dark and curly, teasing her face with tiny errant wisps, where before it had been brown and straight. Now her face was oval and very pretty with long lashes and a delicate mouth. Before she'd looked . . . Well, she'd been no glamorous model, but she'd been presentable, sophisticated, very nineties.

She pulled the nightgown over her head and stood naked, staring at herself. Her body was curvy, voluptuous, a little heavy by modern standards, where before she'd been a greyhound, lean and sleek, narrow hips and shoulders, small breasts.

"Well, I might get to like this," she said with a chuckle. After all, this *was* a dream, wasn't it?

Remembering the satchel, she pulled the nightgown back over her head and turned up the lamp she'd left burning low, fearing she could never light it again. She sat down on the bed and pulled the tattered bag to her. It contained an ordinary assortment of things: stockings, a blouse, a long dark skirt . . . and a wedding dress. She lifted the lacy garment out of the bag and held it against her. The neck was high and edged in lace. More lace fell from the shoulders as an overlay to underfabric drawn in tightly at the waist. The skirt fell to the floor in a lacy flow.

"It's beautiful," she breathed. She had no recollection at all of buying it.

Laying the dress aside, she lifted out a parcel of letters bound together with a delicate pink ribbon. Flowing script arched across the front of the envelopes. *Miss Leigh Hunter.* In the upper corner was *M. Sutton*.

She opened the packet, then paused. Was she delving into something she shouldn't? These didn't feel like her things or her letters. She glanced down at the stack in her lap and selected one.

May 3, 1899

My dearest Leigh,

Leigh ran a finger over the dried ink. *Dearest.* Again she had the eerie sensation of having crawled into someone else's skin.

> *I wish you could see the morning dew on the field from my window. The sun is peeking over the horizon and every blade of grass is aquiver with life as the first rays of light turn the droplets into diamonds. Do you suppose God grants us the beauty of dawn to ready us for what the day will hold—a promise to sustain us through any ill that will befall us? Or do you think that the world simply turns on its axis, oblivious to the simple thoughts and hopes of man?*

The beauty and the intimacy of the thought he chose to share stunned her. Who was this Matthew Sutton—a philosopher or a dirt farmer? And where was this other Leigh if she was here in her place? Guiltily, she returned to the letter.

> *I think of you all through the day. Each time I see a bird wing across my field, I marvel at the idea of flight and wish you were here so I might share it with you. Each time the wind blows through my hair, I imagine you at my side, the wind caressing your cheek as I so long to do. I am counting down the months until October when my wishes will come true.*

She opened another letter. It too was filled with thoughts so intimate she blushed as she read them. If only she could know what this Leigh had answered. Was she as enamored of Matthew as he was of her? On and on she read, letter after letter, each one cataloging his thoughts and his hopes for happiness, long life, children.

He had lost someone once, he wrote, a woman destined to be his bride. His sorrow had been deep and lasting, and then he had met Leigh, though only by letter.

You represent my life rising from the ashes, as the phoenix did. You are my rebirth and my future.

Leigh dropped the letters and rose to cross to the window. She stared out at the horizon, where dawn was a pink shadow encroaching on the night. Her headache returned with full force as she desperately searched her mind for some recollection, some hint, as to where she was, how she'd gotten here, how she could not remember a love like this. Her former life—as she was beginning to think if it—seemed more and more like the dream and this the reality. Things were so *real* here, she thought, running a finger across the rough wood and then the smooth, cold glass of the window. People, too. She remembered Matthew's expression there with her in the twilight—the want in his eyes, the love. She couldn't remember ever seeing emotion so stark and raw in any of her lovers. Lust, maybe, but not true emotion. That was kept behind a carefully constructed mask of noncommitment. She herself wore such a mask.

Matthew's poignantly penned words haunted her. She felt as if she had peeped through a keyhole, as if she had seen into his mind without his knowledge. She knew intimate secrets he had told no other living soul, entrusted to no one except the woman he loved. Did she deserve such trust? Was she worthy to take on this privileged woman's identity?

And what if she *had* slipped into someone else's skin,

taken someone's place in time? What was it Sherlock Holmes had said? *When everything else has been eliminated, what remains must be the truth?* Well, then, she had traveled in time or between planes of existence, or she'd made some other transfer she didn't begin to fathom. She was living an honest-to-goodness science-fiction story. And there was no way home. No magic portal to step through. No magical red slippers to click together.

Was this other soul back in New York, living her life? And what of her name? Could she have moved through time and *still* be Leigh Hunter? She smiled to the darkness, imagining Bryan's surprise when he tried one of his kinkier bedtime antics on some prim miss from 1899.

She returned to the bed and searched farther into the bag, finding a small leather book carefully tied closed with more ribbon. Eagerly, she opened it, turned to a page dated May 3, 1899 and began to read.

Received letter from Matthew today. He seems anxious for the wedding day.

"Anxious? The man's pouring his heart out here." Leigh turned the page.

Purchased eleven yards of lace for wedding dress and twelve yards of silk. Material should arrive three months before wedding. Matthew mentioned wind. I should see to purchasing a variety of hats.

"Is that all she got out of his letter?" She read on, each passage as flat as the next. Not once was there a mention of her love for him, her hopes for their life together, no secret thoughts about their wedding night.

The last entry was dated October 28, 1899.

> *I am writing this from the stage en route to Aurora, so that accounts for the unevenness of the lines. I do hope that Matthew is pleasant and is not expecting too much of me. I fear from his letters that he is a passionate man, and never having met face to face, I cannot judge the depth of his "secret side," as Mother terms it. Autumn is a dreadful time for a wedding and I am trying to keep up my spirits.*

How horrible to live life so passionlessly, to neither see nor feel what was before one, Leigh thought. Then she realized with a jolt that that was exactly the way she had lived these past two years. Plunging ahead, meeting life on its own grounds, yet never seeing nor acknowledging the small things that made up the big picture.

Leigh closed the book, but held it in her lap. Was she dreaming in terms of Charles Dickens? A sort of *Christmas Carol* experience brought on by too much alcohol and sushi and too little peaceful slumber? *No,* some small voice whispered, and she knew deep in her soul that she had been given a gift, that she was about to step across a threshold into the rest of her life.

"Good morning," a singsong voice chanted, boring into Leigh's confused dreams. She jammed a pillow over her head, but someone pulled it away and plopped something on her bedside table with a clatter.

"Rise and shine, sleepyhead."

Leigh raised her head and looked straight into Miss Eva's smiling face.

"You can't sleep away your last day of freedom." Miss Eva snatched away the pillow, gave it a furious fluffing, then wedged it behind Leigh's back as she turned over.

"You didn't have anything to eat last evening and you have to keep those roses in your cheeks."

Despite her annoying fussing, Leigh sensed nothing but compassion from the slightly rotund Miss Eva.

"I brought some toast and jelly and oatmeal." She plopped the tray onto Leigh's lap and whipped off the dishtowel covering it with the aplomb of the best New York maitre d'.

Eva's face was expectant, filled with barely contained excitement, as if pleasing Leigh was the most important thing in the world at this moment. Leigh smiled despite herself.

"It's lovely, Miss Eva."

"Now you eat your meal and we'll go shopping and get you acquainted with your new neighbors."

Leigh picked up the spoon and dipped it into the oatmeal. She grimaced as she put the spoonful in her mouth. She'd always hated the thick gray slime. But to her surprise, it was creamy and smooth with a hint of cinnamon and brown sugar.

"This is very good," Leigh said, dipping up another mouthful.

"Of course it is." Miss Eva unfolded a brilliant blue dress and hung it in the armoire. "It's my own special recipe. I fix it for all my girls."

"Uh-huh," Leigh replied, noting that Miss Eva was now hanging up a brown sprigged calico dress. These clothes hadn't been in the satchel from last night.

Dipping another spoonful, Leigh leaned to the side, as inconspicuously as possible, to see around the end of the bed. A huge steamer trunk sat on the floor, overflowing with a rainbow of fabric.

She glanced back at Miss Eva, now humming to herself as she smoothed and straightened dresses.

"Boy, this chick must have been some clotheshorse," she mumbled.

"What did you say, dear?" Eva turned from the armoire.

"I said I certainly have a lot of clothes." Leigh spooned up more oatmeal and tried to smile innocently.

"Indeed you do. Your father, God rest his soul, provided well for you."

Another valuable piece of information. She entered it into her mental list. No father.

"So tragic to lose both parents like that."

Another piece to the puzzle. No mother either. That would explain why she was now a mail-order bride, she thought sarcastically.

She watched the endless parade of dresses, with their high necklines and tight bodices, and wondered if her new body would fit into any of them.

"Now." Eva smoothed the last dress and then stuffed it into the bulging armoire. "Finish your breakfast and we'll be off." Her voice rose on the last word—lilting, piercing, and all together annoying—but her eyes were sincere.

"Wait," Leigh called as Eva bustled toward the door. "Are there other . . . girls here?" There, she'd asked the dreaded question. Just what kind of "girls" did Miss Eva deal in?

Miss Eva knitted her eyebrows together. "Oh, no, dear. Don't you remember? It was just you and I on the stage. Are you still not feeling well? You shouldn't have gone roaming around last night. You should have been here in bed. Oh dear, oh dear."

She bustled over, genuine concern spreading across her

broad face, and clamped a hand on Leigh's forehead. "You don't seem to have a fever."

"I'm fine. I just meant . . . were we joining any other girls here?" The recovery was stitched together from bits and pieces of tangled information, but seemed to be effective as Eva's concern melted away.

"No, dear. You're my only little chick. I'll be back to collect you in an hour," she flung over her shoulder as she hurried out of the room, closing the door behind her.

Leigh set aside the tray and again crossed to the mirror. She turned to the side and pulled the nightgown tight around her. She'd gained at least a cup size and one or two inches in the hips, just enough to give her the hourglass figure she'd always envied.

"Maybe going crazy isn't so bad after all," she said to the stranger in the mirror.

Leigh stared into the storefronts she passed, each one a picture out of a history book. They passed the general merchandise store with horse collars and fresh apples, the hotel with its name painted in baroque script on the front glass, and a lady's dress store boasting the most torturous garments imaginable.

"Leigh dear, I saw the most wonderful thing in here." Eva caught her by the hand and dragged her into the small shop.

Dress forms modeled the owner's latest creations, yards and yards of material gathered and tucked and bustled. *Heavy* was the word that sprang to Leigh's mind.

"Esmerelda?" Eva called.

A tiny woman emerged from behind a curtain, a tape measure draped around her neck. A pencil jabbed through the light brown bun atop her head and pins crisscrossed the front of her dress.

"Esmerelda, this is Leigh Hunter." Eva hauled Leigh out from behind her and thrust her forward. "She'd like to see that item I was admiring yesterday."

The little dressmaker raised her eyebrows and smiled. A little too slyly, Leigh observed. Esmerelda wove through the crowded shop, then stepped behind a counter topped with delicate laces and filmy material. She rummaged around under the counter, then produced a silky white garment—the tiniest of laces adorning the neck and the most delicate of rosebuds stitched into the neckline.

"It's beautiful," Leigh said, fingering the soft fabric. "What is it?"

Esmerelda cast an incredulous glance at Eva and Leigh knew she'd done something else wrong. "Why, it's a nightgown, dear. A very *special* nightgown," she said with excruciating patience.

"Yes, special," Leigh repeated, her mind whirring. Obviously Eva thought she needed this. For Matthew of course.

"I think you should buy it," Eva said without preamble and with a none-too-gentle nudge of her elbow.

"Oh, I don't know." Where on earth would she get the money for this—Or for anything else? The thought crashed over her. She had no money and no means of obtaining any.

"Here." Eva thrust a pouch into her hand. "This is the money you sent me to hold for you. As your advisor in the ways of love"—Eva waggled her eyebrows knowingly—"you need this nightgown."

As if I couldn't seduce him on my own, Leigh thought. She glanced back at the gown. Well, it *was* beautiful and she *was* dreaming.

"All right, I'll take it. How much?"

"Two seventy-five."

Leigh opened the pouch and poured the coins out into her hand. They were twenty dollar gold pieces, according to the mint mark. She counted out fourteen and plunked them onto the counter. Esmerelda stared openmouthed at her.

"That's two dollars and seventy-five cents, Leigh," Miss Eva said, whisking the extra money away and depositing it back into the bag. "Bride's jitters," she said to Esmerelda, who nodded dumbly, then closed her mouth.

Esmerelda carefully wrapped the garment in brown paper, all the while sneaking glances at Leigh from beneath her lashes. When Esmerelda handed Leigh the package, Eva took her elbow and led her out of the shop.

"My dear, have you never been shopping before?" Eva asked when they were outside.

Leigh stared at Eva, trying to come up with some explanation that would work, something that only sounded half as incredible as the truth. Two hundred and seventy five dollars was a steal for a custom-made negligee, she wanted to say, but instead said, "Not often."

Eva took her elbow. "Then I make it my duty to acquaint you with the fine art."

An hour later, Leigh emerged from the general store, packages stacked to her chin. Eva had overseen the purchase of new linens for her new home, new clothes to wear with her new husband, and new kitchen utensils for the food she could not cook.

"Leigh dear. I'll just take those packages for you." Eva hefted the load into her ample arms. "I have an appointment with Mr. Edgar Thornton back at the hotel and I'll take these back for you. I believe that he and Miss Susan

Jones would make a fine couple and I've asked him to come for his interview today. It's such a nice morning, I thought you might like to look around our little town."

Eva turned and headed off down the sidewalk, her head bobbing from side to side as she struggled to see over the load in her arms.

Leigh turned full circle, taking in all of Main Street. After all, she was surely due to wake any second, and she wanted to remember this strange and vivid dream. Down at the end of the street, a small crowd had gathered, and Leigh headed in their direction. When she arrived, a woman carrying a basket of corn pushed past her. A man carried three ripe tomatoes. Suddenly craving fresh vegetables, Leigh waited her turn until the crowd ahead of her thinned out.

The produce stand was of weathered wood and a cheerful sign proclaimed that someone named Wooten sold the best produce in town. A good feat when autumn had long since stricken down vegetable gardens with a frosty hand.

When the crowd ahead of her cleared, Leigh saw a small man behind the counter. He was in animated conversation with a customer. He waggled a heart of celery and said, "Now celery is silly. Who needs celery?"

Déjà vu slammed into Leigh, staggering her for a moment. A woman frowned at her as she stepped backward unexpectedly. Regaining her balance quickly, Leigh pushed through the last people and shoved her way to the front, despite the grumbling that followed her.

Ian.

He looked exactly the same as when she'd last seen him grinning at her on a dirty Manhattan street.

"What the hell is going on?" she growled at him.

The smile reached his lips before he turned his attention

to her. When their eyes met, he smiled more broadly and reached across the counter to take her hands in his small, gnarled ones.

"Now, child, we will set things right."

Chapter Four

"Sometimes the soul is lost. It takes a wrong turn and ends up someplace it should not be," Ian said.

"A soul is not a rental car. It does not take a wrong turn," she forced out from between clenched teeth. "You are part of a bad dream. I will wake up soon and you and your crazy notions will be gone." She snatched her hands out of his grip.

He smiled serenely, her anger lost on him. "You were not meant for the twentieth century, Leigh. You belong here with Matthew."

"And what exactly is your role in all this?"

He shrugged his shoulders. "I correct mistakes," he answered simply.

"How do I get back? I want to go home."

"You are home." He leaned forward and gently took her hands again. "You were not meant for the other time. Your future was not there, your happiness was not there.

You were meant for here. Unfortunately, I do not have the power to turn back the pages of time to undo the pain you have suffered." His smile was angelic and mesmerizing. "But I can promise you much happiness here."

She was about to yank her hands away again and demand once more an explanation that didn't sound like a bad episode of *The Twilight Zone* when a hand touched her shoulder.

"Leigh," Matthew's gentle voice said in her ear.

She turned toward him, startled.

His eyes searched her face, his brows knitted together in consternation. "Is anything the matter?"

"No, I was just talking to . . ." She turned back to the vegetable stand and found it deserted. Ragged sheets of canvas twisted in the wind, unused and old. Dust covered the narrow ledge where moments before cucumbers and tomatoes had rested.

"He was just . . ." Robbed of words, she waved an ineffective hand toward the old stand.

"A family named Wooten once ran this business, but they moved away years ago," he said gently.

Leigh looked up at him, confusion numbing her mind. He brushed back a lock of her hair. "I came into town to remind you about the Halloween dance tonight." He took her hand and together they walked down the street.

"Matthew?"

"Yes?"

"Do you think you can dream while you're dreaming?"

He chuckled, a warm throaty sound. "I don't know. Do you dream that way?"

Leigh shrugged. "I guess I do." She was dreaming right now, she wanted to say, but his touch felt very real, warm, and right, and Ian's words swam through her thoughts.

*   *   *

Lanterns bobbed in the trees and children clad in home-made Halloween costumes chased one another. A wooden dance floor had been laid and ropes festooned with more lanterns were strung across it. A few adults wore costumes, but most left the pretending to the children.

Matthew handed Leigh down from the wagon. He was dressed in clean denim pants and a white shirt. Leigh straightened the skirt of the brown calico dress and wished for a pair of jeans and a T-shirt.

Three witches clustered together on the other side of the dance floor and Leigh immediately recognized the Smith sisters. They waved and smiled, then turned in unison and shook their long black capes at a group of children, who ran shrieking in mock terror.

Miss Eva hovered around the edge, a nervous-looking man following in her wake.

"That's Edgar Thornton. Miss Eva's working on a match for him, too," Matthew whispered in Leigh's ear. His breath ruffled the tiny hairs just above her ear, sending a shiver down her back.

"And that"—he pointed to a pale-faced young woman holding a voluminous hat in her hands—"is Miss Susan Jones. The most famous spinster in Collins County."

"She's so young. Why would anyone call her a spinster?" Leigh asked.

"She's not so young. She's almost twenty-five."

Leigh caught her breath. Did he know that she was almost thirty? So what did that make her? Ancient?

"Is she Miss Eva's next target?" Leigh whispered back.

"A repeat target," he answered, leaning even closer.

"Repeat?"

"Miss Eva has an enviable matchmaking record. Miss Jones is her only failure. Seems she's hard to please."

"Maybe it's because she's so old," Leigh answered sarcastically.

"Probably so," he answered with sincerity, missing her meaning.

Ian's words came back again, haunting her the way the tiny ghosts and goblins haunted the birch grove just beyond the circle of light. He'd said he couldn't turn back time, couldn't erase the sorrow living out of her intended time had caused her. So how many years did she have left if she stayed here?

If she was here.

If this was real.

Women did not live long past their fifties in this time, she thought, remembering some worthless bit of minutiae stored deep in her memory.

The sharp sound of a fiddle being tuned stopped her thoughts. Other instruments joined in, then jolted off into a poignant waltz.

"May I have this dance?" Matthew whispered into her ear and took her hand in his warm fingers.

Leigh nodded and stepped up onto the wooden floor. Matthew took her into his arms, one arm snugged around her back, the other hand holding her hand. He moved onto the floor gracefully, swirling her with him as if they'd danced together all their lives. She relaxed and let the music move through her, willing her feet to move of their own accord. Faces passed them in a collage of color and expressions.

"You dance very well for someone who's never danced before," he murmured close to her ear. She looked up, puzzled, then remembered that this was probably some bit of information he and his love had exchanged in their letters.

He smiled wider and pulled her closer, executing an elegant turn that swirled the skirt of her dress around her. Onlookers clapped and she realized they had the whole floor to themselves. With a sigh, she abandoned her doubts and slipped wholeheartedly into her role. She'd either wake from her dream soon or die of old age.

Dusk matured into night and the lanterns cast cheery circles of soft yellow light. Suit coats and ties were abandoned as raucous reels made the musicians fiddle for their lives, beads of sweat glistening on their brows.

Leigh spun around the circle of dancers until the faces melded into a blur. The dance ended as she whirled back into Matthew's arms.

"Let's give the band a break," he said and led her over to a crystal punch bowl filled with a bright red liquid. "May I get you a drink?" he asked, reaching for a crystal cup.

"Yes, please," she answered, loosening the top buttons of her dress.

His hand paused, the glass ladle inches above the punch. His eyes glanced at her throat, then back up to her face.

Leigh flushed to the roots of her hair, both with anger and embarrassment. She'd never learn the mores of this society. She buttoned her dress back up.

Matthew handed her a cup and took one for himself, quickly draining the liquid.

"Would you like to walk? Away from the heat here, I mean?" he asked with a sideways glance.

Leigh nodded and put the cup on the table. They stood beneath the halo of lantern light. Overhead, high, thin clouds scuttled across the full moon's face, stippling the earth with shadows and silvery moonlight, fittingly mysterious for the eve of Halloween. They walked side by side, not touching, down a lane overhung by trees.

"Look there." Matthew suddenly pointed to a tree and left the path, motioning for Leigh to follow. He stepped up to a tree and reached up where a glob of green reflected the feeble light when a cloud released the moon.

"A luna moth," he said, bumping the green glow, which wobbled farther up the tree trunk. "They're a beautiful vivid green with dark brown spots that look like eyes on the ends of their wings. Fools critters who want to eat it." He touched the insect again and it obligingly climbed onto his finger.

Leigh recoiled. The only good bug was a dead bug was her motto. But he held the creature with such reverence, his face solemn and delighted at the same time. "See?" He held it closer and she did indeed see the dark spots that looked exactly like huge eyes.

He carefully placed his hand back against the tree, and the moth stepped off his fingers and resumed its position on the bark.

"Why are you so interested in things like moths, cows, and grass?" she asked as they moved back out into the moonlit lane, but the words sounded condescending and patronizing.

He frowned for a moment as if worrying a thought; then he smiled and shrugged. "All the things God gives us in nature we can never lose."

"What?" Leigh stopped and stared up at him.

"No one can ever take away the sunrise except God. No one can take away the sunset or the sound of frogs before it rains or the locust songs of late summer. All these things are gifts to us."

His deeply private words, penned to another, came to Leigh's mind. That was what he had been trying to say to her. From anyone else, the thoughts would have sounded like some New Age babble, but she knew that he meant them, that the thought was as deeply embedded in him as his eye color or the shape of his lips.

"I think of you at dawn."

The words caught her by surprise, so engrossed was she in her thoughts. "At dawn?"

He stepped closer. "The earth is soft and still, soothed by the night, like a lover would soothe."

larm bells clanged in her head. *Intimacy warning,* the internal voices screamed.

"And the grass is beaded with dew, waiting for the sun to come and wipe it away."

He moved closer still until his breath stirred her hair.

"Then a gentle fog blankets everything, soft, damp, skimming over the ground, its touch light and caressing."

The blood was thumping in Leigh's ears, her heart racing. Desire and arousal poured into her veins while her brain frowned in confusion. *He's talking about grass and fog, for God's sake.*

His arms slid around her and drew her close. "I dreamed of seeing these things with you, showing you the beauty of the world as I see it. I read your letters, then read them again and again"—he bent lower—"and dreamed of doing this."

He kissed her, his mouth gentle, yet demanding. Leigh's body bypassed all thought and responded with simple instinct. She clasped him to her, pulling him tight within her embrace, urging him to kiss her deeper and deeper.

It was Matthew who pulled away first. He let her go, turned away, and paced a short distance from her. His shoulders moved up and down as if he had just run a distance.

"Matthew?" she asked, wondering if she'd again overstepped some boundary. But part of her knew why he'd turned away. She was as aroused as he.

"I'm sorry, Leigh. I got . . . carried away." He put his hands on his hips and tilted his head back to look up at the moon. "We'll blame it on the full moon and Halloween."

Leigh went to him and smoothed her hands across his shoulders and down his back.

"Please don't," he said in a tight voice.

Leigh dropped her hands to her sides. "I'm sorry."

He turned to face her. "You have nothing to be sorry for. I kissed you."

"Oh, no. I was in on that, too. Believe me." She moved toward him, something inside her painfully longing to touch him again.

He moved back one step, just enough to put him out of her reach. "We should get back to the dance, or else we'll have tongues wagging."

Bowing to the mores of the times, Leigh walked by his side, again not touching him, back to the thin strains of a reel. And just for this time, she was grateful for the restraints of 1899 society. For with a full moon and Matthew Sutton in her arms, only the goblins could judge what might have happened otherwise.

They returned to the dance, but the innocence of the event was lost. Matthew stood at her side, his hand occasionally brushing her fingers, making her arm tingle all the way to her shoulder. He was very careful not to touch her too familiarly. The whole orchestrated event now grated on Leigh's last nerve. She was suffering from a bad case of lust brought on by a discussion of fog and grass.

Her tautly stretched nerves silently applauded when the final notes died away and the musicians rose to place their instruments in cases.

"Well, I will see you two tomorrow morning," Miss Eva crooned.

For a moment, Leigh could not focus on her question; then she remembered. She was to be married tomorrow. Wed. Hitched. Permanently attached to Matthew.

What if I wake up before the wedding? With a jolt, she realized the change in herself. She was, for the first time in years, looking to the future, be it dreamed or real.

"Yes. At eleven o'clock," Matthew was saying with a quick squeeze to Leigh's fingers.

"You two are my crowning achievement." Eva clasped her hands together and tears filled her eyes.

Matthew glanced down at Leigh briefly. "Yes. I think so, too."

Eva hurried off after Edgar Thornton, who trudged ahead alone, apparently another hash mark on Susan Jones's tally of unacceptable suitors.

With their hands joined, Leigh and Matthew walked back to the hotel, treading the path of moonlight that powdered the ground ahead of them. Neither spoke and Leigh wondered if Matthew's thoughts were on tomorrow or tomorrow night.

"Well," he said as she stepped up onto the hotel porch, "I'll see you at the church in the morning."

"Matthew." She paused, searching for the right words. "Are you sure you want to do this? I mean, if you don't . . . I'm giving you an out."

He tipped his head and smiled. "An *out?* An odd term. Of course I'm sure." Before she could brace herself emotionally, he had gathered her into his arms. "You are breath and light to me now, Leigh, as necessary as both. I've waited a long time for you, as I hope you have for me, and a longer time for tomorrow."

Then he kissed her again and Leigh knew she was in trouble.

Lust she could deal with.

Love she could not.

"Do you, Matthew, take Leigh here as your lawful wedded wife?"

Matthew turned, a soft smile playing across his lips. "I do," he said in his soft timbre, his voice barely above a whisper.

Leigh waited for her vows, her hands shaking beneath the small bouquet of wildflowers she grasped. For the thousandth time, she wondered at the headlong plunge she was about to take and for the ten thousandth time she turned Ian's words over in her mind. Was this where she truly belonged at this moment in time? Of all the places she could be in creation, was she meant to be here? Now?

"And do you, Leigh, take Matthew here as your husband?"

She stared up into his face, so open and trusting, and a thousand doubts chased by demons of guilt raced through her. A tear slipped down her cheek and she saw his brows knot together briefly. "I do," she whispered.

"Beg pardon?" The minister leaned forward, a moment of panic flickering across his face.

Leigh cleared her throat. "I do."

He leaned back, a broad smile of relief on his face. "You got the ring, Matthew?"

Matthew searched the pocket of his coat and produced a tiny gold band. He grasped Leigh's hand and slowly slid the cold metal onto her finger. "With this ring, I thee wed," he whispered, needing no prodding from the minister.

"Well, then, by the power vested in me by the state of Colorado, I pronounce you man and wife. Kiss her, Matthew boy."

Matthew lifted the thin sheet of lace that covered Leigh's face and kissed her, his touch sweet and shy, but promising more.

The squeaky organ groaned out something akin to the recessional, and Leigh felt Matthew take her arm and gently turn her to face the congregation. A sea of expectant, happy faces grinned at her as she took a step forward, then two, Matthew's hip against hers, his grip on her arm firm, as if he knew her knees were banging together like cymbals.

Together, they navigated the narrow aisle and out into the welcome autumn sunshine. A cold breeze sailed around the corner of the small white church, lifting the lace of her dress and threatening the contents of the white cloth-covered tables set up underneath the small grove of trees, where last night goblins had cavorted.

Matthew smiled down, happiness sparkling in his eyes. He bent closer and kissed Leigh again, his lips grazing hers like the brush of a butterfly's wing.

Struggling to put together two words, she waited for him to say something. But he only squeezed her hand and turned to greet the crowd that was just now catching up with them.

Countless people smiled at her and wished her good luck, some of them squeezing her hand and reminding her that she was now responsible for a favorite son. The wind stopped and the sun shone brightly, almost as if it were gracing them with the last of summer.

She sampled home-cooked dishes, prepared with love and carefully brought in precious china. Children clamored to touch her. Matthew never left her side, a hand

always around her waist or on her shoulder, fingers sometimes entwined with hers deep in the folds of her gown.

A constant presence.

To have and to hold from this day forward.

"I've never seen a lovelier wedding, and I've seen many
of them." Miss Eva's tearful greeting pulled Leigh back
down to earth.

"I've arranged many a match, but never have I seen a
love match such as this." She dabbed her eyes with an
ornate silk handkerchief. "You are a very lucky girl. You
know, not all of my matches are so perfectly suited as you
two."

Matthew's fingers found Leigh's, and he pressed his
palm against her palm, an intentional intimacy that shot
through her like an electrical charge. "Thank you, Miss
Eva," he said when Leigh's mind suddenly went blank.

"You are a beautiful bride," the three Smith sisters
chimed in unison, wearing identical dresses. "Is that your
mother's dress?"

Leigh stared down at the dress, panic rifling through
her. Then she remembered the diary. "No. No, I had it
made . . . at home." She had no idea where she was supposed to have come from.

"It is lovely, child. And you, young man, are quite the
sight." All three sisters plucked at his tie as if he were a
child, and Leigh drew a sigh of relief, but the panic stayed.
She could never pull this off. She had almost no information about this Leigh Hunter except what was penned in
the diary. What if someone knew her? What if someone
started asking questions?

They danced on the same wooden floor that had been
laid for last night's goblin party. The same band played
the same tunes, yet nobody seemed to notice. The decora-

tions had changed though, from ghosts and pumpkins to flowers and white ribbons.

Matthew held her closer than last night, swirled her around, ignoring the good-natured catcalls from his neighbors, openly in love with the woman in his arms. Leigh lent herself to the task, threw away her doubts and fears for these brief hours, and pretended that she was truly, heart and soul, Mrs. Matthew Sutton.

"We should be going," he said as the last notes of a reel died and she stilled in his arms. Happy abandon slipped away, reality sinking into its place. Afternoon was drowning in the purple of evening, bringing with it a prophetic chill.

She listened numbly as Matthew thanked their guests and announced their departure. Gentle jests and good wishes followed them to Matthew's wagon.

They left the cheerful light and moved into the shadows, where the team waited with heads bowed. Matthew lifted her into his arms, pausing for a moment before placing her on the hard board seat. He climbed up beside her and flicked the reins; then they moved away from the church and into the silvery night.

As the last strains of music faded behind them, the vastness of the moonlight-drenched landscape encircled them, making their shared board seat seem intimate.

Disturbed only by the occasional jingle of harness and the constant clop of hooves, the quiet night seemed more frightening than any subway ride she'd ever taken. She felt vulnerable, tiny, beneath the canopy of stars overhead—an insignificant soul in the grand scheme of things. Yet she knew from Matthew's letters that she now represented the very core of this man's world. Suffocating guilt settled onto her shoulders.

"Deep thoughts?" he asked, glancing sidelong at her.

"Just a few butterflies."

He stared straight ahead over the horse's back, seeming to have returned to his own thoughts.

They turned into the lane leading to his house. White ribbons were tied to the trees that lined the lane and to the porch columns. He stopped the team and set the brake with his foot.

"Welcome home, Mrs. Matthew Sutton." The words were said lightly, but his eyes were dark and serious.

He climbed down and held up his arms. Gathering her skirt into one hand, Leigh allowed him to lift her into his arms. He shifted her against his chest and, instead of setting her down, climbed the steps to the porch, shoved open the door with one foot, and carried her into the cool interior.

The dark material of his suit scratched against her cheek and her heart pounded. She expected him to carry her straight upstairs, having steeled herself against the inevitable. He'd probably never been with a woman and must be eager.

Instead, he stood her gently on her feet and backed a step away.

"I have to see to the team. I'll be back in a few minutes." He turned to go, then paused and looked back over his shoulder. "I left some milk in the cooler and there's cake in the kitchen." He smiled. "Welcome home."

The door banged behind him, and through the screen, she watched him take the steps two at a time. Soft, unintelligible words came back to her as he grasped the bridle of the nearest horse and led them around the house.

She dropped her wilted bouquet on a small table and wandered into the kitchen. A neatly iced chocolate cake sat in the center of the table, obviously the gift of some thoughtful neighbor. It looked tempting through the glass cake cover that imprisoned it. She raised the cover and swiped at the icing with one finger, feeling just as guilty as when she'd done the same as a child.

Licking away the stickiness, she moved to the tall cooler, which was much like the refrigerator in her apartment. She pulled open the door and a moist chill coiled out to touch her. A huge block of ice sat in the bottom and a crockery pitcher rested on a shelf. She tipped the vessel forward and peeped in at cold milk.

Cold whole milk and homemade chocolate cake. When was the last time she'd indulged in such decadence?

She drew out the pitcher and poured herself a glass, then sliced two generous portions of the cake and placed each on a delicate china plate with a pink rose pattern. She found a fork in a drawer and sliced off a bite. Closing her eyes, she concentrated on the rush of flavor and the memory of a long-forgotten cake concocted in her grandmother's kitchen.

She raised the glass and sipped the cold, smooth milk, laden with milk fat. A small sound startled her and she opened her eyes. Matthew leaned against the door facing, his arms crossed, smiling. No, he was almost laughing.

"What?" she asked with a shrug of her shoulders.

He shoved away from the door and moved toward her, his tie hanging loose. When he was inches in front of her, he reached out a finger and wiped at her top lip. "You wear the evidence of your sin, Mrs. Sutton."

As his fingers grazed her mouth, the laughter faded from his eyes. His touch lingered on her skin and he moved closer until their foreheads touched. "I'm glad you're here with me, Leigh."

His scent was sweet, a warm honest smell without the aid of cologne. Bits and pieces of his letters floated through her mind, vows and wishes intended for another.

"Matthew." She raised her hands to place them against his chest, but his fingers caught hers.

"You and I are strangers in all ways except our words. I do not expect more of you than you are willing to give," he said carefully.

"Matthew—" she began again, but he interrupted her.

"Come." He tugged at her hand and led her through the house and out onto the porch. Moonlight rained silver on the fields visible beyond the trees that surrounded the house.

Planting her hands on the porch railing, she breathed in, her chest tingling with the cold, fresh air. Her blood began to race and her senses surged with awareness. Matthew wrapped his arms around her from behind and drew her backward into his embrace. She relaxed, allowing her body to mold to his.

"Come with me," he said into her hair. He took her hand and led her off the porch and across the carefully tended yard to the edge of a field. Freshly turned soil lay in gentle ridges, frosted by the light of the moon.

Matthew scooped up a handful of the dirt, crushed it in his fist, then held it to his nose and inhaled. "The only time it smells any better is in the spring when Patty and I turn it for the first time."

He held out his closed fist, indicating that Leigh was to smell. She did, cautiously, but found, to her surprise, that the aroma was pleasant and somehow comforting.

She smiled at the expectancy in his eyes. He was like a child offering a new drawing or some enigmatic creation rendered in clay. He opened his fist and let the soil filter away. Then he brushed off his palms and pulled her to him.

"I can only offer you simple things, Leigh. My love. This

land. Sunrises. Songbirds. I'm not a rich man, nor do I ever expect to be."

Leigh closed her eyes, guilt and joy warring within her.

"You came to me, to strange people and a strange town, leaving behind all you know because I asked you to," he murmured into her hair. "In return, all that is mine is yours: my heart, this land, these fields, and all that is in them. You only know me by my words. You haven't looked into my face and judged me. I hope that, over the next weeks, you will come to love me as I love you."

A tiny voice frantically reminded Leigh that she was an impostor as she tilted her face up and stared into Matthew's eyes, again dark with emotion. He lowered his head and kissed her, drawing her tighter against him until she could feel the work-roughened ridges of his abdomen and the strength of his grip. When he raised his head, his pulse was hammering against her chest and the strong arms that held her trembled slightly.

"You may have the bedroom I showed you yesterday," he said into her hair, his chin propped on her head. Then he released her and moved a tiny step away. "I'll stay across the hall until you ask me into your bed."

Chapter Five

The bluntness and compassion of his words took her aback, robbing her of her self-assuredness. All her worldly knowledge and experience deserted her, leaving her truly a trembling virgin bride and him the experienced lover. She'd been prepared to have to find some way to tactfully fend off his amorous advances, to explain that they needed to know each other better, when in reality intimacy with Matthew was all she had thought about since walking out of the church.

"It's time for bed." He led her back across the yard and held the screen door open. They ascended the stairs and he lit a lamp just inside the bedroom he'd so carefully prepared. Soft yellow light chased the shadows into the corners of the room.

With hands that trembled slightly, he replaced the chimney to the lamp and turned to face her. He removed the veil from her hair and laid it on the bed. For a moment, she thought he might change his mind about separate bedrooms and desire surged to life. But instead, he leaned down and kissed her again, but this kiss was different from earlier. Now his lips moved over hers in a familiar, almost playful way. When he drew away, she wanted more.

"Good night," he said and walked quickly out of the room, closing the door behind him. Disappointment replaced caution, and deep within her, his words left a small knot of loneliness.

Matthew allowed his fingers to linger on the doorknob, a darker side of himself urging him to reopen the door. She'd expected him to sleep with her, to claim her love here and now, forging them together. He'd seen it in her eyes, but he'd seen fear, too. Now a gentler voice explained patiently that they were, in fact, strangers and she needed to be courted and won.

And yet there was something about her he could neither name nor place—something different, mysterious, odd. She seemed to be here with him and then also seemed to be existing in her own world, a private bubble into which he was not permitted.

With effort, he drew his hand away and moved across the hall to his own room, darker and more lonely than it had ever been. Standing in the dimness, he pulled off his tie and removed his coat. A cold breeze was pouring in the window and as he pulled down the sash, he wondered if Leigh was cold. Was her window closed against the night's chill? He should go look, a voice within him urged.

He pushed away the voice and lit his bedside lamp. The furnishings seemed shabby. Uncertainty gripped him.

What can a poor farmer like you, Matthew Sutton, have to offer a woman like Leigh?

Perhaps she had expected more. Maybe it wasn't hesitation he'd seen in her eyes, but disappointment. A thousand worries suddenly poured into his mind, addling his thoughts for a moment. Then a cool breeze through the window calmed his racing mind and heart, reassuring him with its gentle voice. Leigh was a wonderful woman. Kind. Gentle. Cultured. A real lady. And yet she was a farmer's daughter, reared on the land, accustomed to hard work. He would court her, woo her to his side, win her heart. The worry drained out of him and fatigue took its place.

The brightness of the sunflowers was blinding, like tiny suns come down to earth. Someone stepped toward her, out of the light, took her hand, and began to lead her away, deeper into the field of nodding flowers. The hand that gripped hers was firm and warm, and occasionally she caught the timbre of a soft voice, pointing out a flower, describing the softness of its petals, the firmness of its cluster of seeds. Then the dream vanished like a bubble speared by a blade of backyard grass on a sultry summer afternoon.

Soft sounds drew her out of the hazy remains of her dream and into the bold reality of morning. She turned over. Matthew stood at the end of the bed, holding a tray, fingering her veil, which still lay across the end of her bed.

"Good morning," he said, abruptly dropping the veil.

"Good morning."

He sat down on the edge of the bed, the mattress giving way with a gentle groan. "Did you sleep well?" he asked, leaning over to place the tray on the bedside table.

"Yes, I did. In fact," she said, pushing herself up in the bed, "I can't remember when I have slept so soundly."

Dark circles shadowed his eyes and restless sleep had

tousled his hair. His shirtsleeves were carelessly rolled up to his elbows, baring strong, sinuous arms.

"Did you?" she asked, already knowing the answer.

"Yes, I did," he lied, then rose, moved to the window, and stared out across the field. Daylight was just breaking, casting lethargic shadows against the opposite wall.

Guilt, now her constant companion, probed at her again. A confession rose up in her and with it, all the imagined relief at baring her soul. But before the first words left her lips, she looked into his eyes, brimming with love. Love for her. Not for this other person who had written emotionless letters and skimmed the surface of life, never diving into the depths.

The idea that he loved *her*, wanted *her*, shook her so that she moved her hand to throw back the quilt and invite him beneath the covers with her.

"Would you like to see the farm?" he asked before she could speak.

"Yes. I would like that very much."

"I'll be downstairs when you're ready." He strode to the open door. "Take your time," he said, then moved through the door and shut it behind him.

She ran her hand across the quilt that covered her. Every stitch had been worked with love, every seam carefully studied before it was fitted into the pattern. Not a task taken lightly nor a gift given easily—a gift more of oneself than of substance. Was this simplicity what her soul had craved? Was this why Ian had arrived to "save" her?

Shaking off the confused musing, Leigh swung her feet out of bed, wincing as they touched the cold floor. Her dresses peeked out of the armoire, collected and delivered by Miss Eva before the wedding. She selected a heavy wool one, again wishing for jeans and a sweater. Maybe she would buy a pair one day when they were in town. Perhaps with time, Matthew would not be so shocked to see her wear them.

She drained the glass of milk Matthew had brought her and hurried downstairs. Heat rose to meet her at the top of the stairs, along with the aroma of baking bread. Matthew wasn't in the kitchen when she arrived. She turned back through the living room; then she saw him standing on the front porch, a cup in his hand. He wore no coat, despite the fog that rose with each breath, and he stared off across his fields, now dusted with frost.

"There you are," she said, opening the door and stepping out into the cold.

He glanced back at her and smiled. "Our lovely autumn is over, I fear. Last night was the first frost." He pointed to the sparkling landscape. "Winter will be swift now."

He took another sip of the coffee and the aroma coiled up and wound around Leigh.

"Have you got another cup of that?" she asked.

Matthew glanced at her with a quick frown. "Of course. In the kitchen on the stove." Leigh started for the door. "I made it very strong. I thought you didn't like coffee."

Another misstep. Leigh paused with her hand on the screen. "Well, since it's such a cold morning and yours smelled so good, I thought I'd try it. Since you like it so much." The excuse sounded shallow and contrived, but she dared not look back over her shoulder.

"Cups are in the cabinet to the left."

She shoved the door open and walked to the kitchen. Just what other intimate details of this other woman did Matthew know and she did not? From the letters, it appeared the other woman had told very little of herself to him, Matthew doing most of the revealing; yet there must have been some times when the woman told him things of herself, her life.

She poured herself a cup and sipped the coffee, wincing at its strength.

"I warned you," Matthew said, setting his empty cup on the table and moving to her side. She hadn't heard him come in, and she started when he put his arms around her and drew her back against him.

There was a controlled intensity in the arms that bound her to him.

"I love you," he said simply into her hair.

The corresponding words bubbled up into her throat, surprising her with their assuredness. But she bit them back, not yet ready to completely surrender herself to this fantasy.

"You don't have to answer," he whispered, and the note of disappointment in his voice twisted at her heart.

"Matthew, I just need . . . time."

"I know." He relaxed his grip and let his arms fall to his sides. "Well, I promised you a tour. Would you like to walk out to the barn with me and I'll hitch the team to the wagon?"

He started forward, but Leigh caught her arm. "Matthew. Could I borrow a pair of your pants?"

He turned and frowned. "To wear?"

"I wore them at home often. They were so much more comfortable than skirts . . . around the farm." She winced inside, hoping her memory was accurate and that Matthew really had commented on her life on the farm.

He studied her a moment longer. "I have an old pair. Wait here."

Leigh released her breath and said a small, grateful prayer.

Matthew returned and held out the trousers. "I brought a shirt, too."

Leigh took them from him, feeling his gaze on her

back as she turned and headed upstairs. "I'll only be a moment."

"I'll wait for you," he called after her.

She slipped into the trousers, sighing contentedly when the heavy dress slipped away. Standing in front of her mirror, she cinched the pants with a belt from one of her dresses. They were a little tighter than she liked, but she smiled, imagining Matthew's reaction.

Shock rendered Matthew speechless as Leigh descended the stairs, one hand on the stair rail, taking each step slowly and carefully. His old work pants hugged her figure like a second skin, the worn denim doing little to hide the curve of her hips and the smooth lines of her thighs and legs.

He swallowed and watched her close the distance between them, every step, every movement executed with deliberation for maximum effect.

"Thank you," she said, reaching the bottom step. "These are much more comfortable." Her expression was teasing, seductive, and her eyes glittered with mischief.

"What did your father say about your dressing like . . . this?"

Her expression faded, replaced by a frown. "Well, he didn't say much about it." Her eyes narrowed in thought. "I didn't wear pants unless there was no one around except him and Mother."

"What about your brothers?"

She frowned again, deeper this time. "My brothers?"

"Yes. James and Sam?"

She chewed her bottom lip, tiny white teeth nibbling at the pink skin. "They didn't care either."

Funny, Matthew thought. He'd never have pegged Leigh Hunter as a rebel. In fact, this woman standing before him had so little in common with the woman with whom he'd corresponded for nearly a year that she could be a total stranger. Could someone truly be so different in the flesh? Or was there something afoot here?

She stepped down into the hallway, a shadow of a frown still playing across her face. "Are we going to the barn?"

"Yes." He caught her elbow, careful to keep his hands away from her body, even though his palm ached to slide down her side and over the intriguing curve her hipbones made beneath the cotton fabric.

A cold wind scattered her hair across her face in delicate wisps as they stepped from the house. Following the well-trodden path to the barn, they heard the groans before they reached the closed barn.

Matthew dropped her hand and broke into a trot. Leigh hurried behind him, the sounds raising the tiny hairs on the back of her neck, even though she had no idea of the source.

Matthew flung open the heavy doors and hurried down the line of stalls, almost skidding to a stop in front of one midway down.

"What is . . . ?" The words died in her throat as she stopped behind Matthew. The mare, Patty, stood with head drooped forlornly, her back arched in a bow. A tiny, still bundle lay in the hay at her feet.

"Patty," Matthew whispered, moving along her side, his hand gliding across her coat. "Oh no." He dropped to his knees and ran his hands over the foal.

"What's the matter with her?"

Matthew turned a pale face toward Leigh. "Twins. This one's dead. The other's probably a breech."

The breech part she understood only too well. The old, nearly forgotten fear clawed its way out of her insides and settled cold, bony hands around her throat. She backed up a step.

"Go back to the house," Matthew said, his tone broaching no argument.

"No. I want to stay. I can help."

"This is not something you need to see, Leigh."

"I know how terrible this can be."

He frowned again. "You do? How?"

A pretty lie sprang to her lips, an easy explanation. But the truth shouldered past. "My sister," she whispered.

Matthew stared at her a moment until Patty groaned again, the sound almost human. "Go get that rope hanging there on the wall. Then go back to the house and get the bucket of lard on the back porch."

Leigh quickly retrieved the rope, then ran back over the path they'd just traveled to the back porch. She found a tin bucket in the corner. A peek under the lid revealed a thick yellow substance like bacon grease. She heaved on the thin wire handle and lugged the heavy bucket across the yard to the barn.

The mare's reddish-brown coat rose and fell in struggling breaths. Her eyes were terrified. The dark pupils rimmed in white were focused on Matthew, as if begging for his help.

"I have to get her back up on her feet," he said. Then he looked up at Leigh, doubt clearly evident in his gaze, and Leigh knew he judged her lacking for this purpose. He considered her a delicate flower in need of shelter and protection—something to be adored and guarded, but never used.

Indignation flared within her and anger, dark and hot, slowly filled her chest. Then she remembered the woman who had scripted the passionless letters filled with inane details of a protected and privileged life—a hothouse flower, reared to be a pretty decoration on a man's arm.

Leigh narrowed her eyes. *Well, not this gal.* "What do you want me to do?"

Matthew studied her a moment longer. "Take that rope and loop it through her halter. We have to tie her off so she can't lie down."

Following his example, Leigh slid the rope through a ring in the halter and tied a knot. Matthew took the line from her and moved deeper into the stall to stand at the mare's head.

"Back away," he instructed and Leigh moved out into the hallway.

With gentle words and firm pressure on the two lines, Matthew encouraged the horse to stand. She refused at first; then she lunged to her feet and stood on wobbly legs.

"Take that rope and coat it with lard," he instructed, hidden from view by the mare. Then he moved into sight, tying each of the halter ropes to rings on opposite sides of the stall.

Leigh took the rope, dipped one finger into the oozy mess, then plunged the rope into the lard. When she drew the rope out, globs of lard plopped onto the barn floor and her shoes.

Matthew shoved his whole arm into the lard and smeared the grease up to his shoulder. He held out his hand for the grease-coated rope and flashed her a small smile before approaching the back end of the mare. He looped a slip knot into one end of the rope and paused.

"You should leave now, Leigh. This isn't going to be pretty, and it isn't decent for you to see."

"Isn't decent? I'm your wife. What could happen on this farm that isn't decent for me to see?"

Matthew stared at her and she thought she saw a small spark of admiration in his slow smile.

He ran a hand over the mare's hind quarters, speaking

to her in a low, soothing voice; then he pushed his arm, rope and all, inside her womb.

Leigh fell back against the wall, anticipating flailing hooves. At least from her own experiences in the gynecologist's office, that would be what she'd do if she were a horse and could get away with it.

Patty hunched her back and grunted in relief, almost as if she knew Matthew was helping.

"I've got the nose," Matthew said, his cheek against the horse's rump. "And the front feet." He rotated his arm slightly and began to withdraw his arm very slowly. Patty made a feeble attempt to lie down, bending her front knees, but the ropes prevented her from sinking into the hay.

Matthew crooned words of nonsense to her, keeping his voice even and soft; all the while the rope continued to emerge. Then, two tiny hooves and a little black nose appeared.

Patty hunched her back and grunted.

"That's the way. Help me, girl." His voice rose with excitement and the foal slid out into the world, caught by a bed of fragrant hay.

Leigh stared at the scene, knowing her mouth was hanging open. Matthew quickly tore away a huge membrane, caught up a handful of hay, and began to brush the baby as if to scrub away the fur.

"Untie Patty," Matthew said, never taking his eyes from the foal.

Leigh edged her way along the inside of the stall, one eye on the horse and the other on the knot inches from her fingertips. What if Patty decided she'd had enough of this intrusion? Leigh pulled the knot loose. Then she moved around the horse's head and untied the other knot, dashing out of the stall, nearly knocking over Matthew in her haste.

Patty angled her head around to peer at the baby, then wiggled around until she could lower a soft nose and nudge at the bundle in the hay. She nudged more firmly, rocking the baby back and forth. With a mew like that of a newborn kitten, the foal lunged to its feet and irritably switched a stump of a tail. Patty rumbled deep in her chest, rubbing her broad nose over the baby's body, encouraging it to move closer. Then, with joyous tail twitching, the baby found its mother's milk.

Patty leveled kind brown eyes on Matthew and as good as said, "Thank you," with another soft rumble. Leigh glanced at Matthew. Tears ran down his cheeks, pooling in the corners of his smile. Her throat tightened. Together, they'd brought a life into the world, connected intimately with another creature. Leigh closed her eyes for a moment, remembering her sister's struggle to give birth, her face pale against the hospital sheets, her eyes filled with the same pain, the same fear.

When Leigh opened her eyes again, Matthew had his arms around Patty's neck; his face was buried in her soft mane. If anyone else hugged a horse with tears in their eyes, she'd have scoffed at their sentimentality and thought them a fool, but she knew Matthew's emotions were real. Living here, coaxing his living from the land, he and his animals and his land were one, each dependent on the other for survival.

Simple things.

The belief he lived by.

Simple things.

And with her heart pounding from both fright and joy, Leigh realized with staggering reality that was exactly what she wanted—what had been lacking in the life she lived from one great expectation to the next, missing all the good stuff in between.

Matthew released Patty and stepped back, casting a sheepish glance at Leigh. He caught the hind feet of the dead foal and moved it into an adjoining empty stall. Patty was busy with the new foal and didn't seem to notice the loss of its twin.

"I should bury it now before Patty smells it and remembers," Matthew said apologetically, brushing at the smear of blood that streaked his shirt.

"I'll help you."

"No," he answered quickly. "You don't have to do that."

"I know I don't have to, but with two of us, the job'll take half the time." Leigh took two shovels down off the wall. "Then we can take our tour around the farm."

He started to speak, his lips moving wordlessly, but he nodded instead.

Matthew carried the tiny body out to a sun-dappled spot that would be shaded by an aspen tree in the summer. Wordlessly, they dug the grave and laid the foal to rest. The sun was high and shadows short when they finished and started back toward the house. Matthew took her shovel from her and gave her hand a squeeze that spoke more than words.

Matthew leaned his hips against the kitchen sink, his shirt tied around his waist. One finger pulled the skin on his cheek taut as the other hand pulled a straight razor across the angles of his face. Bits and dabs of soap spattered his face, betraying the paths of the razor.

Perched on a kitchen chair, Leigh watched, fascinated, toweling the last of the dampness out of her hair. The whole shaving process seemed so intricate, so complex, and yet so uncomplicated. One of life's smaller joys, her father used to say. A smooth, clean face to start the day.

Simply by feel, Matthew seemed to know where to place the blade for the next pass, the proper slant, proper speed . . . all without drawing a drop of blood. An impressive feat considering she couldn't shave her legs without one or two nicks.

Matthew cut his eyes at her and smiled, never missing a pass with the razor. "Did you never watch your father shave?"

"Huh? Yes. When I was little," Leigh answered, shaking herself out of her reverie.

Matthew swished the razor in a pan of water in the sink, twisted his mouth to one side, and resumed the gentle scraping. There was something very soothing about watching him perform such a mundane task, something very domestic—an ideal Leigh had avoided at all costs . . . until now.

Matthew had removed all his clothes except the suit of long underwear that sagged in the rump, and he'd washed away as much of the lard as possible outside. Now water for his bath was heating. She'd bathed first while Matthew busied himself in the barn. Now the tub stood in the center of the kitchen floor . . . refilled and waiting.

"Is that water hot yet, Leigh?" he asked.

A large pot rattled its lid impatiently as if in response to his question. He'd filled the tub almost full with cold water, bucketful by bucketful, and now all that remained between her and a naked Matthew Sutton was the all-too-cooperative rattling pot.

Leigh knew what she was about to do was brazen and likely to give Matthew the shock of his life, but she refused to cower in the other room while her husband bathed. If she was to live this life as Leigh Hunter, housewife, farmhand, helpmate, she was going to live it under her own terms.

And he *was* her husband.

In all ways but one.

He'd expected to marry a mouse, prepared himself for life with a fragile bit of fluff. Well, she was about to dispel those illusions.

He toweled away the soap remains and laid his razor on a small shelf by the sink. Turning, he ran a hand over his face, jutting out his jaw to test its smoothness. He caught her gaze and stopped, his hand still cradling his chin. "Some exciting first day as Mrs. Matthew Sutton, huh?"

Leigh nodded.

He knitted his eyebrows briefly. "Are you all right?"

"Yes, I'm fine," she answered. "Still a little amazed."

He laughed and loosened the shirt around his waist. "I've seen a lot of foals and calves born and it still amazes me, too." He took two towels from the counter and carefully lifted the steaming pot from the stove eye. Steam clouded around him as he poured the boiling water in the tub. He set the pot back on the stove and turned toward Leigh.

"I'll take you on that turn around the farm as soon as I'm done," he said, a suggestive note in his voice.

Leigh nodded. "Okay."

Matthew waited, but she remained seated. He stared pointedly at her, but she returned the stare coolly.

"I'm going to get into the bath now." He tried again.

She nodded again.

Unnerved, Matthew began to unbutton his suit of underwear, but Leigh didn't flinch. When he reached his navel, he paused and looked up at her. Except for a slight flush across her cheeks, she seemed unaffected. Disrobing in front of a woman, even if she was his wife, was something he had never done before. Somehow, undressing before her in the heat of passion seemed more . . . proper than doing so in broad daylight in his own kitchen.

"When I take this off, there is nothing underneath," he said bluntly. Perhaps as an innocent, she did not realize that once this garment fell to the floor, there would be nothing between them except what *she* wore.

Slowly, she nodded. "I know."

Matthew hesitated. The next move was his. *No one is that innocent,* his common sense warned and his heart began to hammer. She was playing some seductive game with him. After all, she was not all what he had expected from her letters.

Desire coiled in his stomach and his body made its wants known. He felt his cheeks flush, as much from the absurdity of the situation as from embarrassment. He was held captive by his body and his wife in the middle of his own kitchen.

Tension vibrated between them and the air was thick with more than steam. Everything about her, the way her hand pushed back her hair, the way she licked her lips, the slow arch of her neck as she readjusted her spine, seduced him.

If he took the next step, what would happen? Would he send his virgin bride screaming from the room? Or would she uncoil herself from that chair and saunter across the space between them? Drape her arms around his neck? Hold her all-too-evident curves against his bare body? Maybe join him in the bath?

"Leigh, this just isn't done. There's something about it . . . It isn't proper." He shoved his arms back into his sleeves and quickly sat down on a nearby chair.

"What isn't proper?" she asked.

"You there . . . me . . . here." He pointed at the tub, knowing he sounded like an idiot.

She smiled a small, slow cat smile and he suddenly knew how the cornered barn mouse felt.

"Do I make you nervous?"

"No, Leigh . . . it's just . . ." He was babbling again. *Speak, Matthew. You're a grown man.* "It's just not proper for a wife to watch her husband bathe. Especially when they've not . . . not . . ."

"Slept together?" she finished.

"Yes," he answered with a rush of breath.

As he feared, she uncoiled herself from the chair, her movements languid, fluid. She glided across the short distance between them, stopped and looked down at him.

"Then it's time we did something about that."

Chapter Six

Nothing in Leigh's letters could ever have prepared Matthew for the woman who stood before him now, her eyes dark and sensuous, threatening to devour him with their depths. Yet he felt as if he were staring up at a stranger.

Was she toying with him? Teasing him? There was only one way to find out. He rose from the chair and moved back to the steaming tub. He stood for a second, facing her; then he drew his arms out of the garment and paused, the material gathered in his hands at his waist, giving her a chance to back away.

She didn't blink.

He dropped the suit of underwear to the floor and stepped out of it, all the while keeping eye contact with her. She calmly scanned him from head to toe, then returned her gaze to his face.

He stepped into the tub and sat down, sliding down in the water. The air undulated with tension as he picked up the soap and hastily made lather to cloud the clear water. Leigh knelt down beside the tub and spider walked her fingers across the tops of his shoulders, stopping to feel the knots of tension there. He shuddered under her touch and tiny ripples darted away to crash against the tub's side.

She took the cloth from his hand, dipped it into the water and began to lather the soap.

"Leigh, this isn't a good idea."

"Of course it is." She drew the cloth across his shoulders and he closed his eyes. Of all the dreams he'd ever had of family and marriage, this was the one he most craved.

Touch.

The touch of a gentle hand that knew his body, his wants, his needs. Soothing fingers that sought out and caressed some needy part. Hands frantic with passion. An innocent caress at the end of a long day. He sighed and leaned into her hand.

Drawing circles, she covered the fine hair scattered across his chest, the expanse of his shoulders, his forearms, and as her hand dipped below the water, he caught her wrist.

"Don't." He bit out the words, bringing his face even with hers.

"You're my husband," she said softly. "You said I had to ask. Well, I'm asking."

Leigh watched hesitation play across his face. His lips moved as if he were about to speak; then he abruptly pulled her face forward with a soapy hand to the back of her head and kissed her, soap and all. There was nothing of the gentle, proper Matthew Sutton in this kiss. It was urgent, wanting, thinly controlled.

"Leigh." He whispered her name with such naked passion that all her defenses crumbled and the game was no longer a game.

She pulled away, her fingers fumbling at the buttons on her shirt while he watched.

"Yo. Matthew boy," a voice called from the porch. Before she could react, the door scraped open and a man walked into the kitchen, a cloud of pipe smoke preceding him.

His ice blue eyes twinkled at the sight of the two of them, but he didn't appear flustered or even embarrassed, merely amused. Leaning against the doorframe, he crossed his arms, clamped the pipe between his teeth and grinned around it.

"Leigh, this is Isaac Benton, my neighbor," Matthew said with all the dignity he could muster. "Isaac, this is Leigh . . . my wife."

Even that admission didn't ruffle the man casually lounged in the door. "Married her, did ya?"

"Last night," Matthew said pointedly.

Isaac tossed a casual gaze her way, still smiling; then he turned his attention back to Matthew. "Got a new dog yesterday. Drove all the way over to Eldon for it."

Leigh was having trouble fighting down the laughter struggling to get out. *If Matthew could only see his face,* she thought with a new onslaught of internal mirth. He may have had a more embarrassing moment in his life, but she'd bet this one would at least move into the top five.

"Patty had her foal this morning. Twins. One was born dead and the other was a breech. We turned her and she's all right."

Isaac grunted and cast another assessing glance toward Leigh.

"Got dirty, did ya, boy?"

Matthew nodded miserably. "Lard."

Isaac smiled, mischief sparking in his eyes. "Elizabeth sent ya some cake. It's outside in the wagon. I'll go get it." With a final amused smile, he pushed away from the doorframe and sauntered out the front door.

Leigh sat down on a chair and laughed out loud. "Oh, Matthew. Your face."

He grinned crookedly. "Isaac owns the farm next door, he and his wife, Elizabeth. He appointed himself my guardian a long time ago."

"Don't people knock around here?"

Matthew smiled slyly. "Not in the middle of the morning."

"I'll go keep him on the porch while you finish your bath." She rose to go, but Matthew caught her wrist. "We'll finish this later," he said with a smoldering look.

Her head spun from the wave of need that slammed into her. It was as if he had reached inside her and turned on a switch. She imagined her knees wobbled visibly for an instant as his hand fell away and she directed her steps toward the front door, hearing the water splash behind her.

Isaac rocked back and forth in a porch rocker, his pipe resting in one hand. He stared out across the fields, their coat of frost long since melted away.

"Do ya love the boy?" Isaac asked bluntly, continuing to stare far away.

"Yes, I do." The answer just slid out, surprising Leigh with its simplicity . . . and its truth. The conquest had been a sneak attack.

"Humph," Isaac replied, seating the pipe back in his mouth. "Didn't think much of you from yore letters."

"Really?"

"Matthew let me read 'em."

Leigh sat down in a companion chair, covering her surprise at the admission. Old Isaac had nothing on New Yorkers for bluntness—that was for sure. Why would Matthew share something that seemed so intimate to him? And just who was this Isaac Benton that he should be privy to these very personal letters?

"He was took with ya right from the start." Isaac shook his head and rested his pipe on the chair arm. "Matthew's a dreamer, always got his head in the clouds. Couldn't find a better man nowhere's tho'. That's why it's my job to look out fer 'im." Isaac shifted in the chair and turned those chilling blue eyes on her again. "What are yore intentions with this boy?"

A sharp laugh bubbled up in Leigh, but she bit back the sound when she realized Isaac was deadly serious. "I think my intentions are clear. I married him, didn't I?"

"Sayin' words and doin' deeds ain't the same, missy. Any fool knows that."

Leigh chafed under the rude words, but that damned inner voice reminded her she'd answered many times just as cutting and just as intentionally.

"Before I answer your question, answer mine. What business is it of yours?" She raised her chin a bit, anticipating his tart retort.

He continued to stare at her with those icy eyes, then smiled. "I like a direct woman. Like I said, Matthew there's a dreamer. Always sees the good in everybody. Takes in every stray that comes along. Not a better judge of horse-flesh in the county and not a worse judge of people.

"He lost his mama and papa when he was a young'un, 'bout fourteen, as I remember. But he stayed on here, grubbed out a living for himself, finished school, too. Me and the wife, we wanted to take him in, raise him as one of ours, but Matthew'd have none of it. No, sir. It was his farm and he wanted to run it himself." Isaac shrugged and leaned back in the chair. "So I kept an eye on him. Invited him over for a meal once a week at least. Let him do things his own way. And he didn't do too bad for himself. Got one of the prettiest places around.''

Another soul forged in the fire of loss, Leigh thought. Touched, she felt a silken bond coil around her heart, binding her to Matthew.

"Then Mary came along." Isaac smiled. "Sweetest little thing. Matthew acted like a darn fool for months over her. Then her drunkard daddy set the house afire, and Mary with it.''

The sweet little ghost that haunted the house swept over Leigh's soul, reminding her that the house she was beginning to love had been carefully prepared for not one, but two other women, neither of them her.

"Matthew grieved for a year. Then he got this darn fool idea in his head to order himself a bride." Isaac shifted in the chair to stare at her. "That's when yore first letter come.''

Leigh sorted through the letters in her mind, trying to recall the first comments exchanged and came up with nothing. So she remained quiet, certain Isaac would tell her just what she'd said.

"You struck me and Elizabeth as a spoiled, pampered brat lookin' for a husband to give her poor parents some relief.''

Leigh recoiled under the attack, her mind speeding through paragraphs and sentences, searching for some information with which to defend herself.

"Matthew musta been uncertain, too, 'cause he asked me to read yore letters after a few months. Oh, the boy said you were just what he wanted, just the woman for him, but I had my doubts.''

Leigh leveled an icy stare on Isaac, applying her best board room glare. "I assure you, Mr. Benton, that I am neither spoiled nor pampered.''

Isaac made a sound of disgust and returned to staring off across the fields. "Didn't sound that way to me. All them parties you prattled on and on about. All them shopping trips with yore mama. How you were goin' to redo Matthew's house to suit you."

Funny, Leigh thought, she didn't remember even one comment about dreams or plans. But she could remember nothing to refute what he was saying. In fact, her opinion of the other Leigh was just the same as Isaac's, leaving her no argument in her favor.

"That was my former life, this is my life with Matthew." The statement sounded as empty and feeble to her as she knew it did to Isaac.

He turned back to her, a thin line of smoke streaming out of his pipe. "You help deliver that foal today like the boy said?"

Leigh nodded.

Isaac clamped on the pipe stem, making a sharp clicking sound until Leigh longed to snatch it out of his mouth. "Well . . . we'll see."

He rose and Leigh knew she'd been judged and that the conversation was over.

"Isaac. Stay and have some cake with us," Matthew said, pushing through the door. His hair was still damp and the scent of soap trailed behind him.

"Naw," Isaac said with a quick glance at Leigh. "I gotta get on home. Elizabeth said to invite you and the missus over for supper tonight, if you can come."

Panic clamped a cold hand around Leigh's heart. Passing herself off to Matthew was a large enough challenge, but maintaining her charade in front of people who knew Matthew so well might be another.

"We'd love to. See you tonight." With a hand on Isaac's back, Matthew accompanied him out to where his wagon was hitched to a birch tree. The two men stood, their arms draped over the wagon's sides, in conversation. Leigh watched Matthew for a moment, an odd sense of pride sneaking through her at the sight of him. He'd taken a life of ruins and resurrected it . . . twice.

Leigh pushed the rocker and set it swaying back and forth, basking in a sunbeam that arched across the porch. Funny. She hadn't thought about going back home since . . . when? Not since she'd gone to the produce stand and found it empty. Did she still want to? She asked herself the question, then paused, waiting for the answer.

No, she did not.

All she'd ever wanted or needed was here.

But she wasn't entitled to it. She was a liar, an impostor, allowing Matthew to go on thinking he had married his meek little hothouse flower. She had to tell him.

"Isaac keeps an eye on me."

Leigh jumped, startled. "I see that."

Matthew stepped up onto the porch and stared down at his feet. "He's not a rude man." He spoke as if to make certain she understood this person, who was very important to him.

"He doesn't like me very much."

Matthew smiled. "Isaac doesn't like most people. I think he got the wrong idea about you." He glanced up. "As I did."

"Why did you let him read my letters?" She nearly choked on the lie.

Matthew blushed. "I'm sorry I did that. I was uncertain, confused. I wanted his opinion."

So Matthew had had doubts about his bride. "And did I measure up?"

Matthew smiled. "I imagine he told you his opinion."

"He did. And I told him mine. He doesn't think I'm good enough for you. He thinks you've had enough pain and I would just add to it."

"What else did he tell you?" Matthew asked sharply.

"About your parents."

Matthew turned away from her, his hands on hips, and moved to the edge of the porch. "Damn Isaac's meddling," he said beneath his breath.

"He just wanted me to understand you, Matthew."

Matthew turned. "It was my place to tell you about them."

Leigh rose and met him in the middle of the porch, placing a hand on his chest. "So tell me about them now."

Matthew shook his head. "I have to show you." He caught her hand and drew her behind him down the steps and out into the yard.

Morning sun had stolen the layer of frost from the fields and dusty rays slanted through the trees to warm the ground. Hand in hand, they walked the perimeter of the front field, half in shade, half in sun. Golden stubble speared color-spattered leaves, marking the completion of harvest, and a few hardy birds sang in the branches over their heads, warbling sweet hymns for the dying of summer.

Matthew didn't speak, even though Leigh waited for him to elaborate on Isaac's comments. Instead, he strode at her side, guiding her gently up a slight rise and then across the field to a charred spot. He stopped, stared down at the darkened ground, then gripped her shoulders and turned her around.

Leigh inhaled quickly. Spread out beneath her was Matthew's farm. The house sat primly amidst its skirt of birches. The barn was off to the left, and beyond the buildings, the fields stretched like a rumpled patchwork quilt to the horizon.

His breath was quick on her neck as he moved close behind her and put his hands on her shoulders. "Our house used to sit here. Daddy and Mama cleared all this land themselves, and Daddy said he chose this spot because every morning he could walk out on the porch and see all his good fortune spread out at his feet."

"What happened to them?"

Matthew's grip tightened faintly. "Smallpox. Both of them at once. Only God knows why I wasn't taken."

"You stayed here all alone?" Leigh turned and his hands dropped away from her.

Matthew nodded. "No one knows where they got it. Hadn't been a case in the county in years. The doctor insisted we had to burn the house and them in it to prevent an epidemic."

A small muscle in his jaw tightened and relaxed. "Mama used to tease Daddy that he was a foolish man to build his house on the top of a hill, where every bit of wind could blow through the walls. Daddy built the barn down there where it was warmer. It was lucky he did. That's where I lived . . . afterward."

Leigh turned back toward the neat house, the carefully kept yards, the brightly painted barn. All hard won.

And for some reason he wanted to share this with her.

She was not deserving.

"Matthew, there's something I've been trying to tell you." Leigh turned back to stare up into his expectant face. Words deserted her at the tenderness she found in his eyes.

"What?" he asked with a slight frown.

"I'm . . . I'm not who you think I am."

He smiled, a relieved note in the sound. "No one is. I

don't expect to know you, as I want to, in the beginning. Knowing another person takes years, and then sometimes we never completely understand that person.''

"That's not what I mean.'' A thousand words raced through her mind—short, terse explanations; compassionate explanations—none of them adequate. "I mean that I'm really not who you think I am.'' She drew in a deep breath. Her heart pounded and her head swam with the repercussions that would come. "I'm not Leigh Hunter.'' She closed her eyes and waited for the explosion.

When she heard nothing, she opened her eyes and stared at Matthew. He stared back, wearing an expression of patient understanding. "I don't know your reasons, Leigh, but I knew you were not truthful with me right at the start.''

"You did?''

"Of course. You didn't think you fooled me, did you?''

"Well . . . I thought—''

"I knew you were not the woman portrayed in the letters. No one could hold so little passion for life.''

"I beg your pardon?''

Matthew stepped closer and slid his arms around her waist, pulling her against him. "You wanted me to think you were a cold, unfeeling woman who saw no joy in the same things I did. You don't have to tell me why you did it and I'll never ask. We are here now together. That's all that's important.''

Realization dawned and Leigh attempted to pull away, but he held her firmly in his arms and kissed her. As in the kitchen, he kissed her with bone-melting intensity, passionate and rawly wanting. Despite the arguments lining up in her head like an orderly regiment, her body responded to his, and she let him pull her closer.

"Oh, Leigh," he whispered into her hair when he finally released her mouth.

The honest confession weakened her knees as the lethargy of responding arousal poured through her like warm honey. "I know. I want you, too," she whispered back while tiny voices of alarm danced a jig in her head.

All Leigh's liaisons rolled into one had never generated a tenth of the mind-numbing passion this one man did with a caress and a kiss. His lips moved from her lips to her neck and down onto her shoulder, where he nuzzled aside the open neck of the shirt to gain access to the tender skin covering her collarbone.

Leigh laced her fingers in his hair, pulling him closer, molding him to her, as if drawing him closer would hold him there always. She blanked her mind of the guilt knocking to remind her of its existence and concentrated instead on Matthew.

He pulled back and Leigh felt hot everywhere his searching gaze touched her, but she knew there was more than lust in his assessment of her. There was possessiveness and love and wistful longing—things at which she'd often scoffed and frequently condemned as oppressive. But today, she closed her eyes and enjoyed his appreciation.

"Matthew!" someone shouted from the yard below, and when she opened her eyes, a wagon and team sat in the front yard.

"Just how many people do you know?" she asked as he released her slowly and stepped back.

"Seth! We'll be right there!" he called back.

The couple standing on the porch could have been the models for the portrait *American Gothic*. He was tall and thin, and she was short and work worn, her hair pulled back in a severe bun on the back of her head.

"I come fer my wages," the man stated.

"Of course," Matthew replied. "Leigh, this is Seth Taylor and his wife, Effie. They're our neighbors to the north. Seth helped me with the wheat harvest this year."

Matthew left her on the porch and went inside. Effie Taylor looked Leigh up and down, her lips pursed almost as tightly as her hair was drawn up on her head.

"Are you that mail-order bride Matthew was all atitter about?" she asked, her words dripping with disapproval.

"Yes, I am."

Effie and Seth exchanged looks. "We don't hold with no such goings-on," she said. "I come along so's I could get a good look at you."

"And do I pass your approval?"

Effie blinked once. "Wearin' pants like a man. Sellin' yerself to the highest bidder. I figure that makes you a—"

"Thank you, Seth." Matthew reemerged from the house and placed several coins in Seth's hand. "I might need some help next week moving the hay up in the barn."

Seth cast a sheepish look at his wife, then at Matthew. "I'd be glad to help."

"I'll ride over and get you when I'm ready."

Seth nodded and shuffled toward the wagon, casting embarrassed glances at his wife. "Come along, Effie."

Matthew placed an arm around Leigh's shoulders and pulled her close to his side, defying Effie to comment. Effie turned without further words and followed her husband to the wagon, her gait stiff and her head high.

"Seth's a good man, but Effie's one of the most spiteful women I've ever met."

"Another one of your friends who doesn't care for me."

Matthew chuckled. "I guess I did create a bit of a stir with my correspondence with you. Good old Matthew. Never did a spontaneous thing in his life."

"And I, on the other hand, wear men's pants in public."

Leigh turned to face him, longing to pick up where they'd left off in the field.

Matthew glanced up at the sun. "If we're going to Isaac's house for supper, we'd better be getting ready."

Lazy afternoon rays were slanting across the road as Matthew picked up the reins and clucked to the horses. The wagon strained forward with creaks and groans, and they left the shade of the porch and moved out into the warm, dying sun.

Leigh touched the soft knitted shawl in her lap. The warmth of the day would quickly give way to the chill of evening as soon as the sun dipped below the horizon. She passed her hand over the garment again, marveling that three days ago she'd never even have considered wearing such a fluffy thing. But she was here now and lots of things were changing. She glanced to the wagon bed behind them and the carefully placed blankets.

Isaac's house was smaller than Matthew's but cheery with its brightly lit windows and wide, generous porch. Matthew climbed down from the wagon and tied the team. When he reached up to help her down, Leigh leaned forward, letting her hands drift across his shoulders as he set her on her feet.

Casting her a glance filled with sultry promises, Matthew took her arm and led her into the house.

"Leigh, dear. It's so good to meet you at last." Elizabeth Benton was everything Effie Taylor was not. Cheerful, friendly, and kind, she bustled around them offering food and drink, obviously a wonderful hostess. She clasped Leigh's hand firmly and gave it a comforting squeeze. "Welcome to our community, and we hope that you are very happy here."

Leigh smiled, Elizabeth's enthusiasm catching. "Thank you. I'm sure I will be."

Dinner was elegantly served on a table with real china and a lace tablecloth. Despite her heart being in her throat, Leigh enjoyed the food and the light conversation. When the table was cleared and the dishes washed, Elizabeth dried her hands on a towel and turned to Leigh.

"Now, dear, why don't you tell us all about yourself?"

Chapter Seven

Leigh's heartbeat ticked off the seconds she had left to live and the huge slice of chocolate cake in her dessert plate threatened to leap into her lap. She swallowed and glanced at Matthew's serene face.

"Matthew has told us so much about you, I'm afraid my curiosity has gotten the best of my manners." Elizabeth touched Leigh's shoulder. "Of course you don't have to if it makes you uncomfortable."

"No, it's quite all right."

"Well, why don't you start by telling us what it's like to live in a city the size of Denver?" Elizabeth leaned back in her upholstered chair and sliced off a piece of cake from the plate in her hand.

Leigh swallowed and squirmed on the settee. So she'd come from Denver. This she could handle.

"It's very busy and crowded. Very noisy. I find that I much prefer it here."

Elizabeth cast a teasing glance at Matthew. "I'm sure you have your reasons for that other than the lack of noise. What kind of work does your father do?"

Leigh searched through her memories of the letters with speed a computer would have envied. Then she remembered Matthew's comment in the barn. "He's a farmer." She slanted a glance at Matthew, but his face remained placid. She relaxed a bit and allowed herself to slip further into the role.

"How many brothers and sisters do you have?"

She remembered a mention of brothers from Matthew and she'd added the sister today in a slip of tongue. Should she repeat her error or hold with her story? "A brother and a sister."

Elizabeth smiled. "A nice balanced family. And are they still at home?"

"My sister is married but my brother is still with my parents."

"Do you miss home very much?"

Leigh glanced at Matthew. "Not as much as I thought I would at first."

Matthew colored and shifted his gaze away from her. The exchange was not lost on Elizabeth, who deftly steered the conversation to the subjects of crops and weather.

The evening passed quickly for all but Leigh. To her, the hours crept past. Then Matthew was announcing that they should get home and Elizabeth was wishing them Godspeed. Isaac saw them to the door with an invitation for another night and they were alone.

The air was brisk, but not uncomfortably cold and a full moon powdered the landscape with silver. Matthew didn't speak and Leigh rode in miserable silence wondering if she had told the truth, lied, or lied outrageously. They were almost home when Matthew drew the team to a stop and turned to her. Even in the dim light, she could see that he studied her face, her eyes.

"What was that back there?"

The world dropped away underneath her and confusion rose to fill the void. Lie about what? She'd lied about so much, how could she possibly know to which incidence he was referring? "I tried to tell you today."

"Your father has been dead for seven years, or at least that's what you wrote to me."

"My father's been dead a long time," she answered truthfully. "I just didn't want her pity."

"You never wrote to me about a sister. You never mentioned her until today in the barn."

"She died in childbirth." Again she spoke the truth.

Matthew studied her for a moment, his brown eyes serious and thoughtful; then he touched her cheek. "You've already become a part of me, Leigh. These few brief hours together, and I love you as I never imagined I'd love. I don't care about your past, only about your future with me."

Then he kissed her, his body trembling with the intensity of long-neglected wants.

Overhead, stars winked knowingly from their celestial vantage points. Beneath the pile of quilts, Leigh moved closer to Matthew, reveling in the intimate sensation of his skin against hers. She smiled into the darkness, remembering the look on Matthew's face when she'd practically dragged him over the wagon seat and into the back, where she'd conveniently placed a stack of folded quilts before leaving home. But his objections had quickly died, to be replaced by loving words, as he made good on his whispered promises.

"You are not the woman I thought I married," Matthew murmured close to her ear.

Unable to decide if she detected approval or disappointment in his voice, Leigh rolled over to face him. "I'm the same woman who promised to love you."

"That part you certainly fulfilled." He drew her tightly against him until his chest hair tickled her skin. But in the dim light, she could not see his face plainly enough to gauge his reaction.

"Where did you learn to do . . . that?" he asked softly.

Leigh's mind skimmed over the last half hour, most of it a haze of pleasure, and she wondered, with a jolt, what *had* she done? She had a vague memory of a shocked look and a sharp intake of breath on Matthew's part, and after that, decadent pleasure had wiped her memory clean.

"I have a vivid imagination," she murmured against him.

"I'll say." The hint of doubt in his voice rang clear.

Leigh pushed herself up on her hands and leaned over him. "Are you complaining?" she teased.

"No, but I was wondering why here in the wagon?"

"I figured this might be the only place we wouldn't be disturbed."

Matthew wrapped his arms around her and rolled her over beneath him. As she felt his weight upon her and looked up into his eyes, deep and dark with love for her, her heart began to hammer again.

"I had planned for this to happen in our bedroom."

"And it will." Leigh pushed a lock of hair out of his eyes. "Later."

In all her liaisons, no one had ever made her feel with the depth and tenderness that Matthew did. Despite the apparent urgency of his own need, he'd been tender and careful, ever mindful of her wants. And now, as she watched passion cloud his eyes again, she felt somehow disloyal for being more experienced than he.

He began to seduce her again, not with practiced technique or titillating methods, but only with the knowledge that he loved her deeply and truly. And as she was seduced, the guilt mounted.

The wee hours of morning were marked by a deep, thick silence as they pulled the wagon into their yard. Not an insect sang, not a bird stirred as Matthew helped her off the wagon seat.

"I'll put the team up and I'll be right in," Matthew said with a kiss to her cheek and a shy smile.

Leigh climbed the steps, listening to the rattle of the wagon as he led the team around the house toward the barn. The front door scraped open with the same complaining sound and the interior of the house looked the same as when she'd left it this afternoon, but she knew nothing would ever really be the same. She'd consummated this union with Matthew, given herself to him body and heart, and yet she had still not told him the truth about herself.

A sudden panic seized her. Could she live this lie the rest of her life? Could she pretend to be someone else with someone else's past, someone else's memories, until the day she died? Never see home again? Never see another television set? Another automobile? More importantly, could she keep up the pretense forever? *No* was the answer that ricocheted through her thoughts.

Slowly, she climbed the stairs to their bedroom and lit the lamp by the bed. Their bedroom. Where Matthew would love her every night, if she was any judge. Where they would conceive their children. Where their children would be born. Leigh felt the world collapsing in on her, the weight of it almost unbearable.

She ran a hand over the quilt that waited for her to pull it back and climb into her marriage bed. Leigh raised her eyes to the window, where her reflection stared back at her accusingly. *You don't belong here,* it seemed to say with a frown.

Matthew's breathing evened out to a gentle whisper and Leigh turned onto her side to study his face one more time. There was no place for her in his world. One day she would bring him heartache, pain he didn't deserve. Better that she leave now and let him think that he hadn't really known the woman he married. Fueled by the anger of desertion, he'd heal quickly and find someone else, someone who belonged in 1899. An odd twist yanked at her heart at the thought of him loving someone else as he'd loved her tonight. But she pushed the thought away, locked it securely behind a door to a room that would soon become full of banished memories.

Exhausted, he'd fallen asleep quickly, but not before he'd made love to her again—in their bed, as he'd said. Now he slept deeply and she knew that this was a time for her escape.

She crept from beneath the covers, careful not to pull any off him and awaken him with a chill. Then she dressed. The floorboards creaked gently as she padded across them, carrying her shoes. When she reached the door, she paused and turned once more to look back, her heart on fire. All she'd ever wanted was in that room, yet it was denied to her because of a misplacement in time and the nagging matter of a truth she could not tell. Steeling her heart against the ache already beginning in its depths, she turned away and crept down the stairs and across the yard.

The barn door swung open easily and the gentle scent

of horses and hay poured out, enhanced in the moist predawn air. She had to hurry. Dawn was rapidly chasing away the curtain of night in the east.

She slipped a bridle on Dan and led him out of the barn and down the road to a handy stump. She clamored onto his bare back, grateful for riding lessons in Central Park during one of her "back to basics" periods, and punched him into a jarring trot.

The vegetable stand stood gray and deserted, wisps of tattered burlap twining around it like gentle ghosts. Leigh slid to the ground and looped Dan's reins over the hitching post. Ian was here someplace. She felt it.

As she moved toward the graying structure, the first bits of doubt crept through her, whispering fantastic promises in her ears. If she left now, she could return home, take Dan to the barn, and slip into bed without Matthew's ever knowing she'd been gone. Leigh pushed the nosy voice aside and stepped into the stand. Just as she had known, the pumpkin waited on a dusty shelf, all by itself.

Leigh approached it, reached out a finger, then drew her hand back. Hesitation she could not explain nibbled at her determination.

"I knew you would come," said the familiar voice.

Leigh whirled and stared down at Ian.

"So you have decided to return." His eyes were sad; his countenance was defeated.

"Yes. I have no place here. It's not like you said. I don't belong here."

He shook his head slowly. "Yes, you do, child. But you are accustomed to listening to your mind and not your heart. You have not yet learned the difference."

"I just want to go back home."

Ian moved a step closer and looked up at her. "To what do you return, Leigh?"

"To my . . . life, my career, my friends."

Ian jerked his head to one side. "Back there you exist—you do not live. No one waits for you. No one watches or prays or hopes for you."

"You make my life sound miserable. I wasn't unhappy. In fact, I was very happy and very successful."

"If you were taken away and locked up, never to see the light of day again, and you could take one thing or person with you, what or who would that be? What is the one thing you value most."

His question stunned her. Her thoughts churned, her mind sifting through the past twenty years of her life. But always her thoughts settled on one thing. Buried beneath a stack of out-of-date magazines in her apartment was a seldom seen photo album. In it were chronicled the brief span of years that her family was complete. There were pictures from her childhood, pictures of her sister and the rest of her family. All seemingly neglected and dusty, but precious beyond value.

"A photo album of my family."

"And are the pictures mounted on paper of silver or are they printed with ink of gold? Is it the book you value so much or is it how it makes you feel to hold it, to open its cover and see familiar faces smiling up at you?"

A lump sprang to her throat as the memory of those pictures came to her, as clear as if she were holding the old volume in her hand. "Don't play mind games with me, Ian. I see what you're trying to do and it won't work. I can't stay here. Don't you see? It isn't fair to Matthew. He thinks he's married *his* Leigh Hunter. How can I ever tell him the truth and then how can I not?"

Ian smiled. "The heart has ways of overlooking things obvious to one not smitten. You think too much, Leigh Hunter. Don't think. Feel."

Leigh shook her head vigorously. "I don't want to think or feel. I just want to go home and be done with all of this."

She stepped forward toward the pumpkin, which was out of place in the drab shelter. Before her fingers touched its skin, she felt the tingle she remembered from before, the magnetic pull. She closed her eyes, silently praying that, as she moved back through time, her memories would be erased and she wouldn't remember Matthew Sutton or how it felt to be his wife.

"Leigh?"

Matthew's voice rubbed across her skin like warm velvet. "What are you doing here?"

She opened her eyes. She was standing on Main Street, dressed only in her nightgown, her feet bare in the fine dust. In front of her sat the pumpkin, waiting. Dawn had come and gone and so had Ian.

Leigh glanced around, but the little man was nowhere to be seen.

"Leigh?"

"Leave me alone, Matthew," Leigh said, moving a step closer to the pumpkin.

"Don't touch it!" Matthew shouted and she turned.

"How . . . ?"

Matthew spread his hands helplessly. "I don't know how I know, but I know you shouldn't touch it."

Tears flooded her eyes and she felt torn in two directions. "I have to go, Matthew."

"No, you don't."

"I'm not who you think I am." The tears were flooding down her cheeks, muddling her mind and making it hard to explain. "I'm not Leigh Hunter." She reached toward the pumpkin.

"I know you're not." Matthew lunged forward a step,

one hand outstretched. "I mean I know you're not the same woman I corresponded with and I don't care. I don't want to know what happened to her or what went on between the two of you. I only know that I want you to stay here with me. And I don't know how I know, but if you touch that pumpkin, you won't be here with me anymore."

"Go away, Matthew. Go back home."

"I can't. You're here. Home is wherever you are now, Leigh."

The suppressed sobs were choking off her air and her head was aching. Tears fogged her vision. Matthew's face was distorted, but not enough to mask the pain in his eyes.

"Good-bye, Matthew." Her fingers closed around the pumpkin, and she felt its magic seize her.

The skin was smooth and cool and her consciousness began to whirl, colors blending and arching. The world beneath her dropped away, and she floated, suspended in time and space. Fragments of the last few days unraveled within her, speeding through her mind, accompanied by the emotions each had evoked, alternately soothing and stabbing her in the heart: Matthew's whisper that she was his first lover; the trembling touch of his hand as he slid the ring on her finger; the Smith sisters' voices as they'd hovered over her; her last day in the office arguing with Mike; an endless, lonely weekend during which she'd cried over old movies; her sister's face.

A warm kiss on Leigh's cheek roused her, and she opened her eyes to stare into Matthew's warm brown ones. "Where am I?"

He frowned, his brows knitting together. "In our bed."

The memories of making love to him last night rushed

back, and Leigh felt her cheeks redden and then blaze. What had possessed her to do the things she'd done to Matthew? And where had she gotten the ideas?

"I'm glad I made you blush," he said with obvious pride. Then he sprawled onto the bed beside her, fully dressed.

"You're already up?" Leigh asked, observing that he wore his work clothes.

He nodded, twirling a tendril of her hair between his fingers, his chin propped in his hand. "It's long past noon. I let you sleep late." He waggled an eyebrow at her and she laughed; then another memory stole her happiness.

"Was I in town this morning?"

He nodded, his face suddenly serious.

"Why was I there?"

He shook his head, his gaze never leaving her face. "I don't know. I was hoping you could tell me."

Leigh frowned. Her memory of this morning was foggy and confused. She remembered being desperate; she could remember the emotion, but not the details of what spawned it. She remembered an old man and a pumpkin. . . .

Then full recollection returned. She stared at Matthew, his eyes full of love and tenderness, and remembered Ian's words.

"What's that?" Matthew nodded toward the bedside table. An old photo album lay there, its edges frayed and tattered.

Leigh scooted up in bed, tucked the quilt securely around her, and picked up the album. A parade of faces filled the pages, each one bringing tears flooding to her eyes. The clothes and surroundings in the pictures were those of the time period, but the faces were her parents, friends, and sister.

"Is this your family?" Matthew asked, pointing at a picture of a man and woman standing in front of an eighteenth-century house instead of the fifties ranch on Maple Street.

"Yes, they are."

"And this must be your sister?"

He pointed at a portrait of a smiling young woman, large with child. Leigh remembered the day the picture had been taken. Karen had been standing outside her house, a huge white Victorian she and her husband had slaved to remodel. Now Karen smiled from in front of the same house, only her clothes reflected the 1890s.

"Yes, it is. Isn't she pretty? She was so happy here."

Matthew kissed her temple and pulled her back against him. "Tell me about her."

Leigh slowly closed the album and placed it on the table as a rush of happy memories returned. And as Matthew pulled her back against him, she heard the door to yesterday shut with a gentle click.

AN AUTUMN BOUQUET

Linda Madl

Chapter One

wedding. The caterer, the guests . . .

Apple Grove House, Apple Fest Season
Kansas City, Kansas—1999

"For gosh sakes, Brad, the wedding guests are here."
Jennifer Hollis clutched her apple blossom and white rose
bouquet so tightly her fingers crushed the fresh, ribbon-
wrapped stems. Panic welled inside, but she fought it back,
hardly noting the damage she did to the flowers as she
spoke into the parlor phone. "Brad, you can't be serious.
Reverend Gleeson has arrived. The agency video cams are
ready to roll. The caterer has set up the food table. Please
tell me you're joking about not being ready to get married."

Brad replied, but Jen barely comprehended his words
through the static of disbelief. Her head spun and her
emotions retreated into numbness. She had heard all she
needed to know: Her groom had decided he couldn't go

through with the wedding. He was sorry he was leaving her with a mess to deal with. But he'd realized as he sat drinking with his buddies at his bachelor party that he and she did not want the same things out of life. Their marriage would be a terrible mistake.

"You waited until now to tell me this?" Jen asked, still breathless with incredulity.

"Bad timing, I know, but this break is for the best, Jen," Brad replied with only a hint of regret in his voice. "You'll understand that someday. I'm leaving for California as soon as I hang up. So neither of us will have to be embarrassed by running into each other around Kansas City."

There was no avoiding the disaster, Jen realized. The finality of his tone came through loud and clear. Without waiting to hear more, she slammed the phone down. What was there to say to the man who deserted you on your wedding day—a man who'd told her he loved her only a week ago? A week ago! Had it been that long?

The bang of the receiver hitting its cradle echoed through the authentically restored 1850s parlor of Apple Grove House. The noise bounced off the carved walnut fireplace, the brass wall sconces, the wavy lights of the tall windows, and the glass doors of the oak secretary.

Dazed, Jen sank down onto the black horsehair settee, unconcerned about wrinkling her antique wedding gown. Creased satin and rumpled Brussels lace hardly mattered now. But she shifted to accommodate the pressure of the horsehair bustle against her back side. The unfamiliar fashion garment felt strange over her Victoria's Secret underwear. Why on earth had she thought it so wonderful to wear an 1870s gown with a bustle?

Was it all going to be for nothing? All her hard work. Her wedding was about to begin—and a promotional television spot was about to be videoed—and she had no bride-groom.

She glanced around the room, distractedly listening to the murmur of the guests seated outside in the sunny apple orchard. She'd always loved this place. In fact, she'd always loved anything old. Yellowed or faded, cracked or chipped, frayed or sagging. She even preferred vintage clothes to styles from the fashionable Johnson County shops. Old things warmed her heart and filled her with nostalgia for times passed—times she'd never known.

And Apple Grove House was her favorite *old* spot in the world. She'd only been ten years old during that first apple fest her family had joined in years ago. Though she'd been too young to understand the term deja vu, she'd instantly recognized a place that somehow was a part of her. After that first visit, she'd returned to Apple Grove House as often as she could. Then she'd grown up and the luckiest thing of all had happened: Apple Grove House had become one of her accounts at the public relations agency where she worked.

Over the years she'd discovered much about the house's history, about how it was built in 1844 by Moses Grove for his half-Indian wife, Anna. About how Moses had operated the Kansas River ferry for the blue-coated dragoons and cavalry that traversed the military road between Fort Leavenworth and Fort Scott. About how he had operated a post office and traded with the peaceful Delaware Indians. The house was still full of things left behind by the Grove family—Moses, Anna, and their ten children.

Jen, sentimental fool that she was, had used the keepsakes to inspire her wedding at every turn. Even her apple blossom and white rose bouquet was a replica of the one in the bell jar on the mantel. Jen raised the posy to her nose and sniffed the heady aroma of fruit and flowers.

Nobody knew whose bouquet the dried one had been, but Jen had insisted that hers be just like it. The florist had eyed her dubiously, but done his best to comply.

Now she didn't even know if there was going to be a wedding.

"Well, there's the lovely bride."

Jen cringed at the sound of the familiar but unwelcome voice. When she turned toward the door, she saw tall, handsome Ted Neisen stride into the room with that take-charge air that invariably annoyed her. Warily she rose from the settee. "Hello, Ted."

Looking disgustingly dapper in his tuxedo, the fair athletic, fiftyish amusement park developer came to a halt in the middle of the parlor and rubbed his hands together in anticipation. For the first time in her battle with Ted, Jen felt like the fly in the spiderweb.

"I just wanted to extend my best wishes to you and your groom before the ceremony. Where is the lucky man?"

Jen groaned inwardly. She loathed Ted and he was the last person on earth to whom she would admit that Brad had just told her he was walking out on her. The only reason she'd invited the high and mighty developer to the wedding was to show him how she intended to rescue Apple Grove House from his crass profiteering. The man had never seen an orchard or a meadow he didn't want to pave. Jen refused to allow him to violate the beauty and serenity of Apple Grove House with a gift shop and a bevy of high-tech thrill rides.

"My groom will be here any moment now," Jen lied through her forced smile. When she'd invited Ted to the wedding six weeks ago, she'd been certain of her victory. It had all been arranged: the video cam crew to tape the old-fashioned wedding in the apple orchard, period reenactors, authentic country musicians, fine imported apple wine, and—best of all—the TV spot scheduled to raise community support.

Jen's boss at the public relations agency had gone for the plan. He'd loved her strategy for saving the old house and the cider mill from becoming an amusement park. But now Brad had gone AWOL.

"Too bad," Ted said, looking around the elegant parlor as if he'd never seen the room before. "Just wanted to let you know that I'm impressed with what you're trying to do here. Not many people have the courage to go up against me."

Then he shook his head. "But your efforts are misguided. Impressive, but misguided. This may be an interesting old place. But you need more than a romantic publicity stunt to keep the county from handing Apple Grove House over to me."

Jen dropped her hands to her side, the petals of her bouquet brushing against her skirt. Her chin took on a defiant angle. "The wedding is just part of my plan."

"And you are such a lovely bride, with your blond curls and those big brown eyes," Ted said, his calculating gaze coming to rest on Jen again. He'd never hit on her, but she'd frequently had the feeling that he had considered the idea—regardless of his wife and college-age daughters. "Great figure too, even with that damned bustle. Anyway, I still don't understand why you are doing all of this to keep me from developing this area. It's not like I intend to tear down the house or anything sacrilegious like that. And the amusement park will generate jobs."

"Apple Grove House is too important historically to be smothered under the shroud of commercialism," Jen said, her emotions raw at the moment. "I don't want to see the apple orchard standing in the shadow of a roller coaster. I don't want to see the old cider mill turned into a greasy snack bar and the house renovated for a gift shop. People need to remember and celebrate the simple pleasures of picking apples, making cider, and enjoying the fruits of their labor."

"Oh, Jennifer," Ted said with that *tsk-tsk* tone in his voice that always made her grind her teeth. "You sound old and preachy before your time. I should be the old man here and you should be the forward-looking new generation."

"I am looking forward," Jen insisted, her fist crushing her bouquet again. "I'm looking forward to passing our heritage on to my generation and the next one."

Ted smiled patronizingly and shook his head.

To Jen's relief, her auburn-haired sister, Jessica, rushed into the room in a swish of autumn gold taffeta. Her son, Joey, Jen's favorite and only nephew, strutted into the room behind her.

"Jen, the guests are beginning to wonder what is going on," Jessica blurted. "What did Brad have to say on the phone?"

Jessica and Joey halted when they saw Ted Neisen. "Sorry, I didn't mean to interrupt," Jessica said, her eyes growing wide and questioning.

"You're not interrupting." Ted eyed Jen with a look that told her she had a long way to go before she won this contest between the old and the new. "Just wanted to wish the bride good luck. May the best— No, wait. I'd better be politically correct here, right?" He gave a condescending chuckle. "May the best *person* win."

As soon as he was gone, Jen's bravado hissed from her in a long, slow breath.

"What did Mr. Ferris Wheel want?" Jessica asked. "Your face is whiter than your gown. Where's Brad? What did he say on the phone?"

"Ted wanted to gloat, I think," Jen said, struggling against the sense of defeat and despair that was beginning to settle over her.

"Little early for that, isn't it?" Jessica said with a pleased smile. She was in Jen's corner all the way about Apple Grove House. "He'll change his tune soon enough. Good news. Kelly says the cameras are working at last. What did Brad say? Why is he so late?"

Jen took a deep breath and turned to face her sister.

"He has a flat tire, right?" Joey volunteered with precocious gravity. "I bet that's it."

Despite her heartache, Jen couldn't resist smiling at her adorable nephew, who wore a child-size tuxedo coat, unbuttoned and pulled open so he could shove his hands deep into his trouser pockets. Like his mom, he had auburn hair, and pale freckles dusted his nose and cheeks. In his miniature formal clothes—which he'd agreed to wear only after they'd tried to get him into a Lord Fauntleroy suit— he looked eight years old going on thirty-five.

Jen's heart always warmed at the sight of Joey because she knew instinctively that he had a crush on her. So she'd made a special effort to include him in the wedding. He was her little ring bearer. "I wish it was that simple, Joey."

"If that's all, I'll send Mark to pick him up," Jessica offered, clearly unconcerned about offering her husband's services without his knowledge. She and Mark seemed to have the perfect marriage, Jen thought with a frown for the umpteenth time. And she couldn't even get her groom to the altar.

"We'll have Brad here in no time and the guests will hardly notice the delay," Jessica added. "And if we don't have any more problems with the video cams, we'll have this wedding under way. Your friend, Kelly, was about to tear her hair out over the camera problems."

"I know," Jen said, momentarily distracted by the mention of camera difficulties. She'd been concerned about the strange problem when she was setting up the wedding arrangements. "Apparently Kelly didn't believe me when I tried to tell her that cameras sometimes leak light or take double exposures around here. Sometimes video cameras just refuse to operate like they did this morning. One day you'll have trouble. The next day will be okay. Last summer I had to have a whole shoot retaken for promotional materials about the house because of something strange happening with the cameras."

"The cameras are working now, so let's get this wedding on the road," Jessica said, turning toward her son. "Go get your dad, Joey."

"No, wait," Jen said, realizing she couldn't put off telling her sister the truth any longer. Her mind reeled anew with the thought of Brad's defection—and Ted's taunt. "I'm afraid it's not as simple as picking Brad up."

"What then?" Jessica asked, glancing at her watch. "We've got to get things moving. Where is he?"

Jen took a deep breath and opened her mouth to speak. "Brad isn't coming, Jessica. My groom is leaving me standing at the altar."

"Standing at the . . . ?" Jessica's mouth dropped open. "You're kidding?"

Jen shook her head. "I wish I were. For the life of me, I can't imagine where this all went wrong. Maybe this whole wedding and promotion idea was a mistake. Maybe that is what turned Brad off."

"Are you kidding?" Jessica exclaimed. "Publicity turn Brad off? Think about it, Jen. Just when was the last time that handsome ham of yours resisted a camera?"

Jen nodded. It was true. Brad, tan and fit, loved the cameras. She'd seen him grin shamelessly into the lens on the golf course as he praised a charity tournament or he beamed in front of a fashionable new Plaza restaurant as he declared an endorsement. Or happier yet, he smiled at news crews in the lobby of his father's Johnson County–based international firm as he announced a corporate expansion.

No, publicity wasn't a problem for Brad. He loved the limelight and he treasured the trendy. What was the problem then? The answer shined in her brain like a neon sign: Apple Grove House was not trendy enough. It was not trendy at all. *Shoot,* Jen grumbled to herself. Why hadn't she seen this difficulty sooner?

"Don't let it get you down, sis," Jessica said, touching Jen's arm sympathetically. "You're hardly the first bride to be stood up at the altar."

"But how many of them have a video crew, three hundred wedding guests, an old-fashioned country band, and a clergyman waiting to see them walk down the aisle?" Jen rubbed her temple, hoping to discourage the headache that threatened.

"A good point," Jessica said, her dark eyes growing wide. It was a strange expression to see on her sister's face. Jessica was usually the practical one—the one who'd been like a mother to Jen since they'd lost their parents in a car wreck five years ago. "What do we say to all those people out there?"

"I don't have a clue, but I keep thinking there has to be a way to pull this off," Jen said, continuing to shake her head as the sickening feeling of helplessness grew in her stomach. She didn't have a single inspired—or uninspired—idea of what to do. Not one. But she wasn't about to let Brad—or Ted be victorious.

After a long silence, Jessica's face brightened. She

grinned as if the answer had been in front of them the entire time. "Maybe we could find a stand-in."

"A what?" Jen asked, thinking she had heard her sister incorrectly.

"Not a real groom," Jessica explained with a frown. "You know, some gallant soul who would look good—and save the day for us. You could call it a romantic publicity stunt later. All the gifts would have to be returned, of course. But at least the cameras, the food, the flowers, and the reverend wouldn't be wasted."

"But who would be a stand-in on such late notice?" Jen puzzled, though she was warming to the idea. "Who would look good in front of the camera and go along with the promo idea?"

"I don't know." Jessica shook her head. "Not on such short notice. All the modeling agencies are closed on Saturday."

"Any good-looking reenactors in uniform out there?" Jen suggested. She'd been sequestered in the parlor and hadn't seen them yet.

Jessica grimaced and shook her head. "Cute, but all short and bearded."

"Any more ideas, sis?" Jen said, realizing this seemingly simple solution wasn't as uncomplicated as it sounded. Bewildered, she and Jessica stared at each other.

At last Jessica shrugged.

"Have we lost to the enemy?" Jen sighed. Stymied once more, she sank down on the settee again. "Where is the cavalry to ride in and save the day when you need them?"

At the sight of the tall man called Ted, whom his mother and Aunt Jen didn't like, Joey had backed into the shadowy corner by the huge old secretary. His hand in his pocket,

Joey toyed with the small camera he'd sneaked off a guest table earlier. He'd stolen it after he'd asked his mom what the cameras were for. She'd explained that Aunt Jen wanted guests to take "candy" photos of each other.

"Candy pictures?" Joey had repeated, uncertain what that odd term meant, but liking the sound of it.

"Not candy, can*did* pictures," Mom had explained as she'd adjusted the tight cuffs of her dress. It was gold colored and trimmed with dark gold velvet; it stuck out funny in the back with something she called a bustle. "Unposed photos that people are not expecting someone to take. Surprise pictures."

"Surprise pictures?" Joey repeated. "You mean the kind where their mouths are hanging open or they look like they're sleeping when they're supposed to be paying attention."

"Something like that, Joey." Mom's mouth had twisted as if she was trying to keep from smiling. "Or some nice pose that the professional photographer doesn't catch."

Cool, Joey had thought and pocketed a camera when Mom wasn't looking. He'd always thought it would be neat to be a cameraman like the men Aunt Jen worked with sometimes. He could get some good surprise pictures— ones that would make Aunt Jen laugh.

Mom and Aunt Jen had pretty much forgotten that Joey was still in the room. The man called Ted had distracted them. When grown-ups overlooked Joey, things usually got really interesting. Ted didn't really say much or so it seemed to Joey. Soon the man left. Suddenly Joey's mom and Aunt Jen were staring at each other as if something really terrible had happened.

Aunt Jen looked really pretty in her gown of lace, shiny beads, and white satin and with her golden hair piled on top of her head and covered with white filmy stuff and silk apple blossoms, Joey thought. She looked kind of like an old-fashioned princess.

"What are we going to do?" Mom asked. "The ceremony should have started ten minutes ago."

Aunt Jen shook her head. "Give me a minute alone to think, will you? Let me figure about how to pull this off. Maybe we can get some footage for the promotion. I can't do anything about Brad, but I'm not ready to let Ted win this round over the cider mill and Apple Grove House."

"Okay. I'll give you a few minutes," Mom said. "I'll encourage the musicians to keep playing and I'll try to appease the reverend—and Kelly and her cameramen. Don't be long. Maybe we'll just have to pop open the bubbly apple wine and declare a party without a groom. No reason to be embarrassed. This kind of thing has happened before."

"That doesn't really make me feel any better," Aunt Jen said without looking at Joey's mom. She sounded as if she felt really bad. Joey longed to do something to cheer her up.

Mom passed him, walking out the door, her footsteps barely audible over the rustle of taffeta. She did not see him.

The room fell silent except for the ticking of the old clock. When Joey moved out of the corner to get a better look at Aunt Jen, he saw her staring at the brown flowers in the glass-dome thing on the fireplace. After a moment of stillness, she began to touch her hair as if to put it back into place—as if it had ever escaped. Her pearl earrings glistened in the light and some color had come back into her cheeks. She looked really pretty even if she was sad.

This would make a good *candid* photo, Joey thought, pulling the camera from his pocket. Not a fun one, but one the photographer would never catch—just like Mom said.

His movement caught Aunt Jen's attention and she turned toward him, a frown forming on her lips.

"Joey, I forgot you were here," she said, straightening up when she saw the camera in his hands. "What are you doing, Joey?"

Joey sighted her through the view finder. "This will be great, Aunt Jen. You look good."

"No, this really isn't a good time for a picture," Aunt Jen said, a hint of pleading in her voice. She stepped toward him, holding out her hands to stop him, the fragile white flower petals of her wedding bouquet trembling with her movement. "Joey, don't please."

Determined, Joey pressed the button before she could reach him.

The room exploded in a painful burst of radiance. Light too brilliant to have come from a camera blazed. The flash was so powerful, it sent Joey staggering backward. He covered his eyes with his arm and turned away. Then instantly the light vanished. Ceased.

Blinking, Joey lifted his head to look back at Aunt Jen. Was she going to be mad? he wondered.

He gazed in her direction, squinting, anxious for his eyes to readjust to the cool shadows of the room.

"Aunt Jen?" Joey called softly, but she wasn't at the mantel. "Wow, that was bright, huh, Aunt Jen?"

No answer. Balls of light bobbed across Joey's vision, still blinding him. He blinked again, waiting for his aunt in her white wedding gown to appear. But the room remained silent, empty.

"Aunt Jen?" Joey cried, louder this time. Was this some kind of trick, some mysterious custom having to do with weddings that he didn't know about?

He stumbled into the middle of the parlor and slowly turned around once more, looking for Aunt Jen. Maybe she was behind the settee or in the other corner, behind the bookcase. He scuttled around the room, searching everywhere.

There was no one in the parlor—except for him.

Joey stared down at the camera in his hand. It looked just as it had when he'd slipped it off the table. Just the way all those little cameras looked—normal. But Aunt Jen was gone. His stomach did a flip-flop. He knew the sick feeling had nothing to do with the yucky salmon he'd mistakenly snatched from the food table.

Impossible as it seemed, Aunt Jen was gone. What should he tell Mom?

Joey threw the weird yellow-and-black box with a glass lens down into the corner—where he'd been hiding earlier.

Nothing—he would tell Mom nothing, he decided with a shake of his head. She would kill him for making Aunt Jen disappear. Joey started toward the door. Nope, he wasn't telling her anything. She would start hollering for Aunt Jen. She would start asking him questions and want to see the camera.

Joey darted out of the parlor, escaping from his guilt—and his mom's questions. He just wouldn't think about it, he told himself as he dashed out of Apple Grove House and into the sunlight.

Chapter Two

It was a perfect day for a wedding, Captain Bennett Vance thought grudgingly as he glanced out the window at the blue sky overhead. Sunlight glinted off the Kansas River, which flowed at the bottom of the hill. The bright hope that dawned with a new day freshened the fall air. Only the black smoke pouring from the stacks of the steamboat already churning its way back toward Westport Landing marred the horizon.

Yes, a perfect day for beginning a new life with your beloved, Bennett mused, glad he wasn't a sentimental man. Thankful he wasn't one of the grooms standing with him in the hallway of Apple Grove House.

Besides the four brides and grooms gathered in the hallway for the wedding, the little congregation included

Bennett's commanding officer, Colonel Bailey; Judge Tyler who would preside over the ceremony; and photographer Zach Schuster and his apprentice—plus Anna Grove's ten children. Sergeant Dunham, Bennett's subordinate, stood to the side, waiting to do whatever needed to be done. Excitement and expectation filled the air.

"I'm almost ready to take the photograph, Captain," Zach Schuster said, ducking back under the camera's black cape to make some invisible adjustment, "unless you want to wait for the missing couple."

The written list Colonel Bailey had handed Bennett earlier specified four pairs of names and a pair of initials. Present were Private Dick Roberts and his bride, Mary; Corporal Clifford Thornton and Rebecca; Private Bill Moss and Sara; Private Virgil Boland and Amy. The fifth couple was designated by initials only—J and B.

"I'm not inclined to wait for them," Bennett said, impatient with this whole assignment of nursemaiding brides and grooms. *Fine duty for a West Point graduate,* he thought. *Fine duty for an army captain, a decorated hero of the Mexican War about to be mustered out of the army.*

He'd been assigned to take the men to meet their brides, who arrived on the stern wheeler at the ferry landing below. The reunion of sweethearts had been happy and chaotic. Afterward the grooms had escorted the ladies to the house, where they now fidgeted, arranging themselves and their billowing, crinoline-lined skirts so that no lady's ankles would be revealed in the picture. The men in their dress uniforms smoothed their waxed mustaches and grinned at each other like tomcats about to savor something sweeter than cream.

"Let's not waste any more time, Mr. Schuster," Bennett snapped, suddenly annoyed by more than the indignity of this trivial wartime assignment. The timing was lousy. Only a month ago Quantrill had burned Lawrence. Despite the reopening and rearming of Fort Scott, the Confederate irregulars had proven they could attack anywhere, anytime in free state territory. And a Kansas River ferry landing on a military road was a perfect target. The fact that there was a houseful of civilians here—Anna Grove and her ten children plus these new brides—would hardly matter to the likes of Quantrill and his ally, Cutthroat Clive Morrison. This was no time for cavalry officers to be playing Cupid. "Get on with it, Mr. Schuster. Commence photographing at will," Bennett ordered.

"Wait. Is there a problem, Captain Vance?" called the colonel, his words slightly slurred. He sat on a step midway up the graceful stairway winding toward the second floor. Next to him lounged his old friend, Judge Tyler. They both held blue enameled cups filled with Apple Grove House's finest cider.

Below them on the steps perched the gaggle of Grove children, silent and wide-eyed in the presence of uniformed men and full-skirted ladies.

"The colonel and the judge have been at the cider jug since breakfast," Sergeant Jack Dunham murmured in Bennett's ear.

"That's evident." Bennett drew in a long-suffering breath. He and the colonel had already had one tense exchange over this mission. Bailey was one of the most mulish, pigheaded commanding officers he'd had to deal with during his whole military career—with the possible exception of Major Miller. And then there was . . .

Bennett shook his head. So he wasn't good at getting along with commanding officers. But that didn't make this assignment any more sensible. He took a deep breath and forced himself to reply in an even voice. "One of the couples on your list is missing, sir."

"Well, who is it, Captain?" the colonel demanded. "Let's not keep these lovely brides waiting."

"No name is given, sir." Bennett turned to the four enlisted men and their ladies. "Any of you know who this fifth soldier on the list is with the initial J or B?" He was careful to keep his impatience from his face.

The four soldiers turned eager faces to Bennett. Each had shaved with care that morning, trimmed his hair, brushed his hat, polished his boots, and donned his dress uniform for the occasion. They were ready to get married.

"We're the only four we know about, sir, Captain Vance," the shortest one, Dick Roberts, volunteered with uncertainty. "Mary here says there wasn't any other bride on the riverboat from Westport Landing, sir. But with all due respect, sir, your Christian name begins with B."

Bennett scowled at Roberts. "Thank you for the observation, soldier. But I don't believe there's any connection."

Bennett examined the list again. It was carefully penned in Mrs. Bailey's hand. The dainty, resolute colonel's wife considered herself a matchmaker extraordinaire and frequently dabbled in the love lives of her husband's men.

Bennett had been spared only because he'd warned her off early. At his first officer's reception at Fort Leavenworth, he'd made it clear to the colonel's wife over the punch bowl that he was a bachelor, a divorced man, with no desire for a wife. For a moment, he'd glimpsed the gleam of challenge in the lady's eyes, but then she'd retreated, horrified. A divorced man did not rank among the most eligible of bachelors. Who knew what his transgressions might have been as a husband. His tarnished reputation had saved him, he figured. But it was unlike the colonel's lady to be vague, listing only initials where a bride's and groom's name should be.

"The end of the list just states, 'And a fifth bride and

groom, J and B,' Colonel, sir," Bennett called up to his commanding officer.

With a puzzled expression, the colonel set the jug in his lap and looked down at Bennett; then he turned to the judge. "Fifth couple? I can't imagine who that might have been."

The judge shrugged and reached for the cider jug.

"There was some fellow, I think," the colonel said, his brow puckered in inebriated thought. "Eager to do the deed, as I recall. Mrs. Bailey said something about him, but his name escapes me now. He should have ridden from the post with us and be right here. And the lady should have been on the riverboat."

"Not to contradict the colonel, sir," Dunham said softly, in that self-effacing, weaselly way that annoyed Bennett, "but those four men are the only bridegrooms we know about."

The rotund photographer popped out from beneath the black cape of his camera. "I'm ready, Captain. Just give the go-ahead when you and the happy couples are ready."

Bennett turned toward the colonel. "Do we wait, sir?"

"I wish Mrs. Bailey was here." The colonel raised his cider cup to his mouth and took a sip. "She would clear this up. But she just couldn't leave Mrs. Wentworth with her baby about to be delivered and all. Well then, let's get on with it."

"Take the picture, Mr. Schuster," Bennett ordered, secretly relieved that Mrs. Bailey wasn't there to fuss over the missing lovebirds. The sooner this ridiculous affair was over, the better.

"All right, ladies and gentlemen, after I remove the lens cap, don't move for the next twenty seconds," Schuster warned, then ducked under the black cloth again. The apprentice, Bob, held the magnesium wire wheel over a flash pan high above the camera. At a hand signal from Schuster, the boy struck a match and lit the wire. Schuster reached for the lens cap.

Collectively, the couples sucked in a breath and froze.

A weak light from the burning wire flashed, sizzled, hissed, then died.

"Sorry, this type of lighting is experimental." Schuster groped his way out from under the camera cloth. "A colleague from back east sent it to me to try. Bob, what did you do?"

Bewildered, the boy stared at the pan. "I put a fresh magnesium wire in it, Mr. Schuster. I swear I did, and I used the stuff from the new box."

"Don't swear, Bob," Schuster scolded with a weary sigh. "Just get that other box, and let's try it. Sorry, folks. We'll try again, Captain."

"Of course. Proceed, Mr. Schuster." Bennett stood quietly, never betraying his irritation.

Soon the flash mechanism was ready once more. Schuster was back under the black cloth and sighting the soon-to-be-wed couples. All assumed their best dignified poses once more and sucked in deep breaths.

Bob struck the match. This time the flash pan worked.

A mute explosion of light bleached all images into painful oblivion.

The women cried out in surprise and hid their faces against the men's shoulders. The grooms ducked and covered their ladies' heads. The children whimpered.

Bennett jerked his hat brim down to protect his eyes from the searing brightness. Dazzling lightning swallowed the world: a white void, no noise, no odor. Just giant bright nothingness.

Then it was gone, as quick and silent as a falling star.

Bennett squinted in the direction of the four couples against the wall. They huddled, stunned and blinded. On the stairs, the littlest Grove girl began to cry. One of the older girls picked her up and cuddled her.

Schuster jumped out from beneath the cloth. Bob had collapsed onto the ground, his hands thrown over his head. "I didn't do it," he sobbed noisily. "I didn't do it."

"What the hell was that?" shouted Judge Tyler, leaping to his feet as if he was about to seize the culprit. His cider cup clattered down the stairs.

"I don't know," cried Schuster. "It wasn't my flash pan. It was something more than that."

"Must have been heat lightning," the colonel said, slowly straightening from the crouched position he'd ducked into when the light had struck.

"Yep, that was it," agreed Corporal Dunham, his pale blue eyes wide in surprise. "Heat lightning."

Bennett glanced at the clear sky outside. He'd seen a lot of strange things since he'd headed west from Pennsylvania years ago, but utterly silent heat lightning bright enough to sear away a man's sight? On a September day? From a cloudless sky? Not likely.

"Is everyone all right?"

"I'm *not* all right," announced an unfamiliar female voice edged with exasperation.

Bennett stared at the parlor doorway behind the brides and grooms. The loveliest bride he'd ever seen stumbled into the hallway. She wore an unstylish white gown with a narrow lace underskirt and a satin overskirt pulled up into an awkward fullness trailing behind her. A sheer veil covered her rich blond hair and floated out over her shoulders. In her hands, she carried a bouquet of white flowers. Out of fashion as she seemed, Bennett noted immediately that she was older and much more sophisticated than the other four brides. But her age did not detract from her comeliness.

Where on earth had she come from? He charged across the hall to peer into the parlor. He could have sworn everybody in the house except Anna Grove was in the hallway.

"Joey, that silly flash camera has nearly blinded me," the newcomer complained, her hand over her eyes as she lurched into the hall. "Joey? Jessica? Where are you? I can't see a thing."

Bennett brushed past her and glanced into the parlor. She might be on Mrs. Bailey's list, but to his way of thinking, she was unidentified and therefore a stranger who had made a suspicious appearance. He didn't like the unexpected taking place on his watch.

But the parlor was empty, just as he'd thought. No sign of a groom. No explanation of the lady's sudden appearance.

The brides backed away from the stranger, their faces pale. But Corporal Clifford Thornton reached out to steady the newcomer.

"Thank you," she said. Balanced at last, the lovely apparition blinked at all of them as if they were strangers. They stared back as astonished as she appeared to be. Bennett couldn't recall seeing such an exquisite woman in his lifetime. He stood behind her, as speechless as everyone else.

Finally the lady pulled away from Corporal Thornton's grasp.

"Wow, you guys are in the spirit of things. What a great uniform," she said, her voice warm and full of wonder. "You reenactors are always so authentic. You're not like Jessica described you at all."

"Begging your pardon, miss, but we're not actors. We're the eighth cavalry," Corporal Thornton said with pride in his voice. "Formerly the third Dragoons out of Fort Leavenworth."

"Former dragoons. What a great back story. I don't believe we've met. I'm Jennifer Hollis." Then after a pause, she added unnecessarily, "I'm the bride."

"There you are, Captain Vance." Colonel Bailey lifted his cup to the sky as if making a toast to deliverance. "Mystery solved. Miss Hollis is our fifth bride."

"So it would seem, Colonel," Bennett said, feeling unreasonably annoyed that some no-name soldier had won himself such an exceptional female to be his wife.

"And would you happen to know where your groom is, Miss Hollis?" Bennett asked, striding back across the hallway so he could turn and get a better look at her.

"Brad?" The pleasant expression on her face vanished. "Uh, I don't think he's going to be along anytime soon." Then a polite smile of interest lighted her face as she regarded Bennett, appraising him from head to toe as if inspecting the troops. "I don't believe I've met you before either, Captain."

Suddenly overcome with a need to be formal, Bennett swept off his hat, clicked his heels, and bowed slightly. "Captain Bennett Vance, eighth cavalry."

"Out of Fort Leavenworth, of course," she repeated, that delightful tone of wonder returning to her voice. "The plume in your hat is a dashing touch, Bennett."

Her informality surprised but pleased him.

"Regulation, ma'am." Bennett briefly accepted her slender, warm hand, then released it. She was just as lovely up close. She wasn't a dainty, fashionable bow-mouth beauty; rather she possessed a classic broad brow, a delicate straight nose, lively dark brown eyes, and a natural rosy blush on her lips and apple cheeks. He added, "All the officers of the regiment wear plumes. Miss, what we need to know is, where is your groom?"

"He is not going to be here." Miss Hollis frowned, deeply this time. "I'm afraid Brad is on his way to California."

"Nonsense," cried the colonel, who was leaning over the banister above. "None of my men are on their way to California. He's just lost his way temporarily. We'll take care of the situation. Never fear." The colonel paused long enough to hiccup. "What are we going to do, Judge?"

"I have it." The judge swayed on the steps. "It's simple. We'll perform a proxy wedding—you know, like the royals do. All we need is a stand-in groom."

"Of course, a stand-in groom?" the colonel repeated. "Captain Vance, volunteer to be Miss Hollis's stand-in groom."

"Sir." Astonished, Bennett bit back an unwise, hasty reply. The colonel was in no condition to be reasoned with and Bennett was determined to get this wedding business over as quickly as possible.

"Excellent," the colonel exclaimed. "Now we can get on with the ceremony."

"By the time the ceremony is over, I should have the camera problem fixed, sir," Schuster called up to the colonel.

"Superb, Mr. Schuster." The colonel followed the judge, who was threading his way downward between the children on the stairs.

"Stand-in? Proxy?" Miss Hollis muttered. "Okay, but let's be sure the camera gets it all. We won't have a second chance to do this. Where are Kelly and the cam crew?"

"Mr. Schuster here is our photographer, Miss Hollis," Bennett said, ignoring her questions about Kelly. There was no Kelly under his command.

"A proxy wedding—what a perfect solution," the colonel was saying.

"When Miss Hollis's groom finally makes his appearance, he will thank you for getting the ceremony out of the way and making him a husband." The judge halted unsteadily two steps above the hallway floor, where everyone could still see him. "Gather round ladies and gentlemen. Let's get started."

"Wait, wait, something isn't right here . . . ." Miss Hollis protested, her smile gone and her brown eyes liquid dark with bewilderment.

"What isn't right?" Anna Grove hurried into the front hallway from the kitchen wiping her hands on her apron. "Where are the children? I just saw the brightest flash of lightning, but with no thunder. Is everyone okay?"

At the sight of the widowed owner of Apple Grove House, Jennifer Hollis gasped and the color drained from her face.

"Why, there you are, Mrs. Grove," the colonel called from the stairs. He held up his cider cup. "And may I say your cider is nearly as good as it always was before that thoughtless husband of yours died and took his cider-making secret with him."

"Thank you, Colonel," Anna Grove said, a smile of tolerance on her lips as she looked up at the drunken colonel. Then she took in the condition of her children sitting on the stairway.

"We're fine, Mama," the oldest girl said. "The flash scared Annie."

"The light was from the photographer's flash pan," Bennett explained, falling back on the simplest explanation for the odd event. "The children are fine. And our missing bride has arrived."

Anna Grove stepped up to Jennifer Hollis, who was staring at the woman as if she was seeing a ghost. "I'm Anna Grove. Welcome to Apple Grove House, my dear."

"You look just like the picture in the parlor," Miss Hollis stammered, leaning close to peer down into Anna Grove's kind face. "The resemblance is uncanny. Did Jessica arrange this? Brad would never think of such a thing."

"Jessica who, my dear?" Mrs. Grove asked, patting Miss Hollis's hand. "Mrs. Bailey made the arrangements and I'm just happy to help the colonel and his wife bring all you sweethearts together. Nothing like a wedding to warm an old matron's heart."

"All of us?" Miss Hollis said, her brow furrowing as she glanced at Bennett. She appeared more confused than ever. "I don't understand. I didn't plan a group wedding. Where are Kelly and the video crew? The old camera is a quaint prop but—"

"It's a group wedding, Miss Hollis," Bennett tried to explain. The last thing he needed was for a bride to start an argument with the colonel. "Colonel Bailey and his wife planned it for the benefit of the men going to Texas."

"And I'm a witness." Mrs. Grove took off her apron and tossed it onto the hall bench.

Miss Hollis stared at them, her lips parted and her complexion growing paler by the minute. Bennett began to fear she was going to faint.

"You don't have to play your parts so well," she pleaded, her gazing darting from Anna to Bennett and to the other brides and their grooms.

"All right, ladies and gentlemen, come closer," the judge called, ignoring the newcomer's reluctance and opening up a book he'd taken from his frock coat pocket. "Let's get on with it. Mrs. Tyler hates it when I bring a guest home for supper and we're late. Miss Hollis, trust me. Your groom will thank us all later."

Bennett reached for Miss Hollis's arm. She pulled away and stared back at him, her eyes wide and dark with confusion. She shook her head. "No, something is not right here."

Her hesitance wounded him, though he didn't know why.

"Is the prospect of me being your stand-in groom as horrible as that?" he asked in a harsh whisper. "If it helps, I'm not any crazier about this idea than you are. But the judge is right. This way you and what's-his-name will be man and wife when he finally arrives."

"You don't understand." She shook her head again and frowned. "He's not going to arrive."

Bennett studied her, the dismay in her soft brown eyes almost convincing him that she was telling the truth. But he found it impossible to believe that even a fool would stand this woman up at the altar.

"Now don't fret, Miss Hollis, and don't argue with those who know what's good for you," shouted the colonel from above. "Everything is going to turn out just fine. Be quiet and respond when the judge tells you."

Miss Hollis opened her mouth to protest. Bennett put his finger to his lips to shush her. "Just go along with it. The judge and the colonel are drunker than skunks swimming in a cider barrel. Let them believe what they want to believe. And let the brides have their wedding ceremony in peace."

Miss Hollis opened her mouth as if she was about to protest. But after a glance in the direction of the eager brides—their arms linked with their grooms, their eyes fixed on the judge—she seemed to change her mind. "Okay."

"Join hands," the judge intoned.

Bennett reached for her again, noting the perfect fresh-

ness of the white roses and apple blossoms of her wedding
posy. This time she allowed him to take her hand. Her
fingers were icy cold and her lips pale and stiff.

"Dearly beloved, we are gathered here to join these
couples in matrimony." The judge rattled on, his voice
rising in a fine tenor tone as he waxed drunkenly romantic.
"This commitment is not to be entered lightly, but with
certainty, mutual respect, a sense of reverence and commitment to everlasting eternity."

When Bennett glanced at Miss Hollis, she'd turned
whiter—if that was possible—as snowy pale as the first
flakes of winter. He wondered if she'd faint before the
end.

When their turn came to affirm their vows, she softly
mumbled, "I do," along with Bennett to his relief. And
when he went through the motions of slipping a ring on
her finger, she submitted to the charade.

Above them, the colonel beamed approval. Before the
judge could utter the final words, the colonel flung his
arms into the air and shouted as if he was starting a horse
race, "Kiss your brides!"

Chapter Three

Jen had never felt so discombobulated in all her life.

Moments ago Brad had informed her he was a no-show at their wedding and here she was exchanging vows—and a kiss—with a tall man wearing a cavalry uniform whom she'd never seen before. The wedding kiss had been a light one, chaste, obligatory. Nevertheless, her lips burned where the captain's mouth had brushed against hers, and her body tingled. Waves of warmth coursed over her as if she was a schoolgirl who'd just received her first genuine lip lock—and it'd been a tongue-parrying doozie.

Weak and disoriented, Jen leaned against her groom, clutching the arm he'd offered her and trying to get a grip on herself. It wasn't a real kiss they'd exchanged or real vows they'd repeated to each other, she reminded herself. They'd done it to satisfy the drunken, white-haired colonel on the stairs. The captain knew that. But she couldn't resist stealing a glance up at him. He was smiling benignly at his men, obviously pleased with their happiness. The expression softened his strong masculine features.

Involuntarily, Jen licked her lips, searching for the taste of the captain on her mouth. She found nothing. He'd left none of his essence on her lips, yet the warm butterflies he'd stirred in her belly persisted. She clung to him momentarily disappointed and bewildered. Who was this man? Who were these people and what were they doing here?

She was still in Apple Grove House, but she felt as though she'd been transported by the flash from Joey's camera to another place. Everything about the house seemed familiar. Yet she knew it wasn't the same place she had stood in only moments ago. And where were all her other guests? What about Joey? Jessica? Kelly and her camera crew, who were nowhere to be seen?

"Now for your wedding feast," Anna Grove said, gesturing toward the dining room. "Eat, drink, and be merry."

Along with the others, Jen followed the woman playing Anna into the dining room, where the table was laid with cake and fresh berries, apple sauce, fried apples, ham and warm corn bread, melons, green peas, and apple pie.

Over the table hung a coal-oil lamp.

Jen halted. Her heart stopped beating. She knew from her thorough research on Apple Grove House that it had not been wired for electricity until the mid-1950s. All she was seeing was impossible. Impossible!

She hurried to the dining room window and looked out across the orchard. There stood the trees, branches bowed under the weight of rosy red apples. But no wedding reception guest tables sat beneath the limbs, no caterer's truck nor guests were to be seen, and no music from a band was to be heard.

"Don't worry about your bridegroom," Captain Vance

said, startling her out of her thoughts. He took her arm and led her to the table. "Enjoy yourself."

"I don't think I can," Jen said, an absurd suspicion beginning to take serious shape in her head. The idea was frightening and wondrous. Her head was spinning with the thought of it. There was one way to test the crazy theory. She pulled free of the captain and started back out of the dining room, where everyone was sitting. "Excuse me."

"Where are you going?" Captain Vance demanded, following her out of the room.

"I'm going upstairs," Jen said. "I need a breath of fresh air on the walk above the porch."

Heedless of her train and veil, she dashed up the steps and across the hall to the walk above the porch.

The door stood open, allowing the fall breeze to sweep into the upstairs and throughout the rooms of the house. Jen dashed out the door and across the walk. She leaned out over the balustrade, straining to see the Kansas City skyline towering over on the southeastern horizon. She knew exactly where it would be, jagged and shiny against the sky. She squinted at the skyline.

Nothing.

Involuntarily Jen sucked in a sharp breath. That couldn't be. It had to be there. She just wasn't looking at it right. She peered at the vista once more, leaning out farther over the balustrade and narrowing her eyes to better their focus.

Still, nothing. Not a single skyscraper, no telephone poles, no drone of airplanes circling the downtown airport. Only a seamless line of green trees and hillsides burnished with a hint of September gold stretched out before her.

Her breath came in shallow gasps. She clutched at the railing and searched for other familiar sights. Below, along the river, no railroad. She whirled around and peered up the river toward the Highway 7 bridge. The river meandered peacefully westward without interruption. No bridge. No power lines. No sand dredger. It was impossible, her head told her. Yet all the sights and sounds she knew of the modern world had vanished.

Jen felt as if her stomach had just plunged through the floor.

"Who are you looking for?" asked the captain from the doorway behind her.

When she turned to look at him, she saw a frown of suspicion cross his face. "Not who—it's what am I looking for."

Jen returned her gaze to the spot on the horizon where the skyscrapers and communications towers of Kansas City should stand. Where Brad had gone was suddenly the least of her worries. She studied the skyline and saw nothing but an uninterrupted horizon. Nothing. Nothing. Nothing!

How could that be? She turned to stare at the man who stepped out on the balcony with her. What if he wasn't a good reenactor? What if . . . She saw her proxy groom with new eyes this time.

Earlier he had removed his hat and handed it to Anna Grove when the wedding ceremony had begun. Jen noticed for the first time the telltale tan line across his forehead where his hat protected him from the sun's rays. At the corners of his eyes, she spied white creases she'd not seen before, pale skin untanned from hours of squinting at the road ahead. Fear and disbelief churned in her stomach. Nobody got that kind of tan from a tanning bed.

His brown hair lay neatly combed, furrowed by comb teeth and water, not mousse, and the length of it rested a bit ragged around his ears and along his neck—a barber's cut, not a stylist's careful trimming.

Her gaze went to his shoulders, wide and square. No pads filled his uniform where gold badges declared his captain's rank. Shiny brass buttons marched down the front of his coat emphasizing a broad chest, flat belly and his hips . . . his torso and his thighs.

Jen swallowed the tightness in her throat. From a snug black belt at his lean waist hung a shiny dress saber. The dark blue frock coat covered his narrow hips, but failed to disguise his long legs in sky blue trousers and black boots. As she stared at his legs, she knew he hadn't developed those steely looking thighs and calves from working out on a stair machine at a fitness club. The captain was a horseman.

Realizing that her eyes had strayed rudely, Jen glanced up at the captain's face. He stared back at her, curiosity softening his features.

"Is it possible?" she whispered in awe. "You're the real thing."

A rueful smile tugged at his lips. "I'm a real what?"

"You're really a cavalry captain," Jen said, unable to believe the very words she spoke.

"What reason have you to doubt that?"

"None," Jen admitted. Her mouth had gone dry. From shock, fear, or attraction, she wasn't quite certain. He was an incredibly attractive man—in a classic James Dean way—a glint of rebellion in his dark hazel eyes and a twist of sullenness in the curve of his lips. The insolent type had never appealed to her, but this man . . . he was different.

"Lord," she whispered. "I was just kidding when I asked for the cavalry to ride in."

"What?" he asked, leaning closer as if he had not heard her.

"Nothing." Jen drew in a sharp breath. What on earth had happened to her? She turned her back to him, her mind racing to review events. She had been standing in the parlor. Joey had pulled out a camera and aimed it at her. There had been all that light. A blinding flash. Then she'd found herself stumbling out the parlor door and into a crowd of men and women in costume. Or from another time?

She whirled toward the captain once more. "What is the date?"

"September 20, 1863," he said, without hesitation.

"1863," she repeated slowly. "Lincoln is president. The Civil War is being fought and the dome of the Capitol is only half complete."

"You must read a newspaper now and again," the captain said.

Jen ignored the sarcasm in his voice. "And Moses Grove is dead already."

The captain shot her a look of surprise. "Did you know old Moses?"

Overcome by the impact of reality, Jen sagged against the balcony railing. She'd been teasingly told that she knew more about Apple Grove House than the site's professional historian. Moses's photo, a reproduction of the only one known to exist, hung in the parlor beside that of Anna Grove for as long as she could remember. She was almost as familiar with Moses's and Anna's faces as those of her own grandparents.

But there had been no photos of the Grove couple in the parlor she'd stumbled out of today. Anna and Moses wouldn't hang there for the benefit of tourists until much later than 1863. "I guess you could say I know him by reputation."

"I see," the captain said, the tone of his voice assuring her he was satisfied with her answer this time. "He'd been here for a lot of years—first as a ferryman, then as postmaster and Indian agent. Probably the most notable aspect of his reputation was as the best cider maker this side of the Mississippi River."

"Yes, I know. And his secret died with him." Jen studied the captain. Her breathing had become normal at last, but a flutter of excitement beat inside her. In all her reading about Apple Grove House, she never remembered reading about Captain Bennett Vance. Who was this man? Why was he here? Why was she here? And how was she going to get back?

"The camera," she blurted, her mind once more racing over the events that led up to her arrival in 1863. "It all started with that damned camera."

Her profanity made him blink.

"Sorry. Bear with me," Jen said, a glimmer of sympathy for him stirring. After all he'd never met a woman from another time either. She touched his hand and started back into the house. She didn't see any point in trying to explain to him what she didn't understand herself. Excited that she'd discovered a possible escape route from this nightmare she called over her shoulder, "Let's go get our picture taken again. The photographer must have gotten his camera fixed by now."

Downstairs in the hallway, they found that Zach Schuster and his apprentice had finished their cake and cider and were once again working on the camera.

"Sure we will try again," the photographer said when Jen insisted on posing for a photo. "I know everybody is disappointed. Brides always like to have a remembrance of their wedding day."

"I mean, I want a photo of me in this special dress," Jen explained. "That's all."

"Perfectly understandable," Mr. Schuster said, shoving a fresh plate into the wooden box and ducking under the black camera cloth again. "I'm just sorry that this new lighting source is so unreliable. Now stand right there. That's it."

Jen stood against the hallway wall, her bouquet clutched in her hand feeling as if she was standing before a firing squad rather than posing for a camera. The other brides gathered around to watch. By the stairs, the captain stood clearly unmoved by her determination to be photographed. Who knew what would happen this time? Who knew if this would work, but she had to try to get back to her century.

"Ready, Bob?" Schuster asked from beneath the black cloth.

"Yes, Mr. Schuster," the apprentice replied.

"Now," Schuster ordered.

The apprentice struck the match and put it to the wire lying in the flash pan. A small white flame flashed, then fizzled. The disappointed brides and grooms groaned. The captain remained stoic.

Jen tried to swallow the lump of apprehension in her throat and silently prayed for the camera to work next time. *What if it doesn't?* Jen whispered in the back of her mind. *What then?* She cleared her mind of the thought and forced a smile to her lips. She didn't even want to go where that doubt resided.

Again the apprentice struck another match and put it to a second piece of wire that he had ready, but as before nothing happened.

Jen's shoulders sagged. "Once more, please," she pleaded.

"Sure," Schuster said. Twice more he and his apprentice cut a fresh piece of wire, and they all went through the same motions: Schuster's head under the cloth; Bob striking the match.

Each time Jen prayed that the blinding flash would whisk her out of this surreal nightmare and back to her real wedding. Each time the wire fizzled or refused to light at all.

At last, Schuster fumbled his way out from beneath the camera's black cloth shaking his head. "I'm so sorry, Mrs. Vance."

The realization that the photographer was addressing her by her new name took a moment to register with Jen. Then she jumped and glanced in the captain's direction. He shrugged as if it was of no concern of his.

"I'm sorry, ladies and gentlemen," the photographer continued. "This method has worked for me before, but today—well, the material must have drawn some moisture. So sorry."

Jen released a long sigh of disappointment.

The colonel emerged from the dining room. "What are all the long faces about? Ladies, your husbands leave for Texas tomorrow morning. Are you sure you want to waste your time in front of a camera that won't work? I believe Mrs. Grove has arranged for dancing outside. Let's get this party rolling."

The new brides and their grooms all started talking at once, their dismay vanishing with the prospect of more fun to be had. Laughing in agreement with the colonel, they followed him hand in hand out of the back door of the house toward the orchard. The sound of lively fiddle music drifted into the house.

Jen sank down on a step and leaned her head against the banister in despair. The flash of the camera was the only way she could think of back to her real wedding. If she couldn't get back to the present through the camera, then what?

She vaguely heard the clank of a saber and the soft creak

of leather as the captain crouched down on the floor beside her.

"Well, Miss Hollis," he began, "or do I call you Mrs. Vance?"

"Don't call me that," Jen snapped. "Just call me Jen. Everybody does."

"Jen? For Jennifer?" He shook his head. "No, I like Jennifer fine. So, Jennifer, the day has hardly turned out like I expected it. And I know you're disappointed about your groom not being here and about not getting your picture taken, but that is no reason to waste the festivities the day has to offer. There's still cake on the table and there's dancing music outside. Why not enjoy what is at hand?"

Jen looked down at him. His invitation wasn't an especially seductive one, but it had a certain practical merit. He offered her a placating smile, certainly more than he owed her. His effort lightened her mood. What red-blooded woman could resist a reasonable offer and a pleasant smile from a cavalry officer as dashing as this one?

"What happens after the dance?" Jen asked, smiling back at him despite her gloom and confusion. "Are you going to Texas, too?"

"No. I'm staying here to guard the ferry crossing and to chaperon you new brides until you leave on the paddle wheeler when it comes again Friday for your return trip home."

Jen wondered if there was a way home for her.

He held out a hand to her. "And I'll probably give Anna a hand with the cider making. Until then, we might as well enjoy ourselves."

Laughter reached her from the celebration going on outside. Light and musical, the sound was a balm to the dark confusion that swirled inside and left her feeling so totally at a loss. The delight of the revelers was impossible to ignore.

"Come on," he tempted, stretching a strong callused hand toward her.

"Sure, why not?" Jen said with a shrug. There seemed little that she could do about getting home to save Apple Grove House at the moment. Accepting his hand, she rose from her place on the steps, followed him out of the house, and surrendered herself to dancing among the newlyweds in the shade of the apple orchard.

Chapter Four

That evening the newlyweds' tents glowed briefly with the light of the coal-oil lamps, then went dark. Muffled laughter and low murmurs barely audible over the crickets' song drifted to Bennett's ears. He briefly considered sleeping in the unused tent set up for the fifth couple, then decided against it. He was unlikely to get much sleep lying near all that marital bliss while thoughts of his mysterious bride, Jennifer Hollis, ran through his mind.

A bedroll spread out on Anna Grove's porch would do him fine. The weather hadn't turned too cold for sleeping outside yet. And there was no point in getting too comfortable. He had more work to do tonight.

The afternoon spent in Jennifer's company had left him more attracted to and mystified by her than he'd been the moment she'd stumbled out of the parlor. At first she'd danced with him as if she'd never done a reel before in her life. But she soon seemed to get the hang of it.

And when Corporal Thornton's bride had asked her about her gown. She'd explained that it was the latest fashion from Paris—a Worth gown, whatever that was. She'd gone on to say, to all the ladies' amazement, that crinolines would soon go out of fashion and narrow skirts with a bustle to fill out the back of the dress such as she was wearing would become the rage.

When asked where she'd learned all this, she'd stammered that she'd read it in the newspaper.

Bennett had allowed her to go on until she began to speak about women wearing breeches or something called pantaloons. Apparently intrigued, the young ladies moved closer around Jennifer to hear more, but their bridegrooms began to frown. Bennett quickly dragged her off for another dance.

Then there had been the episode about the outhouse. She had returned from the privy looking flustered and quite pale.

He was about to ask if she'd seen a snake when she said, "It's ridiculous to have to go to a place like that with all this clothing to manage. How do women put up with this? And what do *you people* do for TP?"

She paused to wave her hands in the air. "Never mind. I don't think I want to know. And as if that isn't enough— nobody told me there would be spiders. There was a big ugly one in a web up in the corner." With a shiver, she went silent.

Bennett decided to refrain from mentioning the occasional snake along the path. Where had this woman lived all her life? he wondered.

Satisfied that the night watch was in its place and the brides and grooms were settled for the evening, Bennett strode back to Apple Grove House through the darkness. The moon would not rise for a few hours yet. He found

Anna Grove and Jennifer sitting on the back porch in the dark. As he neared, he heard Anna talking about the house.

"There's a little room upstairs at the back where you can sleep," she was saying. "I know it must be a letdown that your groom was delayed. Tomorrow he'll probably come riding up with an adventure to tell that will explain everything."

"I don't think so." Jennifer sat on a stool with her elbows resting on her knees. She cradled her chin in the palm of one hand and sipped from a cider cup in her other. Before her on the floor lay her discarded white satin shoes toppled on their sides. Her feet were tucked out of sight underneath the stool. At her side on the floorboards lay her wedding bouquet.

She'd been sipping cider all afternoon. That sad little-lost-girl look had come to her face as soon as the music had ceased and the party broken up, Bennett noted.

"No, my groom is not coming, but thank you for your kind thoughts, Mrs. Grove," she added.

"Call me Anna," the daughter of a Delaware Indian princess and a white missionary said. Even in the darkness, Bennett could see the Bible lying open on the widow's lap. "Everyone knows me as Anna, don't they, Captain?"

"That's right," Bennett said, stepping up on the porch and offering the woman a smile. He'd met Anna years ago, not long after he'd first arrived at Fort Leavenworth, and he'd taken a liking to her immediately. They had cider making in common.

"Everything settled for the night?" she asked as she gestured toward an empty chair for him.

"Yes, appears to be quiet," Bennett said, dropping into the chair.

"I honestly don't think all these military precautions are necessary," Anna said.

"After that bloody raid on Lawrence in August, I don't think we can be too careful," Bennett said. He'd known two of the recruits who had died when the Confederate guerillas rode into the free-state town at dawn, murdering city leaders and Union recruits as they charged up one street and down another. "This river crossing and the military road are a vital link right now. Quantrill and his rabble would love to break through the flow of communications and supplies."

"Surely he won't try anything like that now," Anna said, folding her hands over her Bible. "He knows everyone is prepared for an attack."

"We thought we were prepared before the Lawrence attack," Bennett reminded her, the shame of the Union camp being caught unprepared still stinging his pride even though he hadn't been in charge. Rumors of the raiders' intentions had been circulating all summer, yet the town had been caught off guard. Bennett wasn't going to allow Apple Grove House to be so vulnerable.

"Quantrill's raid on Lawrence?" Jennifer's head came up and she turned toward them as if she'd heard their conversation for the first time. "You're talking about Quantrill's raid on Lawrence," she repeated, awe in her voice. In the darkness, Bennett could see the whites of her eyes had grown wide with the mention of the raider's name. "It happened just a month ago?"

"You've heard about it, haven't you?" asked Bennett, astonished by her reaction. The bold raid had been in newspaper headlines across the nation. Where had she been?

She nodded. "Yes, of course, I heard about the raid. It's quite a historic event."

Bennett sensed that she wanted to say more, but decided to hold back. He doubted he would learn much from her with direct questions. Earlier, as they danced, he'd asked where she'd come from, but she'd refused to meet his gaze and replied Johnson County. That wasn't very far away, considering the other brides had traveled from as far as St. Louis.

When he asked her where she'd met her fiancé, she'd thought for a moment before she replied in Westport. At the beginning of the war, the Missouri River town had been a rowdy jumping off point for wagon trains. He had difficulty imagining her with her fine clothes seeking and finding a husband in such a roughneck place.

As she danced in his arms, she was soft and pliant to his touch. Her lively dark eyes and broad smile made him want to stare at her and drink in her vitality. Her answers to his questions had been less than satisfactory. Yet, he told himself, if she were an informant or a spy, surely she would have concocted a more logical cover story.

"The raid was well organized and well executed," Bennett continued. "A feat some of our commanding officers didn't believe the guerrillas were capable of."

"Overconfidence is a terrible mistake," Jennifer agreed as if she had personal knowledge of such a fatal blunder. "Life is full of so many surprises."

Bennett and Anna exchanged glances. Anna seemed to be as mystified by the girl as he was.

Anna shrugged and changed the topic of conversation. "And such a shame about the photographs today. Mr. Schuster has had problems here before and there was another photographer who came once to make a photograph of a Delaware powwow and of our church congregation.

"The young people all lined up to get their picture taken out on the front porch. It was quite an event. The young men wore ties, and they borrowed coats from anyone they knew who had one. The girls put on their crinolines and piled their braids on the top of their heads. The camera never captured an image of any of them."

"It wasn't a problem with the light?" Bennett asked.

"No. He took the photograph right out on the steps in the sunlight," Anna said. "But when he developed the plates, there was no image. The photographer swore he'd done everything right and that he'd mixed his chemicals properly."

"Odd," Bennett said.

"Did anyone disappear?" Jennifer asked.

"No, nothing like that." Anna shook her head. "But you know what the old ones say about having a photograph made."

"What do the old ones say?" Jennifer demanded. Bennett realized they finally had won her full attention.

"That to have your picture made allows the camera to steal your soul," Anna said.

Bennett listened in silence. He'd heard of the old Indian superstition before.

"Steal your soul?" Jennifer suddenly sat up straight as if that piece of information answered something for her. "So the ancient ones knew that cameras are more than just boxes with lenses. Do you think they knew that cameras can do even more than monkey with your soul?" She stopped as if she thought she'd said too much.

"Do what with your soul?" Bennett asked, startled by the harsh slang out of the mouth of such a ladylike girl.

"You know, what if a camera could tamper with . . ." Jennifer stammered, a hopeful expression coming to her face as if she was about to discover something important. "Tamper with time."

"How?" Bennett asked. This conversation was giving him the willies.

She paused. "What if a camera could drag a person from one time to another?" she finally said as if she'd just put the entire thought together for herself. "What if that is what the old Indians were afraid of?"

"Sometimes the old ones are right about things," Anna agreed more readily than Bennett liked to hear. "They share old, ancient memories. Perhaps they did understand something about cameras that the rest of us have overlooked."

"You bet they did." Jennifer drained her cider cup and set it down on the porch. Then she picked up her bouquet. "I'm beat. And these flowers are almost as wilted as I feel."

"Such a lovely bouquet." Anna reached over to take it from Jennifer. "Let me dry it for you so you may have it as a keepsake."

"Would you?" Jennifer asked. "That would be nice. The florist and I went to a lot of trouble to get this made."

"I know just what it needs." Anna took the bouquet. "Now you go on up to bed. You know where the room is. Get a good night's rest. You'll feel better in the morning."

"Yes, you're right," Jennifer said, getting up from her stool. "I hope everything looks different in the morning." She disappeared into the house, the soft rustle of her satin and lace gown whispering with her every move.

When Jennifer was gone, Anna stared down at the bouquet.

"What was she trying to tell us?" Bennett asked, unable to shake a chilly uneasiness settling over him. "Tampering with time? It's like she is trying to say that she's not just from another place, but from another time, too."

"I don't know about that." Anna shook her head. "But look at this bouquet. It is full of white roses. Do you think there's a greenhouse somewhere in Westport Landing that grows white roses? Or maybe they were shipped by train from St. Louis. That's possible, especially these days. But look at this." Anna pointed at the smaller more delicate flowers in the posy.

Bennett leaned closer to get a good look. Even in the growing darkness he recognized the flowers with a start. Was it possible? He'd seen those blooms on the trees every spring since he could remember. "Apple blossoms."

"In September?" Anna asked. "Now where does anybody west of the Mississippi get apple blossoms in September?"

The next morning Colonel Bailey returned from his overnight stay at the judge's home up the river. His face was haggard and his eyes bloodshot, but promptly an hour after dawn, he rode out at the head of the southbound column of cavalry. The four bridegrooms rode with him leaving tearful brides behind—and a detachment of envious soldiers who wanted to be riding to the Texas front, too.

Bennett wasn't exactly bright eyed and bushy tailed himself. After the light had gone out in Anna Grove's room the night before, he'd lain in the dark on the porch until a saucer-size yellow moon had risen and he heard the grandfather clock in the hallway chime midnight.

Then he'd roused Sergeant Dunham and two men and gone to work. Digging by moonlight, they had buried the stash of rifles and ammunition that had arrived on the ferry that day. The munitions soon were hidden in a deep hole behind the cider mill. Only the four of them knew where the guns were. Bennett would have liked to limit the knowledge more than that, but they needed the manpower to get the job done before dawn. If Quantrill came looking for the guns, he'd have a difficult time finding them buried deep underground—and under the apple harvest.

So that morning, as the last of the colonel's contingent disappeared beyond the river, Bennett set about double-checking his orders and plans for the safeguarding of the ferry crossing and Apple Grove House.

By midmorning, when he started back to the house, he saw that Anna had set the brides and her children to picking apples. He stopped to watch them. The girls were subdued, no doubt because they'd just said farewell to their husbands. Two of them yawned frequently as they worked.

But when he spied Jennifer, she was standing on a ladder high up in a tree as she picked apples. She and little Annie, her helper, were laughing. The laughter lit Jennifer's face; the gloom of the night had vanished. She was wearing a baggy blue calico gown at least four inches too short for her—probably borrowed from Anna Grove. Her blond hair was pulled back and tied at her nape with a blue ribbon.

Each time she stretched up to capture another piece of fruit, calico hugged her small firm breasts and clung to her tiny waist. Her skirt hiked up enough to reveal trim ankles in white stockings and dainty feet in white satin bridal pumps. No high-top boots for Miss Jennifer Hollis. She worked, plucking apple after apple from the heavy boughs as if she'd harvested before. Bennett wondered at the contradictions of the girl.

Inside the cider mill, he found Anna herself setting things to order.

"Are you ready to start the cider making, Captain?" Anna asked, putting the last of the press screens into a stack ready to be spread with apple mash when the time came.

"My sentries report the apple wagons are on their way," Bennett said, hanging his hat on a peg and rolling up the sleeves of his blue uniform shirt.

"Yes, several farmers told me they would be bringing in harvest today," Anna said. She worked on in silence for several more minutes. "We'll be getting some pumpkins, too."

Then she added, "Are we going to make cider as good as Moses's this year? We sure could stand to get ten dollars a barrel for it like we did when Moses was making it."

"We'll keep working toward that," Bennett said, reluctant to make promises. Cider making had been one of his favorite activities when he was a boy, and he'd helped his family in Pennsylvania with the fall production every year until he'd gone off to West Point. Then he'd discovered the older widow and her children laboring in their cider mill shortly after he'd arrived at Fort Leavenworth. Moses was long in his grave by then. Bennett had offered his help and Anna had gladly accepted it. Over several years they'd improved the cider recipe, until it was once again in demand in the towns along the Missouri River.

"We're already getting a premium price again, thanks to you, Bennett," Anna said. "But it's not quite like Moses's cider."

"I know," Bennett said with an amused shake of his head. "Who knows what secret that Vermont husband of yours had discovered?"

That Moses had kept his recipe for the best cider west of the Mississippi secret from his wife did not surprise Bennett. He'd known Yankee cider makers who guarded their cider recipes with their lives, not even parting with their secret on their deathbeds. "Did you get the barrels from the Weston bourbon distillery like I suggested?" he asked as an after thought.

"Sure did," Anna said. "Stacked in the corner over there. Cleaned with soda ash and lye and ready to fill with good apple cider. We're going to make the best cider ever this year."

"That's my plan," Bennett said, his concentration already shifting from the war raging beyond Apple Grove House to the cider making chores at hand.

Now that the guns and ammunition were safely buried, his only serious concern was Jennifer Hollis. Who was she? And why was she at Apple Grove House? A mere distraction? A time traveler? A spy?

Bennett frowned to himself. He had no answers to those questions, but he wasn't about to let her keep him from his purpose. He reached for the grease can to take care of the squeaky screw on the cider press. "Yep, Anna. We're going to make the best cider ever."

Chapter Five

"Aren't we about to start grinding the apples in the mill?" Jennifer asked, setting down the basketful of fruit she'd just carried inside the door of the mill. Her eyes were hardly accustomed to the cool darkness, but she thought she could see the forms of the captain and Anna standing near a wooden piece of equipment that looked like a huge old-fashioned cider press.

Jen shook apple leaves from her long, voluminous skirts, which she hated. She missed the denim jeans, sweatshirt, and sneakers that she usually wore for outdoor work. But she'd arrived in her wedding gown and she had no choice but to wear borrowed skirts.

She'd decided that morning that Anna had been right. Things looked better in the sunshine. She'd just told herself as she'd dressed in Anna's borrowed clothes that she should consider her stay at Apple Grove House as an adventure, for now. She'd get home somehow. But for the time being, she'd learn what she could.

"Are those apples washed?" Anna asked.

"Yes, the girls are washing everything we picked," Jen said.

"Then put those apples over there," Anna directed, pointing toward another part of the mill where baskets of apples were stacked. "Those are pippins and we want to keep all the same kinds of apples together."

"Of course," Jennifer said, slightly embarrassed by her ignorance. Her knowledge of cider making consisted only of what she'd learned from twentieth-century apple fests each fall. She set the apples where Anna had told her.

Then she looked up at the interior of the mill again. The structure was larger and loftier than the modern reconstructed mill she knew at Apple Grove House. A lot larger.

Autumn sunlight streamed between the rough board walls and striped the wooden floor with shadow and light. The scent of fresh-picked apples filled the air. A pyramid of wooden barrels towered in one corner and a maze of wooden flumes crisscrossed where Jen was accustomed to seeing stainless-steel pipes in the modern-day mill.

The captain was working on the press. He nodded a curt greeting toward Jen and returned to his work. Today, he looked different. Without his dress uniform and his saber, he looked less formal, less glamorous, but more practical. He'd taken off his hat and rolled his sleeves up to his elbows as if he was prepared to work and work hard. The muscles and veins in his forearms stood out as he labored over the press. There was no mistaking the solidness of his muscular shoulders and the fine length of his legs. And his face? He was completely absorbed in what he was doing. He was devoted to the task at hand and he would obviously expect anyone around him to be just as devoted and focused.

"Will we be starting to mill soon?" Jen ventured.

"Oh, no, not yet," Anna said. "We haven't selected the apples for one thing, and we never start the milling until after dark."

"After dark?" Jennifer repeated, startled by such strange scheduling. "Why after dark?"

"It will be cooler," the captain said, looking up from the press. "Fewer problems with bees. They love this stuff. And when you let the mash stand overnight, it gets a better color, deeper, more amberlike."

"Cooler and color, right," Jen said, realizing that they hardly had the benefit of refrigeration yet—a fact she'd faced over breakfast, too. The milk she'd drunk—with her fresh-baked bread smeared with spicy apple butter—had been full of fat, fresh and warm, straight from the cow. A first for her. She'd had to wipe away a real creamy mustache like those people in the magazine ads. She wasn't certain that she liked milk that way.

"Moses always said the mash is best if the wind blows from the north," Anna said. "But it's hard to predict that."

"Wind from the north?" Jennifer laughed. "I never heard of such a thing. Why would a north wind be good?"

"Temperature, I suppose," the captain said. "Cider makers all have their own strategies and secrets. We always preferred a west wind and a waning moon when I was a boy in Pennsylvania."

This time Anna laughed. "I think ripe apples, clean barrels, good timing, and careful blending are the most important ingredients."

"Sounds good to me," Jen said, wondering how else old-fashioned cider making might differ from modern methods. "How does the mill work?"

"The apples will be shoveled from the wagons into the mill from up there," the captain explained as he worked. He gestured toward the platform almost a complete story above them. A door on the other side of the building opened out onto a hillside wagon ramp where the apples from neighboring orchards would be unloaded. "They drop down into the mill hopper and then are crushed."

"After the mash stands overnight, what happens?" Jen asked.

"Then we start putting the mash onto the press," Anna said, wiping her hands on her apron. She looked from Jen to the captain. "I've got to get back to the house to check on the kids. Why don't you two sit down here and taste the apples? I trust you and Jennifer to make the selection, Captain."

Before Jen could think of an excuse not to help the captain, the widow bustled out of the mill with the conspiratorial air of one leaving newlyweds alone together.

"Have you tasted apples for cider making?" the captain asked, sealing up the grease can he'd been working with.

"No," Jen said, unable to imagine why he would care to have her help. "I've helped pick apples and watched the mash being pressed in the cider press, but that's all."

"Well, then you can learn about it from the apple selection on." He set the grease can back on a shelf and wiped his hands on a rag. "Apples are best if they are ripe, firm, and picked up from the ground after no more than a day."

"Really?"

"Nothing overripe or green," the captain continued, his voice ringing even and calm with the authority of one who knew exactly what he is doing—and loved it.

"The Jonathans are here," he began, pointing to different stacks of laden apple baskets. "Rome beauties are here. They give sweetness. The Jonathan, Winesap and Northern Spy add a tart flavor. Golden and Red Delicious give the cider a nice aroma. Pippins add to the color. And for tannin, a few crab apples."

"Crab apples?" Jen repeated, her mouth twisting with the memory of sourness. "I tried those as a kid and they were awful."

"But blended with the others the tannin in the crab apples helps make the cider keep longer and better," the captain explained. "We won't use many and you don't have to taste them."

"Thanks for that," Jen said with a laugh. "How do we begin?"

"Sit here." The captain gestured toward a bench next to the door.

Jen sat. He soon had several baskets of apples setting at her feet. "This seems like strange duty for a cavalry captain," she said.

"Cider making?" He sat beside her, pulled a knife from the sheath on his belt, and began to cut up a Red Delicious. "Helping out Anna is the one thing that makes this assignment worthwhile. That and keeping her and her family safe from the raiders. Here, I think these look pretty good. There's a wagonload of them arriving today. And try this." He deftly sliced a generous piece and offered it to her on the blade of his knife.

Jen noticed a powerful flex in the muscle of his upper arm as he held out the slice of apple to her. She snatched the slice from the blade, careful not to touch his fingers. She knew the contact with him would burn. Her reaction was silly; she knew that, too. A regular schoolgirl response. But her face grew warm anyway. She prayed that he could not see the irrational blush that flooded into her cheeks. She ducked her head and popped the bite of apple into her mouth.

"Something wrong?" he asked. "You're blushing."

"I feel, ah, I feel like Adam and Eve," Jen blurted.

"Eve gave the apple to Adam, remember?" he said with a chuckle and put a slice into his mouth. Jen wondered what it would be like to have those lips kiss her again. She watched him out of the corner of her eye, incredibly aware of sitting next to a real man—not a sports-car-driving golf-course denizen, but a man who knew who he was inside and accepted his responsibilities. A good-looking hunk of a male. A man who was her proxy husband.

"True," Jen admitted, her voice an octave higher than normal as she gulped down the sweet fruit. The raw apple slice went down in a painful lump. She didn't know if she was going to be able to sit next to him and do this or not. She had to make herself think of something different. "You know, the apple shows up in a lot of other old stories too."

"Sure, the old Atalanta versus Hippomenes race story," the captain said, picking up an apple from another basket. "Of course there is the story of Paris giving an apple to Aphrodite and her rewarding him with another man's wife, Helen."

"And so began the Trojan War," Jen finished, amazed at trading Greek stories with this man. And her college advisor had thought the mythology course she'd insisted on taking was a waste of time.

"Then there is old William Tell shooting the apple off his son's head," the captain continued. He offered her another slice of apple. "That story ended with a war, too, a revolution of the Swiss against the Austrians. We could go on and on."

Jen laughed and accepted the slice with her fingers. "You sound like you know all the stories about apples."

"I educated myself on the subject when I was a kid," the captain admitted. "I thought it didn't hurt to learn everything including history. These Red Delicious are going to do very nicely, I think. What do you think?"

Jen nodded, her mouth full of fresh crisp apple again.

"Captain?" Sergeant Dunham appeared in the doorway, dust swirling in his wake.

"What is it, Sergeant?" The captain never looked up from the apples he was sampling.

Obviously excited, Dunham stumbled into the cool darkness of the mill and came to a halt in front of the captain. "The sentry on the road south just reported that there are rumors of Quantrill moving up this way again."

The captain paused in his apple slicing. "Any specifics? Has Quantrill been sighted at a certain farm or crossing any particular creek?"

"No, sir," the sergeant said. "Nothing like that. The sentry just said that a farmer had come by looking for a lost cow and said he'd heard that the guerrillas were moving this way, looking for horses and firearms."

"The sentry kept his mouth shut, didn't he?" the captain asked without looking from the apple he had just selected.

"Yes, sir, Captain," Dunham said. "The men know better than to let on that we're guarding a large stock of rifles and ammunition here."

The captain cut a quick glance in Jen's direction as if he hadn't wanted her to hear what the sergeant had just said. "Good. Tell them to keep their eyes and ears open. If they hear more rumors, get as much specific information as they can. I want everybody to stay on alert."

"Yes, sir." Sergeant Dunham gave the captain a salute, turned on his heel, and left the mill.

"Are you really afraid that Quantrill will raid here?" Jen asked as she racked her memory for details about the Confederate raider's activities and any relationship to Apple Grove House.

"He might if he gets wind of what we have hidden here," the captain said, slowly picking up another apple to slice.

A chill settled over Jen. "And you didn't want me to know about the rifles, did you?"

"It's best if that kind of information is kept quiet." The captain turned toward her. "Anyway, you're not leaving here until after the guns are shipped out at the end of the week, so all I have to do is keep an eye on you. Nobody should be the wiser about the rifles and ammunition."

Jen hesitated a moment, astonished by what she realized he implied. "You think I'm a spy?"

The captain shook his head. "Maybe you are. Maybe you aren't. You have to admit, your appearance yesterday was rather strange. And where is your groom?"

"I explained that," Jen said, knowing that her vague explanation of Brad being on his way to California must sound fishy to a practical man like Captain Vance. The full impact of what he was saying brought Jen to her feet. "How can you even dream I'm a spy? I would never do anything that would endanger those sweet girls out there or Anna and her family or this place. I love Apple Grove House. I've loved this place my whole life."

"Then why haven't I ever seen you around here before?" the captain demanded, gazing up at her, one hand on his hip and his knife in the other. "I'd remember you."

"I'd remember you, too." Jen took a deep breath and met his gaze steadily. He had the darkest, most golden green hazel eyes she'd ever seen. A strong brow and long dark eyelashes. He gazed back honestly, but without warmth. She didn't blame him for his suspicions. What was a man to think of a woman who appeared out of nowhere and hinted that she came from another time?

"Why don't you tell me the truth instead of some nonsense about time and cameras?" he asked.

"I've told you all I can tell you," she said and balled her hands into fists. "So am I a prisoner?"

"You mean, am I going to lock you in the corn crib?" he asked without rising from the bench. "No need for that. But you're not going anywhere until the end of the week when the patrol from Fort Scott arrives to take the store of guns and ammunition and the paddle wheeler from Westport shows up to take you and the other brides back where you belong. The least you can do until then is earn your keep. That's what the other ladies are doing."

"They don't know about the guns, do they?" Jen asked, glancing out the door toward the orchard. Among the fruit trees she watched Rebecca Thornton, the corporal's bride, carry her ladder to an untouched tree, place it against the trunk, climb up, and begin picking as she talked with the other girls. The brides were all so young, not a one of them over nineteen and so innocent. Jen felt protective toward them. She was older and she knew more. She knew the future. She'd never dreamed that knowing what was to come would be such a burden.

"No, they don't know about the guns and ammunition," the captain admitted. "I know exactly who they are, where they came from, and why they are here. However, you are another matter. So you can sit in the corner where I can keep an eye on you, or you can pitch in and help us get Anna's cider made by the end of the week. What will it be?"

Jen stood there, uncertain what to do or say. She was innocent. Never in her life had she done anything so two-faced as spying. She certainly would never have anything to do with the low-life guerrillas like William Quantrill. But how could she explain that to Captain Bennett Vance? "I'd rather be making cider than sitting in a corner. Will you allow me to help with the milling tonight?" Jen asked as if she had the luxury of driving a bargain with him.

"Sure," he said, preoccupied with another basket of apples. "Where I go, you'll go. We'll be milling apples tonight. And tomorrow we'll start spreading the mash on the frames for the press and then pressing. We'll need all the hands we can get."

"I'll do my part," Jen said with an indignant, self-righteous shake of her head. She would prove herself to him—somehow. "I'm no spy. You'll see."

"Good," the captain said, slicing off another piece of apple and offering it to her with a skeptical smile. Her declaration obviously left him unmoved. "Until then, don't leave my sight."

That night the milling went well. Bennett set the older Grove boys and two cavalry volunteers to shoveling apples into the mill hopper by torchlight. Below, Anna's old gray mare plodded steadily in the circle, turning the gears that operated the mill. The stone mill wheels crushed the fruit into the pomace necessary for the press. Bennett liked the looks of the pomace, but it was impossible to tell at this early stage if this batch of cider would get Anna ten dollars a barrel.

Even better than the success of the milling, the sentries reported no unusual sightings of suspicious travelers or of raiders near the ferry crossing. But Bennett never allowed the quiet to lull him into over confidence. He'd seen things change too fast too often to let down his guard. He kept the sentries posted day and night and he personally instructed them to be alert and prepared for anything. Quantrill was known for his lightning strikes. Unless they kept a good watch, the guerrilla could ride in, kill them all in their beds, and be gone with the guns and ammunition before any of them knew what was happening.

To the brides and Anna, he said little. He didn't want to worry them. Not that he thought the women incapable of handling the knowledge. He had come to have the greatest respect for frontier women. He'd grown up with a ladylike mother who had been coddled and protected by his father. And Bennett found himself inclined to treat women that way even after his brief unfortunate marriage.

But on the frontier he discovered women who enjoyed being treated like ladies, but who thought nothing of working beside their men, fighting at their men's sides, and making the men's decisions when necessary. Bennett liked frontier women. And he knew if a fight came to Apple Grove House, Anna and the women could be trusted to be more help than hindrance. Until then, guarding against a raid was his soldiers' job, and he'd tend to it himself.

But Jennifer remained a mystery to him. The suspicions he'd voiced about her being a spy had offended her. She'd responded to him with all the testiness and indignation of a pretty little tabby cat who'd been dunked in the rain barrel. That didn't surprise him. How else would an accused spy react? But other things about her didn't make sense.

As much as she claimed that she knew about Apple Grove House, she treated the most everyday occurrences as if each was new to her. Butter making fascinated her. She'd watched little Annie perform the task on the back porch with great curiosity and took a turn at the churn herself.

Later, when Anna's older boy brought in a couple of chickens with wrung necks to be plucked and stewed for supper, Jennifer had turned so pale, Bennett and Anna thought she was going to faint. When she'd dropped a bowl of flour on the kitchen floor, she'd cursed a blue streak and muttered something about where was a Dustbuster when you needed it. At the supper table—Anna had invited Bennett to dine with her family and the brides— Jennifer failed to hide her horror when she learned that they each used their own cloth napkin for a week before getting a clean one on Sunday, whether they needed it or not. A strange girl.

Then there was the matter of her odd underclothing.

Early on the third morning after the weddings, Bennett had walked into Anna's kitchen to get his morning coffee—the widow's brew was much better than that of the cavalry company's cook. Bennett took a couple of strides into the dim room when something stringy and cool flopped in his face.

"What the—" Startled, Bennett grabbed at the attacking item only to seize a handful of something sheer and satiny.

Anna, who was standing by the fire, straightened up. "Oh my, Captain. Don't fight it." She chuckled and started across the kitchen to his rescue. "Sorry. That's just a little laundry that Jennifer hung up here to dry. She absolutely refuses to wear the cotton underthings I offered her. Too bulky, she complains. I'm not giving up my Victoria's something she told me. You don't think Queen Victoria wears anything like that, do you?"

"How would I know?" Bennett stammered. He'd never remotely considered what the English queen might wear under her gowns. He held up a strange-looking figure-eight strip with satiny conical cups and narrow straps. In the other hand he held an odd triangle loop of the same smooth shiny fabric. "How? I mean where . . . Surely this isn't—"

"All?" Anna finished for him. "I'm afraid so. She said all the girls wear this where she comes from."

"Is that so?" Bennett turned the garments in his hands, trying to figure how they would fit on Jennifer's slender body. The straps would go over her shoulders and the cups would hold . . . And the loops of the triangle would . . . Parts of him stirred shamefully.

"Now, now." Anna snatched the garments out of his hands. "It doesn't bear too much thought, Captain."

Bennett surrendered the clothing without protest. Anna was right. How those things fit Jennifer did not bear too much thought.

"Where on earth do you think a nice girl gets things like that?" Anna asked, obviously a bit outraged as she examined the garments herself—but also curious and amused.

Bennett shook his head, still trying to put erotic images of Jennifer in the triangle thing out of his head. "I wouldn't know anything about it," he snapped as he ducked under the impromptu clothesline and marched across the kitchen to the coffeepot on the stove.

Whether she was a spy or not, Jennifer was obsessed with Zach Schuster and his camera. Once she'd gotten over her first fit of indignation with Bennett for suspecting her of spying, she absolutely beleaguered him about two things— neither having anything to do with rifles and ammunition. First, she asked endless questions about cider making, and second, she asked about when Zach Schuster was going to return with his camera.

He enjoyed sharing his cider knowledge. Her questions

were bright and insightful. She soaked up his every word as if she was filing it away for some future purpose. That was all right with him. But the questions about the damned photographer annoyed him.

"Like I told you before, Schuster will be back with his camera at the end of the week. He said he would try to get photographs again then. He thought maybe something in the weather might have changed and he'd have more success."

"Yes, that's it," Jennifer said with a distracted nod. "The problem never lasts. Something will have changed by the end of the week. The camera will work. Then I can get back where I belong."

The idea that Jennifer didn't belong there jarred Bennett. In the last few days he'd come to find her company natural and almost essential. She'd made herself invaluable. He liked her questions and smiles. He liked having her close and watching her work.

"I can't imagine why you think Schuster will have anything to do with you getting home. I will see that you get on the steamboat along with the other brides and return home safely. That was the arrangement made by Colonel Bailey and his wife with the men and their brides."

"I'm afraid it's not that simple," Jen said, smiling up at him so innocently that he had to turn away. He didn't like what her insistence about seeing Schuster made him think. "I didn't come on the steamboat, and it won't take me where I need to go. But Zach Schuster and his camera can," she maintained.

Bennett shook his head. That a photographer's camera was Jennifer's way home made no sense. Unless he believed her tale of time traveling. Or—unless Zach Schuster was her spy contact. *And all this time travel nonsense is just to distract me,* Bennett speculated over the barrel of apple juice that he was blending. The spy-contact theory was logical. It relieved him of believing in the impossible, but three days in her company believing that Jennifer was a spy was almost as absurd as believing she traveled in time.

Chapter Six

In the late afternoon of the sixth day after the weddings, tension hovered, tight and expectant, in the cool darkness of the cider mill. Rebecca, Mary, Sara, and Amy had crowded through the door and pressed close behind Jen. In hopeful silence, they all gazed at the glass jar of cider that Bennett held up to the shaft of sunlight streaming through the doorway. Anna stood at his side gazing up at the container also.

"It's time," the widow whispered at last, her gaze darting to Bennett's face, then back at the jar.

Jen nodded in silent agreement.

This was the moment they'd all worked toward for the last five days. This was what they had picked, crushed, pressed, and strained all those apples for. They'd eaten and slept—and Bennett had seen to his responsibilities as captain—but every other waking moment had been devoted to preparing for this first taste of the blended apple juice that would ferment to perfection—and become the best cider in the state of Kansas.

"What do you think, Bennett?" Anna asked, her eyes resting on the captain.

Jen was as excited as anyone in the mill, but she forced herself to keep quiet.

"I'm not sure I like the looks of it," Bennett said without taking his gaze from the jar.

In the light, the cider shone a rich, murky gold—totally unlike the anemic, ultrafiltered pasteurized stuff Jen was accustomed to seeing in the supermarket. Bennett's blend looked so much more intriguing and substantial—like liquid gold velvet in a jar. The sight made Jen's mouth water. Surely it would taste as sumptuous as it looked.

"I think the color looks good," Anna suggested.

"Yes, the color isn't bad," Bennett conceded, still scrutinizing the jar as if looking for something that none of the rest of them could possibly see. "But the body? I don't know."

Jen's impatience grew. "Well, are you going to taste it or not?"

"Sure looks good to me," Mary offered from behind Jen. The other girls nodded.

"It's time, Bennett," Anna repeated.

Bennett glanced at them, a wicked grin crossing his face, white teeth flashing against his gorgeous tan. "What impatience, ladies! Great things are not to be rushed. Even this blend will not taste like the final product, you understand."

"If this is good," Anna began with a warm chuckle, "the final brew will be delicious. Taste, master cider maker. Give us your verdict."

Bennett put the jar to his lips and took a sip. Everyone watched in silence. Much like a wine taster Jen had seen in a wineshop, he mulled the cider around his mouth in a long, slow, deliberate action—savoring what, she couldn't imagine. She'd never understood wine tasting either.

He swallowed, but still said nothing.

Anna reached for the jar. "Let me try it."

Bennett relinquished the glass container to her, then smiled at the girls, as if he knew something they didn't.

Jen could hardly wait to hear the verdict. Nobody had ever been particularly fussy about the cider that came out of the modern cider mill at Apple Grove House. The beverage had been made to meet certain standards. If it did that, it was good enough.

But Jen knew after working with Bennett for long hours, that if he had anything to do with it, this blend would be something special. He had worked too long and hard, overseeing every detail to not have produced something exceptional.

Anna sipped from the jar.

Still, no one made a sound. Not even an intake of breath could be heard among the seven of them.

The widow, too, took her time, rolling the cider over her tongue and around her mouth like a wine taster. Jen had never thought the making of cider could be as complicated as that of wine, but after the last five days, she was beginning to reconsider. Like the girls, she waited eagerly for the widow's opinion.

When Anna swallowed, a big smile spread across her face. "I think we are close, very close to having rediscovered old Moses's recipe."

Bennett's grin flashed into a broad smile again and he nodded. "I think so, too."

"Hurrah!" Rebecca said, laughing. The other three cheered and danced around in a circle. Everyone had put so much effort into the entire process that they felt the victory was theirs as well as Bennett and Anna's.

Jen laughed with pleasure, excited to have been part of the process. "May I taste?"

"Sure." Bennett reached for another jar on the board-and-sawhorse table they'd set up in the mill. Jen waited anxiously as he tapped the barrel for a sample, then handed it to Jen. He handed one to each of the girls.

Jen put the jar to her mouth and took a small sip, imitating the tasting process she'd seen Bennett and Anna perform.

"What do you think?" he asked, leaning closer as if her opinion truly mattered to him.

Rich, spicy—almost buttery—apple flavor floated through her mouth and filled her head. It was heaven in a jar, completely unlike anything Jen had ever tasted. She stared at the sample to get a better look at it.

"Well?" he repeated. "What do you think?"

"I think it's wonderful," Jen said, convinced more than ever that old-fashioned things were better than new. "No wonder it gets a premium price. This would be wonderful to serve at parties and in the evening in front of the fire or— Golly, I'd drink this anytime."

"It's unanimous, you see," Anna said, touching Bennett's arm

Bennett shook his head as if he wasn't quite satisfied. "It's good, but not quite as good as Moses's."

With a smile, Jen realized what a perfectionist Bennett was. How like him to feel the least fraction of perfect had been missed somehow. What an asset a cider maker like him would be to modern-day Apple Grove House.

"You expect too much, Captain," Anna said with another chuckle. "Ladies, I think we've done a day's work

out here. Go wash up and we'll start supper. You'll be
along soon, won't you, Captain?"

"Sure," Bennett said, peering into the barrel. "I'll finish
cleaning up out here."

"I'll help." Jen had grown accustomed to washing up the
wooden cider making utensils at the end of each workday.

"Then let's go, girls," Anna said, leading the young
brides out the door with her as if they were an extension
of her gaggle of children.

"Last one to the spring is a crybaby," Mary challenged,
and they were off, racing up the hill behind the mill.

Smiling to herself, Jen turned to the dishpan full of dirty
utensils already on the table.

*Funny how accustomed to new and different things you can
become in a short time,* she mused. She'd only been at Apple
Grove House for five days, but she was beginning to feel
as if she'd always lived there. Chamber pots, long skirts,
boiled coffee, and dishpans held no terrors for her now.
It was almost a magical time—like walking into a TV episode of *Little House on the Prairie* or *Dr. Quinn, Medicine
Woman.*

"These won't take long," she said, as much to herself
as to Captain Vance—or Bennett, as he'd given her permission to call him several days ago.

"I'll be finished over here soon, too," he said. "I just
have one more barrel to fill."

Jen went to work, musing over all the new things she'd
discovered and the few things she truly missed, like ice
in her iced tea—Anna Grove had never heard of such a
beverage—sandals on her feet, a good hot shower, and
her family—especially her family. There were so many little
things she would love to share with her sister, Jessica, or
with Joey. Her nephew would love watching Captain

Vance's cavalrymen groom and saddle their horses and perform sentry duty.

But Captain Vance—Bennett—fascinated her. It was more than just the fact that he was her proxy husband. She'd genuinely grown to like him. She liked the sound of his voice when he explained things or gave instructions. She liked the feel of his solid shoulder against hers as they worked. His touch never failed to warm her, but she tried not to show it. She liked that keen concentration that came to his face as he worked. She admired his even hand with his men and his gentlemanly conduct toward Anna, her children, and the girls.

If she was truly a modern woman, those qualities wouldn't be so attractive to her, she told herself. But they did appeal—proof she was old-fashioned and probably a fool. But why not enjoy his company? Because he seemed determined to think badly of her. A spy, indeed.

Remembering Bennett's implied accusation, Jen fumed once again. Now why did she find him attractive?

Every night in bed she'd racked her brain to remember the details of Apple Grove House's Civil War history, searching for some clue that would help her prove her innocence. The best that she could recall was that there had been some trouble during the war. But it had not come from an attack by Quantrill. What exactly had happened? She never could quite recollect.

Then in the morning she would wake to see the sun burning the fog off the river below and the trees on the hillsides turning to autumn hues. Thoughts of war evaporated like the river mist. Living at Apple Grove House was like living in an enchanted place and time. It was like being at Camelot, the mythical kingdom in the musical stage play where it never rained until after dark. The river fog was always gone by eight in the morning and by nine at night the moon shone high above.

Whatever threat the Confederate raiders might pose, as far as Jen knew, Apple Grove House would survive. She'd accepted that Brad and her wedding were a loss. She could live with that. But she couldn't bear to think that Ted Neisen's theme park scheme would destroy this beautiful place. She had to return to 1999.

"I've filled the last barrel of the day," Bennett said, coming up so close behind her that Jen could feel his breath on her neck. "Are you about finished cleaning up?" he asked.

"Yes, about finished," Jen said, grateful for his interruption. She didn't like spending too much time with her own thoughts these days. It was too confusing, drifting in time.

"Then let's walk up the hill to the spring and wash up like the others did," he said. There was a pump behind Apple Grove House where everyone frequently washed up, and the spring trickling into a hillside pool was a favorite place to go, too. In addition to the cold, clear water, it offered the respite of cool shade and a spectacular view of the river and valley below.

"Good idea." Jen hung the last of the wooden utensils to dry on the tool pegs. Then she followed Bennett out of the mill into the last of the twilight.

"So you're satisfied with the blending of the cider?" Jen asked as they walked along the path. Outside, the air was cool and fresh, and a full moon already glowed overhead.

"Yes," Bennett said. "Now time will tell. I don't think we've quite rediscovered Moses's recipe, but it's tasting pretty good. I'm confident Anna will get a good price for it."

They passed the girls returning from the spring. All four were laughing, their faces bright and cheerful. "Don't stay too long now, you two," called Sara Moss. The others giggled.

Jen grinned at the girls and waved. "They think we spend so much time together because you like my company."

"I could do worse things with my time," Bennett murmured without looking at the brides. In a flutter of skirts, they began to trot back to the house, their spirits high and their energy renewed now that their work for the day was done.

Surprised at the remark, Jen stared at him.

"So tell me, how are you feeling about your missing fiancé?" Bennett asked. "Are you getting over the disappointment? Are you going to fall into his arms and believe whatever story he tells you if he shows up?"

"Brad is not going to show up," she said with a wry laugh. "Funny you should bring that up. Actually I haven't given Brad much thought."

"As a matter of fact, you look as though you're recovering from the disappointment very well." Bennett smiled in a way that revealed he meant what he said.

"The first night I was here, I gave him a lot of thought, and I decided that I must not love him as much as I thought I did," Jen said, recalling her first sleepless night at Apple Grove House. Had that only been five days ago? It seemed like a lifetime had passed. "Obviously he didn't love me."

"At least he showed you enough respect to recognize the fact and not marry you," Bennett said, a curious tone in his voice.

Jen hesitated in her tracks. "You sound as if you have some special knowledge of that kind of disappointment."

Bennett who had strode on ahead of her stopped and turned. "I was left at the altar, too, once."

"No kidding?" Jen exclaimed, startled by his admission.

She hurried to catch up with him. "Then you know that sick feeling of astonishment."

"I know the sick feeling," Bennett echoed, turning to walk on down the path to the spring. "It was my former wife who left me standing there, red faced, in front of a chapel full of people."

"But who on earth would leave you at the altar?" Jen shook her head. "Wait a minute. You just said your former wife?"

"Yes. Fool that I was, I made it my goal in life to change her mind," Bennett said. "Pride, I guess. But I was successful. She eventually married me. Biggest mistake I ever made. She hated army life. Eventually we hated each other. Does that shock you?"

"No, it's just too bad," Jen said, truly sorry. What a disappointment it must have been for him—a man who had prepared himself for a career in the military—to have a wife who hated the very life he'd sought. "Children?"

"No children," Bennett said. "She went home to her family and remarried a few years later, once the scandal of the divorce had died down."

"And you?" Jen asked, trying to glimpse his face as he walked slightly ahead of her. Did the subject still cause him pain? "Did you marry again?"

"No, don't care to try that again," he said, his face expressionless. "Women find a divorced man suspect. Besides, I learned my lesson the first time."

How like a man, Jen thought. *Denies the pain, but refuses to ever open himself up to the experience again.*

"Where I come from, everyone has some kind of baggage," Jen said with a shake of her head. "I probably have *not* learned my lesson. I won't go after Brad—that's for sure. I'm starting to see what a mistake he and I were from the beginning. We cared about entirely different things.

He wanted to build a life around the country club and his golf game. Funny how plain it is now. But dunce that I am, I want to marry someday. When the right man comes along."

"Golf game?" Bennett stopped and looked at her. "He must be a strange man. There's not much golf around here."

There will be, Jen thought, then brushed the questions away with a wave of her hand."

Bennett didn't persist, but turned and headed up the path. "Marrying is not foolish for you. I never meant to say that. You'll find the right man or he'll find you. Here we are."

The sound of the trickling water reached Jen's ears. They had arrived at the spring.

"This is going to feel good," Jen said, dropping down onto a rock and immediately peeling off her shoes and stockings. Her white wedding shoes and stockings were serving her well, because the high-top footwear that Anna had loaned her was impossible to get on her feet. Before she put her feet into the water streaming out of the pool, Jen studied her bare legs for a moment. "Bennett, do you happen to have a spare razor?"

He glanced at her and quickly turned away as if he was uneasy with the sight of her skirt pulled up over her knees. "Do I have a spare what?"

"Never mind." Jen decided not to press the question. She scooped water up onto her face. Its coolness soothed away the heat of the day.

Bennett sat beside her and did the same. For a moment, there was no sound but the splash of their hands in the fresh, clear water and the last song of the day as the birds settled in their nests. The sun had dropped below the horizon. Twilight gathered in the shadows around them.

The tensions of the day eased from Jen as the cool water refreshed her.

When she got back, she'd have to go look for this spring, but she suspected that it had dried up by 1999.

She glanced aside at Bennett. He, too, appeared to relax. "You love this place, don't you?" she asked, suddenly realizing that they had that in common. Jen smiled at her feet and wiggled her toes, pleased with that knowledge.

"Yes, you could say that," he replied.

Suddenly she felt Bennett's hand on her shoulder. She glanced back at him in surprise. They had touched before, but they had not touched intentionally since the day they'd been proxy bride and groom. He put a silencing finger to his lips, then pointed across the spring and back up the hill. Jen turned in that direction to see a white-tailed doe standing statue still in the deep shadows, her liquid brown eyes fastened on them, her ears cocked in their direction, her head up and alert.

Neither Jen nor Bennett moved. She was afraid even a gasp of pleasure would frighten away the beautiful wild thing. Ever so slowly, one dainty foot, then another, appeared from out of the underbrush until a fawn stood at the doe's side, peering in their direction. The young deer was old enough that its white spots were beginning to fade.

Jen sucked in a breath of pleasure and awe. But the grip of Bennett's hand on her shoulder warned her to remain silent. As if one miracle wasn't enough, another dainty foot appeared and another set of perked ears appeared until the fawn's twin stood looking at them, too.

Jen was about to open her mouth to whisper admiration when yet another movement caught her eye. Behind the doe and her fawns, a buck strutted out of the shadows, the prince of the forest. A full rack of antlers crowned him, a ten-pointer.

As a suburban girl, Jen had caught a fleeting glimpse of a wild deer or two, but this sight was a wondrous feast for the eyes. The buck did not stop to inspect Jen and Bennett. He moved on through the brush, his restlessness communicated to the doe, who soon followed with her twin fawns trotting along behind her. In a moment, as silently as they had come, the deer vanished.

"Did you see that?" Jen gasped, her hand at her throat. Her heart pounded with excitement. "The whole family."

"Beautiful, aren't they?" Bennett said. "Sergeant Dunham is going to be sorry to hear he missed them. He's partial to venison."

"He wouldn't shoot them, would he?" Jen stammered, turning to Bennett. "That's like shooting Bambi."

"Who?" He looked at her as if she were crazy. "Don't you ever see deer where you're from?"

"Only when the car lights shine into their frightened eyes," Jen said, desperate to save the beauty of what they'd just seen. "Don't let anybody shoot them."

"Game is game, but I admit they made a pretty sight. And Anna's larder is well provisioned. If it will put your soft heart at ease, we don't have to tell the trigger-happy sergeant about the buck he missed."

"Good. We won't tell him," Jen said, reluctant to let go of what seemed to be a special moment meant for them to share. "Promise?"

Bennett laughed indulgently. "Promise."

"Cross your heart," Jen prompted, uncertain where that childish phrase had come from.

"Cross my heart," Bennett said, drawing his finger across his heart, then leaning closer to her, a sudden smile of insolence on his lips. "And seal my lips with a kiss?"

318	*Linda Madl*

Jen stared at him, taken aback by his unexpected flirtation, yet pleased and oh so tempted. She shrugged to cover the pleasure that ran through her. "Why not?"

She leaned forward to brush her lips against his—prepared to give only what had passed between them on their wedding day. She didn't even pucker seriously. He was only getting a quick peck on the lips. Surely a man who accused her of being a spy expected nothing more.

Chapter Seven

Unwilling to allow Jennifer to change her mind, Bennett captured her face between his hands. The sudden movement seemed to surprise her, but she did not pull away. He lowered his head a fraction, then hesitated. She did not move. He studied her lips, tantalizingly pink and invitingly moist from the cool spring water. He refused to look into her eyes. He didn't want to find doubt or hesitation where he wanted to see passion in the velvet brown depths of her gaze. So he focused on her lips, almost as blushing red as an apple. Under his gaze her mouth began to tremble. Then nervously her tongue darted across her lower lip. Bennett's body reacted to the gesture.

He bent to touch her lips with his. He found them pliant, but cool. Yet she did not withdraw from his hold. So he pressed his lips more firmly against hers, then pulled back, releasing her.

After a moment, she opened her eyes and gazed up at

him, a soft boldness in her dark gaze. "Well, is that all it takes to seal your lips?"

Bennett studied her. "That's just a practice exercise."

"I thought so," she said, leaning closer again. She spread her hands on his knees, tilted her face up toward his, closed her eyes, and offered her mouth to him.

Bennett didn't hesitate this time. He seized her by the shoulders and kissed her with all the pent-up desire that had been building up in him day by day as they worked next to each other in the mill. Her lips separated willingly. Hungrily his tongue slipped between them to taste her fully. The inside of her mouth was delicious. He explored deeply, thoroughly, before nibbling gently on her lower lip.

Making a low sound in the back of her throat, she kissed him back. As he teased the corner of her mouth with his tongue, her hands inched up his thighs, setting him afire to possess her. With a last shred of sanity, he grasped her hands and pulled them away.

"Jennifer, you are not an old-fashioned girl," he muttered, his forehead resting against hers. "Believe me. You are not."

She made a strange, strangled sound. He could feel her breath against his jaw.

"Not that I'm complaining," he hurried to add.

"How would an old-fashioned girl behave under these circumstances?" she asked, pulling away slightly and looking up at him.

"She would slap me," Bennett said with a rueful smile. He couldn't imagine Jennifer slapping anybody, but he could see her telling him in no uncertain terms what she liked and didn't like.

"What nonsense." Jennifer giggled softly and pulled away smiling. To Bennett's surprise, she reached up and drew her thumb across his lower lip. "Why slap a man after he's given you the best kiss you've ever had?"

Bennett joined in her laughter. "You don't slap him for the kiss. You slap him for what he's thinking."

"Maybe you'd better tell me what it is you're thinking?" she baited, her smile broadening. Her dark brown eyelashes fluttering against her rosy cheeks.

If Bennett's life had depended on it, he couldn't have put into words the strange combination of lust and sweet need that flooded through him. He drew her to him again, intent on having another kiss.

The crack of gunfire shattered the evening's peace.

Instinctively, Bennett shoved Jennifer to the ground and covered her with his body. They hit the ground with a thud. Beneath his weight, Jennifer groaned. Bennett shushed her and lifted his head to hear whatever more he could. He heard a few shouts from his men on the riverbank. He waited, counting on the brush surrounding the spring to serve as cover.

In rapid succession, several more shots rang out. Then he heard the one cry he didn't want to hear: the bone chilling Confederate war cry. He cursed aloud.

"What is it?" Jennifer asked, struggling to get out from under him.

"Raiders. Stay down," Bennett ordered, rising enough to peer over his shoulder down toward the ferry landing. In the last of the twilight, he could barely see puffs of gun smoke floating over the river. Several more shots were exchanged.

He glanced toward Apple Grove House below them. The house was lit up already with coal-oil lamps.

"Douse the lights, Anna," he muttered as the firing continued. Jennifer struggled to rise, but he pushed her down again. Then he jumped to his feet in the next instant, peering down at the house. As if Anna had heard him, the lights rapidly went out one by one.

"Who is firing?" Jennifer asked, sitting up. "What was that funny yell?"

"That's the famous Rebel yell," Bennett said, eager to find Corporal Dunham and find out just who was where. "Don't move until I come back for you. I'm going to see what is happening."

"You're not leaving me here alone," Jennifer cried, scrambling to her feet and grabbing her shoes.

Bennett didn't have the time to argue with her. "All right then, but don't question anything I say."

"Yes, sir, Captain," Jennifer said, striving to get her shoes onto her wet feet.

Bennett ignored the mockery in her voice. He grabbed her hand and started back down the path toward the house and the cider mill. She kept pace with him. Their dark-colored clothes and the underbrush made them difficult to see. If there were only a few attackers, the gunmen would be too occupied with the firing at the sentries along the river to take shots at them above.

By the time they had skirted around an outbuilding, run along behind the wood pile, and made it down to the riverbank, the firing stopped. The sharp stench of gunpowder hung in the air. In the moonlight, the soft innards of shattered pumpkins littered the riverbank.

"Report, Sergeant Dunham," Bennett demanded the minute he ran up behind the men using a stack of pumpkins for cover. "Casualties? Number of attackers?"

"Yes, sir, Captain." Dunham appeared out of the darkness, breathless and making a hasty salute. "No casualties,
sir. We think there were only three or four gunmen, sir.
Irregulars from the sound of them. You know that god-
awful hollering they make. Probably a scouting party."

"No, wait," Jennifer gasped, clutching her side and
bending over slightly. She held up her other hand as if
asking for a moment of patience. "Lord, I've got a stitch
in my side. I've never jogged down a hill like that before."
She gasped again, then drew in a deep breath and straightened up to face Bennett. "I remember now. I remember
what happens at Apple Grove House."

Dunham's gaze shifted to Jennifer with interest.

Bennett whirled around and stepped toward her. Suddenly suspicious of the unexplainable knowledge she sometimes displayed about things, he regretted that she'd
overheard their conversation about the guns and Quantrill.
It wasn't wise for her to be on the riverbank with him and
the men. Yet if she knew something, he wanted to know
what it was. If she was a spy, he wanted her to reveal herself.
"What do you mean? What's going to happen to Apple
Grove House?"

"The attack isn't going to come from the south," Jennifer said with a shake of her head. "It won't be Quantrill
who attacks. He's already headed back south. It's going to
be another Confederate raider."

Bennett exchanged a skeptical glance with Dunham.
They both knew that was not the intelligence that the
colonel had received on the Confederate irregulars. They
fully expected Quantrill to reappear to press his advantage
in Kansas at any time. But Bennett was curious enough
now to listen to all that she had to say. He regarded her

through narrowed eyes and folded his arms across his chest. "Go on. Tell me what's going to happen?"

"The attack is going to come from the north," Jennifer said, her eyes bright with excitement even in the darkness. "The leader will be Cutthroat Clive Morrison from St. Joe, where the proslavery sympathizers are strong. He's going to be well armed and he's going to be looking for the guns. He knows about them."

She paused, putting a finger thoughtfully to her lips. "Yes, he is informed about the guns. He's going to be damned determined to find them."

Pleased with herself for remembering her history at last, Jen couldn't resist smiling at Bennett. Now he would realize she wasn't a spy.

He didn't return her smile. "What about these scouts?" Bennett asked, his face shadowed and unreadable in the darkness.

"They're Morrison's men, a diversion," Jen said, searching her memory for details of the brief Civil War episode written up in Apple Grove House's long history.

"You don't happen to know the time and date of the raid?" Bennett asked, a strange edge in his voice.

"Shoot, I don't remember," Jen said, wishing she'd paid more attention to the particulars of the historian's account. "But Cutthroat Clive already knows the guns are here. He's been informed by a spy."

The silence that followed her revelation made Jen uncomfortable. She'd just told them what they needed to know to defend the place. Why were they—Bennett and the sergeant—staring at her as if she was a two-headed cow? She looked from one man to the other, but neither offered her a smile or a look of gratification.

"You wouldn't happen to know who that spy is?" Bennett

asked, scrutinizing her with what she realized was skepticism.

"Wait a minute," Jen said, astonished at the turn the conversation was taking. "I'm not the spy. And I happen to know Apple Grove House will survive this raid. Could a spy tell you that?"

"Don't prove nothing," the sergeant said with a gloomy shake of his head. "Seems to me a spy could tell us anything she wanted to."

"Cutthroat Clive was last reported in Oklahoma Indian territory," Bennett said as if he regretted giving her that news.

"Well, Morrison must be back from Indian territory," Jennifer said with certainty. Her historical research had been confined to the event at Apple Grove House. She hadn't pursued Cutthroat Clive's notorious career. She could not explain away Bennett's information. "I don't know how Clive does it or who your spy is. But Clive will lead the raid."

Anger flashed in Dunham's face. He drew himself up and turned to Bennett. "Captain, you know there ain't a spy among us men. Each and everyone here is as loyal as the day is long. Begging your pardon, miss, but there's no traitor among the captain's men."

When Jennifer turned to Bennett again in the gathering darkness, she could just barely see a frown on his face. She realized that he didn't believe her either.

"I'm aware of the men's loyalty, Sergeant," Bennett replied. "Take Miss Hollis into custody."

Dunham snapped a sharp salute and a grin spread across his face. "Yes, sir."

"What?" Jen cried.

"Lock her in her room," Bennett ordered, his voice suddenly unfamiliar and cold to her ear.

"You can't be serious," she said.

"I'm very serious," Bennett said. "I know my men, and I trust them. Sergeant."

"Yes, sir."

"Bennett?" she pleaded, too shocked to physically protest. "You can't really believe I'm the spy."

Next thing Jen knew, Dunham had seized her wrists and ordered rope to be brought to tie her.

"You know too much, Jennifer. What am I supposed to think?" With a grim frown, Bennett turned to Dunham. "Sergeant, there's no need to restrain her, not as long as she goes peaceably. Just lock her in her room. See that the curtains are drawn and the shutters locked so that she can't send any signals and post a twenty-four-hour watch on her."

"Promise me you'll set an extra watch on the north road," Jen found herself insisting, suddenly frightened that somehow she might have changed history. What if her being there somehow meant that Cutthroat Clive was successful in his raid and burned down the house?

But Bennett remained silent as Dunham led her away.

When the door of her room slammed behind her, Jen almost wept. She was a prisoner in Apple Grove House. Bennett had been a gentleman about it. The shutters on the window in her room were locked, but she was not tied or restrained anyway. Nevertheless, what fun she'd had in being transported back in time had vanished. The joy of the adventure was over. She stood suspected of spying. She was ready to wake up from this bad dream—or jump down a sci-fi wormhole or walk through an enchanted mirror—or do whatever she needed to do to get back to the year she'd come from.

Frustrated, Jen turned away from the door.

A small lamp burned on the bedside table. By its light,

Jen saw an open hatbox sitting beside the lamp. Whoever had left the lamp had apparently left the box. It had not been there earlier in the day.

Curious, Jen moved across the room and peered into the box. There lay her dried wedding bouquet, the ribbons carefully arranged around the dried posy. Anna had dried it so that the flowers, though yellowed and edged in brown, still held their shape. Jen could see the curling rose petals and the wide, delicate apple blossom petals. It was still a lovely bouquet.

Jen stared at the posy, then replaced it in the box and dropped down on the edge of her bed. What had happened to her wedding? she wondered. How had Jessica managed? Poor Jessica. What a story Jen was going to have to tell her—if she managed to get back to 1999.

Jen frowned. What if the raid came and the house was burned down and the photographer never came back and she never got home? What if she was hanged as a spy? What if—Jen swallowed her self-pitying sob before it escaped her. What if something happened and she never saw Bennett again?

Thoughts of being separated from Bennett brought her rioting speculations to a halt. Tentatively she licked her lips, longing to know his kiss again. It had been a tender kiss with just a dash of passion. Warm and promising. She had felt the passion quicken in him, in the strength of his grip on her shoulders, and she'd wanted him to surrender to it so she could surrender, too. The thought of that kiss brought a renewed tingling to her belly.

Heavens, if she didn't know better, she'd think she was falling in love with the guy—this man who thought she was a spy. No, it wasn't love, just infatuation, maybe lust, she told herself as she lay down on the bed without pulling back the counterpane. It was too soon after Brad's betrayal to fall in love again.

No, what she felt for Bennett was just infatuation. Who wouldn't fall for a guy who swaggered like a nineteenth-century John Wayne, flashed a dimpled smile like Brad Pitt, and dished out attitude like James Dean? Jen nodded to herself. Just infatuation. That was all that funny feeling in her belly was. A schoolgirl's crush.

She sighed. Her head felt heavy and she let it rest on the feather pillow. What a mess she'd made of things. Just when she thought she knew how to prove herself to Bennett, he took her knowledge to mean she was a traitor. Now she was at a loss about what to do.

Despite the tension and irritation of being locked up as a prisoner, Jen fell asleep and dreamed of going home. But even in her dreams she couldn't get there.

A single cry awoke her—the warbling screeches of the Confederate raiders. The Rebel yell.

Jen bolted upright on the bed and listened, her heart pounding in her throat. She heard the reassuring sound of Bennett's voice shouting orders. Then the gunfire began. It came from the north. Cutthroat Clive was here. Jen dashed for the door and yanked it open, prepared to talk her way out of the room. She had to do something to help.

In the dark hallway, the sentry's chair was empty. He'd deserted his post, gone to find his place among the men, no doubt, she thought. Then she saw that the door to the attic was open and she heard the firing from above. He was defending the house.

Anna appeared in the doorway of her room across the hallway, her long, dark, graying braid tossed over her shoulder. Already, the children in the room next to Jen's were beginning to whimper.

"Get the kids. Stay with them and don't light any lamps," Jen ordered. She knew Anna and the children would be all right in the house. But she wasn't certain about the girls who had abandoned their bridal tents to sleep in the mill since their husbands had gone. "I'm going to find Mary, Rebecca, and the others."

"Be careful, Jennifer," Anna warned, already gathering her children around her.

"I will," Jen said, galloping down the stairs and bolting out the back door toward the mill.

Outside in the dark, the moon had set. Jen could see very little at first. The gunshots were coming closer. She could hear unintelligible shouts from the men and the whinnies of horses, but the fighting seemed to come from the road toward the north. Satisfied that there was little to fear at the moment, Jen raced across the yard to the mill.

The door was bolted. She pounded on it.

"Let me in," she cried. The sound of the fighting was coming closer. She could hear the sound of horses' hooves on the road now. The last thing she wanted was to be caught outside. "Open up. It's Jen. Let me in."

Instantly the door opened and Jen stumbled into the safety of the mill and Mary's arms. Rebecca shut and bolted the door behind her.

"Is everyone okay here?" Jen demanded, regaining her feet and counting the four girls: Mary, Rebecca, Sara, and Amy, each dressed in a long white night rail and hovering around Jen like ghosts in the darkness.

"Yes, we're all right," Rebecca said. The girls nodded in agreement. She seemed to be the natural spokesperson of the group.

But pounding began on the mill door immediately. "Open up," the thwarted raider shouted.

Jen glanced around at the other girls. None of them recognized the voice of the man outside. Between the boards of the cider mill wall, they could see and smell the flames of his torch. Jen could hear firing from the house. Anna and the children were safe, but Jen and the girls had been cut off.

"Come on," the man said. "Your gallant captain is off on a wild-goose chase. Open up."

"There's nothing in here that you want," Jen called. "Just cider."

"I'll be the judge of that," the man said. "Open up or maybe I'll just set the building afire. I have a feeling you're more attached to it than I am."

Jen hesitated. Where was Bennett? Then between the boards, she saw the light of the torch move closer. Smoke drifted into the mill. The light arced downward toward the bottom of the door. Jen gasped. He wouldn't, would he? She stared in fascination as an orange flame licked under the door and up the inside of the wood.

The girls gasped and stepped back.

Jen gulped. According to the official history of Apple Grove House, the mill would not burn down for another thirty years. Another flame appeared licking up higher than the first. Then another.

"All right," Jen cried, unwilling to tempt fate or the Rebels. "We'll open up, but only under a flag of truce."

"Seems to me you don't have much choice about your terms," an eerily familiar voice said.

Jen watched the flames licking up at the bottom of the door. The uncanny feeling she'd met this man before overwhelmed her, but she couldn't imagine how she could ever have met a Confederate raider before. "Who are you?" she asked.

"I'm Cutthroat Clive Morrison, missy, and I'm going to burn this place down if you don't open up." Cutthroat Clive emphasized his demands with another blow to the door. It rattled on its hinges. The flames licked higher. "Open up or maybe we'll set fire to the house, too."

Chapter Eight

"No, wait. There are innocent women in here," Jennifer called, unable to take her eyes off the threatening flames at the base of the mill door. She hoped her admission would appeal to any chivalry Cutthroat Clive might still possess.

She heard him mumble something, but the torch was withdrawn and the flames disappeared. A sigh of relief hissed from her and the girls standing behind her in the dark mill.

"Hurry." Jen turned to them. "Get dressed and put your shoes on," she ordered, suddenly aware of how vulnerable and defenseless the ripe young brides would appear to the excited men outside.

Without argument, the girls obeyed. All the time the distant crack of gunfire grew closer. Jen wondered if Bennett was in the midst of the fighting. "Where are the captain and his men?"

"There are the guards in the house. The others are down by the river and a few rode up north with Captain Vance," said Rebecca, the corporal's bride, as she shoved her arms into the sleeves of her bodice.

So Bennett had heeded her warning, Jen thought, relieved to know that, but wondering how the raiders had gotten to the house in spite of him. She heard the thunder of more horses outside. Men shouted and cursed. Someone let out another Rebel war cry. The shout was so near it sent shivers down Jen's back.

"Come on," the raider outside shouted. "Open the door or the bonfire begins."

"All right, hold your horses," Jen called back in her best stick-it-in-your-ear tone of voice. She didn't want the man to think they were intimidated. She glanced around at the girls. "Ready to run for your lives?"

The girls were respectably dressed. In the dark, their faces were pale ovals—eyes big and mouths small with apprehension. But they bravely nodded that they were ready to face the foe.

"Remember, they want the guns, not us," Jen whispered to the girls over her shoulder. "When I say to, go straight to the house and lock up as soon as you are inside."

"What about you?" Rebecca asked.

"I'll join you if I can," Jen said. "But don't wait for me. Understand?"

The girls nodded.

"Mr. Morrison, I'm opening up," Jen called through the door. "But I expect safe passage for the women to the protection of the house."

"Agreed," Morrison said.

Jen threw open the mill door and found herself staring up at a dirty, bearded man. In the torchlight, she had a good view of his face. With a lewd grin on his lips, he raked his gaze up and down her figure, making her feel as if she was undressed—even though she was fully clothed.

He stood a head taller than she, spare and grizzled, a feather in his hat and gun belts crisscrossing his chest. Jen gulped back her fear. He grinned, showing his stained and dark teeth, but in that instant—poor dental hygiene aside—she knew exactly who he reminded her of.

Her fear of the guerrillas vanished. Anger welled up inside of her. Yet irony brought a harsh laugh to her lips. She was staring at the spitting image of Ted Neisen, the theme park developer.

"You scum bag. You greedy-livered dipstick," she spit out, half laughing and half cursing, completely confusing Ted Neisen and Cutthroat Clive Morrison. "You selfish, ritzy old goat. I might have known: Once a villain, always a villain."

His grin froze into a cold glare. "You Yankee women can't keep a genteel tongue in your head. I'm Captain Morrison to you."

He reached for Jen's throat, but the girls grabbed her arms and pulled her beyond his grasp.

Cutthroat Clive charged into the mill after her. But the minute the torchlight fell on the barrels, he seemed to think better of pursuing Jen. Turning away from them, he marched across to the cider barrels. "Sam. In here. Quick."

Another man carrying an ax entered the mill.

"Start over there," Cutthroat Clive ordered, gesturing toward several cider barrels Bennett had just filled that afternoon.

Jen winced as the ax split the barrel end. Fresh cider splattered the mill walls and gushed out, flooding across the wooden floor.

"There isn't anything here, Captain Morrison," Jen said,

her eyes telling the girls to keep quiet. "Just barrels of cider."

Cutthroat Clive grunted and grinned, advancing on the girls again. "Then where are the guns?"

"We don't know anything about guns." Jen pulled away from the girls and stood up to Morrison again. Where in the hell was Bennett? she wondered. Off on a wild-goose chase? Or hurt—lying somewhere wounded, in pain, and without help? Jen's mouth went dry. But protecting the girls was up to her now. "You agreed to let the ladies join Anna Grove in the house," she reminded Morrison.

Cutthroat Clive kicked at the broken barrel, then glared at her again. "Sam, where do you think Vance might have hidden the guns?"

The man with the torch nodded his head toward the outside. "They might have buried them."

"Start searching," Cutthroat Clive shouted with impatience.

The man dashed out the door.

"Now let's get acquainted," Clive said, that lewd grin returning to his face. "Just who are you ladies?"

Rebecca gulped and started babbling despite Jen's frown. "I'm Rebecca Thornton, and this is Mary Roberts. That is Sara Moss and Amy Boland."

"And who is this pretty blond lady?" Cutthroat reached out and tugged on Jen's loose hair.

"That's the captain's wife," Mary blurted.

"No, I'm not," Jen declared.

Rebecca pinched Mary's arm.

"No, she isn't," Mary cried, realizing her mistake too late. "No, oh, I'm sorry Mrs. Vance."

Jen almost groaned at the sound of Bennett's last name. The girls had teased her about her unique married status all week.

Clive turned on Jen, his eyes narrowing with renewed interest. "So you're the captain's lady. And he's run off and left you here undefended."

"Vance isn't worried about me," Jen said, actually wishing that he was concerned, at least a little. "And he isn't my husband."

Clive regarded her for a silent moment. "You." He pointed at Rebecca. "You lead the ladies to the house. My men won't bother you. We don't have any argument with Anna Grove and her brood."

Rebecca glanced in Jen's direction as if looking for permission.

"Go," Jen said to the young bride while her gaze held Clive's. She prayed he meant what he said. She knew from her reading that sometimes the Confederate irregulars were surprisingly gallant toward women. Sometimes they were not. "Go on. Get out of here."

Without further delay, all four girls ran out the door and turned toward the house. Jen peered out to watch them. None of Cutthroat Clive's men made a move to stop the women. On the back porch, the door opened quickly and the girls disappeared safely inside.

"Now," Clive said, pulling Jen back into the dark depths of the mill. "I just bet you know more about where those guns are than you're owning up to."

"I honestly don't know anything," Jen parried, playing for time now. Bennett and the rest of his men must be somewhere near. Or something was wrong. He took his responsibilities too seriously—and he loved Apple Grove House too much—to have deserted them. "Why would the captain tell me where the guns are? He doesn't trust anybody. I saw the cider barrels filled as we worked. That's how I know there are no guns in them."

She started to add that Bennett thought her a spy but

thought better of it. Instead, she added, "If you want to know where the guns are, why don't you ask your spy?"

A malevolent grin suddenly lit Clive's face. "Just what do you know about my spy?"

"Only that there is one," Jen said. "If he told you the guns are here, he must know where they are."

Morrison went to the door and called out to one of his men. "Bring me the sergeant."

"Dunham?" Jen gasped, stunned at the sight of Clive's men dragging the sergeant into the cider mill. His hat was gone and his uniform ripped. His shoulder glistened in the torchlight. She realized Dunham was wounded. A sickening feeling curled in her gut.

If they'd wounded and captured Dunham, what about Bennett? The historical account she'd read claimed nobody died in the raid—she was certain of that. Nor had the account identified the traitor.

"All right, sergeant," Clive said, as soon as his men halted before him. Dunham sagged between the two raiders, held on his feet only by their grip on each arm. "Where are the guns? You sent us a message saying they are here. Where?"

"Where's my pay?" Dunham rasped as he raised his battered head. He seemed little concerned about Jen's presence.

Clive slapped him. "I ain't got the money now. Fess up."

The sergeant's head snapped back, then forward again. But Dunham made no sound.

Jen's neck hurt just at the sight of the violence. She began to ease her way farther back into the shadows, hoping Cutthroat Clive had forgotten her.

Clive stepped up to the sergeant, grabbed the man's hair, and yanked his head up until they stood eye to bleary eye. "Spit out the location or I'll take you out to the orchard and hang you from one of those pretty little trees. You'll dangle there with your toes just touching the ground until you scream it out."

"You'll never be able to get the guns out before Vance gets you," Dunham muttered between swollen lips. "They're buried too deep."

"Getting them out isn't what I'm here to do," Clive said between barred teeth. "Where are they?"

"Clive?" shouted one of the men in the yard. Rifle in hand, he ran up to the door. "Clive, they've spotted troops coming up from the south. And I don't hear any gunfire on the north road either. Vance may have broken through."

Had Bennett been trapped up north? Jen wondered, relieved to think that he was all right.

"I don't have any more time to waste." Clive returned to Dunham and hit him again. The smack echoed throughout the mill. Then he yanked the sergeant's hair once more. "Where, damn it? Where are the guns and ammo buried? You best tell me, traitor, because you ain't going to get nothing for your silence but sorrow."

"Behind the mill," Dunham whimpered. "We dug into the hillside and buried the boxes there."

"All of it is there?" Clive demanded.

"Yes," Dunham said. "Guns and ammunition in the same hole."

Clive stepped back. He made a quick motion with his hand. The men holding Dunham immediately released their prisoner and backed away from him. Before Jen realized what was happening, Clive drew his gun and shot Dunham. The sergeant's body jerked. Then he dropped to the ground like a boneless scarecrow.

Bile rose in Jen's throat and she choked it back. She swayed for a moment in a nightmare world of darkness and guilt. She clutched at her throat. A sob of terror escaped her. Nobody was supposed to die. She had been sure of that. Nobody died in this raid. Was this her fault?

She dashed toward Dunham, daring to believe that he might still be alive, but Clive seized her arm and swung her around to face him.

"Lead the way to the back of the mill, missy," he demanded, his revolver flashing in the torchlight as he slipped it back into his holster. Gripping her by the upper arm he shoved her toward the mill door. "The sergeant don't need your help anymore."

Jen stumbled out of the door and into the night with only Clive's painful grip to steady her. In the yard she could see that the house was shuttered up. On the roof and at the attic windows, she could see the gun barrels of Bennett's four men, who were holding the guerrillas at bay. She was thankful for that. The girls, Anna, and the children were safe in the house.

Morrison gave her another little shove so that she stumbled out into full view of the soldiers in the house. But he held her in front of him.

"Fire on us and you'll hit the captain's lady," Clive shouted to Bennett's men.

The man on the roof waved. "We'll hold our fire as long as you hold yours. Don't you hurt the lady. Captain Vance would take exception."

"I bet he would," Clive called back. Then he twisted one of Jen's arms behind her back and leaned so close she smelled his rotten breath. "Keep me safe, missy."

He pushed her again, but without releasing her. Jen stumbled along toward the back of the mill. Angry and ashamed of being used as a shield, she marched, her head bowed. She racked her brain for a clue about what she should do next. She didn't have a single idea. What's more, she was uncertain about Clive's plan. Was he going to dig up the guns and the ammo and load them on a wagon or what?

At the back of the mill, he stopped to gape at the pyramid of apple baskets next to a towering stack of orange pumpkins. All week, farmers had been arriving with wagonloads of the fall produce to sell to Anna or to ship downriver. If the firearms were buried here, they were under the stack of pumpkins and apple-filled baskets.

Clive cursed aloud. He shoved Jen away from him now that they were out of range of the house.

"Tom, get more shovels. Bill, you and Dave start throwing the pumpkins over there," the determined raider ordered. "Get more men and start moving those apples."

"Yes, sir," Tom said.

Clive turned to another man. "Sam, where are those troops you said were sighted?"

"They're nearing the river," Sam said.

Clive cursed viciously again. "Forget the pumpkins, Bill. Look for loose dirt and dig there. Dave, get the dynamite."

"Yes, sir," Dave said. "It's in my saddlebags."

"Sure would have liked to have these guns," Clive said. "But if we can't have them, the Yankees ain't going to have them either."

Dave disappeared in the direction of the horses being held by the other guerrillas.

In the meantime, another man joined the first two. They were digging hastily at the edge of the apple-basket pyramid. The excavation deepened rapidly. Jen prayed they found nothing, but she was almost certain the guns were there. She remembered the dirt being disturbed just before Bennett's men began to help the farmers unload their harvest onto the ground.

Jen had no idea what Clive planned to do. But if it had

to do with dynamite, it wasn't going to be good for Apple Grove House or the people in it or Bennett.

"Why wouldn't they bury the arms down by the river?" Jen said, trying to gain time. "Do you have men looking down there?"

Clive cast her a skeptical glance. "I believe Dunham. Enlisted Yankees don't have enough imagination to be good liars."

A shout from the direction of the digging distracted Clive.

"We hit something, Clive," one of the men said. "A wood box. This has got to be it."

"Let me see." Clive charged off in their direction and jumped down into the hole they had already dug.

Now was her chance to run to the house and gain safety. But if she did she'd never know what they were doing or what Clive planned. Jen turned toward the river for a glimpse of the troops Clive's men had said were on the way, but she saw nothing.

"Wire it," Clive shouted, climbing out of the hole. "Do it quick."

Jen saw Dave jump down into the pit. He carried a saddlebag over his shoulder. Then she understood. They were going to dynamite the guns and ammo. They were going to blow everything up—maybe even the cider mill and Apple Grove House.

She stood frozen, frantically searching her brain for a way to stop this madness. She started to go back to the mill for a shovel. Around her commands were shouted. Clive's men began to come out of hiding and find their horses. The raiders were preparing to make their getaway.

When Jen turned back toward the hole, she could see the four men's hats bobbing as they worked at whatever had to be done to make the explosion happen. Hesitant at first, then with growing determination, Jen raced to the hole. When she reached the edge, the men began to climb out, shoving her aside and scrambling as if their lives were threatened.

Clive grabbed her arm and pulled her away from the pit with him. "Now, you don't want to be anywhere near this place in a minute or two, missy."

Jen tried to resist him, but his grip was so firm he almost lifted her off the ground. She tiptoed along beside him, deciding perhaps it was better to waylay his suspicions by seeming to do what he said.

"Now, Clive?" Dave called by the time Jen and Clive had almost reached the lower corner of the mill. "You want me to light it now?"

Clive turned, swinging Jen around with him. She had a plain view of Dave standing with a torch in one hand and a long string she realized was a fuse in his other.

"Now, Dave. Light it now and let's get the hell out of here." Clive shoved Jen in the direction of the house. Suddenly she could hear the sound of galloping horses and of gunshots growing nearer.

Clive released her and mounted the big black horse Tom had brought up for him. "Give the captain a kiss for me, missy."

Then he reined his horse around and spurred it down the lane. His rabble of men followed, dust flying, hooves thundering, and torches glowing bloodred against the night sky.

Jen never spared the retreating raiders a second look. She hiked her skirts up above her knees and raced up the hill. Every step of the way she searched the darkness for the burning fuse. If she was quick enough, she could do it. She could do it. She could save the mill.

At the edge of the pit, she halted. For a moment, she

still did not spot it. All she saw was the corner of an ammo box jutting out of the dirt. Then sparks flashed against the darkness. She could hear the soft sputter of the gunpowder flaming its way closer and closer to the ammo box.

"Shoot!" Desperate, she scrambled into the hole, stepping over the edge, sliding down on her bottom, and ruining her shoes. But she paid no heed to the damage. Her feet-first plunge had sent soil flying. Without the torches, the hole was inky blackness. The fuse disappeared. Where was it? In the dirt? Under her? She scrambled to her knees, her fingers searching through the dirt. Nothing.

But now she could hear the fuse burning. Panic clutched at her heart. Fingers spread, she sifted through the dirt, again and again. But no fuse.

Then something thumped her soundly on the back of the head. She glanced up over her shoulder in time to see a basket of apples from the pyramid above, descending on her. She ducked, but was inundated by an avalanche of fruit. But she kept digging. Apples pummeled on her back, but she refused to be deterred.

"I will find it," she muttered over and over. She reached for the edge of the box. Time was growing short. She ignored the apples pounding down on her. "I will find it. I will."

"Jennifer?" Bennett's voice reached her in the darkness. "What the hell?"

Relief rushed through her. She had no idea where he had come from, but she needed his help. "The fuse," she shouted. "I've got to pull the fuse. But it's so dark. And the apples. It's here somewhere."

Suddenly the pit was crowded with Bennett's solid body. Immediately the pounding of apples against her back ceased as he sheltered her from the onslaught.

"Get out of here," he ordered, pulling at her shoulders.

"No. I can find it," she insisted. Still, she groped. Then she felt it. Tight and sharp against her palm. The fire stung her, but she didn't care.

"I've got it," she cried in victory. With all her might, she hauled back on the fuse, throwing herself against Bennett and yanking the burning fuse free of the ammo box. The sparks sputtered in her hands, then died.

Jen released a long slow breath and collapsed into the bottom of the pit.

Bennett's arms surrounded her and she felt his lips against her temple.

"I did it," she whooped, elated and exhausted all at once. "I did it. I saved the cider mill. We're going to be okay." Then she remembered where she was and whose arms were surrounding her. Her head came up so quickly that she caught his chin.

With a groan, he released her and rubbed his jaw.

She leaned back against the dirt wall of the pit and regarded him with pure indignation. "Where in the hell have you been?"

Chapter Nine

"You were right about Morrison's raiders attacking from the north." Bennett unbuttoned his shirt and pulled it off as he prepared to wash. Just enough light streamed through the kitchen window onto the porch for Jen to admire the contours of his muscular chest and robust biceps. Perched on a stool with a fresh towel in her hands, she was eager to find out just what had happened, but she didn't mind enjoying this intimate view of Bennett either.

She'd already bathed and then helped Anna settle the brides on pallets in the parlor. The girls were remarkably calm after the raiders' attack, but none wanted to return to the mill for the remainder of the night.

Bennett had already met with the major of the troops from Fort Scott and together they had posted additional sentries for the rest of the night, though no one expected Cutthroat Clive to return. The household was settling down to get a few more hours of sleep before dawn.

Bennett reached for the cake of soap on the washstand and began to lather his face and arms. Jen watched, hypnotized by the rivulets of soapy water trailing over his collarbone, down his bare chest, and dripping from his dark curly chest hair. She sighed and licked her lips. His maleness never failed to thrill her.

"I won't ask you how you knew the attack would come from the north," Bennett continued, scrubbing behind his ears and down the back of his neck like a schoolboy, unaware of his fascinated audience. "I don't think I want to know. But on the chance you were right, I rode north with several men. We practically rode right into Morrison. We were outnumbered and they pinned us down for longer than I'd expected. But if we hadn't been up there and run into them, Morrison would have taken us by surprise in our beds."

"Do you still think I'm a spy?" Jen asked, her back straightening with pride.

"You are *not* a spy," he admitted, pausing long enough to meet her gaze, honestly, openly.

A smile of relief crept across Jen's lips. His expression was the closest thing to an apology she'd get from him, she suspected. But she was satisfied.

He scooped up a handful of water and splashed it onto his face. "Dunham is going to pay for what he did."

"I can't believe he's still alive," Jen said with a shudder. The sight of seeing a man—even a spy—shot before her eyes had left her chilled and shaken. It reminded her that things could have turned out much worse. "I thought Dunham was dead for sure when Clive fired at him."

"It's a bad wound, but Anna thinks he'll live," Bennett said, reaching for the towel. "It was probably dark and Morrison was hurried and careless. All to Dunham's benefit."

"But when I saw him lying there and thought he was dead," Jen said with a shiver, "I thought it was my fault. I thought I'd changed history somehow."

Bennett paused, the towel in his hand, and water dripping from his strong jaw. He studied her for a long, significant moment, his eyes narrowing. "You're not going to give up on this time thing, are you?"

"Whatever made you think I would?" Jen asked, realizing that she might be cleared of espionage, but Bennett didn't necessarily believe everything she claimed.

Bennett put the towel to his face and continued. "And Will Johnson will face charges for leaving his post."

"Will? He was just trying to defend the house," Jen protested, shocked that Bennett would be so harsh on the young guard, who had unwittingly allowed her to escape. "It was chaos around here, Bennett. There was no way that poor boy was going to keep me in that room when I could hear the shooting outside. You can't hold him responsible for what happened."

"If he'd been where he should have been, you wouldn't have been held hostage by Morrison or have crawled down into that pit after the dynamite fuse." His voice had become harsh with anger. "You could have been killed, Jennifer."

Shocked by his vehemence, Jen stared at him. "Bennett, we all could have been killed. There was nothing special about my particular circumstances."

He lowered the towel and glared at her as though he wanted to argue more, but thought better of it. "If you'd been in the house under guard as I'd ordered, everything would have been different."

"If I'd been in the house where you wanted me, the cider mill would have been blown to smithereens," Jen replied, annoyed with his refusal to recognize her help.

"Your precious guns would be mangled and there would be no ammunition."

He glared at her a moment longer, as if she were a willful child who was not to be reasoned with. He threw aside the towel and reached for the clean shirt she held for him.

"There was nothing I could have done for Dunham," Jen said, mentally reviewing events. "But you've got to admit that I saved your guns and I did save the mill."

"You did save the mill," he agreed, as he pulled on the fresh shirt and began to button it without looking at her. "But you took a terrible risk."

"You take risks every day," Jen said.

"I'm a soldier and that's my job," Bennett said, his eyes flashing with anger again.

"And is your job to protect me?" Jen snapped though she was amused by his old-fashioned male protectiveness— and a bit touched by it, too.

"Is there something wrong with that?" Bennett snapped back, clearly offended.

"Nothing, except it's ridiculous." Jen said, becoming offended also. "Especially when I remember that you thought me a spy only twenty-four hours ago."

"I thought *you might be dead* only an hour ago," Bennett threw back, his voice low and husky. He met her gaze again. The pain in it astonished Jen. "And I didn't like the feeling."

Instantly she recalled her desolation when she thought of him hurt somewhere along the road and she couldn't get to him. She whispered, "I was afraid for you too."

"Jennifer." Bennett knelt down on one knee and took her hand. He held it firmly as he spoke, his head bowed over their clasped hands.

Jen stared down at the top of his head, his dark hair still wet and mussed.

"I can't begin to tell you how I almost panicked when I realized Cutthroat Clive and his men had managed to pin us down and skirt around us," Bennett said. "I knew he was here at the house. I didn't give a damn what happened to Apple Grove House or the guns and ammunition. All I could think of was you. I should have known you weren't the spy. I knew you'd talk back to Morrison. I knew he'd threaten you if he fancied you were my wife."

"Everything turned out all right," Jen reassured him, the depth of his words almost bringing tears to her eyes. She touched the top of his head gently, his hair warm and coarse between her fingers. "I was afraid for you, too. I knew how this raid was supposed to turn out, but I couldn't be sure . . . and I thought if you had . . . Oh, Bennett."

He turned his face up to hers. She bent over him, longing to brush her lips against his, this time with the passion his lips had promised earlier at the spring.

"Well, you two," announced Anna, emerging from the kitchen with a coal-oil lamp in her hand. "I have a full house."

Jen withdrew her hand. Bennett sprang to his feet.

"I've got Sergeant Dunham on a cot in the kitchen," Anna said, a smile of indulgence on her lips. "I'll watch over him during the rest of the night. The new troopers are bunking on the porch, Captain. So you've lost your cot out there. Unless you want to sleep with the snoring enlisted men when you have a perfectly lovely wife in a bed upstairs."

At the suggestion, Jen and Bennett stared at each other.

A blush stung Jen's cheeks. She prayed it wasn't evident in the dim light. But the idea of spending the night in Bennett's arms didn't trouble her one bit. But what did he think? Apologizing for thinking that she was the spy was important. But it was hardly a declaration of love. She turned away, fearing that he would see the eagerness in her eyes.

Bennett shook his head. "Anna, you know that was a proxy wedding."

Anna laughed. "Only if there is a husband to show up and fill your place. And I sure haven't seen anyone. Is there someone in that room up there that we don't know about, Jennifer?"

"No, of course not," Jennifer said, but she would not pressure Bennett into sharing a room with her. "Perhaps I could sleep in the children's room or with the girls in the parlor so the captain can have a good bed for the night."

"No, no need for that," Bennett said, suddenly restless and moving away from Jen. "I'm sure we can come to some arrangement."

"Of course," Jen stammered, baffled by what he might intend.

"Here's a lamp to take up to your room," Anna said.

Bennett accepted it. Then he took Jen's hand and led her into the house.

Upstairs Jen stood in the middle of the tiny room, while Bennett closed the door behind them. Without saying anything, he set the lamp on the table and blew it out.

"We can make a pallet for me to sleep on the floor," Jen offered hastily. After all, the man had not said that he wanted to share a bed with her.

Jen watched him make his way across the room toward the bed and sink down on the edge of it. His shadow was barely discernible against the others in the room. He reached out, pulling her down beside him.

"Why worry about a pallet when we have a perfectly

good bed right here," he said. "After tonight, I'm not entrusting you to another guard or a lonely bed."

Relief flooded through Jen. "That works for me."

He bent his head down over hers. His beard was rough against her temple. Eager to feel his warmth, to have some hint of the expression on his face, she inched her hand up his chest to touch his face. Her finger lightly grazed his lips.

He moaned. The sound rumbled from deep inside him, a faraway sound. Possessively he drew her against his chest. She could feel the solid beating of his heart. He held her there for several heartbeats. Then he tilted her head back. Jen allowed her head to fall back in wanton invitation. His mouth descended on her throat, trailing hot kisses upward along her jaw and to her mouth. Jen gave herself up to the power of the passion.

He paused when he reached her mouth; then his lips parted. His tongue delved into the most intimate depths of her, exploring secret places, stroking with feverish heat. Jen clung to him, her senses humming deliciously. The kiss went on, gaining in ardor with each sweep of his tongue until she thought she had no existence, no being beyond this sweet moment in time.

Suddenly he released her. She gasped for breath and a chill swept over her. Only the warmth of his hand soaked into her bare shoulder. She realized that somehow Bennett had slipped her dress and her bra straps from her shoulder. He bared her breast and lowered her to the pillow. A moan escaped her as his hands brushed over her nakedness, molding his fingers to her shape. His thumbs grazed her nipples, teasing them to aching peaks. Then he lowered his head to her. The hot wash of his tongue tugged at her, a torturous caress, delivered with agonizing slowness that left her mindless.

She longed to hold him against her, but she couldn't because he had pinned her arms to her sides. Her blood pumped hot and quick through her veins, but she had neither the strength nor the will to move against his restraint. Under his mouth, her breast swelled and grew heavy.

When he eased himself on top of her, she welcomed his weight. His lips found hers again. His tongue stole into her mouth, but gently this time, a cunning intruder. He was delicious: apples, leather, and soap; heat and passion.

"Have you been wanting me as much as I've wanted you?" Bennett breathed into her ear, his tongue teasing her lobe.

"Yes, oh, yes," she whispered. "From the moment I saw you."

"And to think we've wasted all this time," his said, his voice full of amused regret. He sat up briefly, stripping off his shirt. Jen heard the clang of his metal belt buckle being unfastened, then watched his dark outline as he stood long enough to step out of his trousers.

Then he was with her on the bed again, his skin warm against hers. His hands slipped downward, encouraging her to raise her hips and allow him to slip her dress, petticoats, and panties off. Suddenly she was naked and vulnerable beneath him. But his touch was tender. Every contact with him sent fiery thrills through her body—even his kiss brushed along her collarbone and tingled in her toes. She gasped when his hair tickled her belly. When his tongue warmed her navel, she arched against him, longing for more. He did not disappoint her. He touched every part of her, even the secret parts, encouraging her to open for him so he could kiss the insides of her thighs.

The endearments he whispered made her feel sexy and loved. When he opened his hand over her mound, she pressed against him again, relishing and cherishing the slow, circling caress that consumed her in a fiery sweetness.

Gentle, investigative fingers stroked her, drawing surprising wetness from her depths and bringing swirling pleasure to her belly. And the overwhelming desire to find her completeness by holding him inside her grew and morphed into a need so strong she ached for him.

She reached for him, tugging gently on his hair and drawing him to her mouth again. He released her arms and kissed her briefly before he covered her—completely this time.

Penetration was slow and sweet. She savored it. The sweetness of it made her sigh. She moved with him, rocking. With a final thrust, the exhilaration of his steely manhood buried tightly inside her snatched away her breath.

Weak and supple in the glow of her pleasure, she let him gather her beneath him, positioning her for comfort and the utmost sensation. Random kisses fell on her throat, her face, her breasts, burning against her skin. She reveled in their heat.

She lost herself in the rhythm that rocked their bodies together in oneness. His strokes were sure and deep, slow at first, deliciously erotic. Then their rhythm gathered momentum. Sweet demand urged Jen on, seeking the completion she knew he could give her. Suddenly the spiral wound tight inside her burst free.

Jen cried out softly. Her body convulsed. Waves of glorious release swept over her, again and again. She thought it would never end. She prayed it would never end. Her life would forever soar at this pinnacle of pleasure. Then, slowly, it slipped away. She gasped for breath. Bennett's voice reached her, tender and reassuring.

His body tensed. He groaned, his breath hot against her ear. He whispered her name. Against the walls of her womb, she felt each eruption of his love. Replete, but greedy, her body fused around him.

They remained locked in each other's arms for a long time. Jen even fell asleep, then awoke when he moved to her side. He gathered her up in his arms and both fell asleep with his lips pressed against her shoulder.

They awoke just as the watery light of dawn crept between the slats of the shutters. They made love again. No words. Slow, sweet, and tender caresses. Incredible pleasure. Where had Bennett been all her life?

Jen awoke. Her eyes snapped open, but she did not move. She did not want to disturb Bennett. She did not want to lose the pleasure of his arm lying heavy across her waist and his knee inserted between hers.

"Zach Schuster comes back today with his camera," Bennett said without opening his eyes.

"I know," Jen said, surprised that he was awake.

"That's what you've been waiting for all week," he said, still without moving.

"Yes, well, I know now that the danger is over here." Jen closed her eyes and longed for their lovemaking to have changed the world as it had changed her heart, her life. "But where I came from the danger still exists. I think."

She opened her eyes and a small laugh escaped her. "I have seen the enemy and he's a Confederate raider. Wouldn't Ted Neisen love that? But I'm sure he'd trade in the ammo belts for something more dapper, like a uniform with shiny buttons and gold epaulettes."

Bennett opened his eyes at last. He regarded her solemnly, the hazel of his eyes dark, soft, curious. "What are you afraid this Ted is going to do to Apple Grove House?"

"He will turn it into a gift shop full of Beanie Babies, coffee mugs, baseball caps, and gummy bears," Jen said.

"Beanie Babies?" He raised a questioning brow and smiled. "As bad as that?"

"Never mind. You have no idea," Jen said as her frustration with Ted Neisen took shape in her head once again. "He's not going to destroy the house per se. Not at first anyway. He's just going to destroy the essence of Apple Grove House. The tradition of understanding our heritage will disappear. The pleasure of savoring the smells and the joy of working in an orchard and being close to the land. The satisfaction of learning how to make good use of what is at hand. I suppose if you've been shot at and about blown away by dynamite, the house being turned into a shop doesn't seem like such a terrible fate."

Outside the rooster crowed and the bugler sounded reveille, but still Bennett did not move. "You know what else will be on that steamboat today?" he asked with closed eyes again.

Jen rose on her elbow so she could see his face, so she could admire that strong jaw with the dark overnight dusting of a beard on it. "What?"

"My mustering-out papers."

Jen hesitated. She wasn't certain what he was talking about.

"My discharge papers," Bennett explained. "Believe it or not, this country is willing to be shed of me, even during a war."

Insulted on his behalf, Jen sat up, clutching the sheet to her breasts. "But why?"

"I've served my time," Bennett said, still without moving. "I could reenlist, but I've had my fill of the army and its arrogant officers. I've risked my life and spilled my blood once for this country in the Mexican War."

Jen stroked the long scar on his thigh, wishing she could have been there to help him.

"I have nothing to prove to the military anymore. I'd rather stay here, near Apple Grove House, or go west."

"Don't you have family or someone in Pennsylvania?" Jennifer asked, troubled by the thought that he was so alone in this world.

"No. At least no one close," Bennett said. "My brothers took over the family farm, and they are busy with their own families. There's no one who would be glad to see me."

"Then come with me," Jen suggested softly, almost unwilling to believe how perfect the solution was. Bennett Vance was just what Apple Grove House needed. He was just what she needed. "Come back to 1999 with me."

Chapter Ten

Bennett opened his eyes at last to look at the first woman he'd ever loved enough to spend the rest of his life with. Everything that had happened to him before—the first courtship, the marriage, the divorce—that had all been youthful folly. But Jennifer was the real thing. At last he understood that funny old saying married folks used about their better half. The feeling defied logic, but he knew Jennifer was his.

Strange how she'd appeared at this turning point in his life. It was as if the army had been taken away and Jennifer given to him instead. The thought of parting from her was distinctly unpleasant—almost frightening. But she had this crazy notion. "Jennifer, what you are telling me about yourself and time is impossible. Surely you understand that."

"I would have said the same myself a week ago," she said, sitting in the middle of the bed with the sheets gathered close. Excitement lighted her oval face and womanly satisfaction glowed in her cheeks. Her golden hair hung over her shoulder and drew his gaze toward the sheet pressed to her breasts. Bennett took a deep breath to still the desire that stirred in him. Reveille had been called, but he wanted to pull her down into bed with him again. Duty be damned. He reached for her.

"Bennett, listen." She grinned that vital grin of hers and playfully swatted his hand away. "Now think about it. There is something about this place that allows for weird things to happen in time. It has to do with cameras. But besides that, think! If you were with me in my time, we could save Apple Grove House from becoming another side show at an amusement park. We'd get the cider mill to produce a drink that would bring people from all over Kansas to buy it. Maybe we could start a restaurant and expand the craft festivals. Halloween events. A Thanksgiving connection. Private parties. Hayrides."

She was gazing off into space, spinning plans for things he barely understood. "We'll find quilters and wood carvers. A blacksmith. That would be good and a ferrier so the kids could see him shoe a horse. I never knew there was a difference between a blacksmith and a ferrier until I came here. We'll make coming to Apple Grove House a trip back into time for the whole family. A journey to meet our heritage."

Pleased with her own ideas, she grabbed Bennett's arm and attempted to shake him. "Bennett, you have to come with me."

Bennett freed himself from her grip and laid his forearm across his eyes. She had a valid point when she brought up the camera and the light. "What troubles me is I almost understand what you're saying."

"Then why the hesitation?" she asked, her winged brows

crowded together in puzzlement. "You don't have any obligations here. Get your mustering whatever papers and come with me."

"Jennifer." Bennett shook his head. "Even if the time thing is true, what makes you think Zach Schuster's camera can do it this time when it couldn't before?"

The light went out of Jennifer's brown eyes and the joy vanished from her face.

Bennett muttered a curse but went on. "Think this through. Even if you could stand up in front of Schuster's camera and the magnesium light again and it does flash you back to where you came from, what makes you think I could do it, too? What if the light only takes one of us?"

"I don't know." She frowned in confusion. "I know it sounds crazy. Believe me, I know. But it's the only explanation I have. And why wouldn't it work for you, too?"

"I don't know how or why it happened in the first place," Bennett said, as unhappy with the prospect as she appeared to be. "You've got to admit there are a lot of unknowns here."

"I never thought of the limitations." Jennifer shook her head. "No, no. Don't even think that you can't come with me."

"But it is a possibility we would have to consider. We could stand in front of that camera and be parted forever."

"Bennett, I have to go back," Jennifer said. "I don't know what to expect when we get back. Lord, I wonder if my sister Jessica has reported me missing. Old Ted Neisen is probably rubbing his hands together in delight. With no opposition, he has probably ordered his theme park engineers and banking team to move full speed ahead. He probably has a groundbreaking scheduled."

It was a crazy story—an amusement park and a high-handed land developer—but Bennett had come to almost accept it himself—because Jennifer so sincerely believed it, if for no other reason. "You're Neisen's only opposition?" Bennett asked.

"There are others," Jennifer said. "But none of them have the resources to pull things together like I've done. The media, the fund-raising, the support from celebrity names. Saving Apple Grove House in 1999 isn't going to be as easy as pulling a fuse off a couple of sticks of dynamite."

Bennett closed his eyes against the heart-stopping vision of Jennifer turning to him with the explosives in one hand and the broken fuse in the other. Everything could have ended in that one moment, but it hadn't. It hadn't. "So you think I can help by making cider in 1999."

"Oh, yeah, and by posing for some of the publicity," Jennifer said, a curious smile returning to her face. "There won't be a woman in Kansas City who will be able to resist those good looks of yours."

Bennett laughed, surprised by how easy it was to banter with her. "You can't win me over with flattery."

"I'll win you anyway I can, Captain." Jennifer leaned nearer and kissed him on the nose. "Come with me. Come with me and I'll show you the wonders of the future," she pleaded.

"Jennifer, if I go with you, assuming this moving in time is possible as you claim, it won't be to see the wonders of the future," Bennett said, finally getting to the point that troubled him most.

She sobered. "What then?"

Bennett took a deep breath. He'd confessed his feelings once before to a woman—to his first wife—and he'd been sorry. Painfully sorry. "Jennifer, if I stand in front of the camera, if we make the attempt to go back to where you came from, it will be because we love each other."

"Is any other reason acceptable?" she asked lightly, then leaned close once more. There was no mistaking the love shining in her velvet brown eyes. "I do love you, Captain Vance. I don't know where you've been all my life or how I got here to meet you. But I love you. If you want, if doing what I ask seems too crazy— Heavens, I can't believe I'm saying this." She paused to take a deep breath and she touched his face, cupping his chin in her hands. "But I mean every word, Bennett. If you want, I'll stay here with you."

His heart lurched. He closed his eyes and kissed the thumb that pressed against his mouth. *I must be crazy,* he told himself, but he smiled. Then he whispered against the warm pads of her fingers, "Sweetheart, I suppose you want me to wear my dress uniform for the photograph?"

"Oh, yes," she whispered as she leaned nearer and pulled the sheet away from between their naked bodies. "Wear your dress uniform and your hat with that glorious *big* plume."

"Now, I can't promise anything," Zach Schuster said for the third time as he steadied one of the legs of the wooden tripod that held the huge box camera. At his side, Bob, his apprentice, stood ready with the light-making machine. In front of the camera, Jen and Bennett stood posed against the hallway wall.

Jen was dressed in her wedding gown, with her hair up, and her veil on, just as she had been a week ago. Her white stockings were beyond repair, but Anna had loaned her a pair that would do. She'd brushed her stained shoes to make them presentable. They hardly qualified. But they'd have to do. All she cared about at the moment was that Bennett was beside her.

He looked fabulous in his uniform with his hair brushed back and his hat set rakishly at an angle. His mustering-out papers were signed and tucked into his pocket. His discharge was official and he was holding her hand, their fingers intertwined. Whatever happened, they were going to face it together. That was all that mattered.

"I may have no more luck getting a photograph this session than we had last week," Zach Schuster continued. "You can never tell here at Apple Grove House. Nobody has ever been able to explain why photography is so difficult here." He glanced in Anna's direction. "No offense, Mrs. Grove, but some photographers think there's some kind of Indian curse on the place."

Anna chuckled. "The Indians think photography is some kind of white man's curse."

"Can we just get on with it, Mr. Schuster?" Bennett said, squeezing Jen's hand. She didn't blame him for being apprehensive about what was about to happen. She had no idea what to expect either.

"Certainly, Captain," the photographer said. "Bob, light the machine."

"Yes, sir," the boy said, striking a match and putting it to the wire feeding from a wheel over a tray. A flame sizzled into brightness, then glowed unsteadily.

"Now, remember," Schuster called from under the black camera cape. "Don't move for twenty seconds from the time I tell you."

"Okay," Jen said, drawing in a deep breath and praying that this was going to work. Beside her, she felt Bennett tense. She reached for his hand. He accepted hers, his grip tight and resolute. Time would have to rip them apart, but Jen prayed silently that they would not lose each other, whatever was to come.

Anna stepped forward. "Wait, Jen, do you want your

wedding bouquet? I know it doesn't look pretty like a fresh one, but a bride should have her flowers in her picture."

Jen started. She wanted her bouquet. Even if it was dried and crumbling, the fresh beauty of it gone forever, the memories would still cling to it.

"Too late, Mrs. Grove," Schuster said as he snatched the cover from the camera lens. "The light is burning and we are exposing the plate. Don't move. Four. Five. Six . . ."

Jen stiffened and held her breath. Bennett squeezed her hand.

The magnesium wire sputtered; the light wavered. Jen thought it was about to go out. But it continued to burn, sputtering, then flaring. She held her breath and kept her gaze on the camera lens. She didn't know what else to do to make this work. Bennett's hand still gripped hers. A sudden pop cracked from the light machine. Then a white light washed all images out of Jen's vision.

Joey stared at the camera lying on the floor in the parlor corner, where he'd thrown it only twenty minutes earlier. He'd come back to the parlor to see if Aunt Jen might have come back somehow. His mom was so upset about being unable to find her that Joey knew there was going to be trouble if he didn't do something fast. But the parlor was empty. Aunt Jen still wasn't here.

Outside, the video camera crew was everywhere taking pictures. That Kelly lady said the cameras were working now. The wedding guests were already eating and drinking. Mom had given them the go-ahead. Joey pouted. Earlier she'd told him he couldn't have anything until after the ceremony.

"Just a slight delay," she'd explained to the guests and given them that polite smile of hers. "Nothing serious."

Then she'd turned away, frantically searching through
the house, the cider mill, and even the caterer's van—but
no Aunt Jen. She'd finally told Dad. When she had, her
face was white and all worked up as if she was going to
cry—Joey had never seen his mom cry. That was when he
really got scared. That was when he knew he had to do
something.

In the parlor, Joey looked around to be certain that no
one was watching him. All the grown-ups, except for his
mom and dad, were at the food table or at the fancy cider
fountain, drinking like fish. Slowly Joey bent to pick up
the camera.

It was cool to his touch. In his hands, it appeared just
as innocent as it had before Aunt Jen had disappeared in
its flash. Joey turned it over again. Nothing about it seemed
strange or weird. It didn't glow or hum or throb like weird
things did in the movies or on TV. It just looked like an
ordinary camera, like all the other ones on the guest tables.

When he'd been outside he'd watched that Ted guy
whom Mom and Aunt Jen didn't like pick up a camera
just like this one and aim it at some of the guests. Joey
had waited with his heart in his throat as Ted aimed it at
the smiling people. Joey had almost hollered, "Wait, don't
do that." But he hadn't. He wanted to see what happened.
The people pressed together with glasses raised and toothy
grins. *Flash.*

Not a one of them had disappeared. Joey frowned. They
were still there, eating all the cheese puffs—his favorite—
and talking too loud as grown-ups did when they'd been
drinking.

No one had left. No one had disappeared. They were
all still waiting for Aunt Jen and that Brad guy to show up
so Reverend Gleeson could marry them.

Joey knew he had to do something. Aunt Jen would be

so disappointed to have missed her own wedding. And he couldn't bear to see his mother so upset. Hesitantly he walked to the spot where he'd stood when he took the picture. Raising the camera to his right eye, he peered through the viewfinder at the mantel, where Aunt Jen had been standing. He remembered that the brown flowers in the glass dome thing had been in the frame. He adjusted the view so he could see the dried thing inside the picture box.

"Well, here goes," he muttered to himself. Taking a deep breath to steel himself against the explosion of light, he clicked the button. A flash. The camera made a sound as if taking a normal picture, then . . .

Nothing. The parlor remained empty.

"Shoot," Joey grumbled, examining the camera in his hands again. Then he put it to his ear, listening carefully. "Shoot and double shoot. Are you in there, Aunt Jen? I'm trying to get you out."

But the camera gave no hint that Aunt Jen might be inside.

"Okay, I'll give it three tries," Joey said. "That was one. . . ."

"Joey? What are you doing?"

He whipped around to see his mother standing in the parlor doorway. "I'm just taking some pictures of Aunt Jen's favorite room."

"Okay," Mom said, glancing down the hallway and out the door at the wedding guests. "You haven't seen her, have you?"

Joey shook his head.

"If you do, you tell her to see me right away," Mom said.

"Sure, Mom."

When she was gone, Joey aimed the camera at the mantel. "Please, Aunt Jen. Come back. Pleeease."

Click. No flash. Nothing.

"Oooh," Joey cried in frustration. He glared at the camera again, wondering if there was a special button to push—a setting—to make people who'd disappeared come back. All he saw was the little light that told him the camera was ready to take another picture. A terrifying thought descended on him. What if Aunt Jen never came back? Impossible. He looked at the little window and saw that there were three more pictures to take. Surely that meant he still had a chance to bring her back. "Okay, I'll do this until she comes back. This has got to work."

He braced his feet on the very spot where he'd first photographed Aunt Jen, put the camera to his eye, adjusted the viewfinder so that he saw it was exactly the same picture frame as before. He snapped the button twice more. Nothing. Only one picture left.

"Here goes nothing," he muttered and clicked the button for the last time.

Poof! The room went bright white.

Chapter Eleven

Joey dropped the camera and tried to shield his eyes from the blinding light. It almost hurt, just like before when Aunt Jen had disappeared. And there was no sound.

"Aunt Jen?" he called, his hands pressed against his eyes, leaving him still unable to see. "Aunt Jen? Are you back?"

"Joey?" a strange, faraway voice called.

Joey froze, uncertain that it sounded like Aunt Jen.

"Joey, is that you?" Closer this time. And sounding more like her. It had to be Aunt Jen.

Suddenly tears filled his eyes. Arms wide, he stumbled in the direction of her voice. When he encountered a set of legs, he wrapped his arms around them and pressed his cheek against the warm, firm thigh. "Oh, Aunt Jen. I'm so glad to see you. Where have you been? Mom is looking for you. And she's so upset."

"Uh, son?" questioned a deep voice.

A big hand descended on Joey's head. He opened his eyes to see blue cloth and black boots. Not Aunt Jen's white satin skirt.

Instantly he released the leg and stumbled backward, staring upward. "Who . . . ?"

Before him stood the neatest soldier with a wide-brim hat and a plume. Shiny brass buttons gleamed down the front of his blue coat, and a long silvery saber hung from the red sash at his waist.

"Cool," uttered Joey, impressed. "Who are you?"

"We made it," Aunt Jen cried, throwing herself into the soldier's arms. "I told you we would."

The soldier laughed, hugging Aunt Jen to him as if he knew her real well. "We made it, just like you told me," he repeated, then kissed Aunt Jen—a big smack right on her lips. Then they grinned at each other like smoochy grown-ups.

"Where have you been, Aunt Jen?" Joey demanded, tugging on her skirt and feeling a little betrayed. Obviously she'd been off having a good time somewhere.

Aunt Jen whirled around and looked down at him. She smiled that warm smile Joey knew was meant for him. "Joey, you're still here at Apple Grove House?"

He grinned back. "I'm glad you came back, but who is he?"

"This is Captain Bennett Vance," Aunt Jen said. She was standing with her arm tucked around the captain's. "Captain, my nephew, Joey."

"Hello, sir," Joey said. Inspired by the distinguished uniform, he stood up straight at what he thought was attention and saluted the captain. With all due gravity, the captain saluted back. Joey grinned. The stern-faced soldier grinned back at him. Joey liked the captain.

"What's going on?" Aunt Jen said, looking around the

parlor as if she'd not seen it for a long time. "It doesn't look like Ted Neisen has done anything to the house yet."

"Mom is in a panic about you disappearing," Joey said, wondering about the strange look of surprise in Aunt Jen's eyes. She would clear everything with Mom, wouldn't she? "Where'd you go?"

"A long way away, but I'm back now." Aunt Jen turned back to him and smiled as if she was really glad to see him. "Have I been gone long, Joey? Did your Mom notify the police?"

"No, not yet," Joey said, looking from Aunt Jen to the captain. They were acting really strange. "She's trying to keep the wedding guests happy. But if we don't tell her you're back soon, Reverend Gleeson will leave. Then she'll be really mad and there won't be any wedding."

"Joey, do you mean it's still my wedding day?" Aunt Jen asked, her eyes wide and her voice breathless.

Joey shrugged. "Well, what other day would it be?"

"Is it possible that I lived a week in 1863, but no time passed here in the present?" Jen exclaimed, unable to believe that her wedding guests still awaited her outside. She glanced at Bennett.

"I don't know. I just arrived here," said Bennett, who was looking around the parlor, his hand still holding hers fast. "How can you tell this isn't 1863?"

"Joey is here and there's a phone on the wall," Jen said, just as she noted that Joey was looking at her as if she was crazy.

"Mom is about to have a cow because the ceremony is going to be late and all the guests are already eating the food and Brad hasn't shown up. Reverend Gleeson said he has to leave soon, because he has another wedding today. Dad was trying to calm her down. We better go find her."

"Poor Jessica," Jen said, knowing her sister would expect a good explanation. "She must be frantic. What did she say when you told her the camera made me disappear?"

Guilt clouded Joey's face. He stuck his hands in his trouser pockets and toed some invisible speck on the floor. "I didn't tell her I made you disappear." His head came up. "I didn't mean to do it, Aunt Jen. The camera just—"

Moved by his confession, Jen reached out and touched Joey's cheek. "I know you didn't, Joey. It's okay. You don't have to say anything to your mother. I understand. We're here now, Captain Vance and I. Let's keep this our little secret for now."

His sweet freckled face brightened. "And we'll still have the wedding? I'll still walk down the aisle with the ring? See. I've got it here."

To Jen's astonishment, he pulled the wedding ring out of his pocket. The circle of diamonds she'd chosen for Brad to put on her finger glittered in the autumn sunlight falling through the windows.

"How did you get that?" she exclaimed, hardly aware of the sudden squeeze Bennett gave her hand. "Jessica wasn't supposed to give it to you until just before the music starts."

A devilish grin spread across Joey's face. "Oh, I have my ways." Then he seemed to think better of his bravado. "Mom doesn't know yet. She's been too busy looking for you to look in the ring box. You're still going to let me carry it, aren't you?"

"You may still carry it, soldier," Bennett said, smiling at Joey. "You shouldn't have taken it without your mother knowing. But your aunt and I trust it to your keeping. Go find your mother and tell her her sister wants to see her."

"Cool," Joey cried. then he snapped a boyish salute. "I mean, yes, sir." He dashed out of the room.

"You handled that well, Captain," Jen said, glad that Bennett and Joey liked each other. They were kindred arrogant male spirits. "But am I still discombobulated or did you just agree to go ahead with this wedding ceremony?"

"Why not?" Bennett said, smiling down at her. "Actually, we were married once. Remember Judge Tyler?"

"Of course, but— This is all happening so fast," Jen said. "This time-travel stuff is worse than any jet lag I ever had."

"Jet lag?" Bennett shook his head.

"We'll have to start a list of things for me to explain," Jen said, ready to accept going ahead with the wedding— with Bennett as her groom.

Jen looked up into his dark hazel eyes. She loved the depth and strength she always saw there. He was a courageous man, not just as an army officer. He had courage above and beyond the call of duty. He'd braved the mystery of traveling across time to be with her. "There's no going back from this wedding, Bennett," Jen said, remembering that he'd been married once before.

Bennett swooped down swiftly, giving her a light, sweet kiss. "I knew that last night."

"Well, there you are," rasped a familiar male voice Jen disliked. "Do you know your sister is looking for you?"

Jen jumped. She pulled away from Bennett and turned to find Ted Neisen standing in the door and holding a flute glass of bubbling apple wine in his hand.

Bennett turned, too. When he saw the man standing in the door, his face transformed into a mask of fury. "Morrison!" he snarled. "You son of a—" His hand went to his saber.

Ted paled and backed out the door.

"No, no." Jen put a hand on Bennett's arm to keep

him from drawing the weapon on Johnson County's most famous developer. "Bennett, this gentleman is Ted Neisen. It's all right, Ted, really. I'd like for you to meet my groom, Captain Bennett Vance."

"You're carrying the old-fashioned promotional theme a bit far with the soldier's thing, don't you think?" Ted said without making any effort to shake Bennett's hand. "I thought you were marrying Brad what's-his-name."

"Change of plans," Jen said, waving her hand airily and inwardly relishing the challenges ahead of her with Bennett. Life was miraculous. She'd found the love of her life, and with him, they were going to whip old Ted. Jen hugged Bennett's arm. "I rather like the soldier thing."

Ted looked nonplussed, but Jen didn't care. He'd find out soon enough that his plans for Apple Grove House were about to turn to dust.

Before Ted could reply, Kelly, the head of the video crew, rushed in.

"Here you are," Kelly screamed and jumped up and down like a tiny, mad jumping bean. Jen frowned at her undiluted joy.

"Kelly, get ahold of yourself," Jen said, trying to calm her photographer friend, who was as devoted to the Apple Grove House cause as Jen was.

"Hi, Ted," Kelly said, a malicious grin spreading across her face. "Just wanted to let you know the KSWB-TV's news truck just pulled up. Jen, your wedding is going to be aired on the six o'clock news!" Kelly began to screech and jump up and down again.

The confident grin fell from Ted's face. "Shit."

"I'll thank you to mind your language," Bennett warned, his hand inching toward his saber again. "There are ladies present."

Ted stared at Bennett as if he thought they'd all gone

mad. "You've gone too far, Jen. You're taking your own publicity too seriously. If you think a couple of minutes of airtime on the six o'clock news is going to save Apple Grove House, you're mistaken."

Ted turned and left the room.

"Oops, just ruined old Ted's day," Kelly said with a giggle. "A couple of minutes of airtime on the six o'clock news is exactly what we needed. And isn't old Brad going to be sorry to miss out on putting his face in front of the news cam. Oh, excuse me. I'd better go show the news boys where to set up. I know these guys, Jen. They'll do a great job for us. We'll get the city and the county behind us, and we'll save Apple Grove House yet. Hang in there, Jen."

As Kelly vanished out of the door, Jessica dashed in.

"Jen, where have you been?" she cried. The lipstick had been chewed off her lips and a strand of her brown hair stuck out from behind her ear. "The guests are about to mutiny. A few more minutes and the food will be gone and the band will be packing up. And who are you?" she concluded when she got a good look at Bennett.

"Captain Bennett Vance of the cavalry has come to my rescue," Jen said, smiling up at him. "And I'm going to marry him."

Shock robbed Jessica's face of its exasperation. She drew herself up to her full five-foot-five-inch height—the same as Jen's—and scrutinized Bennett. She studied him from the toe of his gleaming black boots to the tip of his blue plumed hat. "You mean in the place of Brad? Jen, don't you need time to think about this? No offense, Captain."

"None taken," Bennett said, a smile of amusement on his lips.

Jessica went on. "I mean with the upset of Brad— You know? On the rebound? Are you certain, Jen?"

"We've had all the time we need," Jen said, looking up at Bennett for confirmation.

"Joey has the ring," Bennett said, putting his hand over Jen's. "And with your permission, we're ready."

"Absolutely," Jen said, her conviction slowly growing that this alliance was meant to be. She prayed Jessica would accept that, too.

Jessica drew in a deep, weary breath and nodded. "License?"

Jen grinned. Her sister was back to her practical self again.

"Here," Bennett said, producing some papers from his coat pocket.

Jen gaped as he displayed the license and certificate Judge Tyler had signed the day of the first ceremony.

Jessica nodded. "They look strange, but official enough." Her expression cleared and she began to give Jen the once-over again.

"Your shoes look terrible. And where's your bouquet?" Jessica said, staring at the hem of Jen's gown. "Heavens, Jen. What have you been up to?"

"Saving Apple Grove House," Bennett said in a low conspiratorial voice.

"Yeah, what's new? I get a full explanation of all this later," Jessica agreed with a dismayed shake of her head. "And what have you done with your bouquet?"

"I forgot my bouquet," Jen said, recalling that instant when Anna had asked the same question. Then she glanced at the bell jar sitting on the mantel. Her breath caught in her throat. The dried flowers in the jar were the exact ones that Anna had dried and placed in a hatbox for her.

Jen knew with absolute certainty in that moment that her meeting with Bennett had been fated by some wrinkle in time. "But there's a bouquet right here. I'll carry this one."

She exchanged a glance with Bennett. She saw that he understood and approved that she would carry the same flowers she had the day they were wed—as proxies. Jen turned back to her sister.

"That's fine with me, but the ladies of the historical society will have a fit," Jessica said. "You'll have some explaining to do."

"I can handle the ladies of the historical society." Jen gingerly lifted the bell jar cover from the bouquet. With great care, she took the dried flower posy into her hands. It was surprisingly sturdy, the flowers intact. The satin ribbons were still smooth and shiny and had only yellowed slightly, just enough to give an elegant antique patina. The greenery still provided a nice contrast to the off-white dried flowers. A faint fragrance of roses and apple blossoms filtered into the room and tickled Jen's nose.

Though the dewy freshness of the flowers was long gone, the posy remained as full and lovely as any dried autumnal bouquet.

"You know, it doesn't look bad considering," Jessica said, eyeing the posy critically. "I can get some fresh flowers off one of the tables for you."

"No, this is it," Jen said, silently thanking Anna for her careful work. "This is perfect. This is the bouquet I want to carry down the aisle."

Bennett's arm tightened around her waist.

"Okay," Jessica said with a shrug. "What else do we need to see to before I cue the music?"

"Our vows," Bennett murmured to Jen. "They should be something special. Not the usual love, honor, and cherish words. This is a special ceremony. It's the real thing. Right, Jen?"

Jen nodded, reminded of the vows she was about to exchange with Bennett. They would say real vows this time. No proxy charade. Today they'd recite their real commitment to each other. "And there's one thing we'd like to change in the ceremony. Will you tell them to Reverend Gleeson for us?"

Jessica agreed.

Unbelievable as it seemed to Bennett, they had done it, just as Jennifer had insisted they could. They'd flashed through time. Transported by light. He had no other explanation for it.

The year 1999 was noisy. The new century assaulted Bennett's ears with the voices of wedding guests, the jumpy music of the musicians in the orchard, and a strange drone from the sky overhead. He'd have to ask Jennifer about the noises after the wedding. Yet the house and the orchard seemed familiar enough to be reassuring. He even saw some guests in military uniforms nearly like his.

But the most important thing to Bennett was that they were together.

Soon all the necessary arrangements had been made to get the wedding under way. When they walked outside and he saw the strange glittering vehicles without horses, the video crew with their cameras, and the women in short skirts, the only thing he said was, "I'm going to have a lot of questions later."

"I'll answer all of them gladly," Jennifer said. "I think we should postpone the honeymoon in Hawaii until we get you the proper identification and coach you on what to say at the security gates."

Bennett didn't want to speculate about what that meant. It was a perfect wedding, unlike the first one. Bennett was glad of that. Reverend Gleeson was sober, though the guests weren't. He could hardly keep his mind on the reverend's words because of all the new things he glimpsed around him—and the distraction of the people Jen had called the news crew.

Joey had the ring when it was needed. The jeweled band slipped onto Jennifer's finger, a perfect fit. To Bennett's surprise, her tears splashed down onto their joined hands as they exchanged their vows—real, binding ones at last. Bennett just smiled at her—a comforting smile, he hoped.

Jennifer's voice was shaky as she repeated their vows, but Bennett made his strong and clear. He held Jen's gaze as he recited his vows. She hung on every word he uttered.

"I, Bennett James Vance, love and cherish you, Jennifer, for being all that you are, all the things you are not, and all that you can be. Your pain will be mine, and your joy will be mine as well. All I ask of you is your love, your trust, your caring."

Then he paused before repeating the phrase they had agreed on. "I choose you to be my wife till *time* chooses to part us."

"You may kiss the bride," Reverend Gleeson intoned.

Bennett took her firmly by the shoulders and bent to kiss her. Then he was making love to her mouth ardently in front of the TV news crew—and two hundred wedding guests.

He concentrated completely on his new bride, kissing Jennifer mouth to mouth, wetly and passionately. He'd come too close to losing her not to appreciate this moment. He was glad to claim her anytime and anywhere. He never broke contact with her lips, not even when they needed to breathe—or suffocate. He allowed her to have her way until she angled her head up and the tip of her tongue teased the inside of his upper lip. Bennett uttered a low groan.

The wedding guests began to applaud. Jennifer gently pushed him away, saving them both from embarrassment.

Jennifer smiled up into his face—that beautiful bright-eyed smile of hers. "Hold that thought," she whispered.

Bennett slipped his arm around Jennifer's waist and pulled her closer just as they were thronged by wedding guests.

"Well, you are quite a surprise, Captain Vance," said one of the white-haired ladies Jennifer had introduced as her great-aunt. "Jen never told us about you. Just what do you do and where did you two meet?"

"I'm a cider maker," Bennett said without hesitation. "And Jenni— Jen and I met at another wedding."

"How nice," the lady muttered. "How like you, Jen. Always up to something different. I must have a photo of you for Aunt Martha, who couldn't come." She raised a strange small black box to her eye and aimed at them.

With rude swiftness, Jen snatched the box from the lady's hand. "Not right now, Aunt Lizzie. If you don't mind, we've had enough of the cameras today."

"Well, of course, dear, if you say so." Aunt Lizzie looked surprised and puzzled. "But I promised your Aunt Martha."

"I'll send a wedding photo to Aunt Martha," Jen said with an ingratiating smile. "I promise."

"Yes, that would be nice, dear." Aunt Lizzie smiled uncertainly and hurried off to join her friends.

Jen held the box up for Bennett to see. "This is a camera. I don't think we should allow anyone at Apple Grove House to take our picture."

"I agree." Bennett wondered how that little thing could

be the same kind of mechanism Zach Schuster had used. "Who knows what another photograph might bring?"

"I've crossed time twice to marry you," Jen said, looking into his face, "I'm not taking a single chance of losing you again."

Jessica appeared with two glasses of bubbly wine and shoved them into Jen and Bennett's hands. "Here, you two. Toast each other."

"Thanks, sis." Jen looked at the wine, then up at Bennett. "But let's not toast here. Bring the wine and come with me. I want to show you something."

Perplexed, but willing to desert the crowd of guests, Bennett followed her back into the house and up the familiar winding stairs to the balcony over the front porch.

Jennifer went straight to the corner and leaned out over the balustrade, peering into the distance. "Yes, it's there. Come see it."

Bennett joined her and squinted into the distance. Without any difficulty, he saw the tall gleaming towers of a city on the southeast horizon.

"That's it. Kansas City of 1999," Jennifer said.

Bennett heard pride and relief in her voice. She was glad to be home.

"Of course, there is other evidence of progress," she added.

He followed her gesture toward the Kansas River below the house. It looked different, too, narrower, with a road and streetlights lining it. And up the river stood a tall, wide bridge.

"I see a lot of things have changed in a hundred and thirty some years," Bennett said. "But I'm willing to toast the future, to Apple Grove House, and to us."

He lifted his glass.

"Hear, hear." Jen lifted her glass and looped her arm through his.

Then they took their first sip of wine as man and wife.

The sweet, bland taste evaporated on Bennett's tongue, leaving him disappointed, unimpressed. He held the glass up to the sunlight for closer examination. "What is this?"

"It's a special apple wine that I had shipped in especially for the wedding," Jennifer said without looking at him, her voice noncommittal. "What do you think of it?"

Bennett tried not to grimace. After all, she had gone to a lot of trouble to serve this stuff at their wedding. "I don't know a lot about wine, but I know apples. I think we could do better than this."

A wide grin lit Jennifer's face and Bennett knew he'd said the right thing. "I think we can, too. We'll start producing a good cider. When its reputation is established, we'll develop our own wine."

"I like the plan," Bennett said, certain he was going to like the future with Jen.

She leaned toward him to bestow a kiss.

He wrapped an arm around her and accepted her kiss, feeling the specialness of Apple Grove House and the orchard blooming around them. It mattered little that he did not understand what had just happened with the lights and the camera. Love was what was important. "Time brought us together, but love will keep us united," he whispered against her lips.

"Forever," Jen said, flashing that joyous smile at him.

Bennett lost himself in kissing her once again.

Put a Little Romance in Your Life With
Fern Michaels

__Dear Emily	0-8217-5676-1	$6.99US/$8.50CAN
__Sara's Song	0-8217-5856-X	$6.99US/$8.50CAN
__Wish List	0-8217-5228-6	$6.99US/$7.99CAN
__Vegas Rich	0-8217-5594-3	$6.99US/$8.50CAN
__Vegas Heat	0-8217-5758-X	$6.99US/$8.50CAN
__Vegas Sunrise	1-55817-5983-3	$6.99US/$8.50CAN
__Whitefire	0-8217-5638-9	$6.99US/$8.50CAN

Call toll free **1-888-345-BOOK** to order by phone or use this coupon to order by mail.

Name_____

Address_____

City _____ State _____ Zip_____

Please send me the books I have checked above.

I am enclosing	$_____
Plus postage and handling*	$_____
Sales tax (in New York and Tennessee)	$_____
Total amount enclosed	$_____

*Add $2.50 for the first book and $.50 for each additional book.
Send check or money order (no cash or CODs) to:
Kensington Publishing Corp., 850 Third Avenue, New York, NY 10022
Prices and Numbers subject to change without notice.
All orders subject to availability.
Check out our website at **www.kensingtonbooks.com**

Put a Little Romance in Your Life With
Rosanne Bittner